Blood Curse

Thomas S. Mulvaugh

This is a work of fiction .All characters, places, businesses and incidents are from the author's imagination. Any resemblance to actual places, people or events is purely coincidental. Any trademarks mentioned here are not authorized by the trademark owners and do not in any way mean the work is sponsored by or associated with the trademark owners. Any trademarks or real places are used specifically for descriptive capacity.

ISBN 978-0-9794767-0-9

First Edition

© 2015 Thomas S. Mulvaugh

Golden Roads Publishing, a division of PAH Publishing

Acknowledgements/Dedication

There are many hands that touch a book beside just the author. I would like to thank Connie Davis who took the time to read through the manuscript and make all the corrections, unfortunately my imagination gets ahead of my fingers. Also thanks to Sandy Bouray for being the model on the front cover, and to the Barry County Historical Society for letting us use the Bayless House for the shot, it truly fit just what we were going for. Last but certainly not least to my wonderful wife Karla who is always there to never let me give up.

This book is dedicated to all law enforcement officers who each and every day risk their lives so that we may be a little safer in a turbulent world. To those officers who have lost their lives, let us take a moment each day to stop, remember, and let us never forget that 'heroes do come in blue.'

THOMAS S. MULVAUGH

BLOOD CURSE

"First came the fall off man, then came the fall of mankind-murder. The sixth sin, there are only three reasons to murder, money, revenge or passion which drives you?"

Chapter 1

The crack of gunfire sounded loudly from an AR-15 rifle. Ryder quickly slid down to the ground, folding up his athletic frame as he pressed his back up against the steel door of a Barry County Sheriff's department cruiser. Another blast of gunfire rang out, ripping into the emergency light bar, sending a shower of bits of red and blue plastic down over him and acting Sheriff Thom Thompson. Ryder's fingers gripped tighter around the butt of the Glock G30 pistol clenched firmly in his hands. He leaned his head back against the cool steel of the door as he glared up at the sharp shooter positioned at the apex of the old weathered barn across the road.

How many times he had played in that barn, tossed down bales of hay to his father waiting on the snowy ground below. He turned and looked at the old house, the flagstone long stolen; this had been his home when he was a kid. He had played cops and robbers here, but he never dreamed he would be living it out for real.

There was another blast of gunfire. As it shattered the door glass he tried to shield his face, but Ryder felt the sting as a small piece of glass cut his cheek just below his left eye. Then it was still, the only thing he could hear was a deep breath of the man next to him. Ryder turned and saw the heavyset man with a round face and thinning gray hair, heavy plastic framed glasses covering his eyes, which he reached up and adjusted in a nervous way.

He was the county coroner: Thom Thompson, better known by his nickname Teeny Tiny or Double T for short. According to Missouri law, since the former sheriff had to be removed from office, the county coroner was now the acting sheriff until a special election could be held. That couldn't come fast enough for Double T; he had no idea what he was doing.

"Don't shoot back!" Ryder told him. "I can talk him out of there." Ryder wasn't a cop, well not anymore. Once the best homicide detective on the force in Kansas City, he was instrumental in tracking down one of the most ruthless killers the city had ever seen. The Kansas City Butcher-now, after winning a billion dollar payoff from Powerball, he took on investigations for those that couldn't afford them, charging only a dollar a day. His latest client- Simon Peters- was the person shooting at them.

1

Ryder slowly rose to his feet and gazed across the hood of the black and gold county cruiser SUV. He aimed the Glock towards the old trailer on the other side of the road. An older pea green mobile home, one time the home of Bubbie, the grandmother of his girlfriend Yakira Rosen, now was surrounded by a barb-wire fence.

Just a few feet away from the trailer, menacing like a hungry wolf stalking a lamb, was a D-9 Caterpillar bulldozer. Its huge blade like shining teeth ready to take a bite out of the metal siding, of the trailer. He glanced out across the once meadow-like field. The towering trees that once gave shade in the summer and cash in the fall, when picking up the bumper crop of black walnuts, had fallen victim to the bulldozer's blade, stacked up and waiting for their cremation and burial.

"I say we take him out. He is dangerous." Ryder heard another voice say."

Ryder hunkered back down behind the fender and turned and looked at the round-faced man who looked like Double T, just not as heavy. It was Double T's brother Deputy Brian Thompson. Clutched in his hands was a Mossberg pump 500 tactical 12 gauge shotgun, his face covered by a riot shield and helmet. "He is going to hurt somebody; do you want one of these guys to get killed?"

"Of, course not!" Ryder drilled back. "You know that my blood still runs blue. But why have it end it like this, when I can talk him out of there?" Ryder paused for just a moment before he added. "Or do you really want to fill out all that paperwork?"

"All right Thom," Deputy Thompson said his shotgun point down to the ground. "You are the acting sheriff; make a choice."

"I am a Medical Examiner, not a cop." Double T said, his head turning from Brian to Ryder, then back to Brian, and said. "All right, we are going to let Ryder go down field." Deputy Thompson opened the door of the cruiser, reaching inside the SUV he grabbed the radio mike and handed it to Ryder, as he switched the radio over to PA setting.

Ryder gripped the Glock with one hand and the mike with the other as he gazed out across the hood again. Ryder brought the mike to his lips.

2

"Simon! Simon Peters," Ryder said as he pressed down on the key of the mike and his voice boomed over the speaker on the SUV in the middle of the broken light bar. "This is Ryder, what is going on?"

"Ryder. Rick Ryder?" The voice replied from the trailer. "I didn't know that was you. What are you doing with them?"

"These are my friends and you know how I feel about someone trying to hurt my friends." All his life Ryder had always been a protector for his friends.

"Look around!" The man shouted back. "All these bloody dozers, they are getting ready to tear all this down."

It was true. The Fletcher Egg Company had used eminent domain to take over his childhood farm, a huge yellow power shovel perched at the top of the hill behind the old pond, its bucket already tearing into the ground to make way for a storage tank for waste water for the factory that was being built. Every place that held memories was going to be wiped away in the name of modern progress.

"What does that matter to you?" Ryder asked, still clutching the weapon in his hand. "This is not where you grew up. These are my memories, not yours."

"But you told me all about them, how you grew up here with your best friend just down the road. How you and she would ride your bikes to Snake Creek to go swimming, how you would spend the day just walking around the farm. I grew up in freaking Chicago!" The man's tone was becoming angry. "You know what it is like to grow up there? Where there is no peace, no quiet!" The man sobbed. "Look around, just peace...." The man's voice grew still for just a moment, Ryder could hear the man crying before he spoke again. "I just want peace." He said softly. Ryder saw the torn lace curtain in the trailer move back and saw Simon appear in the window. "I just want Annie to have peace, a place I can bury her." The curtain dropped down again and they heard a voice emit from the insides of the trailer. "Everyone thinks I murdered her."

"I don't," Ryder said into the mike. "Let's talk." There was silence before the reply came.

"All right, but only you."

"Okay."

"You can't go in there!" Deputy Thompson said as he grabbed Ryder's arm. "He is unstable and I got a warrant from Eureka Springs for the murder of his wife."

"Brian, I don't think he did it. I can talk him out of there."

Brian set the shotgun down on the ground, resting it against the side of the SUV. "I don't like it Ryder; you recognize that smell?" Ryder knew that awful nose burning, eye watering aroma of cat pee- it was a meth lab. "Have you ever seen one of those things blow up?" He turned to Thom and said. "Order him not to do it!"

"I am not a deputy. You can't order me not to." Ryder replied, turning and looking at the trailer and then continued. "Unless you are going to arrest me…" Ryder's voice was low and calm. "…Well, what's it going to be?" The acting sheriff didn't say a thing. Ryder began to step out from behind the vehicle when the zipping sound of Velcro made him turn back. Deputy Thompson was removing his bulletproof vest. He lifted it off over his head and handed it to Ryder.

"Put this on!"

Ryder grabbed the vest from the deputy's hand and laid it down on the hood. He removed his sunglasses and sports coat and the empty shoulder holster, before slipping the vest over his head and then using the straps to snug it up around him.

Ryder walked around the car and over to the barb-wire fence, he pushed the top wire down and slung his leg over and followed it with the other one. He took a couple of steps toward the trailer. "Simon, come on, just throw your gun out and come on out."

"Not till I bury Annie; that is what I am here for," Simon said, as the curtain pulled back again and Ryder saw the man standing in the window. He was less than six-foot, medium built, his head shaved cleaned, as was his face save for a triangular-shaped patch on his chin, just below his lower lip. Ryder watched as the man drew up a Desert Eagle pistol in his grip; it quivered in his grip. Simon sobbed as he added. "Don't you get it, Ryder? If she is buried here those guys can't build here."

4

Ryder knew very well there was no law. If he did bury her, she would be just end up being moved. "Simon, I found her," Ryder said as he took a step through the tall fescue grass towards the trailer. "I found her, the student at Crowder College in Neosho, she remembers you talking to her. She is giving you an alibi. She is making a statement right at this moment. Come on, just give it up."

"It doesn't matter Ryder," Simon said. "I just don't feel like..." Simon dropped the curtain down again. He must have sat on the floor next to the window, as Ryder could still hear him but he couldn't see him. "I hate this damn life. I don't want to fight anymore."

"If you just come out I can take you somewhere that you can find peace." Again there was silence so Ryder called out to him. "Simon! Simon! Are you there?"

"I am here." He replied before he appeared in the window again pulling the curtain back. "I have something for you. "

"What is it?"

"A note, it is a note that is addressed to you."

"Me?" From who?"

"The Kansas City Butcher."

"WHAT!" Ryder shouted back. The name of that serial killer brought him back to one grisly murder after another, each body slit open from the breast bone to the belly button, an organ removed as a trophy by the killer, wrapped in freezer paper, placed in the deep freezer. Ryder shook his head in hopes of erasing the memory of this killer, but also to disagree. "That is not possible! She is in prison, I helped put her there. She's facing execution in two months." Ryder took another step towards the trailer; he was now about a hundred feet away. The wind whirled around changing direction, drifting a strong chemical smell and burning his nostrils. Ryder placed his hand up over his nose trying to block the smell.

"She left this message for you," Simon said as he tossed a red colored piece of construction paper out the window, just the mere sight of the child like writing made his feet like clay; he had to make himself move.

He bent down and picked it up and unfolded it, he hadn't seen anything like this since almost four years ago, hand printed with a black crayon. He began walking away from the trailer as he read:

> My darling Rick Ryder
>
> You thought you had reached the end
>
> But what if it is just where it begins
>
> The heart wants what it must need
>
> Now it time for true love to bleed
>
> This is the first darling that you will see

"Where did you find this?" Ryder furiously demanded as he turned around to face the trailer once again.

"It was shoved under my door the day after Anna was killed."

"Why didn't you show me this?" Ryder shouted as he folded up the paper and tucked it into his pants pocket. His mind flashed back to that night as he and FBI Special Agent Isabelle Alexander enter the house and found the killer, painting the last victim's blood on her face. It was after that trial and the verdict came down-'Guilty. Death.-' that Ryder walked out of the department, and with his last dollar bought a lottery ticket and won the biggest jackpot of all time- one billion dollars. He didn't want to hear about this killer any longer; he just wanted to forget.

"Annie is gone." Ryder heard Simon speak as a shadowy image appeared from behind the curtain. "All because you couldn't stop her. Time to pay, Ricky!" His hand appeared out the window- there was something in it.

"Detonator!" He heard Brian yell. Ryder took off running, but his weak knee gave out on him. He collapsed to the ground just as the trailer erupted into a fireball, sending a plume of black smoke towering up into the sky. The percussion wave tore over him screaming like Banshees drawing souls into the grave, as flaming chunks of the trailer spun as if it were a wicked fireworks display, landing in the grass and creating small fires.

Ryder rolled over onto his back and gazed over at the trailer. The only thing that remained was the twisted frame peeking through the orange and red flames, dancing behind a thick black curtain of smoke. It wouldn't be long before every neighbor would come to see what had happened. He thought he heard a chopper in the air, he looked all over the sky but he couldn't see one. He felt someone grab him by the shoulders and pull him to his feet. They spun him around, it was Thom and Brian, Thom's mouth was moving but Ryder couldn't hear a thing, it felt as if he were underwater, and his ears were ringing. "What?" Ryder yelled, even his own voice sounded odd. Thom yelled as loud as he could.

"You okay?"

Ryder put his hands over his ears and tried to unstop them, but they were still ringing.

Ryder shook his head and said, "I can't hear anything."

Chapter 2

The screaming siren gave a little a comfort to Ryder because at least he could hear, but still he felt that throbbing in his ears, as if he had just gotten out of a rock concert, front row over to the side, right in line with the speakers. He watched as Thom braked hard and guided the cruiser off of the main highway to what would quickly become the main street through the middle of town. He whipped the steering wheel around and guided the SUV into the parking lot of Cassville Mercy Hospital, sliding to a stop under the covered emergency entrance.

The glass door slid open and Thom guided Ryder into the emergency room. Thom began speaking to the staff there, and Ryder struggled to hear. The best he could make out was that Double T was arguing with a nurse about paperwork. The world would come to an end if there was no paperwork. Ryder thought to himself as Thom grabbed Ryder's wallet from his hip pocket and handed an insurance card to the nurse as another nurse grabbed Ryder's arm. Ryder turned to her and he quickly recognized her as one of his favorite nurses, Tracy Katz.

"You like me that much that you just can't stay away from here?" She said with a laugh as she guided him over to a cubicle that had the curtain pulled back. Ryder sat down on the cot and watched as Tracy went about setting up the instruments that were needed. She opened a sterilized bandage, poured an antiseptic on it and dabbed it on the cut just below his eye, it stung but he tried not to react. The curtain swung open and the second act had begun, as another nurse appeared rolling a cart with enough goodies for drawing blood that it would have any bloodsucker feel they had entered vampire heaven. She asked him to remove his jacket and rolled his sleeve up; all the while she prepared the needle and vials to collect her prize specimen. She wrapped a rubber tube around his arm, making his veins pop up. Ryder looked right into her eyes and said.

"Don't dare say it!" He wrapped his hand around her wrist. "I want the truth."

"All right. It is going to really hurt. Satisfied?" She had to yell to make him hear.

"As long, as I get the truth." Ryder's voice winced as she jabbed the needle into his vein and drew out the blood. He turned to Tracy. "Let me ask you something. I come in here because my ears are ringing; why are you taking blood?"

"Because we are vampires and we are hungry," Tracy replied in a mocking vampire like tone, before her normal voice return. "It is just the way things are done." The other nurse placed a bandage on his elbow and pushed it up. "Well, we're done." She grinned as she patted his cheek. "It was great for me. How was it for you?"

"Wonderful, maybe we can do this again sometime. " Ryder joked, raising his voice because he was still having trouble hearing as she rolled the cart out and let the curtain fall behind her. Then it was off to X-ray to check it there were any broken bones, then off to for a CT scan before returning back to the same cubicle, or as Ryder called it the ER go around- it was not merry.

The curtain pulled back again, in walked a man with a clean-shaven head and a beard showing the salt and pepper of middle age. It was Dr. Crowley. He walked in front of Ryder and spoke. "Can you hear me?"

"A little. It just feels like my ears are stopped up." Ryder answered as the doctor pulled out a penlight from the pocket of his smock. Using his fingers he held Ryder's eye open shining the bright light into Ryder's eye. The doctor moved his grip and the light over to Ryder's other eye. He was checking to make sure Ryder did not suffer a concussion from the explosion. Ryder's didn't know if it was the bright light, or the strong smell of the doctor's aftershave but his eyes began to water. The doctor moved back and turned off the light. Now came the questions. Ryder had answered these things so many times he knew them by heart. "You feel dizzy? Any nausea? Feel sleepy?" With each one Ryder shook his head.

The doctor went to the tray that Tracy had prepared and picked up an otoscope and pulled on the upper part of Ryder's ear lobe, to straighten the ear canal. The doctor pushed the instrument into Ryder's ear and examined it. He moved over to the other ear and pulling on the lobe to straighten it the canal. He turned to Tracy and spoke. "Let's try the pneumatic reading and test the TM for any damage." The doctor was speaking low and Ryder struggled to hear him. The doctor clapped his hands together.

"Did you hear that?" The doctor asked, standing next to him. Ryder turned to him and nodded. Ryder turned and faced the curtains, somehow he knew she was out there, waiting for news about him, it hadn't been the first time he had been in the ER, and she was out there waiting for him. No other woman affected him this way; there was not that connection, that feeling that she was part of him.

"Guess who is here?" Tracy asked with a smile, before handing the doctor a small rectangular shaped box, which he placed on the metal tray.

"A cute little Jewish woman, driving nurses mad, trying to get answers. Even threatening bodily harm if she isn't allowed to come back here? I thought she might be." Ryder said his ears still ringing.

The doctor opened the lid of the box. Inside was a siegle spectrum, a small instrument attached to a colored rubber tube with a matching squeeze bulb at the end. Beside the red tube was three small silver funnel shaped objects of different sizes of which the doctor was sorting through, it was used on the tympanic membrane- the ear drum.

"You might feel a little pressure in your ear." Dr, Crowley said, as he used his hands to position Ryder's head to the side. The doctor chose the correct siegle, and placed it in Ryder's ear, finding a good fit he attached the silver funnel to the tube. The doctor took his hand and pushed Ryder's head over. Again the doctor inserted the object into Ryder's ear making a tight seal with his fingers wrapped around the small funnel; the doctor carefully squeezed the rubber bulb. Ryder felt a slight pressure on his ear drum, such as when you go down a large hill too fast. The doctor watched as his ear drum moved. After that the doctor moved the instrument to the other ear, again Ryder felt the pressure inside his ear. With testing done the doctor returned the instrument back to the box and shut the lid before he turned to Tracy and said. "You can let Yakira in now."

Ryder could imagine her out there waiting, impatiently. Sitting in those ungodly torture chamber chairs. Her legs crossed as she thumbed through a magazine with frustration, getting to the end, tossing it down on the seat beside her, before she uncrossed her legs and crossed them again the opposite way. Looking out across the room, smiling at the others there waiting for their news. Standing up, letting out a huge sigh as she runs her fingers through her hair, before tramping over to the vending machines and complaining they have nothing kosher, for a Jewish girl. Selecting a Dr. Pepper from the pop machine and taking a couple of sips, then stamping over to the nurse's desk to demand answers, getting the same answer of 'she will have to wait', she flops back into a chair, picks up another magazine and starts all over again.

"The good news is there no damage to the stereocilia hairs, the ringing should stop with a little bit of time. You just need to take it easy the rest of the day." The doctor placed his hand on Ryder's shoulder and he added with a grin as he turned and looked at him "And no excitement."

"That means keep your hands to yourself, Yakira." Ryder heard Double T joke as he entered the cubicle. Standing beside him was a woman, a little over five feet tall, thin, with very little feminine curves to show for her nearly thirty years of life. Her hair was dark and long, flowing down over her shoulders and complemented her olive like skin against her pastel pink blouse. Her face showed no age, looking more like that of a teenager, just getting a day off from biology class. "Right, Doc!"

"Well," the doctor drew out. "It might be better if he just got a good night's sleep." He moved past her and stepped out of the cubicle. "I will get your discharge papers ready." Yakira walked in, at first her dark-colored eyes narrowed at him in frustration that once again she was meeting him in the Emergency Room, before she smiled and her eyes filled with life as she wrapped her arms around his neck. She kissed him, and then pushed him back.

"What were you doing out there?" She asked in a strong motherly tone. "You could have got yourself killed! She grabbed him in an embrace again. Ryder lifted his gaze up over her head at Thom standing behind her.

"Simon?"

"It was a meth lab; the only thing we have found of him so far is an upper plate of a pair of false teeth that had his last name on it." His phone buzzed and he looked at it. "I've to get to get back out there."

"As Sheriff?" Ryder again placing his hands over his ears, trying to get them stop ringing."

"No, Coroner," Thom replied. "They just found some body parts, three fingers. Also Rick…" Thom said, calling Ryder by his first name, anytime he called him this he knew it was going to be serious. "…the Fletcher egg company is going to begin breaking ground for their plant tomorrow on your old place."

11

"Doesn't matter anymore, but there is something I have to get out of there before they tear it down," Ryder said as he stood up and pulled the tail of the dark blue jacket down. He drew his hand over onto the empty holster, feeling nearly naked without his old service weapon.

"Your service weapon is at the nurse's desk," Thom said as Ryder reached into the inside pocket of his jacket and pulled out the black frame sunglasses and put them on before obtaining his weapon, checking it, he stuffed it back into the holster. Ryder walked out of the cubicle with Yakira by his side. Passing by the reception desk, the woman called out for him. "Mr. Ryder," She handed him a flower, a single red rose; its stem twisted and tied in a bow. "She said to tell you. Now it begins."

Chapter 3

Ryder was under doctor's orders not to drive so his chauffeur for the rest of day was Yakira in her Chevy pickup- a two-tone C-10 short bed four-wheel drive, dark gray metal flake over dark pink metallic, with chrome roll bar. It wasn't exactly subtle going through town, but you could always spot a foreigner in town as they would stop, turn, and look, while all the locals would do was wave.

He sat in the passenger seat looking out the window watching the truck being reflected in the store windows, feeling the warmth of the early spring air flow over him. "Can you take me to the old house?"

"Okay, but after that, I need to go to the shop."

The smoke from the rubble was still drifting up from the remains of the trailer but the Butterfield Fire Department had it all under control. Yakira stopped the truck and Ryder got out. "Just stay put. I won't be long." He said, reaching into the glove box and getting a flashlight. He walked through the tall grass and opened the old screen door. It had been years since he had been in here.

He stopped in what was the living room, its sheetrock walls with the simulated wood covering. He gazed over into the corner where the Christmas tree always stood, over to the chimney where he would warm himself by the wood stove. He closed his eyes. For just a moment in his mind he was a child again hearing his mother's voice calling him in for supper. He walked through the doorway into the kitchen and looked at the old yellow Formica-topped table, the chairs turned over; even though it wasn't there he could still smell her fried chicken and fresh baked apple pie. It quickly came back to him that was not what he was here for.

He switched on the flashlight and walked through another doorway that led to a back porch. Pushing hard he opened another door, which led to a small room barely wide enough for a bed in width and twice as long. With its gray paisley print wallpaper, this had been his bedroom. He let the flashlight shine around the room over the walls. He kneeled down and tapped the wall and a part of the drywall fell over revealing inside the wall, a small metal box. He removed the box and returned to the kitchen, where he set the box on the table and flipped up a chair and sat down.

Getting his keys out of his pocket, he located a small key next to the penlight that he used as a key fob. He opened the box. Inside were

13

several red colored notes, all with black crayon writing. "What is all that?" He heard Yakira ask. He quickly slammed the lid down, grabbing the box he stood up.

"Nothing," he said marching towards the front door.

"But they looked like love notes." She said following behind him. "Are they from…"

"Believe me, they are not love notes." He said holding the box under his arm and the old faded green painted screen door in his hand. "Besides, didn't you want to stop by the shop?"

Ryder just held the box on his lap, holding on to it with both hands as she drove back to town. As they exited town on highway 112, passing by Yakira's old gun shop with the sign over the window that read "WE HAVE MOVED TO HILLTOP!" they began to pick up speed, he glanced over at her but didn't say anything.

"I just want to check on the shop." She said, letting her gaze drift from him and the highway, as she guided the truck down the road. Hilltop, as the name implied, was on top of the hill just outside of town. It was the last spot one could fill up with gas and buy goodies before heading to Roaring River State Park.

Yakira pulled the truck into the graveled parking lot of a brand new building, long and wide enough to allow a complete choice of guns from home protection handguns to a wall of hunting and defense rifles in a glass display cases. Also in the store was a line of sports equipment, offering everything from fishing poles and bait, to equipment for every sport imaginable, including, Ryder's own personal K.C. jersey- number 7- over the cash counter, plus a full snack and coffee bar. But it was the large reinforced cement block rooms at the back, which included an indoor shooting and archery arena that really made this place special.

"You coming in, Sweetie?" She asked as she pushed the gearshift up into park and turned off the truck. Her tone showed that of a Jewish woman mixed with pure hillbilly.

"No, I am going to stay here." He said, reaching into his jacket pocket and pulling out his cell phone. "I think I will check my emails."

She got out of the truck and walked into the store. He reached in and pulled the folded up red construction paper out of his pants pocket, unfolded it and laid it on his lap. Using his phone he took a photo of it, and attached it to a message and sent it.

He just sat there staring down at the piece of paper, looking carefully at the writing. The mix of lower and upper case, where it was not needed, the slant of the T's, the fact that all I's were with a dot, the crowding of the letter L's that ran the lower bar into the next letter and the rhyme scheme. It all seemed like it did four years ago when they first appeared. Just as before, it began with a note attached to a murder victim, then notes sent to him. It couldn't be her, we arrested this killer. It can't be the Butcher. He thought, trying to reassure himself.

He saw her heading out the glass doors of the shop and quickly lifted his head, and just as quickly folded up the paper and placed it back in his pocket. "We had a good day!" She said as she opened the door of the truck. "Over a grand in sales. Good idea hiring Jonnie away from the convenience store; she is doing a great job." She continued, stepping up on the chrome running boards. "Now I guess I make dinner?"

"You are kidding, right?" Ryder said, raising one eyebrow in puzzlement, remembering the thick veil of smoke and destroyed pots and pans the last time she tried to cook. "You do remember our deal? I cook. You clean."

"I know," she said as she started the truck, and it roared to life. "But your ears…"

"But nothing…I don't care if I had a bullet in me. It is still safer if you don't cook. I made a promise to the fire department. You don't cook."

"Well then, how about a Texan burger at the Family Steak House? I sure could go for one." She said offering a sneaky little grin that she hid by lowering her head and only letting her eyes turn to him.

"Had that one in mind for a long time didn't you?" He placed his hands on his ears, "Ears are not ringing as bad. I could go for a burger."

The interstate killed the American soul, the astronauts, the man in the moon, and the want of need slain the small town. Monett was no different. The downtown that once was a display of different shops;

restaurants, doctor's office, shoe shops, even chain stores like J.C. Penney, and this wonderful little stand where you could get the greatest tasting hotdogs, it was all gone; either disemboweled by the properties of progression or suffocated by a collection stores stuffed into the confines of a mall. Occasionally a name of a store will remain, like Modern Variety, where everyone has a memory of a special toy coming from there; others have just wilted away, only to be a memory of those old enough to remember. Yet others were hiding their old age beauty under the masks of modernizations; while even others were like a well-loved woman married many different times, with many names. The Family Steak House was like that; under its bright colors that it wore on the outside, it hid its broken unions, but the latest was just what Ryder needed on a day like today.

Yakira wheeled the truck into a parking spot and hopped out and quickly walked over to his side, and opened the door for him. "What are you doing?" he asked.

"Is it not what you do for me?"

"Yes, but..."

"You told me it wasn't because I am a woman, but because I am worth it. Are you not worth it?" Her question made a small grin come to his face.

It may have been a little secret known by the regulars, but the entrance was at the back on the side, up a ramp through another door. It was brightly decorated with arched openings. Kathy, one of the regular waitresses saw them. "If it isn't my favorite couple," She said patting Ryder's arm. "Third booth, from the left." She said guiding them to the back room. "Sweet teas, a half twist of lemon. Texan burgers with pickles no onions and plate of date fries."

"Are you saying we are that boring?" Yakira asked as she slid into the booth across from him.

"You two boring?" Kathy asked lifting her eyes in amazement, wrinkling her freckled face. "If you two are boring, I don't want to see exciting. Heard about the trailer that exploded, everyone saying it was a meth lab."   Ryder didn't reply, he just sat with his eyes fixed to the red painted wall. Yakira nodded letting her know that it was what she thought it was. Kathy walked away to place their order before she returned with two glasses of iced tea and set them down on the table in front of his He was still engrossed in the red wall.

"What is on your mind?" Yakira asked as she picked up the glass of tea and took a drink. "You are so far away."

"I was thinking about Anna's murder," Ryder said breaking out of his own self-induced trance and picking up the glass of tea. He took a sip of tea,perfectly sweet.

"I thought you said you found someone who saw him at Crowder College that cleared him." Yakira said as she reached across the table, placing her hand on top of his."Isn't that what we wanted?"

"Any other time yes, but now if he didn't kill her, it means someone else did, and I fear who that might be."

"The rose? The one that you got at the hospital?"

"Yeah," Ryder answered, pulling out his cell phone and scanning through to check if there were any messages. Not finding any he laid it next to him on the table.

"Is it from the killer?"

"I don't know." Ryder said as he picked up the phone and sent Private message through Facebook that read "CALL ME!!"

"Ricky," She said letting her fingers tighten around his in a devoted grip. "You seem frightened."

"I am," Ryder said, just as Kathy returned with the burgers and fries. All though supper Ryder would periodically glance at his cell phone, checking for messages, checking Facebook. It just seemed that it was more important than talking to Yakira or even eating. After they ate, he paid the bill with a fifty, leaving the rest for a tip for the server.

The sun was beginning its descent, slipping down past the hills of the 'town of the seven valleys' as they drove past a growth of trees, their shadows blinking, like the flashes of cameras, Ryder again felt that he was facing their questions about the serial killer, they always demanded more than he was willing to give, some things he never gave them. Again he checked his phone.

"Who are you waiting to hear from?" Yakira asked, as she flipped on the headlamps of the truck.

He reached up and pulled his sunglasses off, pulling down the sun visor and looking into the mirror. His dark sapphire-like eyes were reddened from the smoke and there was a bandage on his cheek. She turned and faced him, still guiding the truck down the road, passing by the rodeo grounds. He pushed the visor back up. "Alex." He said without any sign of emotion. Ryder flipped the temples of the sunglasses over and shoved them in the inside breast pocket of his jacket as he added. "I have to talk to her."

The Rosen house was located on Tenth Street, a few blocks from Main Street, on a corner lot. Yakira carefully guided the C10 off the street and parked in front of the garage door. He got out, grabbing the box. As they walked around the house to the front door, Ryder noticed something strange.

"The house is dark," Yakira said asking the question that was running through his mind. "I wonder where everyone is." It was odd; there was always someone here, at least Bubbie. It was odd to see the house draped in darkness, it was almost eerie. A little comfort broke through as Yakira used the small flashlight on her keychain to guide their way up onto the front porch. She fumbled through the keys. Finding the door key, she unlocked it and they went inside.

This was nearly like home to Ryder, even in the dark he knew right where to reach for the light switch. In an instant, they were bathed in the gleaming light of the chandelier that hung down from the open foyer in front of the grand staircase. Even before the front door closed behind her, Yakira began calling out. "Mom, Dad, Bubbie." As she went from the living room to the dining room, the family room, the kitchen, turning the lights on in the rooms as she entered. Ryder noticed a note taped to a mirror of the hall tree in the foyer. The note read.

Yakira

Aunt Lisabeth fell and broke her hip, she is at Cox Hospital in Springfield, and we have gone to see her and are going to stay at her place tonight. You know how bad a housekeeper she is, going to clean it up will be back home late tomorrow. Love Mom.

Yakira walked back into the foyer and began to continue her search upstairs, she had placed one foot on the runner when Ryder handed her the note. "I guess we are on our own." She said, folding up the paper and dropping it down on a small table at the bottom of the stairs.

"Guess I'll see you, then?" Ryder said, turning and grabbing the door knob.

She quickly placed her hand on the door and said, "Do you not remember doctor's orders? No driving!" Letting her arms tighten around his waist and snuggling closer to him. "You are all mine tonight." He didn't return the embrace.

"You also remember no excitement."

She pulled back from him. "What is wrong?"

"I have to hear from Alex." He said, placing the box down on the table to remove his jacket, and hanging it up on the coat rack. He removed the holster from his shoulder and then placed the gun down on the table below the coat rack. "She is the only one that can help me." He grabbed the box and walked away.

He walked to the family room at the back of the house and flopped down on the loveseat that faced the flat screen TV mounted on the wall behind a pair of wing chairs. He once again opened the box and pulled out one of the notes. It was on red construction paper, written in black crayon:

WHERE LOVE LIES IT HAS NO MEANING

A ROSE IS BUT THE TOUCH

NEVER IS BUT TOO MUCH

CLOSE YOUR EYES AND YOU WILL SEE OUR BEGINNING

He unfolded the notes and laid them down on the table and examined the writing. Yakira picked up the remote and turned on the TV that was tuned to a cable news program. The host was talking, speaking about the upcoming election.

Ryder rolled his eyes up to look at two politicians and mumbled: "A devil is a devil no matter what face you put on it." She muted the sound and again his attention turned to the notes on the coffee table. She sat down beside him; he could smell the sweetness of her perfume-honeysuckle, the warmth of her body next to him, that comfort that he was not all alone in this world, the softness of her hair on his face as she leaned over and placed her head on his shoulder. He lowered his head and snuggled against her for just a moment before he lifted his head again. She lifted her head and looked into his eyes. Letting his hand slide down behind her neck he pulled her close and began to kiss her as the reporter on TV told about an earthquake hitting Eureka Springs, leaving a large hole in Spring Street revealing the underground town. Then it switched to a scene in front of the courthouse in Eureka Springs with another reporter.

"What the...!" He quickly picked up the remote and turned up the sound as the reporter spoke.

"Just as in the case of the Kansas City Butcher, the E.S. Independent, a local newspaper in Eureka Springs received a cryptic letter just before the body of Anna Peters was found. I read the quote from the letter received by the newspaper. 'The body of love is but the host. Once in the city of Chiefs, I now hold the city of ghosts. Now listen and you shall hear, one will die and soon the city will fall with fear.'

If our viewers will remember the famous case that held Kansas City in terror for months, even to the point that there were no Royal and Chief night games played, and nightclubs shut down around nine o'clock. The grisly murder reign was brought to a conclusion when former Kansas City Detective Rick Ryder and Special Agent Isabelle Alexander of the FBI arrested Velour, her face painted with the victim's blood. Velour is considered one of the most vicious female serial killers of all time. Brutally murdering and dismembering, thus, the Star gave her the name the Kansas City Butcher...

"It is it believed that the wrong person could be in prison?" The host asked the reporter, "The notes are very similar, are they not?"

Ryder turned the TV off and tossed the remote onto the coffee table. Yakira slipped her pink cowboy boots off and curled one leg under her so she could sit slightly sideways to face him.

"Are you okay, Sweetie?"   He could feel her fingers running through his sandy colored hair, pushing it back. "He closed his eyes and was still as she continued to stroke his hair. "You want to do something? Maybe watch a movie?"

"No, "he said softly, his eyes still closed. Suddenly his phone rang to life. He picked it up and saw the screen; it was the photo of a pretty woman in her late thirties with long light brown hair with golden highlights. Under the photo was the name Alex. He pressed the home button and answered as he headed for the front door.

"Where did you get it?"

"Where did we get the first one?"   Ryder said as he stepped outside onto the front porch. "It was shoved under the door at the vic's home."

"And the rose?"

"Left for me at the hospital, just like it was before. She is watching me," Ryder said as he stood gazing out into the dark. "And the note is on red construction paper."

How can she be? She is in prison I know what you are thinking, and stop it! We got the right person, Ryder. We caught her with blood on her face. It was a DNA match. It was the vic's blood, it was... "

"Red construction paper?" He asked, interrupting her. "

"I know, Rick!"

"We agreed to tell no one about that. Not the press, not the AJ, DA not even Captain Grosstree. I still have them."

"I know, Rick." She said calling him by his first name. Then there was silence at first waiting for her answer; he rubbed his free hand over his chin as she replied. "Since we did that I can't just walk in and have someone compare the handwriting. But I found someone else who can. He said he can let us know in 48 hours, for a price."

"Whatever it takes."

"The lab here is comparing the notes from those sent to the Star and those to the Independent. They should have the results back soon. Suddenly her tone changed from hardened FBI agent to soft and kind, a voice that he remembered showed him a softer side to her, "...Okay honey, I will be right there."

"You not alone?"

"I have some special company I really need to get back to."

"You know what we have to do?"

"I will pick you up in the morning."

"I am at Yakira's parent's house in town," Ryder said as he heard the front door of the house open.

"So I am assuming she is coming with us?"

Ryder turned and looked at Yakira standing there and grinned as he said. "She is part of my team. I will see you in the morning. Around seven. I will buy you breakfast."

Chapter 4

There is something about the morning, that point in the day that the night is still holding on tightly, the calm before the storm, before the bustle of a town coming alive, overwhelmed. The feeling when one could stand embraced in the stillness and know that the new day is beginning. The aroma of the pot of freshly made coffee, drifting up like a heavenly scented cloud to guide one's way through the maze of the working day.

Ryder clutched the mug of coffee in his hands, enjoying its warmth and its taste. He had already showered, shaved and was dressed in a dark navy sports coat, pants to match, and a white long sleeved shirt. He pulled the curtain back and looked outside, he saw a black Chevrolet Suburban pull up and stop in front of the house. He quickly walked back into the kitchen and set the empty mug down on the counter.

"She is here." He said, looking at Yakira rising and holding out her own mug. Dressed in black jeans and a pink blouse she turned to him. "You ready?" He added. She nodded and followed him outside locking the door behind her. He opened the rear door of the SUV and held it open as Yakira climbed into the back seat. Ryder opened the passenger door and seated himself in the front seat.

The driver was Isabelle Mary Alexander, Special Agent for the F.B.I. in the Springfield resident office. Her long hair, highlighted with blonde streaks, framed a long thin face that seemed to belong more on the runway, modeling the latest fashion instead of a badge. Her fashion was typical federal government, plain and bland, dull gray pants and matching jacket with a white blouse, the collar pulled out over the collar of the jacket. Her eyes were covered with aviator style sunglasses, the lenses large and mirrored. She turned to him and her face showing no emotion.

"You promised me breakfast, where to?"

"I know a place, it is on the way. Just drive."

Alex fired up the SUV and drove out of town back through Roaring River State Park, past Eagle Rock and at the top of a hill, turned onto the split personality highway, as it was known as P till it reached the Arkansas state line when it suddenly changed its name to highway 23, and its personality as the pavement changed color and texture.

"Yakira, see you still like pink," Alex said glancing up into the rearview mirror.

23

"You should try it. It might give you a little color," Yakira replied back.

"It isn't that I don't like the color, it is just what must be."

"The Independent got another letter," Alex said as she guided the SUV through twisting curves, hills as they pushed further into Arkansas. The sign warned of a hard bend ahead, she pushed down on the brake and guided the vehicle through the turn, barely missing another car pulling a boat trailer that crossed the centerline.

"What did it say?"

"You can find out, they are publishing it," Alex said pausing as she guided the SUV down a long hill. At the bottom of the hill was another sharp twist in the road. Maybe it was the fact that she was concentrating on the road, but Ryder felt it was more, that she was trying to avoid asking the next question. She glanced over at him "You get it online..." She turned back to the road.

Ryder pulled his smartphone out of his pocket and brought up the front page of the newspaper. There, printed in its full glory was the letter sent to them. It read:

Blood is the glue that binds the soul that binds heart that I search for.

My heart is shattered for my love is not fulfilled

There are but stolen glances, give me my love.

Or on the even night blood shall be spilled.

Ryder looked up from his phone. "This is a totally different note. Look at the I's. This isn't the same person. Ryder dropped his attention to his phone again and accessing the Kansas City Star website and pulled up a past photo but it had been removed. He turned to Alex he could see the doubt rising over Alex's face, splashing up on her like a child in a mud puddle with new boots.

"You really think this is her, don't you?" She asked.

"I don't know."

"I think we are dealing with a copycat.

"And the red construction paper?" Ryder asked letting his gaze drift over to her.

"I don't know, Rick. When you told me about that note—." She paused and took a deep breath. "I was—I was...."

"I know. It took me back there too."

"Enough of this!" Alex said, annoyed. "I need a blasted cup of coffee. Where is this place?"

"It is right up here around the corner on the left."

If it were the middle of summer the canopy of trees would have hidden the restaurant from view, but, the wood log structure was exposed to all visitors. A poster that announced the upcoming 'Gala Costume Street Ball in Eureka Springs' hung on the door. The rustic look continued inside with a cowboy theme, with horseshoes tacked up on the wall. The hostess showed them to a table with a red and white checked cloth and seated them there; Ryder and Yakira on one side and Alex across the table from them. She handed them each a menu. The table was already laid out with flatware and large white coffee mugs.

"Coffee?" The waitress asked as she walked up holding a glass pot of coffee.

"Oh god, yes!" Alex said with appreciation, barely looking up from her menu. "Regular" the waitress filled each mug. "Just leave the pot," Alex added.

"Cream and sugar?"

"Yes, for us." Ryder said as he smiled at the young waitress who was just barely in her twenties with blonde hair, "For her, black and strong."

"Our special this morning is huckleberry pancakes. All you can eat."

"Sound good?" Ryder asked as Yakira agreed and Alex grunted, slurping down her bitter coffee. "And make sure they are fresh, just like that smile of yours." A slight rosy color flushed over the waitress's cheeks as she agreed. She quickly returned with a small metal picture of cream and set it down on the table. Yakira reached over and poured some cream in her coffee. Ryder did the same. As he added two teaspoons of sugar and stirred the coffee with a spoon he noticed out of the corner of his eye that the waitress was standing there staring at him.

"You look familiar." The waitress said, getting closer to him. "You are in my bedroom."

Alex choked on her coffee, quickly grabbing a napkin to wipe her mouth as she asked: "Is there something you are not telling us, Rick?"

"The Pale Ryder of the Kansas City Chiefs?" She asked as she stepped back. "Yeah! Number seven. I had your poster on my bedroom wall. Oh lord! You are so dreamy. And now you won the lottery."

"Yes, and he is very much taken!" Yakira piped in, wrapping her arm around his, placing her head on his chest. "Now, what about those pancakes?" The waitress turned and walked away.

Ryder watched as Alex downed the mug of coffee and poured another one. As he picked up his mug he took a sip and asked. "You want something harder? Like a good whiskey?"

"You know I don't drink." She replied as she lifted the mug to her lips.

"You did after we questioned the butcher."

She set the mug back down on the table and looked at him, tilting her head slightly sideways, her dark green eyes glaring at him. "If I remember right I wasn't alone. You were right there hoisting them with me. If I remember right we finished that whole bottle off." Alex lifted the mug back up and started to take a sip, but set the mug back down. "It was a little bit of fear and if I remember right, a celebration too." She said letting her gaze drop down to the mug that she twirled in her hands. She lifted her gaze to him again.

"Yeah, that it was over." Ryder said, "And now it is going to begin again. I have that same creepy feeling I got before…"

"You mean that she is watching you?" Alex said as Ryder looked around the room. There were several other customers there, mostly older gentlemen grouped around one table, talking about things that old men

26

speak of- the weather, politics, and women. A couple pointed at him, but not one person struck him as out of place, but still he had that feeling that someone was watching.

Again Alex dropped her gaze to her mug of coffee, taking the pot and filling it up again from a couple of sips she had taken. "You know what I did when that case was over? I went home, threw my clothes away, and took a hot shower for two hours straight trying to scrub away that evil. After that, I went to a Baptist Church and got dunked, went to the Methodist and got sprinkled, and after that, I went to a priest to have him bless me. Even now, I close my eyes and it is still there." She used the napkin to dab away the tears that were beginning to form in her eyes. "How do you not remember, Rick?"

"I remember," Ryder said dreadfully. "There are I nights I wake up in a sweat and I have to get up and put another sheet on the bed. I hear her voice, and look and see that no one is there." Ryder sat there looking at Alex; she too was not saying anything. He could hear the clank of dishes and clink of flatware as the others in the restaurant were busy eating and chatting. The waitress returned to the table with their orders and set the plates of pancakes on the table. The young waitress smiled and placed a small glass pitcher of syrup in front of him.

"I brought you the last homemade blueberry syrup." She moved closer to him and whispered in his ear. "The gentlemen at that table over there wanted it but…" She smiled even brighter as she placed her hand on his shoulder and added. '…he's just a bank president. Besides, you are cuter." She stood up and reached into her apron and pulled out a pad and a pen. "I was wondering if I could get an autograph?" She asked as she handed him the pad and pen. She pushed her hair back and tilted her head slightly as she timidly added "…and a phone number?"

Ryder took the pad and pen and looked up at her. "Nicole, wasn't it? I would be glad to give you an autograph." He said as he looked down at the pad and wrote his name. He looked back up at her and handed her back the pad and pen and continued. "But no number."

"Yeah you little shiksa, I have his number, you don't get it."

I wasn't trying to hit on him or anything I was just trying to…"

"Don't knock a teakettle at me!" Yakira said, "I know what you were doing. Now leave!" The waitress turned like a scolded puppy and walked away with her emotional tail tucked between her legs. Yakira stood and dismissed herself to go to the restroom.

"Teakettle?" Alex asked clearly confused from Yakira's expression.

"A Jewish thing." Ryder said taking a sip of coffee from the mug.

"Is she the one?"

"Who?" Ryder asked confused, as he picked up the pitcher of syrup.

"Yakira is she the one!" Alex said.

"What one?" Ryder asked as he poured the syrup on his pancakes.

"The one! Come on, Rick. You got that waitress were she is going to have to put ice cubes down her pants because of how you look. You are worth what- a billion dollars? You are over 40 years old and have never been married. Either you can't find the right woman or you are gay." She leaned over the table and closer to him and added. "I know for a personal fact that is not true." She leaned back in her chair and glanced over her shoulder at Yakira walking back to the table. She turned back to him. "So, is she the one? You know, marriage?"

"Marriage!" Ryder drew back nearly choking on his bite of pancakes. "Who is talking about marriage?"

"I think she is the one and you should ask her to marry you."

"Who is getting married?" Yakira asked as she sat down.

"Nobody!" Ryder said, quickly taking a sip of coffee. He wiped his mouth with the napkin as he added. "Hurry up and eat! We need to get back on the road, and ask them about this murder."

"There is something I have always wanted to know," Yakira said as she poured some syrup on her pancakes. "Why was this killer called the Butcher?"

"Two reasons," Alex said, taking a bite of her breakfast. "The bodies were always sliced open." She took another bite and added. "and

28

she took an organ. A liver, a kidney, lungs, the last one…" Alex swallowed and took another bite. She looked over at Ryder as he spoke.

"And the last one a child's heart." He had tried so hard to bury that image in his mind, of that young girl laying there her chest broken up. He swore to himself he didn't want to see that image but here it was again. "I don't want to see another child. Alex if this is her…"

"It isn't her!" Alex retorted back as she finished up her meal and wiped her mouth and tossed the napkin onto her plate. "Come on let's go! We are burning daylight."

Ryder paid the bill and gave the waitress a larger tip and they were on the road. A twisting, turning, strip of pavement known as Arkansas Highway 23, that slithered through the rolling hills. It was a slow trip from steep hills, sharp bends cutting through the hills, and large stones piled up as if they were books on a student's desk. Ryder wondered what stories they had to tell. Another hard twist of the serpent's tail and a railroad track appeared on the left, along with a small stream between the road and the tracks. Another twist in the road and rolling hills, looking as if they were great waves on the sea appeared in front of them.

Passing under the power lines was as if they were entering a time machine, back to the time when large black steam locomotives sat on the tracks waiting outside of the depot to hitch themselves to large green railcars to make up the Eureka Springs & Northwest Arkansas Railway. Slipping deeper into the town the buildings seemed to close in as the street narrowed, right after passing the Grand Central Hotel, the castle-like city hall, where many lives would begin with the issue of a wedding license, and others would end in the courtroom.

As they passed through the old part of town the time trip ended and once again modern intervention began. Shopping centers and hotels all lined up along Highway 62, to East Van Buren which led them to a left on Passion Play Road. As they topped the hill to the left was the Eureka Springs Police Department.

If it wasn't for the signs, and the white SUV's lined up outside, one could just pass by, thinking this was nothing more than a single story home with beige stone-like siding. Alex pulled the black SUV up and backed it into a spot next to two city cruisers. Ryder held the door open for Yakira and Alex and followed them inside. Once inside he removed his sunglasses. They walked up to the information desk sealed behind glass.

A thin framed woman with short cropped silver streaked hair walked up to the glass. She pushed up her thick black framed eye glasses. "May I help you?"

"I am Rick Ryder; this is my associate Yakira Rosen. We want to talk to the detective in charge of the Annie Peters homicide."

"What department are you from?"

"Private; we have been hired to investigate," Ryder said

The woman turned around and looked at a man, who walked up to the glass. He was tall and stocky with platinum hair parted on the side and dressed in a dark blue suit with a gray and red striped tie that gleamed off his light blue shirt. "What is this regarding?" He asked as he sucked in his gut to make himself appear more impressive.

"Are you the detective in charge of the Peter's case?"

"I am Detective Ron Shepherd and yes I am, and it is an ongoing case." He looked each of them over as if he was a food critic for a high style magazine and they were a greasy fast food. "Since I don't deal with private dicks I would advise you to get out of here, or I will have you all arrested for interfering with police."

"I don't think you will do that," Alex said.

"Who are you to tell me that?"

Alex slipped her hand down into the pocket of her jacket and produced a small black wallet. Flipping the wallet open, she revealed her ID and badge. She took a step forward and pressed it up against the glass as she spoke slowly and very firmly. "Isabelle Alexander Special Agent F.B.I."

"How do I know that is real?"

"Simple. I make a call and have agents come in here and take this place over while I personally go through every case you have ever touched. Do you want me to make that call or do you answer my friend's questions?"

"Buzz them in, Teresa." Detective Shepherd said as she stepped back. "I will meet you in my office. Third door on the right." The double doors buzzed and Ryder pushed them forward and allowed Alex and Yakira to enter as he followed them down the hall and walked into the detective's office.

It was typical small town police, a small room dominated with a metal discount desk. Detective Shepherd sat on the edge, his foot dangling above the floor. He picked up a bottle of Diet Pepsi, unscrewed the top and took a swig and replaced the cap. "Okay, what is this all about? Simon Peters killed his wife and now he is dead. It seems to me the case should be closed."

"I am interested in how she died. The method." Ryder said as he reached into his inside jacket pocket and pulled out a small red vinyl notebook and pen.

"Single stab in the back." Detective Shepherd said as he picked up a folder on his desk. "County coroner says a long thin blade likely a stiletto knife at ten inches in length. " He opened the file and read. "Single entry wound to between the 4th and 5th coastal cartilages in the rib cage piercing the left atrium."

"Direction of impact."

"I don't know." The detective replied opening up the folder. "All the coroner reports is 'cause of death due to homicide stab wound in back.' " He glanced up at Alex and continued. "We may not be the FBI…" Letting the eyes drift over to Ryder he added, " but we get the job done."

"Can I see that?" Ryder asked, holding out his hand. He handed the file to Ryder. " I am assuming you have the CSI, search reports, EV list."

"You sound like a cop."

"Use to be," Ryder said, not lifting his gaze from the reports. "Kansas City Homicide Squad."

"Oh, you are that Rick Ryder, the one that played with the Chiefs. My daughter used to have your poster on her bedroom wall."

Ryder lifted his gaze from the report that he held in his hands and asked "A waitress named Nicole?"

"Yes, you know her?"

"A lovely young girl." Ryder dropped his gaze back down to the file and continued to read. "Where was D.B. found?" He asked referring to the location of the body.

"Basin Park, near the fountain."

"Was the body slit open and organ removed?"

"Oh good heaven, no! There was nothing strange like that. It was a typical domestic dispute. If you read in there we have a witness that saw Peters and his wife getting into a fight at the Passion Play. In fact, security had to escort him out. They overheard him threatening to kill her."

"Only one problem," Ryder said as he flipped through the pages of the report. "I have a witness that places him at Crowder College in Neosho when she was killed."

"Peters told us about that person, we couldn't ever find her." Detective Shepherd said as he again picked up the bottle of soda, unscrewed the top and took a drink before replacing the top. "We are not a bunch of dumb hicks. We kicked over every stone. We couldn't find anything and we just figured that he was lying."

Ryder looked up from the file at the man and handed the file to Alex who began to sort through the photos of the crime scene while he picked up the evidence sheet and began reading through it. "You heard that the Independent is getting letters?"

"Yes," Detective Shepherd said opening his bottle of pop, taking a sip and reattaching the lid. "Are you trying to tell me there is some serial killer loose in Eureka Springs?" He looked over at Alex who was flipping through the pages of the file then back to Ryder. "We can't have a serial killer here."

"Do you not thrive on ghost stories?" Alex asked.

"Yes, but not those of tourists."

"What is all of the gab of a serial killer?" A man grumbled as he walked in. He was well dressed, suit, tie, the works, hair neatly trimmed and styled and smelled of Tommy Hilfiger cologne. As he passed by Ryder, Alex looked up from the evidence sheet at the man walking over to the detective, then back down to the sheet as she asked.

"Did you receive a note before the Peter's killing?"

"What is it with all this talk about killings?" The man that entered snorted, turning to the detective as he demanded. "Who are these people?"

"They are investigators Jason; they are investigating the murder of that young lady in Basin Park." Shepherd turned to Ryder and said "This is our mayor Jason Edwards. Jason this is Rick Ryder and his associate Yakira Rosen."

"And this person?" The mayor asked gazing at Alex, who closed the file.

"Agent Alexander FBI," Alex said.

"FBI," The mayor asked puzzled. "What is the FBI doing investigating a murder? What, those damn silly letters that the newspaper is getting? I want this stopped!"

"Typical," Ryder grumbled.

"What does that mean?"

"You are a politician."

"What is wrong with that?"

Ryder tilted his head and laughed mockingly as he said. "You are all the same; it doesn't matter if it is a little town like this or the nation itself, all you care about is what it is going to look like to voters. My gosh, you have someone threatening to murder people in your town and you don't want anyone knowing?"

"My baby girl is getting married; I will not have you interrupting it. I want you all out of this town."

"What part of federal bureau did you not get?" Alex said closing the file as she stressed the word and handing the folder back to the detective. "Arkansas is still part of the United States now unless…"

"I will phone your supervisor."

"Take a chill pill Will," Yakira spoke up. "How about we just leave here." The mayor turned to her placing his thumbs in his belt he grinned as if he had won the grand prize at the country fair. However, as Yakira lips twisted into a cocky grin, his quickly faded as she added. "Then do an interview for KYTV about the possibility of a killer loose in the city. I figure by the end of the day it should hit the national cable outlets, and by tomorrow the AP, what do you think is going to happen when the tourists hear that?"

"Yeah mayor," Ryder said. "And what are voters going to think?"

"All right," the mayor replied. "You can investigate but try to keep a low profile." He turned and began to walk out of the office, but stopped in the doorway and turned back. "Shepherd, you watch over them. If they get out of line, you let me know." The mayor turned back and walked out.

"Wait one dang-blasted minute!" Detective Shepherd said as picked up his bottle of diet soda, opened it and took a large drink. He returned the lid and continued his tone showing the concern. "I remember hearing about this." He pointed at Ryder. "You were on TV about this. The cutting up of bodies…" He paused before exclaiming out. "The Kansas City Butcher she sent notes before murdering but you—she in prison isn't she?"

"Can I see evidence A-14?" Alex asked.

"Sure," the detective said as he walked around the desk and began to search through the papers and folders that were lying in piles. "We figure it didn't have anything to do with the murder. It was just a sales receipt for art supplies. "Finding a clear plastic Ziploc bag he picked it up. "We have a lot of artists around here." He handed Ryder the Ziploc bag. Sealed inside of the bag was a printed out receipt from a local grocery store in a neighboring town, dated the same day that Annie was murdered. Ryder read the items. 2-liter bottle of soda, 1 bag of potato chips, a loaf of white bread, 1 package of deli cut lunch meat, a small box of crayons and one package of red construction paper'.

Chapter 5

It did seem to be a long shot tracing a grocery receipt from a town that was a half an hour drive away, left in the park that saw thousands of people; it could have been left there by anybody. However, it was the oddity of red construction paper that made Ryder want to investigate further. Besides, this was the only lead they had.

Highway 62 led them out of town and through Berryville and to Green Forest. It was a small town, one where everyone knew everyone, and who and what everyone was doing; the type that if one asked for directions it always involved the first or second stop light. So when a gloss black SUV with government license plates rolled into town the rumors began spreading faster than a wildfire across the prairie and suspecting eyes followed their every move as they pulled into the parking lot of Harp's Grocery store just off Main Street, by the time Ryder opened the door of the SUV he could feel the eyes of those standing on the sidewalk standing watching them as they walked towards the store. Men didn't wear sports coats in this town. He turned and faced a woman putting her groceries in her red Ford escort wagon. He nodded at her and smiled. She quickly slammed the shut and got inside her car, but didn't drive away. Instead she watched them. A poster hung on the door announcing the upcoming "Street Ball Gala' at Eureka Springs. He stepped inside and removed his sunglasses as he glared around the store. Aisles neatly laid out with large signs above to guide you, but he couldn't find the sign he was looking for.

However, Alex walked up to a clerk and said, "I need to see the manager." Alex showed her badge. "Right now!" The young clerk never having seen a federal agent before, couldn't say a word, instead, she just raised her hand and pointed to the office on the side of the store. Again the same glazed over stare, like deer in the headlights of a semi happened to the manager when Alex showed him her badge.

The manager had a thin frame, gray hair slicked over, parted on the side. "What is this about, agent?" The manager sputtered out as he fell back down into his office chair. With a shaky hand, he reached up and removed his round wire-framed glasses. Reaching into the pocket of his pinstriped shirt he removed a white cloth and wiped the lenses clean. He slipped the glasses back on his face using both hands.

"Murder!" Ryder said firmly.

"Murrr-Murder? Oh, my lands." He took the cloth that he had used to clean his glasses and wiped the sweat from his forehead. Yakira must have seen the fear in his face, as she pushed in between Ryder and Alex and grinned at the man.

"We only want to talk to you about a customer of yours," Yakira said softly as she reached down and placed her hand on the manager's shoulder. With her other hand, she reached over and took the plastic bag holding the receipt from Alex. She held it up in front of the man and asked. "Do you remember this person?"

The manager took the bag and adjusted his glasses so that he could see out of his bifocals. "This came from Selene's register."

"Where is she?" Ryder demanded. The manager's hand began to shake again.

"Can we talk to her?" Yakira asked as she took the bag back from the man and stood up.

"She is back at the deli today." He replied, removing his glasses and again cleaning them with the cloth.

"You have been a tremendous help. Thank you. Shalom."

Still the eyes of those in the store were watching them as the trio, with Yakira in the middle, walked over towards the deli. "How did you know to do that?" Ryder asked.

"What, be kind to him?" Yakira asked looking up at him. "By watching you…" she turned and faced Alex. "…both of you. If the person is scared do you not make them feel less scared…." She looked back at Ryder and continued "…and act like a friend?" She turned and faced the deli, jutting her chin out, proud of herself as she added. "Didn't I get what we wanted to know?"

Ryder saw a young girl standing behind the counter; she was pretty with long dark hair that would normally flow down over her shoulder but was tied back and covered with a hairnet, busy with a customer picking out pieces of fried chicken from the counter and placing them in a plastic bag.

"You want to question her?" Ryder asked Yakira.

"Nah, I think I will let you two do it," Yakira replied with a mocking grin as she added. "Of course, if you get in trouble I will be there to bail you out.

Selene placed a price tag on the bag of chicken and handed it to the man and just before he pushed his cart away he gave Ryder a quick glance and snarled. "Must be a Raider's fan." Ryder joked about the rivalry between the NFL teams before stepping up to the counter.

"What can I get you today?" The young girl asked her dark eyes smiling as broadly as she was.

"Answer some questions," Ryder said as he reached down and took the plastic with the receipt inside from Yakira and placed it down on the counter in front of Selene. "Do you remember the person that bought these items?"

"Oh yes, I do!" She said firm and surely as she looked down at the receipt.

"You have many customers in here every day, why would you remember this person?"

"Because of the way she was acting. Real creepy! She kept staring up at the lights and talking about how her true love would be coming back to her."

"It was a woman?" Alex asked, "Describe her."

Ryder reached into his inside jacket pocket and pulled out a small notebook and pen and began jotting down the description as Selene spoke. "Long blonde hair and beautiful, I mean beauty like you don't see in these parts; every guy in here was looking at her, the kind of woman that guys fantasize about."

"How tall?" Ryder asked.

"Not too tall , but taller than me, five nine, five ten. Maybe 120 pounds.

"Anything else?"

"Yes!" Selene said, "Her eyes."

"What about them? Ryder asked, looking up from the notebook he was writing in.

"They were bright blue but scary, real scary." Selene's eyes opened wide. "Oh, and one more thing! She had a tattoo on her hand."

"A tattoo?" Alex asked, taken aback by her words, "Of what?"

"One word, 'thirsty,' but it was written out like it was...."

"Running blood?" Alex asked, sounding startled as if she knew the answer without it even being told.

"Yes, and it looked like blood," Selene said then turning to Ryder and added. "At first, that is what I thought it was. You know what I mean? I have seen idiots cut things like that into their hands."

"How old do you think she was?" Ryder asked as he glanced over at Alex who was just standing there; he wondered why she wasn't asking any questions.

"Young mid-twenties, but that wasn't the weirdest thing she did, the thing that made me happy when she left," Selena said as Ryder continued to stare at Alex, just standing there.

"Huh? What? "Ryder asked, turning to face the young girl again.

"I was telling you the real strange thing she did. She took the box of crayons and threw them all away except one, the black one."

They walked outside. Ryder reached into his jacket pocket and pulled out his sunglasses, he flipped the temples open and said. "What do you think?"

"It can't be!" Alex said as she slipped her sunglasses over her eyes. He could feel Yakira's gaze burning into him, without even looking at her he answered her question before she could ask it.

"We only have one witness that ever saw the Kansas City Butcher," Ryder said as he walked toward the suburban. "She told us that she saw the tattoo on the hand." He held the door open for her and looked back at her as she got in. He shut the door and walked over to the other side and held the rear passenger door open for Yakira and she got in. "That read "'Thirsty.'"

*****

Shadows were growing longer when they returned to Eureka Springs. Passing by the police station again, it occurred to Ryder, that the Passion Play should have been his first stop. It was one of the biggest draws in the area, and surely someone else may have seen Simon and Anne fighting; maybe they could get some more answers. Pulling into the lot, there were only five other cars parked there and Alex pulled up next to a tan Ford security vehicle with an amber bar on the roof.

Ryder stepped out and opened Yakira's door, he stood listening to the stillness, only the cool breeze drifting through the cedars, as if it were God's gentle sigh, the wind whipping up and creating a small dust devil, the tail of his jacket flapping like the flag that hung proudly on the pole outside the ticket booth.

"Hey! You can't park here." He heard a man's voice say. He turned back and saw a tall thin man approaching, wearing a security uniform carrying a cloth bag. "You will have to park in the designated areas."

"We are not here to see the show," Alex said, pulling out her ID and showing it to him. "We are here to see you."

"What about?" The guard snapped to attention his eyes widening as he saw the badge.

"The domestic situation you had here about two weeks ago," Ryder said.

"Oh yeah, him, had to escort him clean off the place."

"Do you know what started the fight?"

"No," the security officer said. "I was just called to get him out of there."

"Did anyone see the fight?"

"Jesus did." The man replied.

"I know. He sees everything." Ryder said mockingly, but anyone isn't a Deity"

"I mean the actor who was playing Jesus. He saw the whole thing. You can find him on the main stage. His name is Matthew Blake. Just go in through the gate over here and it will take you down to the stage."

"One more thing, what is with the bag? " Ryder asked pointing to the bag the guard was carrying.

"Oh new thing happening, people are thinking the Christ statue is a wishing well. They say a pray. Toss a coin down at his feet. Every day we get lots of pennies, and other coins. You know tourists they read somewhere that if you do that, then your wish will come true,"

Ryder opened the gate and allowed the women in and they followed the path down to the main stage. It was a little strange entering out of the tunnel onto the huge outdoor set, the gravel crushing under his feet, looking up at the empty sea of red seats, with the concrete bleachers in the back of the seats. The "cheap seats" in the house. A gust of wind picked up again, as Ryder looked across the multiple sets that were built out of what looked like stone. Standing there, he felt so out of place as if he were a visitor from a different time, a different era. He a caught sight of a man wearing a white tunic, with long curly hair and a full beard, that looked just like the photos of Jesus he had seen as a kid.

"Matthew!" Ryder called out as he saw him climb the steps of the stage set dead center. He stopped and turned to them. "We need to ask you some questions." Alex and Yakira followed Ryder up the steps. "We want to ask you about the couple that you saw arguing a couple weeks ago."

"Oh them," He said with displeasure. "They almost ruined the entire show for everyone." He sat down on a small box on stage. "We work hard here. Everyone thinks it is easy, we work a couple of hours a night and that is it, but when we are not performing, we are out here rehearsing. You have to be the best because there is always someone who wants your spot. Right when I am supposed to be overturning all the tables in the temple, they start yelling at each other. And I don't mean just yelling, I mean screaming at the top of their lungs. It brought the whole thing to a standstill; we had to stop the play just to get them out of here."

"So you know what the argument was about," Ryder asked, producing his notebook from the pocket of his jacket.

"Everyone here did," Matthew said as he pointed to the stands. "You see that center aisle? That was where they stood. It was all about cheating."

"Him?"

"No her," Matthew said standing and walking out to the edge of the temple set. "It was about her cheating on him, with some older man."

"Who?"

"I don't know. But I did hear something about he lived in Cassville."

"Do you remember anything else?"Ryder asked.

"Only that just before they drug him out, he said he that 'was going to kill her.' I guess he did because the next day I had heard they found her body in the Basin Park."

"This may sound like a strange question," Alex said, "But did you happen to see a blonde woman around here?"

Matthew looked back over his shoulder and then turned around to face her. "The one with the haunting eyes, oh yes she approached me after the show." He stepped back to the center of the stage with the others and continued. "Okay, we get some strange ones here, some wanting me to bless them and stuff like that, but..." He hesitated to even say it. "She came and asked me. 'Is it true that in death love is forever?' I didn't know what to tell her, so I just said, 'Yes, my child.' And she kissed my hand and walked away."

"You pretended to be Jesus?"

"We are instructed if someone crazy like comes up like that we are to go along with them, not to upset them, and she was freaky spooky. Oh man, she was a beauty, one that you just don't see in real life, but then she walked up to Danny Carr..." He paused for a moment as if he was wondering how corny his next words were going to sound. "The guy that plays Judas, she gave him something..." Again he paused almost grinning as he said. "It was a half-dollar piece. A piece of silver."

Ryder thanked him and gave him a card that had his phone number on it and added that if he remembered anything else to please call him. Ryder folded up his notebook and placed it back in his jacket pocket. He began following Yakira and Alex back down the steps

Matthew cried out. "Does this have anything to do with the letters the newspaper is getting?"

Ryder stopped and turned to him as he pleaded with Ryder. "I have a wife and two kids if there is a killer on the loose, I would like to know."

"You got a gun?" Ryder asked and Matthew nodded his head as Ryder added. "I would keep it close."

Ryder and the women continued making their way back to the exit when Matthew yelled out. "Hey, there is one other thing!" Ryder stopped and turned back to the man on the stage. "The girl who plays Mary Magdalene, she talked to her too; she said the woman was staying at Crescent."

Chapter 6

In the 1800's all through America towns were starting up, many due to strikes of gold, silver, or other riches to made, but the cozy little town known as the little 'Switzerland of the Ozarks' rose up because of legends. The tales of miracle healing waters that cured all kinds of alignments from the sniffles to restoring the sight of the blind, even bringing peace to warring Indian tribes. To the Native Americans this was sacred land. To the white settlers it was to become the kingdom of the 'first class' and every kingdom needed its castle- that was the Crescent Hotel.

As with all castles, it was placed high up so that it may not only look down upon its subjects but also so that they may look up at its majesty. The Crescent Hotel towered on the West Mountain. The 78 room hotel with its eclectic array of architectural styles, complete with overhanging balconies with large supporting columns, and towers rising up above the five stories, with large windows that allowed the sunlight to shine in. An eighteen-inch thick wall of magnesium limestone, large open airy rooms, and a gala ballroom all added to the castle- like a dream. At one point it was considered the grandest resort hotel in America.

Like all palaces, this one too had its tales of ghosts roaming up and down the hall, opening doors, and tossing items on the floor, which all drew back to a time when a man named Norman Baker arrived on the scene and bought the aging hotel for the purpose of opening a cancer hospital and health resort. Just as the miracle healing water claims drew people there, it was his claims that patients would walk away from the "resort" cancer-free that drew the hopeless there. It seemed that it worked. Those that were ill would check in and would mysteriously be cured and walk away in the middle of the night. The truth was more sinister; the patients died an agony filled death, sometimes down in the basement, which served as the morgue, lying all alone on a cold examining table so those in town could not hear their dying cries, and the myth of Dr. Baker's lie could not be exposed.

Ryder wasn't sure if he believed the tales of playful spirits moving around the Christmas gifts, or a ghostly waiter carrying a tray of butter in the hallways, and that wasn't even on his mind as they climbed up the steps that led from the street to the hotel.

He held one of the large French doors open and allowed Yakira and Alex to enter then followed them in. Once inside he removed his sunglasses and gazed around the huge Victorian style lobby. To the right was a sitting area with red button tufted Victorian style wing chairs facing each other over a rich wooden coffee table and a high back sofa that faced a huge stone fireplace that seemed to dominate their entire lobby. It was the perfect place to just sit and enjoy a glass of wine, or just stand and warm one's self in front of the fire, but that wasn't why he was here.

"I will handle this," Alex said, reaching for her badge in her pocket.

"No." Ryder said as he grabbed Alex's arm and looked over to the left. Behind the large dark colored check-in counter was a tall young man, with a sign above his head that read 'Register'. With his neatly trimmed chestnut hair and a diaphanous growth of whiskers trying to appear on his chin, Ryder knew he was likely in high school, most likely a senior. "You will scare the hell out of him. He will call the manager and we won't get anywhere."

Ryder looked down at Yakira; maybe her youthful appearance could come into play here. He reached into his pocket and pulled out his notebook. "Tell him you are looking for your friend. And you want to know if she is here before we check in."

"And what do I say when he asks me who my friend is?"

Ryder quickly scribbled a name on a piece of paper and pulled it out and handed it to her. Alex leaned over and read the name before looking back at Ryder and lifting an eyebrow. "If she is here, I am out of here," Alex said before Yakira began to walk over to the counter.

Yakira was perfect, charming and smiling. Just as Ryder thought, the young man was putty in her hands. He gave up the information. "Celeste Valor, yes she is here, in room 420. Can I get your name? So you can get checked in? " He smiled.

Alex must have heard him too, as she was busy searching through her smartphone. He could see she was online trying to bring up photos. She got to the one that she was looking for. A blonde haired woman dressed in a bright orange jumpsuit. Alex marched up to him and held the phone up for the young clerk to see.

"Is this her?" She demanded.

"Yeah, I guess, she doesn't look quite that old, but—." The young man looked closer at the photo and then added: "Eyes aren't right."

"What do you mean the eyes aren't right?" Ryder asked his tome hinting that he knew what the young man was hinting at.

"They are not freaky looking."

"What do you mean freaky?" Alex asked.

"Freaky bright blue, almost..."

"They are not bright blue." They are not like..." Ryder said interrupting him as he remembered. Arresting Celeste, the aroma of fresh cut flowers as he pulled her near him as he snapped on the handcuffs on her, the sensual flip of her hair as she looked back at him, a small grin. "She is so beautiful...," He sounded as if he was mesmerized. "...I would do anything she ..."

"Ryder!" Alex question snapped him back to reality.

"Is she in her room?" Ryder asked interrupting his thoughts.

"No, she took the trolley. " He said, his voice returning to normal. "She said she 'was going to go downtown for awhile.' Do you want to check in?"

"We are going to see if we can find her," Ryder said glancing out the door and seeing the flash of dark green outside. It was the trolley. "Can you save us three rooms, hopefully right next to hers?" Ryder knew money doesn't just speak, it screams. He pulled out a hundred dollar bill, folded it into thirds and slid it across the counter, keeping his fingers on it but letting the domination be clearly visible. "It is simple. You take care of us...?" Ryder fished for the young man's name.

"Chad. Chad Bingsworth, sir." the young man said, not taking his eyes off the bill.

"I will take care of you, Chad." Ryder lifted his hand from the bill. Folded in between the bill was a business card with Ryder's phone number on it. "You see her before I do, you give me a call. And save me those rooms."

45

Looking like a green bus with wood trim, Number 1 Red Loop District sat outside the hotel. The doors of the trolley were wide open and the driver, a medium built man with a mustache sat in the driver's seat. He welcomed them aboard with a friendly smile and greeting, asking to see their pass. "Is this good enough?" Alex said, showing him her badge.

"F.B.I.? " He asked, stunned, glad that he was sitting down. "What are you doing here?"

"I am asking the questions," Alex said holding up her phone again with the photo of the blonde woman on it. "Have you seen this woman? Was she on the trolley today?"

"Not today." The trolley driver said, looking at the phone. "It looks like her, but that is not her."

"Let me guess. The eyes are not right?" Ryder asked again pulling out his notepad and pen and began writing. "The woman you saw is younger and eyes are bright blue?"

"So, how did you know?"

"I am great mystic," Ryder joked. "When did you see her?"

"Earlier this week. What is all this about?"

"Murder," Ryder said plainly, not looking up from his notepad.

"The young woman that was killed in the park?"

"Did you know her?"

"The woman that was killed? Some, she was a regular on the trolley; she would always sit in the same seat." He stood up and pointed to the back, the second seat from the back. "I was shocked to hear she was married."

"Why is that?" Ryder asked.

"She was always meeting some man. They would sit together and just ride around; they never got off." He sat back down in the driver's seat. "Talked to other drivers, they would do the same on the Blue and the Yellow routes. And just like they did here, they would get on or off together."

46

"Does this man have a name? Can you describe him?" Ryder said as he raised his head and looked at the man.

"An older gentleman."

"Are you sure?"

"Positive, but it never seemed like it was romantic. It was more like a father and daughter; he seemed to be comforting her."

"Her father is dead," Ryder said knowing the Anne's family history when he took the case.

"Well, they would just talk and pray together." The trolley driver said, " But aren't you going to ask me about the other woman, the blonde with those eyes? I most certainly will never forget her." Again he pointed to a seat this time, the third seat back. "She sat right there. It was cool that morning and the windows steamed over. She drew a face on the window and started to talk to it as if it were her mother. 'Asking if she could help her get her true love again."

"True love?" Alex broke into the conversation. "Did she happen to mention a name?"

"No, señora, she never used a name but she did say she was going to marry him, that she had room ready and once they were married they could be together forever." He set back in the seat.

"Where did you let her off?"

"I didn't." The bus driver said turning around and staring out the windshield, his hands resting on the steering wheel. He leaned slightly forward and gazed up at the tree through the top of glass. He let out sigh before continuing. "She got on at the hotel, rode the whole route and back to here. I told her she had to get off. But she told me 'her true love was coming to Eureka Springs soon, that she would bring him here.' I got off to report to her, we are not to do it in front of the passengers. When I got back on she was gone." The driver leaned back in his seat still holding on the steering wheel.

"Thank you, Mr.....?" Ryder said has he stood and closed his notepad

"Martine Gomez." He said, twisting his name tag around so Ryder could read it. Then he turned back and looked up at the clock, it was time to go to another stop but he looked up into the mirror above his head at Ryder, starting to exit. "Ryder, there was one other thing."

"You know who I am?"

"Everyone knows the Pale Ryder."

"You were saying?"

"That blonde woman, I saw her one time with a young man, a teenager. They were having lunch here at the hotel."

Ryder stepped off the trolley and walked over to where Alex and Yakira were standing.

"So what do we do now?" Yakira asked as the trolley drove away.

"We check in and wait for her."

"I can't do that!" Alex insisted "I can't spend the night here."

"You don't believe these stupid ghost tales do you? It's just a way they make a buck. Everyone comes here expecting to see one and...."

"No!" she said cutting him off, "It isn't that, it is..." Alex's phone beeped, she was getting a text message. She looked at the screen and smiled brightly and then lovingly wiped her finger across the screen before she looked back up at Ryder. "I have paperwork to do. I have to go back to the office. I am not officially on this case. I am just doing it because of you because you are my friend. I'll get fired if they find out."

"Okay, but we are going to check in and wait for her." Ryder looked at Alex; he almost dreaded adding this next part. "You know where we've got to go tomorrow." She nodded unenthusiastically. "Can you arrange it?"

"I can," Alex said hesitatingly as she reached into her jacket pocket, pulling out a bag of M&M's ®, popping a piece of candy into her mouth. "I will pick you in the morning."

"No need to do that. I will have Gene bring the Killer Bee down. We will meet you in Chillicothe." Again she popped another candy into her mouth and chewed on it nervously. Alex went back down the steps to her vehicle while Ryder and Yakira walked back into the hotel. "We will take those rooms." He told the young man behind the counter. "But we only need two of them."

With that the young man turned and grabbed two keys, there were no electronic cards, just good old fashioned keys on a brass fob with the room number on one side and the words '1886 Crescent Hotel' on the other. Ryder just couldn't get it out of his mind how this town did seem like a step back in time. As if instead of the Glock strapped to his side, it should have been a six shooter Peacemaker, tied down, of course, tipping his Stetson to the lady as she passed by.

"Which one of you would like room 419?" Chad's question snapped Ryder back to reality, but it was the question as much as it was the tone. It was as if he were a dental assistant asking who is next to enjoy a root canal.

"What is so special about Room 419?" Ryder asked, looking at the young man.

"It was Theodora's room when this was the Baker Hospital. They say she haunts it."

"You take it," Yakira said looking up at Ryder.

"Don't tell me you believe in this stuff?"

"You don't, sir?" Chad said, still holding out the key. Ryder mockingly grinned as Chad reached over the counter and grabbed the key and said."I can tell you I use to not be a believer till I worked here overnight. There are strange things that happen. Doors that open by themselves, shadows that suddenly disappear. "

"The only the things that scare me are the thing I can see," Ryder said frostily as he paid for the rooms.

Chad gave Yakira room key number 421. "Any luggage we can help you with?"

"No, we are just staying the one night." Ryder said as he texted a message 'Please bring the Killer Bee to the Crescent.'

"If you are hungry may I recommend our Crystal Dining Room, or if you are in the mood for pizza, the Sky Bar on the fourth floor. Your friend Ms. Velour, she liked going there a lot."

Ryder twisted his head slightly sideways at the young man, staring directly into his eyes, watching for any sign of deceit, that this was just a ploy to get them to eat here. Not seeing any he dropped his gaze to his phone that was laying on the counter as it dinged and the screen read 'new message'. He picked up the phone, tapped the screen and read the message. 'It read 'leaving in an hour.' Ryder texted back 'see the clerk at the front counter ask for Chad.'

"Anything else I can do for you, sir?" Chad asked.

"You have an envelope?" Ryder asked. The young man handed him a white envelope with the hotel's address on it. Ryder took two one hundred dollar bills and slipped them into the envelope, sealed it shut, and wrote Gene Weston on it and handed it back to the young man behind the counter. Ryder then took another hundred dollar bill and held it up in between his fingers. "Two things, a man will deliver a Dodge Charger, you give him this envelope." Ryder slid the envelope across the counter to the young man and then continued. "The other thing, if you see our friend come in, let us know." He handed the bill to the young man. He and Yakira headed for the elevator.

The elevator doors opened onto a long narrow hall, the walls painted in a tone that gave it an orange- like glow in the light of the ceiling fans that hung down from the eleven foot high ceilings. Walking along the low pile carpet with its green and golden tones, it was the road that was taking him further back in time, leaving him with the feeling that someone was behind them, watching. He wondered- could it have been Chad? He glanced over his shoulder; nothing was there, except their images reflecting in the multiple pane windows. Alongside the hall wall was dark painted panel doors. He came to the one that had the brass number '419' tacked on it.

"Yours is over there," Ryder said with a nod of his head towards Yakira's room. "Go on in, and I will meet you here and we will go get some pizza." She nodded and walked over to her door, giving one quick glance back at him before she unlocked it and walked into her room. Ryder started to unlock his door, but he turned looked over at the room marked with the brass numbers of '420.' He put the key back into his pocket and stepped over in front of the door. There was something inside of him that was telling him to try it.

It was so still, just so deathly still, the other guest must have been gone. He reached down and his fingers gripped around the knob, he could feel the coldness of the brass as he twisted it and the door groaned as it began to open by itself as if an invisible hand was pushing it. Ryder reached down to his side and slipped the Glock from its holster. His fingers gripped around the checked butt grips of the pistol, his index finger laid alongside the trigger guard as he stepped inside.

The room was only dimly lit by a single brass lamp that set on the nightstand next to the bed. He brought the pistol up in front of him and let it sweep across the room. There were signs that someone was staying here, an open blue hard vinyl suitcase. Draped over the lid was a sheer black peignoir with Chantilly lace. Ryder picked it up. Holding the collar up to his nose he took a sniff. It smelled of flowers, he felt light –headed. Over on a small dresser, was a foam head with a dark colored wig, and next to it was a makeup box.

"What is going on?" Yakira asked standing in the door. With the light from the ceiling fan beaming in behind, she appeared like an angel. "What are you doing?" Disappointment showed that the love of her life would be holding another woman's nightgown.

"Nothing," he said as laid the nightgown back down on the suitcase exactly as he found it and carefully looked over the room. He noticed a pair of black pumps with small bows on the toes that were lying on the floor just under the edge of the bed, covered with dust. He picked one up. "Size seven." He looked at Yakira as she stepped inside the room. Without even turning to her, he asked. "What size shoe do you wear?"

"A five and a half, why?"

"Nothing."

"Ricky, we are going to get caught in here," Yakira said as she walked over next to him, as he placed the shoe back down on the floor. His eyes caught sight of a glimmer, a sparkle of light; it was under the lamp on the nightstand. It was a wine glass. It had just a little red wine in it; just enough for one more swallow. Kneeling down and twisting his head as if he were a puppy looking at a ball that was just thrown, wondering 'what do I do', he thought: what secrets do you hold? He turned the glass toward the light and could see fingerprints on the glass.

"She really is smart." He said, slipping the Glock back down into the holster and standing back up." I doubt there are any prints at all in this room. I don't why she would leave a glass with prints on it."

"Can we get out of here?" Yakira asked, grabbing his hand. "This place gives me the creeps."

"Yeah," Ryder said letting go of her hand as he looked at the black negligee again, , as he reached into his jacket and pulled out a handkerchief that he always kept for times like this. He wrapped up the glass. "I am going to have Double T check this."

"Why?" She asked as he closed the door behind them.

"I don't know it is just a feeling." He added as he placed the glass in his room. "Sometimes you just have to go with your gut." They walked down another hall to where there was a pair of rooms on to his left and one to the right. One was the start of the ghost tour, where one could learn all the tales of all the ghosts, even venturing down into the basement where the morgue was when it was a hospital. Ryder had his own ghosts swirling around in his head, he didn't need to learn of any more, besides it was the aroma of freshly baked pizza, from the other side of the hall that was pulling him in. Right under the large oval sign with the words 'Dr. Baker's Lounge' and the symbol of the rising sun rays. He held the large French door open for Yakira and followed her in.

Also known as the Sky Bar, it was cozy, not overwhelmingly huge, or so small it caused panic and wanting to get out. While the rest of the hotel was thrown back to the Victorian age, the bar was a step back to different age. A time of bright neon colors radiating off the walls, bathed in light like a comforting warm hug, wrapping you in a blanket of pressed tin ceilings, with a round light of a ceiling fan twirling with guiding breezes, like being on a sailboat guiding you back to the bar with a tin embossed front panel and bright purple accents. Your eyes are quickly drawn over to the large painting on the wall. Clasped in the grip of two groups of sun beams painted on the wall, what the painting was what each individual would see in it. Someone might see two beautiful women, one nude, one dressed, one dark haired, one light-haired. He stood staring at the painting, not understanding why. Maybe it was the symbolism of good and evil, one dressed in purity, one dressed in darkness, one ready to love, and one ready to kill.

"Would you prefer a table inside or out on the balcony?" He heard a woman say. He turned from the painting and saw a young tall woman with hair that was nearly like snow, yet she was young as if she should have pom-poms in her hands instead of flatware.

"Outside," Ryder said, as she guided them through the maze of tables with checkered black and white tablecloths through the glass doors. It was the vantage point in the hotel, high up on a concert balcony, looking down on the entire old part of town. The edge was guarded by a black iron fence with gas- fed lamps interweaved as if they were watchtowers. At one end of the balcony was a towering chimney. The tables were made of wooden planks, weathered and beaten down from the baking of summer sunshine and the bite by the nipping teeth of winter, arranged along the edge of the fence. She seated them there, the third table from the left.

"Menus are in front of you." She said. "And your server will be right with you."

Ryder looked at the menu; there were several pizza choices from all veggie to supreme when suddenly he heard a voice that he recognized. "My name is Ginger; I will be your server tonight." He glanced up and saw a young woman standing there, her ginger- like hair pulled back in a loose ponytail that flowed down her back. It was Ginger Weston, Gene's daughter. As she recognized him she smiled, wrinkling up her small button like nose, the glimmer of the gas lamps spread over her face, revealing her speckling of freckles along her cheeks.

"Hi, guys!" She said brightly. "So you are the high roller that everyone is talking about? I should have known. So what can I get you to drink?"

"Coke?" He asked, looking over the table at Yakira and she nodded. He looked back up at Ginger. "And can you get me the kind with sugar?"

"For you, I am sure of that." She jotted it down on her pad. "So what is it going to be?" She turned to Yakira and asked.

"Oh, sweetie," she looked at the menu that was printed out on a card and read her choice, "hamburger, mushroom, green peppers, olives, red onion and extra cheese on a thin crust."

"I am sure when they find out in the kitchen who you are, they will hurry this up."

"No need. We're here all night."

He turned and glanced out across the rolling hill in the distance, watching as the light began to peek out between the trees like lighters being held up during a ballad at a rock concert. The statue of the Christ of the Ozarks towering up, arms stretched wide. Below them, the hotel pool now left alone, and St. Elizabeth's light up spot lights beaming upon each station of the cross.

"Is there a song you would like to request?" Ryder heard a man say as he walked up between the tables and leaned his hands down on the rail. Ryder stood up and towered over the man as he again looked down at the church at the bottom of the hill. "I am the guitarist here. If there is something you and your lovely lady would like to hear."

"How about 'Love of My Life ' by Queen, that is my favorite song," Yakira said.

"So you are here almost every night?" Ryder asked as he turned around and started to hand the man a fifty dollar bill, before pulling it back at the last moment and asked. "Where you here the night the young girl was murdered?"

"Yes, sir." The man answered. "In fact, she was sitting right at the same table you are."

"Was she alone?"

"No, she was with another young lady." The man said as Ryder handed him the fifty.

"Blonde and bright blue eyes?" Ryder asked.

"Yes sir, they had a glass of wine and she got sick."

"Which one? Was it the one that was murdered?"

"Yes sir," The man replied. "The blonde woman and a teenage boy helped her back downstairs." The man carefully and quietly strummed his guitar checking to see if it was tuned properly, finding one string slightly out of tune he twisted the tuning knob. He looked at Ryder and added. "And before you ask, I don't know who the young man was. I have seen him around a few times, and I think I heard her call him Jay maybe once." The man turned to Yakira and smiled as has he said. "I think I can play that for you." Soon the melodic chords began ringing out and Yakira began swaying back and forth and singing the words.

"Did you I hear you say something about a blonde woman", Ginger asked as she set the bottles of coke down in front of them, "that was acting strange?"

"Did you see someone?" Ryder asked lifting the bottle to his lips to take a drink of the sweet dark liquid.

"Stupid old witch! She made me have to pay for a glass that she took."

"A wine glass?"

"Yes, how did you know?"

"Just a guess," Ryder said calmly as he set the bottle back down on the table and looked at her. "She acting strange?"

Ginger's gaze drifted away from Ryder, out across the rail and the rolling hills to the large statue in the distance. Ryder's gaze followed hers to the statue of Christ. "She talked to him out loud." Her gaze drifted back to Ryder as she continued, and he looked back at her. "Saying she needed him to stop the sixth sin. You know, I wouldn't have thought anything about that, but…"

"But what?" Ryder asked.

"Well, that Sunday Father Anthony gave a sermon at Mass about 'The Ten Sins of Man,' like you know, the Ten Commandments? And the sixth one is…"

"Murder," Yakira said as she suddenly stopped singing as she took a drink of pop.

"Yeah." Ginger replied turning and facing her. "He made a point while we can ask for forgiveness and we can make up for most sins and be forgiven, it was the only sin that could not be undone by man, only God could forgive that sin."

"Was she with someone?"

"Yeah, another woman. They each order a glass of wine."

"Chilean Carménère?"

"Yes, how did you know?"

"It goes well with pizza," Ryder answered as he again took a sip of the soda. "Were they talking about anything?" He asked holding the bottle of pop in his hand.

"Men," Ginger answered. "One in particular, her true love."

"The blonde?"

"Yes, she kept talking about what she was going to do was going to bring her true love back to her, and that the other woman was going to help her get him. That is when the woman, the one that was murdered got sick. I got get back to work, is there anything else I can get you?"

"No," Ryder said and Ginger left, after a short time she returned delivering the pizza to the table. She had started to leave when Ryder asked. "Ginger, one thing the glass she took, which one was it? Hers or the other woman's?"

Ginger though before answering. "That was what was really odd. She never touched her glass it was full, but the she took the other glass." Ginger left.

"What is with the wine?" Yakira asked. The pizza warm and fresh, the aroma was overwhelming demanding as she took time to give thanks. Afterwards she took a piece and gave it to him and then served herself. "How did you know that wine?"

Ryder picked up the pizza and took a bite, the cheese stringing out from the edge of the slice back to his mouth. He wiped the cheese from his mouth with a napkin before he replied, his mouth still full, he mumbled out. "When we arrested Velour we found a half drank bottle of that wine in her place with one glass. When I tried quizzing her on wines she didn't know a thing about them. In fact we found out she is allergic to fermentation any kind, vinegar and..."

"And wine that means..." She stopped in mid-sentence as she gazed over Ryder, making him turn and watch as Ginger approached the guitarist with another request from another couple. "There was somebody else in that house?" Ryder turned back to Yakira as the guitarist began strumming out another song, the 'Long Run' by the Eagles.

"You said she confessed to those murders."

"I know, I always felt there was someone else in that house," Ryder said as he got another piece of pizza and placed it on his plate. "But I never found anyone. No matter how much we tried she kept saying she was alone. We found no prints except hers."

Ryder took yet another drink of the pop and stared across the table at Yakira. "There is something I need to tell you about Celeste Velour. I put a lot of murders away, but this one..."

"Crazy?" Yakira asked.

"No crazy doesn't know what it is doing. She knew very well what she did she—"she seem to enjoy it. She is—well you seen how Alex is acting?"

"Are you telling me she is evil"?

"She will find your weakness and she will use it against you. Tomorrow just be on guard." Ryder warned. They finished up the pizza; Ryder paid the bill and left a big tip for Ginger responded with a hug. Then they returned to their rooms.

Room 419 one of those legends, haunting spirits wandering the hall searching for peace; peace was all Ryder wanted as he opened the door and stepped inside. Immediately he was taken aback by the bright colored wallpaper with it star light patterns and darker blue-green trim. It was a small suite, two rooms with sloped walls; an outer sitting room with a red velvet Victorian style easy chair and chaise lounge in the turquoise paisley fabric. In between them was a brass stand lamp with a fringed white shade. In front of the chaise lounge was a round walnut table.

The other room was separated by a large doorway, this was the bedroom and it continued the same wallpaper. The bed was pure Victorian style with a highly carved headboard. On each side of the bed were Victorian style night stands and brass lamps with Tiffany style stained glass shades. Ryder turned on both lamps, revealing at the foot of the bed a red tufted settee.

He removed his jacket and draped it across the settee, then removed his pistol and holster and slid them into a drawer in one of the nightstands. He removed his shoes and stretched out on the bed, then looked across the room. To the left was a sign that he was not back in the 1800's, it was a color TV and an apartment size refrigerator. However, it was the sight to the right, tucked up next to the sloping wall and between the closet doors, that drew his eye; it was a dresser with a mirror on it. In front of the dresser was a round-backed chair. He got up and walked over to it and sat down on the chair. He noticed how low it sat and how the top of the dresser nearly hit his knees, he felt as if he were a grown-up in a child's playroom. He moved the mirror back as far as it would go to see his reflection. He got up and walked over towards the bed and back past the slope in the wall, where he saw a photo hanging in an oval picture frame.

He looked carefully at her. The picture was old, she wasn't that bad looking, but the deathly stare she was giving him just made him look even closer. Though there was no name on the frame he just figured this had to be Theodora. "Well, Theodora," he said, drawing back from the frame and beginning to unbutton his shirt. "If this is your room, you can come and join me if you want." He removed his shirt, exposing his bare hairy well- toned pecks and tossed the shirt down on the settee. There was a rap on the door.

"Room service." He heard a sweet kind female voice say from behind the door. He opened the door. Before him was a young woman, with long dark red hair. She stood holding a silver tea tray with a teapot, along with a china cup and saucer on it. "Your herbal tea, sir," the young woman said as she carried in the tray. He had forgotten to order it but guessed that Yakira remembered that he always like a cup when he was sleeping in a hotel or a strange bed as it helped him sleep. She placed the tray down on the nightstand. He thanked her and gave her a twenty, and led her back to the door. "May you sleep well, Mr. Ryder."

Ryder removed his pants and threw them over the settee, then poured himself a cup of tea, propped the pillows up behind him, and leaned back, enjoying his tea. He had just about finished the tea when suddenly he heard a low moan and watched as one of the closet doors opened all by itself.

"Coming out of the closet, huh girl?" He yawned and placed the cup back on the tray, he could barely keep his eyes open as he placed two pillows under his head, fluffing them up before he crawled under the covers. He reached over and turned off the light and lay down, again he heard another noise in the room. "I must warn you, I have a girlfriend and she is just next door, and she can get very jealous." Just before he closed his eyes he could swear he could smell a strong sweet fragrance, but before he could think any further he closed his eyes, fell asleep and began to dream.

He was walking down a long narrow hall. It was dark, only an occasional flicker of light would break through allowing him to see that there was someone in front of him. It was so cold, and what looked like the thick fog was growing thicker. Suddenly a bright light appeared, he was able to make out where he was, the hallway; it was the Crescent Hotel. The light was beaming down on a woman; she was dressed in a dishabille fashion, alluringly in a sheer black negligee, that openly revealed her womanly curves. She turned to him. A face painted with a brush of beauty and framed with hair of gold that flowed down on her shoulders. Waving a finger of seduction, she invited him closer to her. He didn't want to go, but for some reason, he just couldn't refuse.

They stood in front of a door. It was room 419. It was his room. He felt her fingers entwine in between his as she led him into the room and over to the bed. She stood in front of him. He felt so weak, so helpless, when she pushed him, he just fell back on the bed, spread-eagled. Like a tiger stalking her prey, she crawled up from the foot of the bed and onto him. Pinning him, she laid down on him, bring her face to his. Again he just couldn't move. It as if he was here, but he was standing outside of his body watching all this happen. She moved her head down to his and he could feel her hair falling down and tickling the sides of his cheeks. As she moved her lips closer to his he could smell her perfume, the scent he had smelled before falling asleep.

"It is you!" He said in his dream, watching as it appeared the woman floated above him like a ghostly spirit.

"Of course, baby! It has always been me. It always will be me." She lowered herself and kissed him on the lips, the moved over to his neck where she kissed and then gently sunk her teeth into his flesh. He cried out in pain. She drew back up and reached over, and turned on the lamp next to the bed. He could see her now, it looked like Celeste but younger, much younger, like the photos they had taken from her house.

"The Spirits of Night are calling me again; I listen to them." She said as she reached down between her breasts and produced a small folded red colored note. She held the note up and continued in a beseeching matter. "Only true love can stop me, a love that will last forever." She lowered her head to his chest and kissed him again. She slowly moved her head up towards his face, with her dark red lips barely touching his skin. He could feel her warm breath on his lips as she stopped and with blazing eyes she stared down at him.

"I need it again; I need to taste it again." She said as he felt her slip the folded up paper into the pillow case under his head. Using her hands she gradually slithered her way back down off the bed, letting her fingers trace down over his body. She picked up a dark red rose, using the flower; she traced it back up his body, placing the stem in her mouth, as the thorns, bit into her lips. Leaving the blood in her mouth, she lowered her mouth to his and kissed up the short stem, leaving the flower petals in his mouth. She stood up and seemingly floated across the floor and out the door into the hall, and the door slammed with a bang.

Ryder suddenly awoke with a scream; he was breathing hard. He got out of bed; the sheets were soaked with sweat. He hadn't had nightmares like that in a long time. He sat back down on the bed and noticed his underpants were sticking to him; they too were drenched in sweat. It was also when he noticed that the light was on. He swore he had turned that off. It was just old wiring or a faulty switch. He tried to reason with himself as he got up, knocking his pillows onto the floor and walking into the bathroom. Flipping on the light switch he grabbed one of the folded up wash cloths and began running cold water in the sink to cool off. He ran the rag under the water before he wrung it out. He washed his face, and he looked up into the mirror. As he saw his reflection he dropped the washrag into the sink. His face and chest were covered with dark red lipstick.

What the...? He thought as he picked up the cloth and began wiping the lipstick away. He turned his head and gazed at the bite marks on his neck. Suddenly there was a hard rap on the front door to his room.

"Ricky, Ricky! Are you okay? Let me in!" It was Yakira; she must have heard him scream out. "Open up this damn door before I kick it in!" Ryder took the wash cloth and wiped the lipstick from his chest as he opened the door. She burst in with an M&P Body Guard 380 Semi-automatic clutched in both hands. Her trigger-finger perched alongside the trigger guard. "What happened? Did the dybbuk get you?"

"I told you, there is no such thing as ghosts,"Ryder said as wiped the rest of the lipstick off of him. As he stood there with the door wide open, many other doors were now open and other guests were standing gawking at him. He would have said 'take a picture, it will last longer' but a pair of young women who were roommates were already doing that.

"She tried to have her way with me," Ryder said with a mocking grin as he looked at a middle-aged couple standing in the hall. "Maybe you should try this room next time, that way you can get lucky." With that, he slammed the door shut.

"I heard you scream."

"I just had a bad dream." He said as he walked over to the red easy chair and sat down. He looked up at her as she slipped the safety back onto the weapon. "You think it was a ghost and you bring a gun? " He rubbed his neck where the bites were as he continued. "Honey, they are already dead."

"So? I will kill them again." She said, looking down at the washcloth in his hand and asked, "Is that blood?"

"I wish." He said as he stood back up and walked back towards the bed. He stopped and turned to her and noticed she was wearing a pink baby doll nightie, her long hair messed up yet still flowing down behind her. She stood with the gun clutched in her hand dropped down to her side. "Did you hear any other voices?"

"Like ghosts?"

"Like a woman," Ryder said as he sat down on the bed and placed the cloth on the back of his neck.

"A woman!" She demanded, grabbing the washcloth and examining it. "This is lipstick! You had another woman in here?"

"I had no one in here, but it seemed so real."

She turned his head, revealing the bite marks on his neck. "Well, those are real! Someone had to be in here. WHO WAS IT?"

"You won't believe me if I tell you."

Yakira laid the gun down on the nightstand and sat down on the bed beside him; he could smell the honeysuckle perfume she wore as she laid her head down on his shoulder. "I will believe you, Ricky. Who was it?"

"It was Celeste at least I think. Well, the one that everyone is seeing, those haunting eyes. I know it sounds crazy. She even put a...." He quickly paused and looked over at the pillows on the floor beside the bed. He grabbed one and stuck his hand inside the case. "...She put a note on my pillow." There was no note, and he grabbed another pillow, again there was no note. Yakira bent down and picked up the pillow lying on the floor. Yakira slipped her hand into the pillowcase. She pulled out a folded piece of red paper, her jaw dropped; she was silent as she handed the paper to him. He tossed the flower on the bed and unfolded the paper and there, written with a black crayon in child like writing with misused words, he read:

TWINKLE ,TWINKLE MY LITTLE STAR
NOW YOU WONDER WHO I ARE
I SEE YOU WHEN THE MOON LEAPS
AND HOLD YOU AS YOU AS ONE SLEEPS
NOW LISTEN FOR THE NIGHT DOVES CALL
SHE LIE WHERE NOT SHE FELL, BUT WHERE MEN FALL.

Chapter 7

After Yakira returned to her room, Ryder took a shower and wrapped himself in the robe that the hotel had provided. He photographed the note and sent a copy to Alex, he had hoped that she would get right back with him, but she didn't. He tried to get some sleep, but he just couldn't. Instead he lay there, resting against the headrest, listening to moans and groans that emitted throughout the hotel and wondering- are these the ghosts? Even watching as the mirror on the dresser that he moved previously fell back down to its original place. Maybe it was ghosts, maybe it was Theodora objecting to him moving her mirror, it didn't matter if he believed in them or not. `What frightened him was the image that would not leave his mind- the woman with the haunting eyes.

Assessing old police files from the Kansas City Police Department, he went back over his files; could they have gotten the wrong person? Could there be two people that looked almost the same except for the eyes?

Celeste was the middle child; she had an older sister, and younger brother. Seemingly coming from the perfect family, well to do father, who worked for the Kansas Highway department, stay at home mom. They lived on a farm just outside of Independence, Kansas. The entire family, aunts, uncles and cousins, would get together on every holiday, and have a big meal. Sunday's they would be at church. Her mother Nellie, would lead the choir, her father Dale, taught a Sunday school class. She made good grades, even graduating with honors, and getting a scholarship to the University of Kansas where she graduated with a nursing degree and was the head nurse on the trauma unit at Truman Medical Center. Ryder never could figure it out, what turned the homecoming queen into a cold blood killer. Now going over this again it still made even less sense than it did then.

He went back over the accounts of all the witnesses that found the bodies. Wilma Dean Larkin's answer to the question, "When you found the body did you see anyone around?" Her reply, "A young woman in a gray college sweatshirt, she was wearing sunglasses, her blonde hair was tied back, she looked like she had come from the college." Body location in a grassy area, the edge of Kauffman Lake, Kauffman Park, it was close enough to UMKC, he just dismissed it and went to another victim.

Body location; putting green of the seventh hole at Mission Hills, Country Club, Kansas City Kansas. Question to groundskeeper when finding the body. "Some college kids, they all had on UK shirts." Describe them. "Typical teen's, one boy, two girls." Were they together? "Two were, the other girl ran away." Describe her. "Thin, wearing dark glasses," Hair? "Couldn't tell, was wearing a sock cap."

He flipped to another report Body location: Martha Laffite Thompson Nature Society Pawpaw trail near the bank of Rush Creek. Home owner near site: "I saw a group of kids from the University." He went on, going through them case by case, all except the last two murders. They had a similar description, either one or more college students being in the area. The last two had no mention of college kids. Next to last murder witness very upset, distraught, afraid that murderer saw her. Bought her coffee and a doughnut, calmed her down. Description "older blonde, pretty with a tattoo on hand that reads 'thirsty.' Describes the suspect as in 40's."

Last murder…. A child. He could see anymore, Ryder closed the file. He had seen enough. Somewhere in the night he must have fallen asleep, only to be awakened when his phone rang. It had been in his hand but he must have dropped it on the bed. It was Alex. He quickly answered and was met with her concerned tone.

"What the hell is going on?"

"I think we made a big mistake, Alex."

"Bull Snot! We did everything by the book."

"Everything, Belle?" He asked using a pet name for her.

"Okay, maybe we broke the rules in some cases. We held on to evidence. We falsified a report where we were. It was nothing that could have freed her, just that would have saved us having to explain what we were doing on those nights. Why are you bringing this up for? We got her dead to right."

"What about the witnesses?"

"What about them?" She replied back, as he slid off the bed and stood up, walked over to the dresser and noticed how indeed the mirror had returned to the original position.

"They were all college kids." He continued, as he opened the closet door and it let out a small moan.

"We checked that all out. Most of the murders occurred around them. It had nothing to do with the colleges; most of the victims were college age, even from the colleges. Like the girl from William Jewell." There was something on the closet floor. He bent down and picked it up, it was a single dark red rose, its stem tied in a bow.

"Uh—mmm...."He hum- hawed about, pulling the phone away from his ear as he said. "Talk to you later," and he ended the call. A knock on the door interrupted his thoughts, it sounded as if someone was knocking with their foot. He got up and opened it.

"I brought breakfast!" Yakira said holding a tray in her hands with two covered plates, a silver coffee pot and two cups along with all the necessary items for breakfast. She entered, a white robe wrapped around her tightly, the hem nearly dragging the floor. She set the tray down on the table in the outer room as Ryder closed the door. She lifted the cover of one of the plates as she introduced it. "Omelet with mushrooms and onions and..." She lifted the other cover and said "biscuits and gravy, toast and jelly, and a pot of coffee."

"Which one is for me?"

"I thought we would do what we always do." Yakira said, as she wrapped her arms around his neck and kissed him on the lips and he lifted her up, her bare feet dangling. "We share." She said with a smile, and he put her back down on the floor. By the time they had finished breakfast and a couple of cups of coffee, there was another knock on the door. Ryder got up and opened it again. It was a man, the concierge of the hotel, Franklin Malloy. He stood holding several boxes. Ryder asked him in.

"The store owner is a friend of mine." Franklin said as he set the boxes down on the chaise lounge. "I had him open up early." He drew himself to attention with the precision of a ROTC cadet. "I hope I have done well for you, sir." He turned and smiled at Yakira as he added "You too, ma'am." He turned back to Ryder. "I do hope you like our choices. And here is the bill; you can just pay it along with your room, sir." He said as he handed Ryder a folded sales slip from a local store.

"And the Charger?" Ryder asked as Yakira sat down beside the boxes and began to open them.

"Your car is here sir, and I gassed it up for you. I must say that is a one of a kind car, driving around everyone noticed me."

Ryder reached into his robe pocket and pulled out his billfold and gave the man a hundred dollar tip. "Thank you, sir." Franklin said heading for the door. "And if there is anything else I can do for you, please let me know."

Ryder was looking over the sales slip, underwear for him and Yakira, light blue Arrow dress shirt, new pink pant suit size 2 petite, and white crew neck top. Ryder looked up from the sales slip. "Franklin, I don't see the pink baby doll nightie here?"

"Sir?"

"She had it on last night, I just figured she had you get it."

"No sir. She asked me to bring up bathrobes last night but nothing about night clothes."

"Thank you anyway." Ryder said as he guided the man out of the room and shut the door behind him. He turned back to Yakira, "where did you get the pink baby doll you had on last night?"

"When I got back to the room it was lying on the bed. I just assumed you had someone get when it when we were eating pizza. You didn't get it?" He shook his head. "So where did it come from?"

After getting cleaned up and dressed and paying the bill Ryder and Yakira walked outside and got inside the Killer Bee, a blood red 1971 Dodge Charger with gun metal stripes that ran up the center of the shark-like nose cone, up the hood and down the sides of the car. At the back was a high wing spoiler.

It was going to be a long drive so they made one stop for bottled water, and some snacks: green onion potato chips, then it was back to Missouri the same way they had come, through Cassville, to Monett, to Interstate 44, to Interstate 49 and headed north. There was something about this trip; heading north into Missouri was like going to a different state. The contour of the land began to flatten out, the soil became richer and trees thinner, this was farm country. Not cows, pigs, or chickens, but crops. Fresh young green shoots sprouting up, lined up as if soldiers parading proudly along the sides of the highway, as far as the eye can see either way.

Soon the greedy hand of conurbation reached out, slowly at first, just a nibble of the teeth of metropolitan. Once green farmland, now an island off the coast of the cement jungle of the city of the fountains. Tranquility has been devoured, by a beast that has its own beauty, towering creatures that only give a glance as you pass by the towering building. Ribbons of pavement spread out as a mighty river, vehicles caught in the stream, as if they were confused salmon, only guided by the light hung above, attacking them as if it they were bait. Ryder had no attention of being caught and turned and head around the city onto Interstate 35, the concrete vines of the jungle thinned, and once again Ryder was able to breathe, the jungle didn't take him.

Chillicothe is derived from the ancient Shawnee Indian words meaning "Principal Place, the home of the principal chief. To anyone who had worked law enforcement it meant the home of the Correction Center. Surrounded by a guard of 12 foot high razor wire sits several different buildings, all without any spirit or cheer. Ryder, seeing Alex's SUV, wheeled the Charger into the parking lot.

He got out and watched as Alex stepped out of her SUV. As he held the door open for Yakira he watched as Alex looked over at the glass doors with the dark green frames. Her eyes were covered with sunglasses and she reached into the dove gray blazer pocket and pulled out a packet of plain M&M's. She poured out a green one and popped it in her mouth.

"Sedative?" She joked, offering the bag of candy. She poured out a blue one for Yakira and a red one for Ryder.

"I don't smoke anymore. So when I get nervous I pop these things."

"What are you nervous about?" Ryder asked looking at the building; it was typical prison structure, basic tan metal, with green roofs, void of humanity and of hope. "We have been to these places many times."

"It is not what it is, it is who it is." Alex said and popped another M&M. "She gives me the creeps just to talk to her." The three headed for the front door. Ryder reached up and removed his sunglasses as they entered.

It seemed almost comical to walk across a large rug on the floor that read 'Welcome to Missouri Correctional Center' and then across the bare tile floor. It was nearly empty except for two men standing next to the counter that ran nearly the length of the room. Behind the larger counter was a large heavy set woman with short cropped coal- like hair. Alex reached into her pocket and showed her badge. "I am Special Agent Alexander; I made arrangements to see prisoner number FD 993312."

Alex closed her ID and stuffed it back into her jacket pocket and continued slowly, turning her head to glare at the two male correctional officers standing next to her, with a glare still hidden behind sunglasses , they could easily still see she was daring them to question her authority in this matter. "This is private investigator Richard Ryder and his associate Yakira Rosen. They are with me." She reached up and pulled her sunglasses down and glared at the woman and she added. "Will that be a problem?" She turned.

"Do you have a weapon on you? If so, you will have to turn those in." The woman said. Alex reached under her jacket and removed her service weapon- A Glock 17; she quickly removed the clip and the chambered slug, before handing it to the woman. Ryder did the same, handing over his pistol. "You have a permit to carry this?" The woman asked.

"Yes I do." Signed by the A.G. himself, Ryder grinned. "I am a special case."

"You have to be nut cases if you want to see that woman." The lady guard said as she took their weapons and locked them away. She turned back to Ryder and asked. "So you are Monsieur Ryder?"

"Excuse me?" Ryder asked, confused that she would use this name to address him.

The woman grinned broadly, revealing the large gap in her front teeth. "Follow me." She turned and led them back behind the heavy security door that went into the prison, They followed her into a large room, with a middle aged woman sitting in front of a computer screen on a desk and on the wall a large bank of monitors, which showed several views of the interior of the prison's women's section, including individual cells.

"Barbara, bring up cell 42D." The guard said and the woman clicked a couple of keys on the computer and they viewed the interior shot of a prison cell. A single prisoner, a blonde woman sitting on a bed, prompted and primped with hands crossed on her lap. "Recognize those photos on the wall?" Ryder looked closer at the monitor as Barbara used the keys on the computer to zoom in tighter. The images were grainy, but he could make them out. It was him. Ryder leaned back from the computer as the woman returned the image to normal view.

"Where did she get those?" Ryder asked, again turning to the female officer.

"Like all the others here. They are sent to her in the mail or a guest brings them." She explained as Ryder narrowed his gaze at her as if demanding 'why would they allow this?' so she explained further. "It doesn't cause her harm, and since we allowed the photos, she is the most model prisoner we have."

Ryder watched the screen as Celeste looked right up at the camera smiled and then blew a kiss; it was as if she knew he was watching her. Ryder quickly stepped back. "Ricky, you okay?" Yakira asked wrapping her arm around his. At the same time Alex pulled out the package of candy and popped three of them in her mouth.

"We tried to take them away from her but she took another female prisoner hostage and threatened to bite through her jugular vein if we didn't give them back." She looked at Ryder and added in a warning tone. "You should know how she is. You brought her here." She looked over at Alex. "Both of you did. I was here, if you remember."

"She's doing it again, Ryder." Alex advised as she chewed the pieces of candy. She swallowed and turned to him. "Are you sure you want to do this?"

"We have to." He said, watching on the monitor as two female guards entered and placed hand cuffs and leg shackles on her. The guards led her out of the enclosed cell; as she passed by a camera she again raised her head and smiled, raised her clutched hands to offer a wave.

"Hard to believe, isn't it?" The female officer asked.

"What's that?" Ryder asked.

"That this is the most dangerous person in the state of Missouri."

"Not if you know who she is." Ryder said softly as he watched her being escorted out of the prison and towards the visiting center. A male officer escorted the trio back through a maze of doors to a small room. There were two plastic chairs sitting on one side and a single chair on the other. Separating them was a piece of glass with a speaker encased into it.

"You know, we are kind of breaking rules here." The guard said as he pulled out one of the chairs and offered it to Alex. "Her attorney is going to have a fit."

"You do what I tell you!" Alex snapped back at him. "Understand?"

"Yes ma'am." He said just as the door on the other side opened.

In walked Celeste flanked on each side by a female guard. They escorted her over to the single chair and helped her sit down. Celeste held her cuffed hands up to one of the guards, with the look of a child at her first day of school; she smiled at her as she begged.

"Please, there is no way I can hurt anyone here. Please, I promise to be a good girl." Celeste's voice was soft and timid like that of an innocent school girl.

Alex sat down in one of the chairs and nodded to the guard to release her hands and one of them did. As Celeste rubbed her hand Ryder noticed the tattoo on the back of her right hand. The lettering was red and read 'thirsty' the lettering appearing as running blood. Yakira sat down in the other chair and Ryder stood behind them. The two female guards moved towards the exit door.

Celeste was in her early sixties but she looked as she was in her thirties. Slim, and even under the bright orange jumpsuit her feminine curves still somehow echoed that she was all woman. Her hair was golden and long, yet seemed to be all in place as it rested on her shoulders. A face sculptured in beauty luscious full lips, a small nose that turned up just slightly at the end, and dark green eyes that seemed to reflect the light and make them sparkle with flakes of gold as she smiled at Alex and said with a fake French accent.

"Mademoiselle Isabelle, I must say you look very beautiful today. The golden highlights you have added since we have last seen each other, they become you. And your figure, you look so trim, it is so hard for us women to get our figures back."

Alex reached into her jacket pocket and yet again pulled out the candy, poured out a couple of M&M's and popped them into her mouth.

"Oh! I see we have given up cigarettes. The candy will pack the weight back on and they will think you are with child." Alex emptied the rest of the bag of candy into her hand and munched down the handful.

Celeste turned and looked at Yakira. "This one is not the Annalisa that you spoke of, it is the sister." She made a made a sound with her tongue, as if she were shaming them. "Monsieur Ryder, we may robbing the cradle, but then with Annalisa you were breaking the rules of God, were you not, you are not to love your own sister."

She turned to Yakira and said in the same fake tone. "What a tangle web you have gotten yourself into, little girl." Celeste leaned closer to the glass and stared at Yakira. "You think he will be yours, but that cannot be." She leaned back and continued. "For you see little girl, he belongs to another; her spirit resides in him." Again she leaned towards the glass and said in her normal tone. "And that spirit is me."

"What do you know about a murderer in Arkansas that was sending notes like you did?" Ryder asked firmly. Celeste looked at Alex, who wadded the brown colored bag up in her hands.

"Just like he always was, all business," she said before looked up at Ryder and asked, "The ones to the paper or to you?"

"What is the difference?"

"Oh Sweet Monsieur Ryder." She said, falling back into the fake French accent again. "If you don't know by now, you will never know, except when it is too late Detective Ryder." Her tone once again changed to her normal Midwestern style. "You want to know this. I will tell you. But only you. The women must leave."

"Go on." Ryder said motioning with his head for them to leave. Yakira and Alex left and Ryder sat down in the chair. He scooted up close to the glass and looked in at her, odd as it seemed, he swore he could smell flowers. Celeste cupped her hands together and rested her chin on her thumbs as she looked over at him.

"So, you want to know about the girl that you can't get out of your head?"

71

"Who is she?"

"She is who she is, and all she is what is?"

"Don't start that crap again!" Ryder warned her. "I just want answers. Who is she?"

"She is me, for it is my Spirit. And her soul and your soul shall be come one. The answers you seek you cannot find, for it is not yet time." She replied, curling her lips up into an evil smile and running her tongue over her lips as she added. "You shall not know till you hear the bells Hera ring, it will be then you take your bride and on the wedding bed sire the child of..."

"I didn't hear anyone ask me to marry them." Ryder mocked, interrupting her. "Was it you?"

"I am but the spirit. She is but my spirit."

"Good or bad?" Ryder mocked her even more, making her bite down on her lower lip in frustration. It was this same tone that made her angry confessing to the murders he figured it could work again.

"Both. I was once an angel in heaven. But I took a step too far and I fell and landed at the gates of Hades. It was there the spirits talked to me." Celeste said as she leaned back away from the glass.

"Stop it, just stop it!" Ryder shouted standing, knocking the chair over. "You may scare others with this stuff. You want everyone to think you are crazy, but you are not. I know exactly what you are." He leaned down on the table and looked at her through the safety glass. His words became short and to the point. "You are a Cold-blooded. Calculating. Murdering. Wicked witch!"

"Don't call me that!"

"What? Cold-blooded like the venomous snake, or is it...witch!"

"He called me that. He didn't have a right to touch me! I was a good girl. He made me a bad girl." She said, huffing, getting madder with each word she spoke.

"You have always been a bad girl. You are filthy disgusting. Give it up to any man that…" As He spoke, Ryder watched her face twitch as her eyes narrowed.

"You shut up!" Her shout brought the female guards forward, but Ryder held his hand up and requesting they stay back. He had to push her just a little further. Ryder grinned devilishly as he added. "They are getting ready to send you to ERDCC, you know what they means don't you. All those morons out here protesting that you don't die. They are going to get disappointed, and you know what I am going to do? I am going to open up the cheapest foulest tasty wine I can fine to toast your death, because you don't deserve anything but the worst. Go to hell and die!" He turned and headed for the door, when Celeste's hand slipped down to her sock and she pulled a sharpened nail file and with one quick motion she slashed her palm open.

"Richard Thomas Allen Ryder! " She screamed at him as she slapped her hand up onto the glass divider and blood dripped down the glass as the female guards pulled her away. Slapping the cuffs on her, they drug her back towards the door as Celeste continued to yell at Ryder, saying. "You bring the fires of darkness upon you. Upon you and all those that love you I place a Blood Curse. All those that died, their lives are upon you. It is their blood that stains your hands."

Ryder walked out of the building and back to the main lobby. He walked back over to the counter to pick up his weapon. Then out the door to the Charger and unlocked the door for Yakira. He shut the door and walked back around to the driver's side and looked out across the roof at Alex getting into her SUV. "How about we go find some place to eat? I saw a place just down the road, it looked pretty good."

"Sure." Alex said as she got into her vehicle. "I'll follow you."

Ryder got into his car and sat down in the driver's seat and Yakira said "Thank you for the flower." She said, sniffing it.

"I didn't get you any flowers." Ryder said, looking over at her and his jaw dropped as he took the flower from her -a single dark red rose, the stem twisted into a bow.

Chapter 8

Ryder didn't have much to say as he drove back towards town, only occasionally would he glance up into the rearview mirror to check to see if Alex was still following behind them, or glance down at the flower lying on the console. It wasn't until they were seated at the quaint little family owned diner, icy cold drinks on the table and hamburgers were ordered that Alex spoke.

"Okay, what did she have to tell you?"

Ryder picked up his glass of sweet iced tea and said. "Same old stuff that she had to tell us when we arrested her, that she is a spirit that we cannot hold. What was it she said she was?" They sat near the back of the single room café, at a wooden table, Yakira next to him and Alex across the table, who was nursing a glass of Diet Coke; he looked at Alex.

"Some sort of Fallen Angel." Alex replied, staring more at the glass on the table instead of him.

"Same thing, that we can't hold her, placing a Blood Curse on me." Ryder said leaning back in the chair.

"A what?" Alex asked, confused. "Rick, she never said anything like that before. What do you mean by that?"

"It is silly. She cut her hand placed her hand on the glass and shouted out that a curse was placed upon me, and my family."

"Are you sure she said family?" Yakira spoke up.

"No, I think her exact words were 'upon you and all those who love you.'" He watched Yakira take a large drink of her tea. His eyebrows knitted down in bafflement, that she could believe this stuff. "You don't believe that hogwash, do you?" He asked with a mocking grin.

"I am Jewish! Curses with blood are a big thing. Exactly what did she say?"

"I don't remember, something about their blood is on me, and stains my hands…"

"Upon you and all those that love you I place a Blood Curse, all those that died upon you, for it is their blood that stains your hands." Yakira repeated the curse word for word.

"Yeah that is it."

Yakira lean back in her chair and held her hands out as she spoke frantically. "She placed it on all of us."

"Come on," Ryder said, disbelieving that she could be falling for the mumbo-jumbo garbage. He looked over at Alex who was twisting the glass in her fingers. "Oh, come on! You too?" He repeated with more disbelief. "We are not little kids telling ghost stories here, this is stupid. She is a freaking nutcase!" He paused as the waitress approached the table with the plates and set them down in front of them. He thanked the waitress, and they gave thanks and he started again. "Are you two telling me that you believe what some lunatic is saying? That suddenly we are going to have run of bad luck? Maybe I should get a rabbits or a four-leaf clover."

"It doesn't work that way Ricky." Yakira said. "You being part Irish you should know this."

"I don't believe the little wee people. Or any of that crap. I am a detective I believe in facts." Ryder removed the top bun and salted his dill pickles and replaced the bun as he looked over at Alex. "And you an agent believing this." He took a bite and wiped his mouth with his napkin and then said. "Let's look at this like real adults. The killer isn't her."

Alex had ordered a grilled chicken sandwich. Instead of taking a bite of it, she munched at the plate of fries that was in between them. "There is something that I need to tell you." She picked up another fry and dipped it in the ketchup that she had pooled on the edge of her plate. Before eating the fry she rolled her eyes up to him. "The Kansas Butcher may still be free."

"How is that possible?"

"There is one way." Alex said lifting one eyebrow as she ate the fry.

"That the wrong person is in jail?" Ryder asked answering his own question with a tone of disbelief, lifting his burger and taking a bite.

He swallowed quickly so he could ask. "I thought you were the one that was sure we had the right person, now all of a sudden you think she is innocent." He paused for second to replay Alex's words in his mind before he cracked back. "NO! We caught her bathing in a child's blood. She is guilty!"

"What about the notes sent to the newspaper?"

"What about them?"

"They don't match either the ones being sent now or those sent to the Star." Alex said chewing on a bite of her sandwich.

"So we are talking about a copy cat just like you said." Ryder said as picked up a single fry. He could feel his face twisting into a frown as he watched her slowly rotating the glass in between her fingers knowing it meant that there was something else she wasn't telling him. "What is it?" He demanded.

"While you were in there, I got a message from Kevin in the lab. The notes that you got back then, and those that you are getting now —." She paused and lifted her head and looked straight at him as she continued. "They match. The same person wrote them both."

"That is impossible!" Ryder said placing his burger down on the plate and leaning back in his chair. He slowly rubbed his curled index finger across his chin as he gazed over the table to his friend. "Celeste confessed to the murders, every one of them. Giving us details that only the killer would know. Why would she do that if she wasn't the killer?"

"There is one way this could all be true." Yakira said as she took a sip of her tea. "You remember when you thought I murdered Congressman Warner? You hid evidence..."

"Yeah, you hid it from me!" Alex blurted in. She quickly looked over at Yakira who was clearly annoyed with her. Alex turned back and picked up her glass and took a sip and Yakira continued.

"You were trying to protect me. Could it be she is trying to protect someone?" Ryder turned his attention from Yakira to Alex and said.

"She does have a sister?" Alex said.

"But we could never could find her."

"Celeste is in her sixties and looks like she is in her thirties. Maybe the sister looks like she is in her twenties." Ryder said, finishing up his burger. "Think you can find her?"

"We never did search for her as a suspect." Alex said. "It was just background on…" Suddenly Alex stopped in mid sentence. "It was when we mentioned that we were trying to find her sister, that Celeste confessed." She turned to Yakira and added. "You may have something. That is good detective work."

Ryder's phone rang. He reached into his pocket and answered it, it was Double T.

"Ryder, you need to get back here right now!"

"What is going on?"

"Where are you?" Double T's tone sounded frantic.

"We are still in Chillicothe. We are just having…"

"You need to get back to your old farm, right away. We found something on it."

"What?"

"I can't tell you on the phone, you…you just have to see it."

Over the years Ryder had seen many of his buddies in the force fall down through the cracks. Many would turn to alcohol, seeking shelter in the bottom of an empty Jack Daniels bottle. Others found escape with drugs, some illegal, other at the mercy of the prescription fairy with whatever relief they could get a doctor to give them.

Yet others found escape through just spending time with their families, holding a child in their arms, instead of a Glock in their hands. However, there was a special breed of cop, they found no comfort slugging down drinks or even in the comfort of love, they were driven by the job itself. It was the thrill of the chase, the wonder of what was coming next, the excitement of making that piece of the puzzle fit, as you slowly realize what the picture of the puzzle is. It was as Ryder darted the Charger back and forth, waiting for a chance to pass the slow moving Lincoln, that he realized he was in that last group. Even though he didn't carry a badge anymore, this was still his passion.

The speedometer pointed to 80 mph, as he zipped past the Lincoln and two other vehicles. He glanced over at Yakira as he pulled the car back over into the other lane. She sat there her eyes fixed on the road, helping him watch for anything that might be ahead of them. He glanced up at the rearview mirror and saw the black SUV that Alex was driving pull in right behind him.

Two hundred eighty miles gives one time to think. If it had been anybody else that told him that, or if Thom had just cracked one joke, he wouldn't be in such a hurry. However, when Double T was serious, it had to be just that. The sun was beginning to set, casting out its long shadows, creeping out farther, the shadows reaching out over the highway. Even running at high speed, darkness was over taking the day when they reached the country road that had led to the old farm. It made it hard to navigate, and to his regret he had to back off the speed, only relying on the brakes.

"Dear God," Ryder exclaimed as he approached and could see the nightscape swathed in a rainbow of flashing red and blue emergency lights. On the hill behind the house was a glowing sea of light radiating into the sky. The fence had been cut down and Ryder guided the Dodge down the narrow path that was being used for a road, passing by the bulldozer. As the tires slipped into holes, the lights of Alex's SUV flashed across the interior of the Dodge, bouncing off Ryder's face as it reflected in the mirror. Ryder fought the wheel, guiding the car off the road onto the grassy field, pushing through the fescue, parking next to the bright white van that had the words "Barry County Coroner" written in black letters on the side and back doors. With the meat wagon here, it told Ryder one thing, there was a body somewhere.

"What the hell?" Ryder asked as saw the bright spotlights that had been set up along a large deep hole that had been dug into the ground. Surrounding the perimeter of the cavity that had been torn into the ground were several county cruisers, an ambulance and the Butterfield rural fire truck.

Ryder got the car. He was so drawn in by what was happening, he didn't even offer to open Yakira's door. She followed behind him. He approached the area, which was guarded with yellow police tape. He lifted it up and held it for Alex and Yakira. Through beams of the flashing lights he saw a large man approaching them.

"You have to see this, Ricky." When Thom used his first name, this way, Ryder knew something serious was going on. He was holding something in his hand. "Ever see anything like this?" He added holding up a piece of clothing. It took a little while and the luck that Yakira had grabbed the flashlight out of the glove box, and shined it on the item so that he could recognize it.

"It is an old Wildcat's letterman jacket." He said as he gazed up on the black jacket with its tan leather sleeve inserts. It was grimy and caked with mud, but he could see the golden foot ball patch on the sleeve with the letters CHS and the digits of a year that was more than forty years ago. Thom turned the jacket around to the front and Ryder could see the Gold colored Letter "C" with its football, basketball and track pins. It wasn't until the beam of the flashlight that Yakira was holding hit the number '19' , that Ryder knew who this jacket belonged to.

It was a tale that anyone who ever wore or, rooted for the black and gold, or stepped through or walked the halls of the Cassville elementary, knew like their own family tales. It was tales of a pair of ghosts roaming the halls, slamming locker and classroom doors. Hearing voices out in the halls when tests were being taken, yet when the teacher would look, there was no one there. It was the tales that made fourth graders pee themselves, and tales that made high school students tempt faith by raising a beer on the opening day of 'trout season' and asking the ghosts to come and party with them.

In Cassville, opening day of trout season is as much of a celebration to the town as Mardi Gras is to New Orleans. The schools are closed and many workers come down with a bad case of rainbowtroutitis-the only cure to catch a rainbow trout. The legend of Greg and Karen began here, over forty years ago; their tale is that something bad happened to them. What happened to them depends on whom you ask. Some say they ran on to a group of devil worshipers and they sacrificed them, burying their bodies deep in the woods. There are still hikers today searching for their graves. The other tales were that a teacher went nuts and murdered them, because he quit the next day and left Cassville, never to be seen again. It was the tale of a tragic love story gone wrong. That he murdered her in a fit of passion, and there were witnesses who stated that the couple got into an argument. After seeing what he did he killed himself, the buzzards, coyotes and black bears carrying off their bodies. It was a tale of two teenagers who disappeared on March 1, the opening day of trout season and a school holiday. It was the farfetched stories that were produced when moans and groans could be heard in the old rock gym; it was here that the legend of their haunting grew. The most likely story was that they ran away together never to return to Cassville but that was unfulfilling, and wouldn't scare grade school kid to death when they heard the heater pop. Seeing this jacket, that last tale was no longer the case.

"It is Greg Anderson's jacket; there is no doubt about it." Thom said and turned and began to walk back towards the hole and they followed him. "When they started digging they ran across bones." Thom looked back over his shoulder at Ryder and added "Naw, not human, cattle." He pointed down into the hole and said. "Then they hit this. Ryder looked down into the hole. In the middle were the remains of a 1970 Coronet R/T convertible, its bright paint hidden under the realms of rust, the cancer eating away the metal body, the canvas convertible top now ripped to shreds of clothing it once wore proudly, and the scoop hood twisted and bent up, revealing the dead remains of the most powerful engine on the street- the hemi.

"We ran the VIN." Thom said. "It checked back to J.C. Anderson, Greg's father. It is his car."

Ryder watched as a deputy crawled down a ladder at the edge of the hole next to the car, wearing white coverall. He and three other men were carefully unearthing the Coronet from its grave, it was the one and only 1970 Hemi R/T convertible. "You know anything about this?" Thom asked as he handed the jacket to another deputy to bag up.

"I wasn't even a burp in my mom's tummy when all this happened," Ryder said. "She was a kid herself." Ryder climbed up on the pile of dirt to get a better look. Across from the hole was a bright yellow John Deere Excavator stopped in it tracks, its huge bucket tucked away in shame up next to it. "In fact I think she told me that these two were classmates of hers." Ryder looked back at Thom and the others standing below him, bathed in the light of the search lamps, only a few feet away darkness surrounded them.

"I might be able to explain the cows' bones. According to tales that Pop told me there used to be a big blackjack tree here. Five cows were standing under it when lightning struck the tree. It killed the cow. According to Pop they buried the cows here."

"That was your grandfather?"

"Of course, there is nobody else I would call Pop!" Ryder grumbled at this question, to even think he would ever call his father this. "My father was my father. My grandfather was my Pop." Ryder climbed down the pile of dirt.

"When was that? When were the cows buried?"

"I would guess around forty-one or forty-two years ago." Ryder answered.

"Could it have been when these went missing?"

"Yeah, but what are you trying to say Thom, that Pop had something to do with the kids?" Ryder asked, as the deputies switched out again and another deputy took over digging.

"Of course not, but when they started digging they found the cow bones first; that means the car was already in the hole when the cows were shoved into it. Who would have been on this farm at that time?"

"Pop, granny, mom, Uncle Tony."

"What about your dad?"

"My father? Yes he worked here on the farm." Ryder said as he looked over the search site. "Where is Brian?"

"Well…"Thom drug out. "Let's just say this is not the only mud pit that is being dug in this county. Sam Beckwith is causing trouble. Saying there is a conflict of interest as he remains deputy and running for sheriff."

"There would be if you were also running, but it is just him and her. What is her problem?"

"All the money you have given him for the election."

"I gave only what I could legally give. I just think he is the best person for the job." Ryder said as he began to walk away from the hole.

"Because she is a woman?" Alex asked; she had to shout over the sound of the power saw cutting through the roof pillars of the car, as a stream of sparks rose up out of the hole as the aluminum oxide disc cut through the metal.

"You know better than that!" He snapped back at her. "No, because she is an outsider. She is a freaking Jayhawker; she was born and raised in Dodge City. "Yakira's flashlight beam was leading them back to the car. "Her training was in traffic and parking control. For most of her career she was a meter maid." Suddenly the power saw became quiet and Ryder lowered his voice to normal. "We have a murder to investigate in Eureka Springs," he stopped walking and turned back to Thom and added. "You need me, you have my..."

Before Ryder could get the rest of his words out a deputy from down in the hole cried out. "Thom, you need to get down in here right now. Not as sheriff, but as County Coroner." With that Thom turned and raced back towards the hole, with Ryder and the others following him. Thom quickly descended the ladder down into the hole, and gazed down at the interior of the car, the passenger side door now had been cut open.

"Ricky," Thom said, looking up at him. "I am calling. Get down here right now." Ryder quickly crawled down the ladder and carefully stepped around the remains of the car. Lying on the remains of the dash was a skull-male-, with a small bullet hole in the forehead. Thom placed his hand on Ryder's shoulder and said. "You have a murder case here now."

Chapter 9

It was a long night, bathed in the spot light, watching and carefully documenting, photographing as the skeletal remains of two young teens were removed from the rotting interior of the mid-sized Plymouth. Two victims; a male, age 18, six foot Greg Anderson, found in the remains of jeans and a Rolling Stones t-shirt; female-Karen James, age 18, height five foot found in the remains of bell bottom jeans and a floral patterned blouse, apparent cause of death, a single bullet in the head.

Lots of coffee and doughnuts were consumed before the sun began to peek up over the horizon. Ryder's knee, which had been blown out in a late hit that ended his career early as the Kansas City Chiefs quarterback, ached as he climbed back down into the pit for the umpteenth time. Dressed in a white coverall and wearing surgical gloves he stepped over the rusted shut passenger side door of the Coronet and began to search the contents of the car.

In the back seat were the remains of two large black 'Modern Biology' books, their pages yellowed and falling apart as they were turned. Also in the back seat a CHS annual, it was tan in color with the word 'Avaunt' printed on it and dated back forty-two years ago. Ryder flipped through the pages, they were yellowed and the ends were rotting out. There were many messages written on the pages from fellow students. As he flipped through to the graduating class that year there were a few faces that he recognized. His mother, Danielle Delaney, Yakira's mother Rebekah Feinstein, there was not even a signature over their photos, but over Karen's was this 'Karen, whose beauty on the outside is only outshined by her inside beauty, forever yours, Ryan.'

"Yeah, dad, we know what forever means with you." He mumbled as he closed the book and placed it in an evidence bag, marked its location and sealed it shut. After documenting their location with a digital camera he picked up and bagged several gum and candy wrappers, and $1.85 in coins. He began to move back into the front seats when his foot kicked something under the passenger's seat. He saw a curled wooden handle; he leaned down and tried to remove it from under the seat, but it was caught in between the seat and floor, crushed by the huge amount of weight that had been on the car.

"Can somebody get a pry bar up there?" He yelled out of the hole. Soon Yakira crawled down the ladder and into the hole and handed him a three-foot bar. He placed it under the seat and pulled up on the bar.

The seat frame gave away from the rusted out floor, and the seat up ended. He could see what it was now that was stuck in the seat springs. It was a revolver. He carefully removed it, it was rusty and the other side of the handle was broken. He pushed the release at the front of the trigger guard, it was mostly encased with rust and dirt, but the gun broke in two, the barrel swinging forward. There was room for nine 22-caliber shells in it, seven were still in it, and two had been fired.

"H&R Model ".22 Special" 9-shot Target Pistol." Yakira said. As he handed her the bagged weapon, she added, "From the serial numbers I would say it is from the 1930's, maybe 1932. Single or double action automatic ejector, good home defense weapon. A 22 caliber would really mess up somebody. I would say this is the murder weapon."

"Can you trace it?"

"Yes, but I doubt it would do any good, in Missouri this far back I really doubt there is any record of it. However, I might be able to find something on my own. Old man Packard who I bought the shop from, kept records of every sale. Because he backed every sale with a two-year guarantee, if it was bought at his shop then there might have been recorded. I am not promising you anything, but I can look."

Ryder pulled the seat back down and crawled over in the front section of the car, the windshield pillars had been pushed over on the dash and the instrument panel was bowed in the middle. Ryder tried to open the glove box door, but it was rusted shut. With his fist, he slammed the glove box door a couple of times and it popped open. Inside was the weathered but still intact owner's manual, a box of condoms, a repair sheet for the Dodge, dated February 27th, and under it a small velvet jewelry box. He opened it up.

"Oh my God!" Ryder said out loud as he gazed down upon the ring in the box. It was unique, with a large tear drop shaped pink diamond as the center stone and smaller white diamonds and emeralds that looked like leaves on the sides of the white gold ring.

"What?" He heard Yakira say, almost breathless, "What is that? It is so beautiful. And just my color, pink!"

"Well, let's get this bagged. He pulled out his pen to write on the bag, but it slipped from his fingers and fell out onto the ground. Could you get that for me?" He asked Yakira. As she bent down, he slipped the jewelry box into the bag and sealed it shut. She handed him the pen and he wrote jewel box, glove box for its location.

I had been a long night and the sun was now playing peek- a-boo with the horizon, the warm rays of the sun beginning to spread across the fields, shadows long an dark, tracing across the remaining fence lines. Ryder followed Yakira up the ladder out of the pit and handed a deputy the bags, then Yakira handed the bag with the gun to the deputy.

Ryder walked over to Thom who had loaded the bodies into bags and placed them in the bright white 'meat wagon.' Double T slammed the doors of the Suburban, revealing the county logo. He turned back to Ryder and Yakira "Well I'm pretty sure I know how they died, but till I get them on the table and get a sample of the marrow I won't know for sure."

"What? No playing how they died?" Ryder asked, knowing usually his friend was always the joker, even in his job. There were two kinds of medical examiners- those that were joking, and those that were deadpan serious. He hoped that his pal wouldn't turn into the latter type.

"No more games, Rick. Just the facts." Thom said as he began to walk around to the driver's door, when Ryder grabbed him by the arm and stopped him.

"You really don't like being sheriff, do you?" Ryder asked as he made the man turn around.

"There aren't enough words in the English language, and I don't even have to say 'watch my French', because there aren't enough dirty words there either to say how much I hate this." Thom said, before he grabbed Ryder's wrist with his hands and pleaded. "You have to help me with this."

"I will do what I can, Double T."

"You promise!"

"Yes."

Double T turned to Yakira, standing next to Ryder, and asked "You too?"

"Sure," she drug out, sounding unconvinced, herself. "But I am not a detective."

"It doesn't matter. You both promise, to help me and Barry County. So help you God."

"Yes!." Ryder said pulling his hand away from Thom's grip.

"Say it! And raise your hands."

"So help me God." Ryder and Yakira said as they raised their hands. At that moment Double T grinned broadly and quickly turned and opened the door of the wagon, reached inside, and returned with something in his hand.

"Here you go." Thom said handing Ryder and then Yakira a five point golden star with the words 'Deputy Sheriff Barry County' with the great seal of Missouri in the center. "You are now both deputies." He turned to Ryder and grinned, relived. That he didn't have to do this investigation anymore. "Ryder, I am placing you in charge of this investigation. I know if there is anyone that can solve an over 40 year murder it is you." He looked at Yakira and added. "Both of you."

"Double T, I did not agree to be a deputy, and I don't want a badge." Ryder said holding out the badge for Thom to take.

"Yes you did!" Thom retorted back. "I heard you! You swore to help me and Barry County, that is close enough, and it was to God. You want to tick Him off?" He looked down at the badge Ryder was holding out and pushed Ryder's hand back. "And yeah, you do need a stinking badge." He added in a fake Mexican accent, trying to reword the line from the movie, 'The Treasure of the Sierra Madre'. With that he grinned even more and walked back to the Coroner's wagon and opened the door, just before he got in, he turned and joked.

"Now I will take these contestants to back to my lab. But first I have to find some sticks and stones."

"Let me guess," Ryder said, rolling his eyes up, "to find out who broke their bones?"

"Ding, Ding!" He said, mocking the sound of a bell. "You win! And your prize is your wages! For being a deputy you receive your standard rate of a dollar a day and you pay the expenses. See you later, deputies." He got in and drove away.

"So what do we do now?" Yakira asked as she wrapped her arm around his waist.

"How about first some breakfast and then we head to bed?"

"Oh, really?" She asked intriguingly, looking up at him and batting her eyes.

"In our own beds. To sleep." He replied as he looked around at the parked cars and then asked. "Where's Alex?"

"She left last night a little while after they found the bodies. Said 'she had to get home, and told me to tell you she would call you tomorrow.' "Yakira looked up at the sky and the red haze over the sunrise as she continued. "Which I guess now is today."

I don't get her!" Ryder snorted as they walked back to the Killer Bee. "When we were hunting for the Butcher, we were up day and night. Now she has to get back home all the time. She is hiding something."

"I think it is a man." Yakira said as he held the door open for her. As she slipped down into the passenger seat she continued. "I heard hear on the phone last night she was talking sweet nothings to someone."

As Ryder and Yakira drove back to Cassville, he saw her look of shock when they drove past the restaurants in town, and headed towards the lake house between Golden and Shell Knob. She asked, "why are we not stopping?"

He just replied "I have something better, just wait." Passing by the pub in Golden he just repeated again, "Something you have wanted to experience your whole life."

"Is that so? " She said, turning her head slightly sideways and looked at him, grinning as she winked. "All my life? Or say, when I became a woman, or am I going to become one now?"

"You have a dirty mind."

"I is what I is." She said, turning back as he guided the Dodge down the narrow road that twisted through the trees and down to his A-frame lake house on Table Rock Lake. He got out of the car and opened the door for her. He led her into the house and guided her to a stool at the bar that separated the great room and the kitchen.

After he thoroughly washed his hands, Ryder opened the refrigerator door and pulled out a package of meat and set it on the counter. "What are you fixing?" She asked as he reached back into the refrigerator and pulled out a carton of eggs.

"Deep fried bacon and eggs."

"What!!! Bacon? Sweetie, I know I hop off the kosher wagon every now and then, mix a little dairy with meat, but pork? That is the big no no!" As he opened a drawer and pulled out a sharp carving knife, he turned to her and said.

"You can with this. It is 100% beef, made by Mother himself." Mother was a friend of Ryder's from Kansas City, once a Hall of Fame running back, known by his dirty word nickname- the defensive line would call him when he broke through, now the owner of one of the best rib joints in the city. He had just made a side of beef bacon from a fatty piece of brisket, hickory smoking it and curing it, before packing it up and sending it on overnight delivery to Ryder.

Ryder opened up the bag and pulled out a slab of meat, deep red and covered with fat. As he took the knife and carefully sliced into the meat, he stopped just long enough to look back over his shoulder to see that she has slid off the stool and was standing behind him. He sliced a long, thin, but not too thin, slice of meat and laid it over to the side of the cutting board and her mouth watered.

He cut several slices, then using a pepper mill sprinkled a little pepper on the meat, dipped it in flour and fried it in oil. While he was waiting for the bacon to fry, he quickly made a pot of coffee and then he scrambled up some eggs, Ryder style. With chopped up chives and a little sour cream in butter. It didn't take the bacon long to cook as he flipped over the bacon; it was a nice golden brown color and crisp. He plated the scrambled eggs on two plates and then removed the bacon and drained it on paper towels; he quickly put two slices of wheat bread into the toaster.

"Get the jelly and butter." He told her as he reached up and got down two cups, filling them with coffee, topping each one with a little cream and two sugars. He placed the bacon on the plate and just as he turned around the toast popped up. He placed a piece of toast on each plate. "Did you get the silverware?"

"It's already on the table." She said as she followed him into the dining area. He set the plates down on the table, his at the head and hers just to his right. They said grace and the first thing each one of them picked up was the bacon. It was so flavorful, like smoky fried steak; the sweetness of the molasses and brown sugar gave it some wonderful bacon-like taste.

"Where have you been my entire life, sweetie?" Yakira said to the bacon as she held the slice out in front of her. "I could just plotz right now." She closed her eyes and took another bite and moaned with delight. "Seriously if I could just die right now, I would...really bacon deep fried... I am one sameah bah'ura." She finished all her bacon and looked down at his remaining piece while he was eating his eggs.

"Go ahead." He said with a nod of his head. "I can see you are a happy girl. There is another ten pounds of it in the freezer."

She quickly picked up the other piece of bacon and began to munch it down. "You said Mother sent this?"

"Yeah, you remember him?"

"Yes, tell him I just fell in love?"

"With him?"

"No silly, " Yakira said with a laugh. "This!" She said, holding up the piece of bacon.

"He is starting to make this; wanted to know if I would give him an endorsement." Ryder said as he finished his eggs and pushed his plate back as he picked up his toast, buttered it and spread strawberry freezer jam on it.

"Tell him I will stand naked at Union Station if he will send more of this." Yakira said, chewing on the last piece of bacon.

"Honey, there is another ten, besides the one pound that is the fridge." Ryder said as he leaned back in his chair and took a bite of toast. "So I think you can keep your clothes on right now."

"I want this every morning. It isn't going to last that long." Finishing up the bacon, she ate her eggs. As she lifted her fork up to her mouth she looked over at him as he raised the cup of coffee to his lips. "So what is up with that ring?"

"What ring?"

"Ricky, I saw you put it in your pocket. Why did you take it?" Yakira said as she scooped up another bite of eggs.

Ryder reached into his pocket and pulled out the ring. He set it down on the table in front of him . "This came from White's Jewelry in Cassville. It was bought by a couple that was just beginning their lives; they wanted something that was unique and as special as they were. So the jeweler did just that." Once again he picked up the ring and held it up; he took a cloth and carefully cleaned it, making the stones sparkle and the white gold shine once again.

"How do you know that?"

"Because I knew the woman who wore it, it was my grandmother, Ellie, my father's mother. She told me that she was saving it for me, that it was to go to the first male grandchild and that he would give it to the one he loved. She said it was locked away in a box. I never opened it till after she died, and the ring wasn't in there."

"The bigger question is—."Yakira said reaching over and taking the ring from him and trying it on. It was way too big, rotating on her fingers, barely fitting her thumb. "How did it get into a car that was buried with two dead bodies?"

"Well there is only one person that could have taken it, my father. He is a thief." Ryder paused, then took the ring back from her, and added. "And now a murder suspect."

Chapter 10

That hole on his old family farm had served as a grave for over forty years. There was just something about opening a grave that left Ryder feeling dirty and grimy. It was unlike a murder scene, where soulless eyes would stare up at him. He could see them begging him to find their killer so that they could find rest. Opening a grave, where there was no stare, just a frozen grin of fright maybe even one of anger their rest had been disturbed.

He gazed at himself in the bathroom mirror that spanned the entire width of the wall. He stood there in his underwear, his hands pressed against the sink counter top. The sound of water pouring from the shower head was like a drenching rainstorm, hitting the bottom of the fiberglass tub sounding like thunder; it was a storm that was running through his mind. That was what was really raging. He gazed down at the Formica countertop, the gold swirls on the gray counter began to turn into faces, faces of all the victims he had seen in his career. He looked back up into the mirror as it began to fog over from the hot water. As he slipped his shorts off, he swore he could see a face appearing in the mirror, a golden haired woman standing behind him. He turned around but there was no one there, he turned back to the mirror, she was still there-it was the woman he had seen in his dreams. He wiped away the fog and as the mirror cleared, her face vanished.

He pulled the white and gold shower curtain aside and stepped into the tub under the shower. It felt so good, like an electric blanket in the middle of February. He closed his eyes and began to forget about the faces, including the one he had just seen in the mirror, try as he might, that was one face that kept popping up and appearing in his mind.

After washing he got out, dried off with a towel, slipped on some sleep pants and a t-shirt and headed to bed. It didn't take long till he was fast asleep. Once again he began to dream:

He was standing along the shores of Table Rock Lake; a thick blanket of steam was rising up from the waters, moving over him like whiffs of clouds being guided by the wind. An image appeared on the water, that of a woman, her long hair glowing as if the sun was beginning to set in the sky. It was the woman he had dreamed of before; she floated over the waters like a ghostly spirit, till she was standing on the bank next to him.

"Darling," the woman spoke, her voice soft and low, "you cannot stop what is to happen. The moon shall rise and when it wears a veil like a bride that shall be a sign that you must prepare for your bride." He dreamed that she reached up placed her arms around his neck and he looked into her cool blue eyes. He wanted to run, but it felt as if he were stuck in muddy clay, not even able to lift one foot. As he dreamed that she kissed him on the side of his face, he could smell the sick sweet smell of flowers. "You must forget the others; I am the one, the only one."

Suddenly the vision faded as he was aroused by his phone ringing. In a sleepy daze, he picked it up and answered it, seeing a photo of a woman on the screen. It was Alex.

"This better be damn good." He said crabbily, as rubbed his hand over his eyes.

"I found Celeste's sister. She is in Lamar, Colorado."

"That is over 500 miles from here." Ryder said as he sat up, putting a pillow behind him so he could lean back on the headboard. "How did you find her?"

"You don't want to know." Came her reluctant reply.

"In other words, you pulled an Alex and looked into something you didn't have permission to. Phone records…banking information."

"She made a purchase at the Safeway Pharmacy. You want to go?"

"No, you can handle it yourself."

"You sound grumpy."

"Well, I am not a morning person if I don't get my sleep; you should know that very well."

"Its three o'clock in the afternoon."

"WHAT!" Ryder popped back; he had only wanted to sleep for a few hours. "Just tell me what you find out. I am out of here." With that he ended the call and got out of bed. As his bare feet hit the cold wood floor, he looked down; his feet were covered in mud, the legs of his sleep pants wet with lake water. He brought his hand up to his face. Remembering the kiss, he dashed over to the mirror on the dresser and gazed into it. Turning his head to the side, there it was bright, blood red lip stick on his cheek.

After washing his face and feet, he quickly dressed in black pants and a dark gray tweed sports coat over a gray and white striped shirt. Before checking his messages and finding out he had missed a call from his uncle, he combed his hair and headed out of the bedroom. He heard music playing from the stereo in the great room. He walked into the kitchen and stopped as he watched Yakira, dressed in pink slacks and a pale pink rose-printed blouse, dancing by herself. He walked up and placed his hand on her shoulder and said. "Mind if I cut in?" He took her in his arms and they began to sway back forth to the rhythm of the music.

She tilted her head back and looked up at him, her long dark mane of hair falling down behind her as she said. "Something tells me you are not just dressed for a night of dinner and dancing."

"Uncle Tony wants us to come for supper. First we have to stop by to see Double T."   As the song ended he dipped her back in his arms and gazed into her dark soulful eyes. He lowered his face to hers and asked tenderly. "You ready?"

"For anything, baby." She said, before he kissed her, holding her there for a moment before he pulled her to her feet and spun her around holding on to her hand; with a quick but gentle snap he spun her back to him and wrapped his arms around her and held her close. The smell of her honeysuckle perfume was almost intoxicating, for just a brief moment he was happy.

"You know how much you mean to me?" He asked tenderly as he rested his chin down on top of her head. "No matter what happens I want you to know that…" He squeezed her tighter and she let her fingers come to his arms. He felt alive; he didn't want to let her go. "There is something I would like to ask but…"

She pulled from his embrace and turned to him and smiled as she said "'…but what?"

"I—I don't know how to say it…" He gazed out the sliding glass door that led out on to the deck, standing there was the blonde woman; he could hear her words in his mind.

"You cannot. For you belong to me."

93

Just like a light being turned on in the middle of the night the moment was shattered as he shouted out, "Leave me alone!"

Stunned, she stepped back, traumatized by his words she said in almost a whisper. "If that is what you want."

"Not you, her!" Ryder said pointing to the glass door. Yakira turned and looked out and then back to him, her eyebrows lifting in surprise.

"There is no one there." As she spoke the vision of the woman faded

Chapter 11

It took about forty-five minutes to make the back into town. He parked in the back behind the Thompson Funeral Home. If it weren't for the huge flashing sign out front that announced funerals and visitation times, there would have been no indication this was anything but an old fashioned home.

Ryder opened the back door and walked in, removing his sun glasses. He looked over at Yakira, now wearing a jacket. They stepped into the elevator and descended to the basement. Immediately they were met with the icy breath of the ceiling cooling ducts. Stretched out on the examining table were the bones of the young woman, next to them on a gurney were the skeletal remains of the young man. Thom was standing behind the table over next to a counter on the far wall where glassware was sitting. Like a mad scientist creating an experiment. There was something dark bubbling in the flask under a Bunsen burner. Thom, using a pot holder, picked up the flask and poured the liquid into a beaker. As he looked back at Ryder his face was blank of any expression.

"Just a moment," Thom said seriously, "I have to get this right." He carefully poured the contents from the flask into the beaker, watching carefully as it reached a certain mark on the beaker. He then poured a white substance from another beaker into the first beaker, using a glass rod he carefully stirred the mixture, then lifted the beaker up and added "Coffee?"

"No thanks." Ryder said. "I have had your coffee before, it strong enough to wake the dead. What do you have?"

Thom carefully took a sip of his coffee and walked over to the examining table. "Something really strange happened here."He said as he took another sip of coffee and set the beaker down.

"Is that not a gunshot wound?" Ryder asked as he reached into his inside breast pocket and pulled out a small note book with a pen attached to it. He began to write in it.

"Without any soft tissue we just have to take a guess." Thom explained as he picked up a pair of forceps from a small tray next to the table. "Since both skulls have bullet holes in them, we can assume they were murdered."

"Could it be a suicide?" Yakira asked

Thom walked back over to the counter with the glass ware, opened a drawer and pulled out an Annie Oakley cap gun. "Most people shooting themselves do it in the mouth, under the chin, or to the side of the head." He said, mocking each movement with the cap gun to his head. He then handed the toy gun to Yakira. "Try to shoot yourself in the back of the head."

It was difficult but she twisted her arm behind her head and pulled the trigger. Thom used the forceps he was holding and pointed at the wound in the skull. "The cranial bone of the left-hand side of the skull was the entry point." He moved to the skeletons hand, and held up the right arm. "She was right-handed."

"How can you tell that?" Ryder asked.

"Whatever arm is dominate, the Humerus bone on that side is slightly wider. The humorous on her right-side is .82 mm wider. She was right-handed. "He turned to Yakira and said. "Using your right hand reach behind and try to shoot yourself in the left hand side of your head." She did as she told struggling to twist her hand around, holding the toy upside down she was barely able to do it. "Now you're the gun lady, if you were shot that close would there be GSR?"

"Gunshot residue? Yes, a lot of it even in the bones."

"Now pull it back at least two feet." He said. She tried, but failed.

"I can't!" She said, dropping her arm down to her side. "She couldn't have shot herself. It had to be someone else."

"Ding, ding, ding," Thom mocked the sound of a bell and the tone of a game show announcer. "We have a first round winner in 'How Did She Die. You have now won the first round would you like to go on to the bigger prize. If there is no GSR how far would the gun have to be away? Tick, tick, hurry the clock is ticking. "

"I would say at least two-feet away." Yakira replied

"We have a winner. Those that have lost don't worry we have a nice box of Rice a Roni for you." Suddenly Thom's tone changed back to normal as he picked up a laser pen and used it to line up with the bullet hole in the back of the skull. "See the angle of wound?" He said as the red beam of light took a steep downward angle. "As you can see it came from a downward slant. I would say the killer was standing behind her. She was either sitting down or you're looking for a seven-foot tall killer."

"Okay," Ryder said, looking up from his notebook. "Another possible way; murder suicide, he shoots her, feels bad, shoots himself."

"Same reason. No GSR on his skull. The angle of the wound shows it came at a low angle, as if someone was on the ground and he was standing. But there is something else about Karen's body that's bugging me." He turned the skull over and pointed to the nasal bone, and then the jaw bone. "You see the fine cracks around the Maxilla? Both nasal bones and the zygomatic bones." He said as he pointed to the cheek bone on the right-hand side? These are signs of old trauma."

"What does that mean?' Yakira asked.

Having seen this same thing on many autopsies from many murder cases Ryder answered. "It means that she was abused."

"I would estimate them to be, possibly a year or more old; they are not the kind you get from a car accident or falling downstairs…" Thom looked up at Ryder and laid the forceps back down on the tray. "He stepped out from behind the table and stood in front of Ryder. "Take a swing at my face."

"What?"
"Just don't hit me. And do it in slow motion."

Ryder swung his right hand at Thom coming next to the side of his head. "See, you are right-handed, so you swung at the left side of my face. He went back to the skull. "This is on the right-hand side, meaning…"

"A left-handed hitter." Yakira spoke up. "Just like in baseball."

"Ding-Ding! Tell that lady what she has won." Thom imitated a bell and with deep tone trying to sound like a game show announcer continued. "Well she has won a trip to the 'that makes sense island.' "His tone changed back to normal and serious once again as he said. "Greg was left handed. Want to know how I know? " He walked over to the old school annual and flipped it open to a page that showed Greg playing softball during P.E; it was clear that he was batting left-handed. "I called Ben Crawford."

"The old principal? He has to be over eighty." Ryder said.

"Eight-seven to be exact, but he remembers both Karen and Greg. Greg being a hot-head, especially against Karen, and he also remembers…" Thom flipped through the pages of the annual, through the juniors till he came to the photo of Karen. He held it up. "You see anything different about this photo?" Ryder looked at it and compared it to the others, all the others had been taken by a professional with a screen behind them, hers was outside.

"She didn't have her photo made that day."

"You got it, Pale Ryder," Thom said, using a nick name that was given to him by the high school football coach, because when he started throwing, it brought death to the other teams' scores. "Also Crawford remembers that she missed that day because she broke her nose in an accident."

"Let me guess: she fell down the stairs?" Ryder said as he closed his note book and placed it and the pen back into his jacket pocket. "So we are back to murder suicide?"

"How does she shoot him, and then shoots herself. Or he shoots her then shoots himself. Let's say it was possible, that is what happened. Explain how they got in the car and then buried themselves in the hole. Find the person who buried that car, and then you will find the murderer."

Ryder turned and started to head back to the elevator and had just pushed the button and the doors opened, when Thom called out. "Oh! The guys found a bullet in the old R/T. I sent it and the gun over to Alex and her pals to see if they can get a match. I'm not sure if they can even get it to fire, but I will let you know what we find out."

"Why me?" Ryder asked looking into the empty car, holding the doors open with his hand. "Why did you put me in charge of this case, why not one of the other deputies?"

"Because of who you are. This is one of the oldest and well known cases in this county. I don't know these other guys. There are two families that have not been able to put their children to rest. I know you will get the truth, and the truth is what they want."

"Truly," Ryder said, glancing over his shoulder at the man. "Sometimes the truth doesn't go down that easy; knowing your son was an S.O.B. may not be the greatest thing."

"Maybe so, but it may be just what Karen's family needs."

Chapter 12

Back in the car they headed north on Main Street and then right on State Highway Y, and then left on Seventeenth Street. There was a slight incline and Ryder pressed down on the accelerator, making the dual exhaust rumble. His Uncle Tony, Father Anthony Delany, was just leaving his office at St. Edward Parish; he stopped and looked towards the street. Ryder pulled the Charger into a parking spot in the lot, stopped, got out and looked across the roof at his round faced uncle. His reddish hair and freckles told of his Irish heritage. His mother's brother, he was the only family he had, well, the only one he wanted to know about.

"Uncle Tony, we were hoping to catch you before you left." Ryder said as he walked around to the back of the car and opened the passenger's side door.

"Yu want me to marry you two?" He asked, and then laughed.

"Why is everybody in this town saying that?" Ryder asked. "We—I—I mean—we are just dating. Nobody is talking about marriage." Ryder stumbled over his words and for the first time since he was back in high school he felt a warm flush come over his cheeks, and hoped that no one else could see it.

Father Anthony kept walking across the parking lot. He stopped in mid stride and turned around. "What are you two waiting for- an engraved invitation? Let's go have some supper."

Ryder and Yakira followed him across the parking lot and the street to a comfortable looking home. It was a simple ranch style with blue siding, a single car garage on one end and a large picture window that faced the highway on the other end. In the driveway was a one of kind vehicle, a 1970 Cyclone/ Ranchero combination. The front was Mercury muscle car, the back was all pickup, with a strip of tail lamps across the tailgate. The father looked at the car as he unlocked the front door, and then back to his nephew as he pushed the front door open. "Thanks again for the car. I have wanted that car ever since I was in high school."

"I found your drawing in a box of stuff that mom had." Ryder said as they all walked inside and Father Anthony turned on the ceiling lights. There was a small living room to the right with twisted wood poles for trim that served as the door way. Ahead was a small walk way to another hallway to the left that lead down to the two small bedrooms, which shared a bathroom and the master bedroom which had its own bath.

Back up the hallway and to the right was the largest room in the house, the family/dining room. Black leather furniture dominated the room; a La-Z-Boy recliner and love seat on one side and a seven-foot sofa on the other. Next to the sofa was a large entertainment center. In the center was a large TV, on the side were bookshelves loaded with books and photos. At the far end of the room was a dark maple drop leaf dining table, with ladder back chairs the same shade as the table.

The father turned on a table lamp in between the loveseat and easy chair and then turned on the TV as Ryder walked over to the table and placed his hand down on it. Memories of him sitting at this table at his grandmother's house next to his mother brought a smile to his face. Hearing that his uncle was going to make his grandmother's fried chicken and corn bread and gravy brought even a broader smile.

"I haven't had that in a long time, Uncle Tony." Ryder said as he turned and looked at him standing the kitchen. He was tying an apron that had a big pair of lips printed on it along with the words 'Kiss the cook'.

"And some sliced tomatoes, and for dessert, apple pie and ice cream." Uncle Tony grinned, wrinkling up his freckled face as he added, "homemade, of course." Ryder glanced over his shoulder at Yakira who was picking up photos from the bookcase and looking at them. She picked up one of a four-year Ryder riding around in his pedal car.

"You were a cute kid." Yakira said as she lovingly rubbed her fingers over the glass. "You even have dimples."

"What happened, huh?" Ryder joked as he walked over to her and his eyes fell upon a photo of his family. It was made to look as if it were taken during the late 1800's, taken at Silver Dollar City, and they were all dressed up as an old fashioned family. "That was right before we found out that mom was sick." Ryder said as he picked up the photo and added. "The last time we felt like a family." He placed the photo back on the shelf and glanced down at the books lined up on the shelf, his eyes fell upon the cover that was familiar to him.

"Uncle Tony, you were a freshman when mom was a senior, right?" Ryder asked, slipping the annual from its place on the shelf.

"Oh. Yes." He heard his uncle reply from the kitchen along with the sizzle of chicken being placed in a cast iron skillet. "And she was the worst! Making my life—if you will pardon the expression-a living hell."

101

Ryder took the book, walked back over to the table, sat down and began to flip through the pages. In the background was the mumble of talking heads on Fox News, and drifting over to him was the aroma of chicken browning in the skillet. Meanwhile, Uncle Tony mixed up the corn bread batter in a large green glass bowl.

Ryder flipped through more of the pages, noticing the comments from his classmates, that how much of a class clown his uncle was back then, from mooning the French teacher to putting shaving cream in the mashed potatoes in the lunch room . He flipped over another page and noticed a bright eyed auburn haired girl with the name Cindy Walker under the photo that had a heart drawn around it with the words 'Tony, the hottest boy in school, Cindy.' "

Who's Cindy?" Ryder asked, looking up from the book. He could see his uncle's thoughts tracing back as he slid the corn bread into the oven.

"I haven't thought about her in a long time." Father Anthony said as he wiped his hands with a towel and walked over to the table. He looked over to the book and said. "She was something special." He pulled a chair out and sat down; Ryder could see the memories that flowed in his uncle's mind that appeared as a grin as he pulled the book over in front of him. "My first love, all the way through high school, I thought I was going to marry her." He stood back up and went back to the kitchen to turn the chicken, making sure to get the skin all crusty and crisp.

"So what happened?" Ryder asked, pulling the annual back over in front of him.

"Just wasn't God's will. He had other plans for me." He looked back at the table as Yakira sat down at the table next to Ryder. "You know, I wasn't born with this collar." The father said with a cocky smile as he straightened his collar. "In fact, I was kind of a stud back then; turn the page." On the next page were more comments from three other girls about how cute he was. Father Anthony stiffened up his back up and pushed his chest out, as he playfully punched his nephew in the arm and added. "Now you know where you get your good looks." He grinned broadly, showing all his teeth as he added in a tone of confidence, "From Me!"

"So what happened, Tony, why don't I have any cousins?"

"She broke my heart. We were both going to go to C of O, back then it was still known as the School of the Ozarks, but it seems she got a scholarship to the University of Arkansas, which came with another man. After that, I just found that God wanted me somewhere else. Last I knew she was living in Eureka Springs; owned one of the artsy shops down there."

Father Anthony returned to the kitchen to turn the chicken; Ryder was beginning to get hungry and the smell of cornbread and chicken was just adding to that, but he had to keep his mind on why he was really here. He flipped through the pages to the senior class. "Mom was sure a pretty woman." He said, noticing her in a photo with a couple of other girls standing in front her locker. He flipped the page over and saw a photo of Karen and Greg listed as the 'cutest couple'. Ryder looked up again from the book.

"Did you know the kids that went missing?" Ryder asked with care, trying not to show that he was looking for answers.

Again his uncle returned back to the table and said bluntly. "Ricky, we are family." He pulled out the chair and again sat down at the head of the table. "If you need to ask questions, ask them. I am your uncle, not some criminal. I heard that you were put on this investigation."

"How did you hear that?"

"It is a small town. You are a big deal to this town. All star quarterback, NFL player. Well before you, there was Greg and Karen, they were the 'it' couple. You asked me if I knew them." Father Delany flipped the book to the back cover where there were many more signatures. One that was from Greg that read 'Keep the greasy side down and the shiny side up 10-4 over and out.' "He was into CB's back then." He pointed to another scribble this time from Karen, 'to a good kid even though you have an awful sister.'

"What is it with her and mom?" Ryder asked as he read his mother's post 'to the best brother a sister could ever have'.

Father Delaney took the book, shut it and looked at his nephew and Yakira. "Your mothers were the best of friends in school, all the way through from the first day of kindergarten to the day Danielle died."

103

"What does this have to do with Karen?" Ryder asked, grabbing and opening the book again.

"Because all through school Karen and Danielle competed against each other, they hated each other. Yes, your mother could hate." Father Anthony said as he stood up and walked back into the kitchen, removed the chicken from the skillet and put it on a platter. "It started with your mother winning the first grade spelling bee, and then being crowned Little Miss Cassville." Uncle Tony carried the platter of fried chicken into the dining room and set it down. On the table as he continued. "Then in junior high things changed, Karen began to fill out and became a beauty. She became a cheerleader, your mother didn't, she became homecoming queen, and your mother was the first runner up. She was Miss Tip-Off, she was…"

"Is that motive enough?" Ryder asked in the tone of a detective and not of a son.

Father Anthony sighed heavily as he turned and walked back into the kitchen, opened the oven and pulled out the cornbread. "You are going to find this out anyway. You might as well hear it from me." The father poured off some of the oil in the skillet to make gravy. "It was the first of March, it was a common thing to go to Roaring River and have a party. Karen and some of the other seniors were there partying; she was drinking Jack and Coke and had way too much when she came on to your father."

"Came on to… you mean….?"

"I mean she walked over and sat down on his lap and proceeded to ram her tongue down his throat. She told him 'yes, she would.' "

"Would what?" Ryder asked as his uncle poured the gravy into a bowl.

"I don't know." Father Anthony said as he set the bowl of gravy down on the table. "No one ever told me. But…" He sighed again, as he regretted telling Ryder this. "…Rebekah joined in the fight. Karen ran off into the woods and your mother and Rebekah ran away screaming how they were going to make her pay for this."

"What about Mr. Ryan Ryder? What did he do? Did he have a thing for Karen?" Ryder said as he began to write in his notebook.

"He wanted her more than anything, she was the class beauty. So he ran after Karen." Father Anthony opened the refrigerator and pullout a plate of sliced tomatoes. He set them down on the table and returned to the kitchen.

"Greg; where was he at this time?"

"He was in the woods with some other girl." The father said to Ryder as he pulled open the cabinet door and pulled out some bright white china, then opened the drawer and produced flatware for the three of them.

"Who?"

"Don't know, I never saw her before, she said she was just 'visiting from out of state.' You know how it is on Trout Day, everyone comes out. I just remember she was so naive looking, and Greg pounced on her like a hungry wolf." After setting the table Father Anthony sat down.

It grew quiet and Father Anthony gave the blessing "Bless us, O Lord and these Your gifts which we…" As he prayed Ryder's mind wandered well away from the table, well away from this year back to a time when his parents were students at CHS, pondering on his uncle's words. He didn't want to, but it was that part of him that he just couldn't leave behind. He began to see his own mother as a possible suspect, what Karen did was motive enough to make his mother kill her. It was the number one motive for murder. As Father Anthony finished up the prayer he said another one in Hebrew so as not to offend Yakira's beliefs. Again Ryder's mind raced with how the two were killed. There was a question that he wanted to ask his uncle, but he had to wait till the prayer ended.

"Amen." Ryder said joining his uncle and Yakira as he snapped back to reality. Uncle Tony, after taking a piece of chicken passed the platter to Yakira. She held it over to Ryder with one hand and asked in a provocative tone.

"Which would you rather have? A leg —," she said with a grin as she reached down and pulled up the pant leg of her pink trousers, revealing her bare smooth calf. "Or a breast." She laughed at him as a little color flushed over his cheeks.

"I think I will take a couple of wings." He said, as she lowered her pant leg and he took the wings and she took a piece of white meat before setting the platter back down.

Uncle Tony passed the cornbread which had been cut into squares and placed on a plate and then the bowl of gravy. Ryder did what he had always done 'fed the chickens' by crumbling up his cornbread. "Did you hear anything that night Uncle Tony?" Ryder asked as he dipped the gravy on the cornbread. "

"Such as?"

"An argument or gun shot?" Ryder asked as he picked up the chicken and took a bite, enjoying its salty flavorful taste, a taste that brought him back to his mother. It was just like she made, just like his grandmother used to make. He just wished he had his real choice, the breast meat, but he was too embarrassed to reach for it without Yakira's mocking tone.

"Yes, I do remember what sounded like a gunshot."

"Where was it, from the woods?"

"In fact, there were two. One from the woods, and then about a couple of hours later one across the park, over next to the Pibern Trail. I thought they were firecrackers, but I guess they could have been gunshots." Father Anthony said as he cut into the cornbread with gravy and scooped up a forkful and added. "Also heard that the woman in prison may not be the Kansas City Butcher."

Like a crack of lightning his uncle's words snapped Ryder's mind back. "Where did you hear that! Around town?" Ryder demanded.

"No," Father Anthony said pointing to the TV. "The news." Ryder turned and faced the TV; a local broadcast reporter was speaking. It was outside the prison. Marching along the sidewalk was a group of forty-five people, some carrying signs reading 'Free Celeste! She is innocent.' 'To beautiful to die!' While others chanted "mental illness is not a crime."

"The report is that a murder occurred in Eureka Springs, Arkansas." Ryder heard the reporter speak as he had to raise his voice to be heard over the protestors. "Murder, just like those that happened in the Kansas City area, when a note was sent to the local newspaper there before the murder occurred. The brutal string of murders occurred in Kansas City almost four years ago. It is reported that the same style of writing with a crayon that was sent to the 'Star' was sent to the Eureka Springs newspaper. We at FOX4 have learned that another note has been delivered to the Independent Newspaper promising that yet another murder is to happen. Officials in Eureka Springs had quoted as saying 'they are taking this to be a serious threat, but do not want residents or guests to the city to be alarmed and they should not feel unsafe. Eureka Springs mayor, Jason Edwards stated 'that additional officers would be placed on active duty.

Ryder used the remote to turn up the TV. As the FOX News national anchor spoke as she asked the local reporter. "We have heard that the arresting officers of Ms. Velour, Rick Ryder and F.B.I. agent Isabelle Alexander visited Ms. Velour yesterday. Is there any indication that possibly Velour may be innocent?"

"No Greta, we have no confirmation of what was asked of Ms. Velour. We did contact the Kansas City Mayor's office and Captain Craig Grosstree of the K.C.P.D; they both gave us statements saying that they believe that the right person was convicted for the murders and the evidence proves that. However, Greta, Mr. Ryder resigned after that case, and went on to become America's biggest Powerball ® winner and now uses his winnings to help those who cannot afford a private detective. We at FOX4 have a source that tells us that the case he was working on was in fact this murder at Eureka Springs."

Ryder turned the TV off. "Great!" He said with grief. "Now they are going to think she is innocent."

"You don't?" Father Anthony asked and Ryder turned to him.

Ryder ran his hand over his face and went to the refrigerator, opened it, and pulled out a bottle of soda, opened it and took a big swig. "Maybe it is time I told you both what it was like." Ryder took another sip of the pop and continued. "Most other serial killers follow some plan. Their victims fit some profile. All women, all men, certain hair color, a certain race, a certain age, but she was different. There was no pattern; it was as if she was trying to get our attention. One was an old man, one a young woman, one white, one black, one rich, one poor, one near a church, and one near a school." As Ryder continued to speak he paced back and forth in the family room, as if he couldn't stay still remembering these things. "The only thing in common was that she would send two notes, one to the newspaper and the other one to me." Again he took a swig of the soda.

"The first two murders were nothing to the city, just another group statistic, but the third and fourth murders rattled it to the core. It was the Star that dubbed her the Kansas City Butcher.

Ryder paused, staring out at the picture window behind the table; the sun was beginning to set, creating long reaching shadows that cast out over the street. "By the fifth killing it brought the city to a halt. The Mayor was screaming bloody murder at me, threatening to have my ass and badge." Again he paused, staring out the windows as the warm glow of the sun quickly faded, and with a blink of God's eye, the night had begun. He stood still for a moment, his mind racing back to those days when The Royals cancelled night games, night clubs were locked up tighter than jail cells. Even the gangs would cease their criminal activities. "Owners of the Royals, Chiefs, even high school principals wanted me and Alex run out of town." Ryder took another sip and turned his back to them; as if he couldn't face them when he explained this horror. "You know how creepy it is being on the streets of K.C, it was if we were the only ones out there. When you shut the car door you could hear it echo off the side of the buildings. No matter how many warnings the city gave there was some moron, some uninformed teenage twit that just had to get to Crown Center, so they could have the latest in fashion." Ryder paused again, turning back to face them. "I swear you could hear that scream from clear across the city. By the time we would get there all we would find was a body in an alley, wrapped in freezer paper, the left hand chopped off with a meat cleaver and taken away."

Ryder downed the rest of the soda and set the bottle down. He rested his hands on the back of the chair where he had been sitting at the table and continued. It was at the twelfth murder, we got a lead that a young woman saw her; but the last murder was the one I can't forget. She was just a baby, six years old, on her way home from school." He turned his back to the table and spoke the next words gritting his teeth together in anger. "I warned them to close the schools. Did they listen? No! All they cared about was getting the state's money. Seeing her tiny body sprawled out by the merry-go-round. But she made a mistake; she left a crayon out at work at the hospital she worked at, as a surgical nurse. We raided her home, and saw her with that hand, blood running down her face. I couldn't do it anymore." Ryder leaned his head down on the back of the chair.

Yakira stood up next to him and placed her hand on his back, and lowered her head on to his.

****

After washing his face in the bathroom, Ryder returned and they finished their supper. They visited for an hour or so, talking about family; his grandmother and grandfather, which Ryder always enjoyed hearing about. Of course tales of when Ryder was a kid and the funny thing that he did gave Yakira a laugh. After that Ryder left, walking back to the church to get the car. Father Anthony took a piece of paper, wrote something on it, folded it up and handed it to Yakira as he said. "This is what he came for."

Yakira took the note and unfolded and read it. It was an address in Van Buren, Arkansas. "What is this?" She asked with worry, looking up from the note.

"It is where Ryan lives." She stood there staring at the man, wondering why he gave her this.

"His dad!" She started to shout out, but quickly lowered her voice. "He hates him! After what he did, I can't say that I blame him."

"Just as he forgave his mother for leaving him, he has to with his dad." Outside she heard the rumble of the exhaust on the Dodge pull up in front of the house.

"Tony I know you believe in forgiveness stuff but…" she lowered her gaze back to the paper and shook her head before she looked back up at him and asked. "Why do you give it to me? Why don't you tell him?"

"That night when you were shot and nearly died, that was the first night I saw him reach out and trust someone other than himself. He reached out to God that night; he will again."

"He was just praying."

"Doesn't matter, if it was God or someone else, he allowed himself to care, but now he is afraid again." He reached down and took a hold of Yakira's hand. "No ring."

"He will ask me when he is ready." She pulled her hand away and became angry.

"He isn't afraid of that. He is afraid to be happy. If he does something, bad might happen and he will be hurt again." Yakira looked down at the paper in her hand, her hair falling down the sides of her face. "It all has to do with his jackass of a father."

"Father?" She asked shocked by his word.

"What he did to my sister makes me angry, but what he is doing to Ricky really makes me mad. "He has to forget him."

She could hear the front door opening as she whispered. Ryder entered.

"When do I—How do I tell..." She tried to whisper, but Ryder asked interrupting her.

"You ready to go?"

"You will know when it is time."

As the Killer Bee traveled down Main Street back towards town, and the car passed under a street lamp, Ryder looked over at her. She was quiet, slumped a little in her seat, biting on her thumb nail, making it click against her teeth. He hadn't seen her do that in a long while, but he knew what it meant. Inside of her was something bubbling like a pot of soup boiling on high, getting ready to pour out, but fear, fear that she would look like a fool or it might hurt someone else would just cause her to cover her emotions and let it boil even harder inside of her. Eventually it would come out.

"I thought we would stay at your mom and dad's house tonight." He said letting his eyes drift back to the street.

"Okay."

"You think they are back?"

"That will be great."

"Because, it is such a long walk back to the lake and we don't have a car."

"Yeah I know." It was clear to him that she was not listening.

"Because your mom makes the best spare ribs I've ever had and when your dad dresses them up in little kangaroo suits, it is so funny."

"What!"

"Why are you so far away?"

"Just thinking." She said as she sat up in her seat.

"How much for your thoughts?" He asked as he guided the car onto a side street.

"I don't think even you could afford them." She said as he pulled the car into the driveway. As he stopped the car behind her pickup, he started to reach for the door handle; she reached over the console and grabbed his arm. "Have you ever thought about what life brings?" He leaned back hard in the seat as she continued. "I mean- if you had things to do all over again would you?"

"Such as?"

"You life, your family. If you had your mother here with here now, what would you say to her?" She asked, pulling her hand back. He shook his head as his finger gripped around the leather rim of the steering wheel. He stared out over the hood, the glow of the security lights mounted on the garage wall glowing casting shadows of the car onto the pavement.

"I don't know. To tell her that I love her, that I think about her everyday seems…" The security lights turned off and darkness surrounded them. "I just don't think there is anything I could say."

"What about your father?" She asked as she let her hand slip down into her pocket where the note was.

"Him! I have nothing to say to." Ryder said as he grabbed the door handle and the dome light filled the interior of the car. "I see the lights are on. Your mom and dad must be back. Let's go inside."

Even though there was a slight chill in the air, he wiped the sweat from "being placed on the spot" as he walked around the car and opened her door. By the time they reached the front door and she unlocked it he could feel the chill of the night air again.

111

" Nechda Ma shlomekh? Her grandmother asked as they entered.

"I am fine, Bubbie," Yakira said.

"And you Motek Ma shlomkha?"

When Ryder's grandmother died it was this woman- Seraphina who took her place. She was his Godmother, a rarity that a Catholic would have a Jewish woman as this, even though it wasn't recognized by the church. As far as he was concerned it was this tiny, round woman with frosted hair that made the best Matzo ball soup in the world. Even though there was no blood kin, she was still grandma and that is what he called her.

"I am good too, Bubbie." He said as he leaned down and kissed her on the cheek.

Reaching up and pinching his cheek she looked over at her granddaughter and said. "Sweetie, you better hold on to this one, or I will just take him away." He tried to grin through her words, not letting her see what was going on inside of him, but like a true grandmother she saw right through it. She patted his cheek and pulled her granddaughter over to her. "I want you two to take those guns off. With them you leave the problems too. You let none of this come between you two." She glanced at each one of them. "Understand?" She looked at them and each one nodded. "Good, because Bubbie knows best."

Ryder removed the Glock and holster and laid it down on the hall tree in the foyer. There was something that was comfortable about removing his gun from his side, but at the same time it felt as if he were suddenly undressed, like he was standing around half naked to the world. Yakira removed her weapon, a Bulldog revolver ,and laid it down next to his Glock on the hall tree.

"Come on you two, we will get you something to eat." Bubbie said, pulling on his hand.

"I can't—I mean we already had supper at Uncle Tony's." Ryder tried to explain, but she just pulled him forward through the dining room.

"Hantarish!" She insisted, meaning nonsense, as she guided them towards the kitchen. "I just made a banana black walnut cake; you can

112

have a small piece. Wouldn't want to hurt an old lady's feelings, would you?"

"Okay Bubbie a small piece."

"And a cup of coffee," Bubbie said as she guided him back through the dining room and into the kitchen at the back of the house. "You can't have cake without a cup of coffee. Don't worry, it is decaf. It won't keep you awake."

Ryder had mixed feelings about that, he wanted to sleep but with it brought dreams, and worse, nightmares. As they entered the kitchen they were greeted by Yakira's parents, her father Pascal and her mother Rebekah.

"Glad to see you back, my boy." Pascal said. He and his wife were both sitting at the small table in the kitchen, having a cup of tea. Ryder perched himself up on one of the stools at the bar, and Bubbie seated her granddaughter on the stool next to him.

Bubbie took a small step stool, and used it to get two small plates and coffee cups out of the cabinet, setting them down next to a 13x9 pan, with a light brown cake. Bubbie cut the cake into eight pieces, and scooped a piece onto each plate. Getting forks out of the drawer she handed the plates to each of them. "See, just a small piece. Besides, it is a light cake; you will probably have to have two pieces." She returned to the counter and poured coffee into the cups, and fixed them both with cream and two sugars.

Ryder knew the only way to make her happy, was to eat the cake, even though it was large piece. Using the fork he cut into the cake, and scooped up a bite. The sweetness of the overripe bananas and brown sugar made it rich and the black walnuts made it complete. Although the chocolate butter cream frosting was a little too sweet for him, if anybody else had made this he would have scraped the icing off, but he couldn't do that to his Bubbie.

"The big talk around town is the uncovering of the missing kids." Pascal said, before he took a sip of his tea. Pascal was in his sixties; a squatty set man with graying hair along the sides of his head and a bald spot on top. It was strange that he hardly ever seen this man when he wasn't in a suit, one of his own, hand tailored, made by himself. He was not wearing a tie so it meant he was relaxing. His wife favored Yakira some in the face, but she too was heavier set, with swept back hair like polished obsidian due to the courtesy of a monthly trip to see Andrea at the beauty parlor for a dye job.

Pascal took a sip of tea and set the mug back down on the table and continued. "That was all everybody was talking about coming into the store. I think they were just making the rounds. Coming out of Tomblin's, Whitley's, then my place." He took another sip of his tea and looked over at his wife. She was quiet, which was strange for her; she always wanted to know the latest gossip that was going around the square. "You knew those kids, didn't you? You went to school with them."

Ryder was raising the forkful of cake to his mouth, when he stopped half-way there as he watched Rebekah suddenly stand up, taking her nearly full mug of tea to the sink and proceeded to dump it down the garbage disposal. He brought the fork up to his mouth, not moving his head, but he let his eyes follow as she washed the plate and mug out and place them in the dishwasher as she replied nonchalantly.

"I knew of them, that is all."

Ryder lifted his coffee mug up and took a sip. He continued to watch her as she washed her hands and then dried them with a towel draped across the dish drainer. She turned to her husband and continued, "Did you know everybody that you went to school with in high school? That was a long time ago."

There was something strange going on, he could tell she was nervous. She opened up a small upper cabinet door that was next to the window. Ryder knew this was where she kept her medicine; those that she had to take every day, like that for her blood pressure and those that she took only when she needed them, such as that for heartburn, or here nerve medicine Alprazolam, ® which she shook out of the bottle into her hand.

"You nervous, mom?"

"Just all this talk about murder," She said as she filled a glass with water and swallowed the pill. She poured out the rest of the water and rinsed the glass out, and started to place it in the dishwasher when Ryder spoke up.

"Who said anything about murder?"

As soon as he said that the glass slipped from Rebekah's hand and shattered on the tile floor. She rushed over to the broom closet at the end of the cabinets and grabbed a whisk broom and dust pan, and quickly began sweeping up the pieces. "Well that is what you two do now isn't, go around solving murders? I just figured...I mean that was the tales being told, they were murdered."

"You okay, mom?" Yakira asked as she slid off the stool and went over to her mother to help. Even from across the bar, Ryder could see the panic on the woman's face. "I will do this Mom, you just take it easy." Rebekah quickly stood and headed for the kitchen door that led back into the hall. Before leaving she spoke.

"All this talk about murder it is just so upsetting, why can't you just have normal jobs. I think I will find something funny to watch on TV." Then she disappeared. Ryder stood up and followed her out and into the family room. She had turned on the TV. There was a rerun of "The Facts of Life." She watched as the character Blair appeared on the screen. She gave a quick jerk of her eyes to notice Ryder standing there beside the loveseat.

"She always reminded me of Annalisa." Rebekah said as she quickly changed the channel. "I think that is what is upsetting me. All this talk about murder is bringing back memories of when Annalisa was murdered." She continued to surf through the array of channels offered through the satellite, stopping on a segment about Royals win over the Detroit Tigers. She laid the remote down on the table next to a pencil and continued, not wanting to face him, just starring down at the floor. "You just can't get over it when your own child is murdered. It is just so hard to lose a child that way. I can just imagine Greg's and Karen's parents pain knowing their children were shot in the head."

"How did you know that? How did you know they were shot?" Ryder asked as he stepped around in front of her. "But you did know Karen and Greg didn't you? Before you speak, Uncle Tony told me about the fight."

She slowly raised her head to gaze at him, there were tears forming in her eyes. "Ricky, you don't want to do this. It was forty years ago. We were all kids back then. It is hard to remember. Some of those that were involved are gone, why do you want to damage their memories?"

"You are talking about my mother, aren't you?" Ryder said as he moved over and sat down beside her. "I have to know."

115

"Karen deserved what she got." Rebekah said, turning to him. "There are some thing about your mother you should not know."

"I have to," Ryder said. Hearing a thump on the door, he looked up and saw Yakira standing there, leaning on the door, watching her mother. He looked back down at Rebekah and added. "How did you know they were shot?"

Rebekah with the loving touch of a mother cupped both her hands over his and pleaded with him. "Please Ricky! I begged of you don't do this. You have such few happy family memories I don't want to destroy what you think of your mother." He didn't reply. He didn't move. He just stood there. Eyes fixed on to her, the woman that was the closest thing to a mother he had after his mother passed away. They had been neighbors, family friends, it her daughter Annalisa that he played with when he was kid. It was Annalisa that he 'first fell in love with' on later to find out that she was his half-sister. It was his digging for the truth that brought up that secret, and now he just couldn't let it go. It was a missing piece of a puzzle that he just had to put back together again. She pulled her hands from his and spoke.

"Dannie told me," she said, using a nickname for his mother's first name. "After the party we went to the old lodge, and sat there and decided what we would do to her to get revenge. We knew Karen was drinking like a fish. Dannie thought we could wait till she passed out and take nude photos of her and hang them around the school, in the bathrooms, in the boy's locker room. We did that to another girl, it destroyed her, and she dropped out of school. But, Karen figured it wouldn't matter to her. If you wanted to see Karen naked all you had to do was buy her a Sonic Burger. Besides..." Rebekah looked up at Ryder before continuing. "Your mom wanted real revenge, to make her pay for everything she had every done to her. That was when I came up with the idea."

"Mom?" Yakira gasped before the question tumbled out of her mouth. "You killed her?"

"Buhheh-myseh!" Meaning false story Rebekah shout at her daughter. " No, I didn't kill her." She said turning, facing her daughter as Yakira walked into the family room. "I wanted to but... carbon-fire her."

"Going to do what?" Yakira asked as she sit down on the love seat next to her mother.

'Pops told me about it." Ryder explained. "It is when you take the distributor cap off and connect all the cylinders with a pencil line, all the cylinders fire at once wrecking an engine"

"We were going to do it to that brand new Z-28 she had."

"I don't understand how that could be getting even with her."

"You said you were going to? You didn't?"

"No, and this is what I didn't want you to know. You mother wanted more, she said she knew what to do."

And what was that?"

"You don't want to know Ricky!" Rebekah snapped back him. "You can arrest me if you want. But I am not telling you anymore." Ryder stood up and walked toward the door, passing by Yakira. Suddenly he stopped in the door and spoke without turning around.

"Why are you trying to protect her?" He paused for just a short moment letting his eyes gaze up at the family photos that were hung from the hallway wall. Those of Annalisa, Yakira when she was young, Rebekah and Pascal's wedding photo, of her and his mother linked with their arms around each other, smiling at their big catch 'a three inch long blue gill perch'. He turned back around.

"Has there been anyone that you would lie, die to protect?' As Rebekah spoke Ryder let his eyes drift over to Yakira. His gaze returned to Rebekah before he said.

"I am going to find it out anyway. It would be better coming from you."

Rebekah just sat there staring at the TV, not wanting to look at, or talk to him. He had to ask his question by answering himself. "She went after Karen to settle the score once and for all." Rebekah didn't answer, she just nodded. "My mother murdered them both."

"She came back about an hour later covered in blood. She was scared to death. She told me she had seen Greg and Karen in his car. Both of them had been shot in the head."

"Did she do it?"

"She said saw someone walking away from the car. They were carrying a gun." Rebekah fought back tears, pulling up a memory that she had long buried hoping to never remember.

"Who was it?"

"It was Monica Howler's father, Leroy."

"Why would he be there?" Ryder asked.

"Greg liked young girls; Monica was in eighth-grade at that time. Karen would find them for him, she got her jollies watching. Monica was only 13 years old." As she spoke Ryder walked back over and sat on the coffee table in front of her. He leaned in toward her and took hold of her hands as he said.

"What are you not telling me?"

"Your mother may have not killed them, but she set it in motion for it to happen. She told Leroy, and he said he was going to kill them. "

Chapter 13

There were sure signs that spring had began, cheerful red breasted robin males fighting each other, hoping to impress the female bouncing along the yard, the rush of bright yellow beaming up in the form of daffodils, the grass beginning to green and those that just couldn't wait for winter to become a memory were out and about tuning up lawn mowers that would soon be a buzz; the weekend was coming.

Ryder stood beside the Killer Bee and readjusted the pistol strapped to his side. As he straightened his jacket, he reached into the pocket and produced the five -point badge. Once again he was holding law and order in the palm of his hand.

Pascal was getting ready to leave for his shop down town, he watched as Yakira hugged her father goodbye. Memories flooded back to him. In Kansas City, every time he left there was no one to say goodbye to, no one to wonder if he was coming home. Now that he had a whole family, again he was wearing a badge. He pinned the badge to the inside cover of his wallet and slipped it inside his jacket.

"Ready?" Yakira asked as she walked up to the car. She was dressed professionally in gray slacks, white button down blouse and a pink jacket, wrapped around her waist was a dark colored belt and clipped to the belt was the deputy's badge.

"There is more to this than just putting it on." Ryder said as he reached down and held the badge on her belt. "The times have changed," He released the badge and grabbed the door handle. He opened the door and held it open for her. As she started to get in, he grabbed her by the arm and added in a firm tone. "By putting that on there will be those that hate you, those that have known you forever will suddenly despise you, just because of that piece of tin." She just looked puzzled as she sat down on the seat, and he shut the door and walked around to the other side and opened the driver's door.

"We have solved other cases before, Ricky." She said as he slid down behind the steering wheel. "How is this going to be any different?"

"When you wear a badge people look at you differently, they don't get near you. They are afraid of you. Afraid they will say or do something that will get them in trouble. While others hate you as if you the filth of hell it's self. They would love to gun you down, let you die in the street alone. That badge changes everything."

119

As he drove down Main Street heading towards First Street, he wondered how she was going to act when she was called a pig, murderer, and words that he couldn't even repeat in his own mind. He turned onto First Street, the Charger's dual exhaust purred as he guided the car up the hill. He wondered- why would anyone do this for a living. Just because that one in a thousand will smile and say thank you. May it was that one smile that made it worth it.

"Where are we going?"

"I found out where Leroy Howler is," Ryder said as he turned the wheel to the left, guiding the car around the strip of cement. This wasn't the yellow brick road, it didn't lead to a bright city of hopes and dreams, instead the dreams here were as dim as the road that led them here. It was a nursing home, for too many of its residents it was the junk yard of souls, where tiring family members would dump off their aging mothers and fathers, walking away and forgetting about them, much the same way one would get rid of a worn out car. Where they are stripped of their dignity and freedom, only occasionally visited by the grandkids, who spend most of their time texting to other friends as the granddad tells stories of yesteryear, only to be forgotten as quickly as they hurry off. Then as they stand over a grave the same kids wonder why 'grandpa never told them about the tales of his youth.'

As Ryder held the door of the parked Dodge open for Yakira his gaze was drawn to an elderly man standing just outside the covered portico in one of the oval openings, his hand drawn up to his forehead, rigid as his body, standing to salute the flag that was rustling in the breeze. Next to him was a middle aged nurse who stood to look at her watch as the second hand ticked around the watch on her wrist.

"Mr. Howler, I have given you a full minute. It is time to go." The nurse said.

Ryder walked up next to the man, drew his heels together and he, too saluted the flag. The elderly man was tall and thin, his clothes were gray trousers and a blue plaid shirt. What was left of his gray hair was slicked back, his face weathered, and beaten by the years of working out in the sun. He turned his head slightly and as he looked at Ryder through his gold wire framed glasses, his eyes were as clear as the sky above and his lips gave a true greeting as he spoke.

"Where did you serve, son?"

"Law enforcement officer, Kansas City," Ryder said as he dropped his salute, "but my grandfather, he was in the big one. 101st Airborne 501th PIR."

"Operation Market Garden ,Normandy, Battle of the Bulge he saw some action. You must be Bob Delany's son." The elderly man held out his hand and Ryder shook it. "I am Leroy Howler, Sergeant Leroy Howler Korea. If you like, we could talk about those days."

"I would like that. But I am Bob's grandson. His daughter, Danielle, was my mother. You remember her?"

"Oh yes, she was a little older than my Monica." Ryder grinned as he remembered Ryder's mother, and his daughter. It wasn't yesterday Ryder was interested in, possibly he could remember, but he just couldn't suddenly spring it on him.

"Well you can come back, when it is visiting time." The nurse cackled like an old hen being expelled from her nest. Ryder reached into his jacket and produced his wallet. Flipping it open and revealing the badge he said.

"Oh, I think it is visiting time right now."

"Is that real?" The nurse bellowed back.

"Why don't you call the office and find out." Ryder said as he flipped his wallet closed and stuffed it back into his jacket as he added. "Be sure to ask for acting sheriff Thom Thompson. You can find us visiting with Sergeant Howler if you have any questions."

Inside the halls smelled with the decaying odor of the façade of humanity, intertwined with the putrid stench of urine soaked sheets. The moaning cries of those whose names have been forgotten, and have become nothing but a number. Empty stares gazing back, wondering- are your someone I know? Someone I love? Followed by a beaming smile, hoping and praying that it would be, and seeing by the fading glimmer that you are not. The nurse led them all back to Sergeant Howler's room that was down the hall, the third room on the right. As they entered, the nurse helped the man onto the bed.

Ryder gazed around the room and saw the photos on the wall, that of his infantry unit in the war, his wedding photo and photos of his son and three daughters. He noticed the man looking at Yakira; he was trying to figure out who she was. "Are you one of my granddaughters? Are Bridgette?"

"No, this is my..." Ryder began to introduce her, but he didn't know how. He could introduce her as his partner, but he might wonder why the cops were questioning him, then he could get rattled and forget. He couldn't introduce her as his girl friend, it just sounded so juvenile, as if they were back in school. Luckily for him, Yakira piped in.

"I am his wife." As she spoke Ryder's eyebrows lifted, but it seemed to satisfy the old man's curiosity as he replied.

"Well you sure got a cute one here. Sort of like my Monica." The old man looked up at the photos on the wall and grinned. "Yeah, I knew Bob really well. You know, he joined out of high school, even before the war began. He was one of the first 50 paratroopers there were. He told me all about D-Day, how they came by and put a mark on their helmets, and the preacher prayed for them because they feared most of them weren't coming back. He told me how nobody wanted to be the thirteenth one out, but that was the spot he wanted. He was the only one to land on the solid ground that night, the rest landed in muck and water. But his good luck didn't last long; he lost all his equipment but his combat knife and cricket. Didn't stop Bob, he just crept up behind a German guard and stuck him right in the heart. Then he took the kraut's weapon and he and his division moved in. Always thought Bob deserved a medal for that, but you know how your dad was. He didn't care, his men came first."

"He was my grandfather, I am Danielle's son, Danielle, and she called you, about something that happened to Monica." Ryder said looking into the old man's eyes, wondering how he could trigger his memory. Ryder calmly spoke and he watched the man's reaction, hunting for any sign that he was remembering before he spoke the name, "What Greg and Karen did." Ryder watched the elderly man, his eyes twitched as if a bolt of electricity was running through him, his hand clenched into fists of anger.

"I made my mind up I was going to kill him that night." Mr. Howler said, turning and looking at Ryder, who had removed his notebook and began writing down the old man's words. "He and that witch, there wouldn't have been anybody that blamed me. You know what the son-of-bitch did to my baby girl? Then to just stand there and laugh about it, even when I had the damn gun pointing at his head. That son-of-a—he said, he told me he would do it again. I couldn't let him hurt her again, that is when I...

"What is going on in here?" His daughter Monica demanded as she burst into the room, interrupting him. "Daddy, don't you say another word!" She rushed over to her father's bedside. It was quick to see where all of her husband's money was going, the plastic surgery to her nose, the collagen injections in her forehead to remove the wrinkles, and to make her lips full and pouting. Teeth bonded, straightened and as white as purity itself, flashing in the smile of adulteration. Her hair, once dark, now had only highlights showing through. As she stood between Ryder and her father, the smell of a mixture of White Diamonds perfume and cheap cigarettes even overwhelmed the strong smell of the nurse.

"These are Bob's kids. It is Tony and Danielle. I was telling them..."

"They are cops, Daddy! Stinking filthy cops! They are trying to trick you into confessing." She turned to Ryder. "I want you two out of here. Right now!" Monica screamed at them, attracting the attention of the nurse. Ryder stood up and closed his notebook, shoving it into the pocket of his jacket as he and Yakira headed for the door to the room. "And I don't want either of you questioning Daddy unless his lawyer is around. I wouldn't have known anything about this if Janice hadn't called me."

Ryder pulled the door to the room open and stepped outside. He saw a woman standing there in the hallway. It was clear by the way she was dressed in black pants, a wild floral tunic top and high-heeled strap sandals that she was not a nurse and that her name tag read 'Janice' Manager. "I guess you are the one who called?"

"You need to leave that old man alone. And I want you to get out of here. I know the mayor, the county commissioner personally; I will have them down here."

"And I know the governor personally and I will have DHSS down here and you better have every,' I' dotted and 'T 'crossed perfectly. Now we are going to stand right here and wait till she comes out. She doesn't come out; I will get a warrant and go over to her house. Lady, we are talking homicide. I don't care if it happened forty years ago or just two minutes ago. Murder is murder; no one gets away with it if I am involved. Now you go back to whatever belfry you flew out of, or you are going to find out what it is like to be deloused at the County Hilton." The woman turned and walked away.

Ryder leaned back against the wall of the hall way so he could face the door as it opened and out stepped Monica. "I thought I told you people to leave." She said as reached into her handbag and pulled out a cell phone as she warned. "I am going to call my lawyer."

"That way we all can sit down and talk about what happened at Roaring River forty-two years ago, when my mother told your father what Greg did to you."

"He didn't kill him!"

"I know that." Ryder said. "He told me 'I made my mind up I was going to kill him that night.' Not that' I killed him' but was going to. What happened, Monica?"

She shoved the cell phone back down into her purse. "Do we have to do this here? This place stinks." Ryder pointed towards the exit and held the door open for her and he and Yakira followed her over to a large shade tree at the edge of the parking lot.

"I was always kind of a plain looking girl in school, especially in Jr. High. None of the guys wanted to go out with me, so when Greg came and told me he would give me a ride home; I thought it was so cool. All the other girls were so jealous. But then he took me out to the woods; he tried to…" Her words stuck in her mouth as if she had a mouth full of rocks and peanut butter. She didn't have to say anything, Ryder knew what was happening. "He tried to take my pants off. I didn't want to, Karen held me down."

"What happened March the first?" Ryder asked as he pulled out his notebook and began to write.

"Danielle called and told him; he was so mad, he grabbed a gun and told me to get in the pickup. He raced all around the park, looking for his car. We went everywhere all through the camp ground, the hatchery, then we found it. At the end of the camp ground road where Pibern Trail starts, it was near there that he found it, and he drove away, I thought we were going back home, but he went down the road and parked, and said he was going to sneak up on them and shoot them in the back. He told me to stay there."

124

A breath of wind swept across them, tugging at the young leaves, swirling around and picking up bits of paper as it swept across the parking lot, tossing Yakira's hair in her face, which she pushed back before she said.

"Daddy's are good at protecting their little girls, aren't they?"

"That was all he was doing." Monica said as she offered a foul simpering smile, "Just trying to protect me."

"Did you stay in the pickup?" Ryder asked.

Again the words stuck in her mouth, only to tumble out like drops of rain along with her tears. "No, I followed. Hiding behind trees. So he wouldn't see me. He walked right up to the car and jerked the door open, then pointed the gun at Greg's head."

"And then?"

"Nothing, he just turned and walked away."

"Why?" Ryder asked, as Monica reached into her handbag and pulled out a small white handkerchief and dabbed her eyes.

"I started to move closer, but that was when I saw Danielle. She walked up to the car and opened the door. She looked inside, and then at daddy walking away, she screamed and ran away. I moved closer, and saw that they were already dead. That was when I heard someone coming back down the trail towards the car. I got out of there."

"Who was it coming out of the woods?" Ryder asked, watching as she dropped her gaze away from him and to the field across the street as she replied.

"I don't know. I didn't see his face."

"You are lying to me; you just said it was a man, who was it?"

"It was your father, it was Ryan Ryder."

Chapter 14

Walking back to the car, there was almost a Mephistophelian grin on his face that appeared just as soon as he had heard that it was his father who was the one in the woods. There was a sense of right and wrong that was shuddering through him, like a river going past its flood stage, as memories came smashing through all the blockades that he had put in since his first disappointment: the pee-wee league father and son dinner, and he wasn't there. Just like the wind blowing its way around the building, Ryder's memories wound around each other. In his mind he could picture slamming a cell door shut on his father. Having him pleading 'You going to be there for me?' and Ryder replying, which he did, out loud, "Yeah, dad just like you were there for me."

"What?" Yakira asked, confused by his comment.

"Nothing," he said, closing her car door. He started around the back of the car to the driver's side when he received a text message. He pulled out his cell phone and looked at the message. It was from Dina Grosstree, his former commander's wife; the message read 'In Cassville at the city park. Need to talk.' He texted back 'OK'.

Ryder flopped down into the driver's seat and let the black and gray leather- like vinyl envelop around him for just a moment before he fired the massive engine up. He turned to Yakira and saw her reaching into the pocket of her jacket. "Do we find your father now?" She asked, slipping her hand out of her pocket.

"Not yet." He replied, and she pushed her hand back down into her pocket. "Dina is in town; she wants to talk." He turned back around and fired up the car. "After that, maybe, if I can find someone who knows where he is."

There was more than one park in town. There was South Park where the city pools were located, memorial park next to the American Legion, but it just made sense that it was the actual City Park, which was just down the street from the Sheriff's Department. As Ryder turned the Charger off the highway he was greeted with a multitude of vehicles, cars, trucks, from brand new, their paint gleaming, to old that were as colorful as a Wasilly Kandinsky abstract that had lost their gleam years ago.

"What is going on here?" Ryder asked as he guided the Dodge down the narrow strip of pavement, flanked by cars on each side. Over to one side in the park was a group of people gathered around a make shift stage. On the stage was a woman, in her late forties, long dark hair that was tied in a loose ponytail. It was Samantha Beckwith; it was a political rally. The crowd was cheering her on. He rolled the window down and could hear her.

"Are you sick and tired of Barry County being run by certain families, including the sheriff's department? The reason we are having this election is that reason. A family, the Warner's, used their wealth to control this county, and buy the position of sheriff. We all know how that turned out, don't we? Not only did Warner and Sheriff Hart sell out Barry County, but they sold out this nation, by selling weapons to those who want to kill us. But there is a new person that wants to buy the county, one that is even richer than Warner. And that is your Rick Ryder. I know he is your town hero, but unlike you or me he doesn't have to worry where his next meal is coming from, or if he is going to have enough at the end of the month to keep the lights on. I am like you. I have to work for a living…" Ryder rolled the window up and continued on down the street, trying to find Dina. He had remembered how she loved to watch the kids play baseball, not having any children of their own, she sort of become the mother to the players in Kansas City. He saw her sitting on the bleachers, next to the dugout; she had her back to him, staring out at the empty baseball field. He pulled the Charger in behind the bleachers, the rumbling of the exhaust made her turn and glance over her shoulder at him. She stood up and Ryder got out, walking around the car he held the door open for Yakira.

Dina walked down the bleachers with the grace of a model and met them next to ball field. She was a stunning beauty; she had been all her life, with her raw sienna skin that always greeted him with a soft silky touch of her hand as she would rub it along his cheek. Her eyes were as cool as the water of a swimming pool, with a smile that made one dive right in to her emotions, and he could see that after the greetings and warm embraces, there was something that was just about to spill out of her.

She buried her face in her hands and wept. "It is Craig, Rick." She said as her long wavy amber streaked hair flowed down over her shoulder. Ryder's mind flashed with the only thing that could come to his mind.

"Was he shot?"

"No," She said, raising her head. "He just…" She reached inside of herself to find the right words as she stood up, the white ribbed sweater and matching skirt hugged tightly to her curves. She turned and walked

127

over to the ball park fence. Her fingers gripped the caged wire as she stared out across the field Ryder walked over and placed his hand on her shoulder. She turned and faced him looking up at him and smiled the best she could. He could see she was wearing a thick layer of concealer on her face as she continued. "Since you left there have been big changes in the department. They want to bring in younger people. They want to move him to traffic, busting speeders. You know he lives and breathes homicide." Again she turned away from him and stared out across the field past the score board to where young children were engaged in play. "Now it is starting to affect our life. They gave him two weeks off."

"He hit you didn't you?" Ryder said as he forced her to turn around.

"He didn't mean too. He just…" Again she turned away from him walking along the fence of the bullpen as she let her long fingers trickle along the links in the fence. "Work is getting to him and then he comes home and I am complaining because the car broke down." She was twelve feet away from Ryder when she turned around again. "I just have to learn to keep that stuff away from him."

"That is bull! And you know it is." He said as he approached her. "No one has a right to hurt you. You don't blame yourself. I don't want to hear that!" He said as he placed his hands on the sides of her face. "What can I do to help?" He released her.

"I just figured if he could go somewhere. Somewhere he could just lay back and relax." Yet once again she turned away from him and continued lowering her voice. "But we can't afford anything."

"How about a second wedding and honeymoon in Eureka Springs."

"What?" She asked confused and turned around.

"Dina, you have been wanting this as long as I have known you. Let me do it for you. The Thorncrown Chapel, a suite at the Crescent, dinner on the train, the whole works. Even the wedding dress you have always wanted."

"Rick, you can't do this! It will be so…"

128

"What- expensive?" Ryder quipped "It is just money. I invest in people. I am investing in you."

"But he will never go for it, with you paying for it…"

"I will grease some palms, get some letters sent out it will look like he won it in a contest. I know him; he could never let something free go to waste." He placed both of his hands on her shoulders and looked deep into her eyes. He noticed dark circles around her eyes. "Now you play it straight and don't give it away." He grinned, then leaned down and kissed her on the cheek. "Who knows," he said, reaching over and placing his arm around Yakira who had walked up next to him and pulling her close. "You might just win the grand prize."

Afterwards he and Yakira walked her back to her car, and each gave her goodbyes followed with hug and watched as she drove away. "That is so nice that you did that for her." Yakira said.

"Yes, isn't it!" He heard someone say from behind him. He turned, and with a grimace hidden under his sunglasses he recognized the voice as Samantha's. "Buying more votes, Mr. Ryder?" She added as her mouth twisted into a teasing smile. "That is what you are trying to do, isn't?"

"You don't have a clue who I am, do you?" Ryder said lifting his lip into a partial snarl.

"And you know nothing of me, either." Ryder began to walk back towards his car but he turned back around and faced her.

"I know very well who you are. You are a child playing a game."

"Because I am a woman?" She said, falling into step beside him. "Because you don't think a woman can do the job."

"I stand corrected." Ryder said with smirk. You are not a child you are an idiot, if you believe that."

"Well, you don't want me to win, do you?"

"Let me ask you something. If you get a call from someone that says their car has been stolen, what are you going to do?" Ryder asked as he again turned and opened the car door for Yakira.

129

"I will send an officer out to get some information, get a report done so that they can turn it in to their insurance company." She replied sounding confident of her answer.

"How are they going to get to work? If they can't get to work they lose their home, they can't buy their children anything to eat." Ryder explained as he walked around the car and opened the driver's side door. "A car isn't just a car to some of these people, it is their life. What if someone is stealing cattle? That just another case for you? That is money to these hard working people. Ms. Beckwith you don't understand "

"So what do you do?"

"Simple. You rattle cages, you rattle them hard, someone knows something, you find the car. If you can't find their car, you tell them you are sorry, you did all you could, at least they feel that you care. In this county that is what matters. Not just some empty promises that you are giving them. " Ryder seated himself behind the steering wheel and fired the car up. "You give the hope where they feel helpless from crime, that is what being a Law Enforcement Officer is about."

"I heard that Thompson made you a deputy. When I win this election I want that badge back." She said. He looked over at her and grinned sideways. Ryder reached into his pocket, pulled out his wallet, and jerked the star free and tossed it out the window.

"You can have that right now." He said as the star landed at her feet. "But that won't stop me from investigating it." Ryder put the car into reverse and backed up; as he started to speed away Yakira's bare derrière appeared out the window, sitting on the door, she tossed her star at her as she said.

"Dachas katzeh!" Yakira shouted as the star bounced off the pavement.

"What does that mean?" The woman shouted back.

"Kiss my… " Yakira words were cut short as she fell back into the car, when Ryder sped the Dodge around the corner.

He stopped by Ramey's, picked up some groceries, headed back to the Lake House, and spent most of the afternoon making a seven course meal. To start was the Aperitif: a Lemon Pressé, the sweet lemon tasting

130

drink, with salted mixed nuts, it was the perfect jumping point to the appetizer; mini crab cakes, a savory mixture of crab meat, bread crumbs and cream cheese with fresh chopped dill and chopped chives on top for decoration.

Followed by the main course: Duck à l'Orange, its skin roasted to perfection, served with a savory yet sweet orange sauce, along with Asparagus with hollandaise sauce, and rice and mushroom simmered in beef broth as sides.

Next was the salad, or as Ryder introduced it, along with each course was the 'Ferme Auberge' a green salad with a simple vinaigrette dressing. It was confusing to Yakira, as the salad was usually served before the main course, but Ryder explained it was to aid in digestion and helped to clear the pallet for the dessert- Chocolate Delight. It looked like a chocolate cake that failed to rise, or maybe brownies. As she bit into it, there was a class 5 river rapid of flavor. It was so chocolaty that she could barely get the last forkful down. She knew it was a seven course meal, and with the coffee that was served with the dessert, she had counted only six. She wondered what was coming next, and if she could get it down. Luckily he told her it would be served on the deck.

She moaned and held her tummy, feeling that she was about to give birth, and made her way to the sliding glass doors that led out onto the deck. She looked back at the kitchen, it was cleaned up. If he was cooking and cleaning as he was going, he was very upset, and really thinking about something. She fell down onto the lounge chair on the deck and stared out at the evening that was breaking across the sobbing waters of the lake, sloshing on the shores.

"Here you go, the last course." He said standing over her, handing her a large round glass. It was fruit flavored brandy. She took it and sipped the strong apricot flavored drink. He stood staring at the glass. Yakira reached into her jacket pocket and pulled out the note. "You don't have to think anymore." She handed him the note. "This is your father's address."

Chapter 15

Ryder couldn't wait for morning to come, he wanted to go right that minute after Yakira handed him the note, and question his uncle, but Yakira insisted that he just wait till morning, maybe giving him some time to cool off. When he wheeled the Killer Bee into the church parking lot, and insisted she stay in the car while he went inside, it was just wishful thinking. He barged right into his uncle's office, pushing the door open.

It' was simply furnished, with a black faux leather couch pushed up next to the paneled walls in front of it a large comfy chair that matched the couch and over to the side ,was next to the door ,was a coat rack with a couple jackets, including one ladies jacket. In front of the walnut desk where Father Anthony was sitting, was a pair of chairs. In was a young Hispanic woman; she was weeping and clutching rosary beads in her hand. He pushed past her and stood there looking at his uncle. He didn't see a man of God, or a minister, all he saw was a man, his uncle that had kept this from him. He turned and looked at her; she was barely a young woman, a teen that looked as if she was going to be late for school, now that it was a few minutes after eight.

"Get out!" He said in a low tone, which frightened her even more than if he had yelled. She quickly stood and dashed outside.

"Rick, that young girl…"

"I don't care!' He slapped the paper down on the father's desk. "How long! How long did you know where he was?"

"Since last year right, after Annalisa was murdered." Father Anthony said, reaching down and pulling opened his center desk drawer. "He showed up with this. He held up an envelope with a card inside. He handed it to Ryder. "He wanted to tell you what had happened and how…"

Ryder started to open the envelope, but stopped and crushed it in his grip. "I don't want to know his lies."

"It is the only way to forgive." The father said as he stood up from his desk, and walked around to the side.

Ryder flung the card to the floor as he spoke. "You want me to forgive this man? There is no way he deserves that!"

"No one deserves forgiveness, Rick. Not you, not I, and not him, but we give forgiveness for ourselves, not them." Father Anthony walked over and placed his hand down on his nephew's arm and looked at him as he continued. "You forgive me?"

"You are who you are, an uncle, you can't help it, but I can..."

Father Anthony smiled and wrapped his hand behind Ryder's neck and pulled him closer to him, then spoke gently "Son, forgiveness is not forgetting, it is just letting go of the hurt." He let go and added. "And you have a bunch of it to let go of."

Ryder walked over and placed his hand on the rack; he leaned down and lowered his head. His mind was reeling with the last time he has seen his father walking out of his life at a football game. "He never cared for anybody but himself, certainly not me."

"The pasture is always greener on the other side of the fence." As Father Anthony spoke Ryder's hand slipped from the rack down to the ladies light green jacket. He turned and faced him and asked.

"What?"

"When we were growing up we had this little calf that always, no matter what got out every day. He wanted to go over to the neighbor's field and eat, even though it was the same grass, he thought it was better. Your dad is the same way, but with him it is women. The next is always better."

"So what did you do with the calf?"

"We made him into a steer. After that, his wondering ways just sort of stopped."

Ryder picked up the jacket, "That could always be an option." He said with a laugh before looking at the name written on the jacket it read Annie Peters. He looked up at his uncle. "It was you, it was you! You are the man she was seeing on the trolley!"

"Yes, she needed to talk. I don't always have to be here, or in my collar to minster to those that need it."

"So she wasn't cheating on him. Then what was it about?'

"I can't tell you that, you know that."

He walked over to his uncle and narrowed his gaze slightly. "She was murdered and it may have something to do with it."

"It had nothing to do with why she was murdered."

"You don't know that! What was it? She was leaving her husband because she was in love with someone else. Another man?' Ryder paused watching his uncle's reactions he showed nothing. "Another woman?" His reactions were slight, just a slow drift of his eyes away from Ryder, but it was enough that he understood. "The blonde, it was the beautiful blonde. That is how she lured her in. I need her name Uncle Tony. Who is she?"

"I can't."

"You mean you won't." Ryder said as he walked over towards the door.

"I mean I can't. I never told the woman's name. she just called her beauty." Ryder walked out the door and back to the parking lot where he saw a familiar figure leaning down on the passenger's side door of his car. His head turned, looking for and finding the black SUV, it was Alex.

"Guess what I found out?" She asked with the excitement of a kitten jumping on a toy mouse. Not even waiting till he could reply she answered her own question. "I found her sister, in a nursing home in Lamar. She broke her hip. There is no way she can be involved in any of this, but..." With an expectant pause which gave birth to a smile that was both triumphant and taunting, she added. "She has a daughter."

"A what?"

"It is true," Alex explained as she began shuffling through the papers she was holding. "Her sister told me." She spoke as she continued to search through the papers. "Her sister also told me that when she was a teenager they went on vacation and she was raped, became pregnant and her parents forced her to have an abortion. She was never the same after that, having nothing to do with the parents or her brother."

"You said she had a daughter."

"She did; she was working at the hospital, and fell in love with this doctor. This led to another baby, he was married…"

"She sure knows how to pick winners." Ryder said and Alex continued to shuffle through the stack of papers, noticing her medical records including blood type of A+.

"Again the she was being forced to do away with the child. This time she took off and had a beautiful baby girl that she named Lillian." Alex handed him the birth certificate and he began reading. The father's name is marked 'unknown'.

"How did we not know this the first time around?"

"Adoption files are sealed."

"She was adopted?"

"By Annette St. John, a friend of Celeste's, legal in every way, but Celeste remained in the child's life." Alex handed him the adoption papers."

"How did you get all of this, this time?" Ryder asked as he studied the document.

"From her sister, just before we arrested Celeste she sent all this to her sister for safe keeping." Alex paused and he watched her fidgeting with the papers, she pulled out another document and handed it to him as she said. "And there is this!"

"She was placed in R.P.C.? " Ryder asked, looking up from the paper. He knew the place, a mental hospital in Kansas City. He looked back down as he flipped through the pages and read out loud. "Lack's self-confidence and an excessive need to be looked after, also a sign of disconnect with creating a passionate love affair with someone she has no contact with. True signs of Dependent Personality Disorder, Record of violent tendencies, when confronted with reality, true cluster B characteristics…" Ryder looked up at Alex as she asked.

"Okay I have been in the NFL and the Police Academy I have never been nor do I played doctor, well once when I was a kid, but what does this mean?"

"DPD is mental disorder where she relies someone else to meet their emotional and physical needs. If out the person it is like they starve to death without love. The report talks extensively about someone."

"Who?"

"The name has been redacted even in the doctor's files, but she does mention her mother a lot. So I am thinking it must be her." Alex pointed at the file and continued. "Do you see the date she entered the hospital? It is the day after the last murder of the Kansas City Butcher, you see the date she got out? Three weeks before the murders started in Eureka Springs. I hate to admit it Rick, but this person could be the butcher."

"Why not follow the same pattern?"

"Maybe it a different method, a different way, some killers change, so maybe..."

"Did you get all this legally, Alex?" Ryder asked interrupting her.

"Mostly...well some...okay, I paid a kid to tap into the state mental records, but—admit it. It could be like Yakira said; Celeste is protecting someone- her daughter." Finding a photo, she stopped and held it up. "Look familiar to you?" She was beautiful, with long blonde hair, bright blue eyes, nose turned up slightly at the end. Ryder looked closer and his memory filled with that night at the hotel.

"It is her!" Ryder exclaimed grabbing the photo. He buried his eyes into the photo. He could feel her touch, smell her perfume all over again. He could feel his heart thumping in his chest, pounding harder and harder, his pulse banging in his ears. There was something so complex, he feared, yet somehow he longed for her at the same time. He took his fingers and lovingly stroked the woman's photo.

"Ryder! Did you hear me?" He finally heard Alex. He asked her to repeat her question. "She was a student at William Jewell College at that time; I thought we would go see her professor at White Science Center.

"Yeah." Ryder mumbled, still letting his eyes devour the image. Alex reached over and took it away from him and asked.

"Are you okay?"

"I think so." Ryder said, suddenly feeling his heart rate come back to normal. Feeling more like his old self, the detective part began to emerge again. "We need to get a copy of this photo over to the Crescent and see if anybody recognizes her."

"I did that already." Alex replied, assembling the papers back into one pile. "It is her!"

******

As if it were a creature of another world, Kansas City had long tentacles reaching out in every direction. At the end of its limb was a hungry mouth, devouring the dividing lines, to where names of towns like Blue Summit, and Sugar Creek are swallowed in one gulp. It was hard to see where the city ended and the town began, reaching out into Independence.

Heading north on Highway 291, the city released its grip; the giant silver guards stood in the middle of the highway spanning the trusses out across the waters. Their grandeur being seen down the highway, growing taller and bigger till they filled the entire windshield. The steel gutters were like the fingers of a great goddess of the river casting shadows over each vehicle that passed over her. Making them cast their eyes upon the muddy water of the Missouri, to give a wave to a barge as it passed underneath, and her last shadow gave a final good bye.

Located just outside of Liberty Missouri, was William-Jewell College. If one were to picture what college should be, this would be it. It was the embodiment of beautiful in every way it could be. From the brick wall, around the fountain with bushes and flowers that announced itself to greeters at the entrance, to a street that was lined with trees, that which had breaks that allowed one to look through see red brick buildings towering up with white pillars, gazing down upon students milling about, juggling books from class to class. Each building was unique, yet each one is family, tied with invisible ribbons of students past, present and yet to come. White Science Center was that, still with the red bricks of learning, with a touch of distinctiveness with its round face.

Ryder, Yakira and Alex walked through the wide open glass doors and into the main hall, the glass display case catching their reflections as he reached up and removed the sunglasses from his face. He turned left and went down a long hallway, and turned again into a large classroom laboratory with metal counters and black topped stools.

137

Sitting on a stool was a woman, middle aged, with soft cinnamon hair worn in a pixie cut. She turned and looked at Ryder. As he entered the room she stood and extended her hand as she said. "I am Dr. Lori Glass. I heard you heard want to ask some questions about a former student?"

"Yes, Lillian St. John." Alex said, handing the woman the photo; she slipped on a pair of red framed glasses with half lenses and gazed at the photo. "Do you remember her?"

"Oh, yes," Dr. Glass said, removing her glasses and handing the photo back to Alex. "She was one of the best students I ever had, possibly even the best."

"What was her major?" Ryder asked, reaching into his jacket and pulling put out his notebook, he wrote it down as she answered.

"Chemistry with a minor in Biology, especially plant biology. She loved working with flowers." The professor said as she walked over to another desk and picked up a folder.

"Like- growing them? Arranging them? What do you mean?" Yakira asked.

"Oh heavens no, she looked for them to make them into perfume. All the girls at Shumaker Hall were begging her to make a special perfume for them." She handed the folder to Ryder. "You know, there are some plants that are very toxic, deadly, in fact." Ryder opened the folder; it was her senior thesis. "She developed a process to take the poison from flowers such as...."

"Oleander," Ryder said, interrupting her as he looked up from the file.

"She could never get it down quite right. The mice always died."

Ryder turned another page in the report, "It states in here that if she wanted to, she could control the dosage, so that it could be used as a hypoallergenic anesthesia with no side adverse effects. What does that mean?"

"No vomiting, no being spaced out and tired all the rest of the day. More pleasant type because the person would never be fully asleep. They would aware, but not feel any pain. Worse thing that they would have would be visual and auditory hallucinations."

138

"Such as you have a dream but you are not sure it is a dream?"

Yes I guess."

"She was also talking about mind control." Ryder shut the folder up and handed it back to the teacher. "Is that possible?"

"I wouldn't know for sure. There was much more to her research, but she took it all with her when she left." The professor walked back over to the windows and gazed out across the lawn at students walking by on the sidewalk. The street lights were beginning to come on. "We get a few kids that come through these doors that are going to change the world; Lillian could have been one of those." She turned around and Ryder was standing right behind her. "But something happen to her. She changed. It was all about..."

"Dr. Glass, did you know anything about her personal life? Did you ever see her with men?"

"That was what I was trying to tell you. Suddenly she changed. Everything became about some man she saw."

"Did she ever tell you who this was?"

"No, she never said anything to me," Dr. Glass said. However, there was one girl she was close to. Debby Inderwood."

"Where can we find her? Do you have an address for her?"

"She is still here. She was a freshman when Lillian was here. She is in Shumaker Hall."

Shumaker Hall was the sorority house on campus, and was fairly new. The larger H-shaped building housed all four of the groups with a large parking lot in back and a circle drive in front. Alex pulled her black Suburban up in front and got out, the street lights were gleaming in the paint. Ryder opened the passenger door and stepped out.

"Are you sure you want to go in there?" Yakira asked as Ryder held the back door open for her, as Alex got out and looked at the building . "It is filled with young girls."

"You will protect me, won't you?" He grinned as he looked over at her and shut the car door.

"Seriously you know what a freaking sorority house is like?" Alex said as she looked up at the Greek letters on the pillars. "I live in one when I was in college. You think a frat house is bad. You haven't seen teenage girls." They proceeded across the sidewalk that divided the neatly maintained lawn. They knocked on the door and a nineteen-year-old girl opened it. She was wearing tight fitting cutoffs and a white t-shirt with the redbird logo in front stretching across her bosom; seeing Ryder she grinned and leaned back against the door and said.

"Hey there cutie, what can I do for you?"

"Need to see Debby Inderwood." Ryder said, which drew a grimace on the girl's face as two more girls, one with long strawberry colored hair and pouty lips, and the other with short spiky blonde hair, with a gap in her front teeth as she smiled at him, came to the door. They each grabbed one of his arms and pulled him into the front room of the sorority; Yakira and Alex barely got in before the first girl slammed the door closed.

Inside, the living quarters were open, spaciously furnished with modern furniture, with a bone colored tile floor and a dark walnut fireplace mantle dominating the room. Ryder couldn't help but look for a spit in the fireplace, thinking that he was the fresh meat to be roasted over the flame.

"He is looking for Debby."

"She is in my room upstairs." The red haired woman said, wrapping her arm around his arm and leading him towards the staircase, nearly taking his jacket off of him.

"All right girls, go take a cold shower!" He heard another woman say. He turned, and saw a woman in her early twenties standing there, holding a French door open and looking through the panes of glass. She stepped out; she was petite in every way, even shorter than Yakira. Her chestnut hair was pulled back in a loose fitting ponytail. I am Debby Inderwood; Dr. Glass said you have some questions about Lillian."

"Is there someplace we can talk?" Ryder asked, straightening his jacket.

"Don't worry about the Alpha Gamma Delta girls, they are harmless." Debby said, "Finals are coming up and the girls are eager for companionship. There hasn't been a guy in here for over two weeks. And one that looks like you...." She looked at Ryder and sighed. She led them into another general area, this time with warmer surroundings, with a carpeted floor and a comfortable soft sofa. Since the sofa had its back to the staircase, there was yet another girl looking leaning back against the arm of the sofa, her bare leg sticking out from underneath her mini robe.

"I am having trouble with my homework. It is biology. You think you can help me do an experiment?"

"Riley, upstairs!" Debby ordered as she offered Ryder a seat on the sofa, but instead he chose to sit in a less comfortable chair with its back to the wall; he felt like a t-bone steak being tossed in a lion's den. He looked over at Yakira who sat down next to Alex on the sofa and he watched as yet another young lady descended the stairs and stopped in front of him, casually glancing over her shoulder and offering a little grin to him as she said with a tone that sounded like the purr of a cat.

"You going to have dinner with us? You can have my dessert."

He again looked to Yakira, begging for help, but she stifled a giggle, she was not going to be any help. Alex was too occupied with her phone to help. His only choice was to ask the questions he needed to ask and get out of here.

"So, you knew Lillian?" Ryder asked.

"Yes, she was a very good friend of mine. She was the one that invited me to join the Delta's."

"Did she have a boyfriend here?"

"That was what was so strange. I mean, she was so beautiful, every guy here wanted her, but she didn't want anything to do with any guy, something about how her mother told her that all men were scum. I met her mother, she and Debby's dad are happy."

"Lillian was adopted, she ever talk about her real mother?" Ryder could tell by the shocked appearance on the woman's face that it answered his own question, that she didn't know this.

"That might explain what she meant. At first she was making all the girls perfume that was only for them, then suddenly she started talking

141

about how all those men were going to pay for what they did to her mother. That the sin of man, the sixth sin..."

"You are sure she said the sixth sin?" Ryder asked as Alex's phone dinged, she was getting a text message.

"Yes, the sixth sin. I never knew what she meant by that."

"Murder," Alex said, looking down at her phone.

"That is the sixth commandment..."

"No!" Alex said, interrupting him. "There has been another one in Eureka Springs."

Chapter 16

'Darkness is truly a blanket, pulling it up over one's head does not stop the evil. It just hides it so you cannot see; it is still there, breathing, a cold heart still beating, waiting for its next move. Light, it shatters the darkness, yet all the darkness in the universe cannot snuff out even the smallest glimmer of light. Don't believe in darkness, but the light.'

It was this that Ryder's Uncle Tony told him when he graduated from college; what he tried to live by. When he would see the darkness of death before him, he always kept thinking that somewhere, somehow, he was there to offer just a little hope-just a little light. They stopped in Cassville only long enough for Ryder and Yakira to pick up the Killer Bee before heading south.

Even with Alex running code, blue lights tucked away behind the grille swinging back and forth across the highway and from the red and blue from the light bar mounted on the dash and the siren screaming, by the time they returned to Eureka Springs the moon was high in the night sky, only the headlights picking out the budding trees reaching out across the maze of streets they navigated through, climbing to the top of the hill before turning left on Prospect Street. In a big city this would have been a one way street, here two-way traffic was only separated by a thin double yellow line. Along the sides were older homes, two, three stories high, mostly wood frame and painted white. Many were now a Bed and Breakfast that waited eagerly for the season to truly begin; to have couples beginning to share their lives, or those just wanting a little get away to come through those doors. One of the most notable faced its side to this street; it was three storied, called Mount Victorian, once a Catholic school.

The flashing of blue emergency lights from Carroll County and Eureka Springs emergency vehicles turned the sky into a glowing sea. At the bottom was the newest crime scene- a murder at the St. Elizabeth Catholic Church. The street was still thoroughly blocked with vehicles, even though the meat wagon was long gone.

A quick show of Alex's ID allowed them into the scene, with Ryder parking behind Alex. He got out and opened the door for Yakira; he stood gazing across to the church, the bright glow of work lights filling the church yard. A sudden gust of wind whipped across, making the tail of his jacket fly up, revealing the Glock that was strapped to his side. He was lucky to have a friend who was an FBI agent, who helped him get a C.C. permit. He watched a large cedar tree in church's yard sway. He glanced up the hill to the Crescent Hotel. Cement steps led from the street all the way to the hotel. Surrounding the church were wooded areas on each side, it was well isolated. It was one of the draws for tourists, at the same time, it made it easy for a murderer to slip in and out without too many people noticing.

As they walked along the edge of the street towards the bell tower, which was the entrance into the church, Ryder noticed the officers had gathered around the white marble figures below them, the fourteen stations of Cross. In front of the seventh figure he noticed a flash of light from a camera.

Entering the bell tower and staring down at them was a large statue of Elizabeth, the Patron Saint of Hungary, and the one whom the church was named for. Turning to the right and going down five steps was a long sidewalk, along the right cemented into place on the hill were the fourteen Stations of Christ, each one gleaming in white marble, spotless, except one. The first; three larger figurines; one seated, with a child holding up a basket. The second one showing Christ taking up his cross, the third Jesus falls for the first time, the fourth Jesus meets his blessed mother. Ryder suddenly stopped and stared at the statue, remembering his own mother, a smile started to crack across his face, then he remembered how it felt when her hand slipped from his, and his father was nowhere around.

"Sweetie, you okay?" Yakira said.

He didn't say a word, just nodded and continued on past the statue of Simon of Cyrene that helped Jesus carry the cross, and Veronica, who wiped the face of Jesus, till he was standing in front of the one statue that was no longer spotless, it had been covered with blood. The ground under it, too, was stained with a dark color. The outline of where a body once laid was now painted on the once spotless gravel.

"What happened?" Alex asked as she approached Detective Shepherd, who was the one taking the photos.

"You again!" he complained, glancing up at them and going about his work.

"Another murder, stabbed in the back." Detective Shepherd was holding a bottle of diet soda in his hand. "But this one was gutted from belly to her boobs. The Mayor is going to…"

144

"Plotz?" Yakira asked.

"Yeah," Shepherd said. "If that means what I think it means." He opened the bottle of diet pop and took a sip, then put the lid back on the bottle. "You know, you were asking if we ever found anything strange. Next to the body we found a brochure from the Arkansas Missouri Railway, and the trip to Van Buren from Springdale was circled, guess she was planning a trip. The one thing I don't get: why here at the feet of the statue?"

"You don't?" Ryder asked.

"Do you?"

"It is the second fall of Jesus. It represents the second fall of mankind." Ryder said as he saw Shepherd open the bottle of diet soda, and again take another sip. He could tell by the man's vacant expression he didn't have a clue, Ryder had to explain further. "The first fall represents Eve taking the forbidden fruit and being cast out from the Garden of Eden, the second fall represents, when murder entered our world."

"Oh Cain and Able, I never knew that. But that sounds just like that guy over there." Detective Shepherd said, pointing across the yard to a man sitting on a bench in the garden. Ryder looked closer. He couldn't believe it, it was his Uncle Tony, he was sitting next to another man.

"What did he have to do with this?" Ryder asked.

"He found the body," Detective Shepherd replied, taking another sip of the soda, and replacing the lid. "But if you ask me, he knew the victim."

"Why do you say that?" Ryder asked with a lifted eye brow.

"He was very upset."

"He found a murdered victim most people would be upset."

"Not shock," Detective Shepherd said as he opened up the bottle and took another sip before continuing. "This was lost." He replaced the cap on the bottle and said. "You were a homicide officer, you should have seen the difference."

"Who was the victim?" Ryder asked.

"A woman, a local shop owner named Cindy Walker."

The man that was sitting next to Ryder's uncle stood and walked towards them. He walked right up to Detective Shepherd and spoke. "Ron, can I take him home? He has been through a lot."

"Okay, Father Norman."

It was George Norman, his name was stitched on his coveralls. By his dress Ryder assumed he was the caretaker, had the detective not called him father. George was shorter than Ryder by a half a foot, his waist was beginning to spread, his hair was thinning, which a comb over tried to hide, but failed miserably. He turned to Ryder.

"I have seen you before." George said. Ryder received this all the time, and he prepared himself. Was it going to be a quarterback, lottery winner, or cop? "You are Father Delany's nephew, the detective? "The man's answer surprised Ryder. Ryder had learned that sometimes a look, a slight twist of the head, could be better than a question to make others answer the things you wanted to know. "We get together every month. He told me about you becoming a private detective. A dollar a day and you pay the expenses." He turned to Yakira. "You must be his partner, the girlfriend? Anthony said you were pretty." A warm glow flushed over her cheeks. Father George turned. "And you are Alex the FBI agent the one who busted the gun runners." He turned and looked up at the clear dark sky and the stars above them. "First Annie and now Cindy." Father George turned back to the figure that was covered in blood. He still stood staring at the figure of Jesus down on his knees, the cross pressing down upon his back, but the tone of his voice increased, "A lot of evil in the world today, are you going to stop it?"

"So you knew Annie and Cindy?" Ryder asked, once again pulling his notebook and pen from his pocket and began writing.

"Yes, they were members here. Annie was a nice girl, but…" He turned back to Ryder and continued. "..Her husband wasn't, he didn't like her going here." The father looked up at the round blue colored roof that was part of the original church that was built here in the early 1900's, and now served as the vestibule as he added, "Or anywhere really, for that matter." He turned and walked down the sidewalk, passing the other figurines in the line of the steps to the cross. Ryder and Yakira followed alongside him and continued to question him, while Alex stayed behind to investigate further.

"And Cindy?"

"Oh, Cynthia." He said using her correct birth name. "She was a good woman too, strong willed, a wonderful lady all the way around. She was actively involved in the church." A small grin made one side of his lips curl up as he added, "Made the best tater salad I ever ate." The grin faded as he said sorrowfully, "Now I will never have it again."

"When was the last time you saw her alive?" Ryder asked as they passed by the figurine of Jesus being nailed to the cross.

"Earlier today," The priest said as he stopped in front of the figurine of Jesus dying on the cross. "She told me that she had called Tony and was waiting for him here."

"Did she say why?" Ryder asked as the father began to walk down the sidewalk again, along the stone wall.

"No." They stopped once again at the point where the sidewalk turned and went towards the front door of the church. He took a deep breath and gazed out towards the small garden that held white marble statues of 'Our Lady of Fatima,' standing and looking down on the figures of small children kneeling and praying. "I would think it would be best if your uncle told you that."

Ryder walked towards the church with its dolomite limestone exterior hand cut from the local quarries, beautiful stained glass windows, and bright red clay tile shingles. Ryder walked up to his uncle, sitting on the bench in the garden. His uncle looked up at him. "It was Cindy, Ricky." Father Anthony said as he dropped his head down.

"I know, but why are you here?" Ryder said

"She called me; she said that she felt someone was following her." Father Anthony said, lifting his head up and looking at Ryder.

"Who?" Ryder said calmly as he sat down beside the man.

147

"She didn't, she could never really get a look at the person." Father Anthony stood up and walked over to the lady figurine before he continued. "She said it was more of a feeling, but she was really scared." He turned back to his nephew and added. "I mean terrified."

"When did you get here?"

"Around eight, she asked me to meet her here…." The father lowered his head, placing his hands over his face and continued. "That is when I found her…."Ryder noticed his uncle's clothing, jeans, tee shirt stained with blood, and tennis shoes, also stained with blood.

"What did you do?"

"I saw her lying there, just staring up at me. I wasn't thinking; I grabbed her up in my arms. I tried to do CPR, but she was gone. I called for an ambulance and the police." He walked back over to Ryder.

"Did she mention anything about taking a trip, say on a train?"

"Oh, no way," Father Anthony replied back. "She got motion sickness real bad."

"Did you see anyone?" Ryder asked. "Or a car?"

"Come to think of it, just before I got here I saw a light blue Prius drive away, but I didn't think anything about it. I mean cars are always coming and going here."

"Where was this car parked?" Ryder asked, and the father pointed at the parking area across the street. He led Ryder over to the parking spot at the end.

"Right here!" The father said, pointing to the spot. "It was parked sideways across two spots. Ryder reached into his pants pocket and pulled out the key chain with the small penlight. He guided the small blue beam of light around the pavement. "What are you looking for?"

"I don't know," Ryder said He stooped down as the beam caught something bright and shiny. He picked it up; it was a piece of foil wrapping, bright on the outside and white on the inside, crimped on the edges. He ripped a page in the notebook and carefully wrapped up the piece of foil as if it were a prime rib steak from the butcher.

"What is that?" Yakira asked as she placed her hand on his back.

"I don't know." Ryder replied as he carefully stood up and placed the paper in his jacket pocket. "Maybe nothing."

"Sir!" The shout of a young officer made Ryder look up as the uniformed officer raced toward Detective Shepherd. "The newspaper! They just got another note." Ryder and Yakira raced back towards the church, and down the sidewalk. The officer started to hand the detective the note, but Alex quickly grabbed it from him. And she read it, before handing it to Ryder. Ryder read and his eyes opened wide.

"Waste not doubt
This was the one that was the way out
It is the game that is fowl
Be still, and you will hear the scream of howl.
 And the Iron Gate demon will grow still.
That shall be time for the kill."

Chapter 17

'Serial Killer Loose In the Ozarks'
'Tourists Flee the Little Switzerland of the Ozarks'
'Hundreds of Other Tourists Cancelling Reservations'

The headlines of the newspaper, the newscasts, the bright colored news vans parked all over town, running up to locals with a microphone in hand, wondering what they thought of the mayhem that was taking over their town. But it was the headlines of a newspaper better known for the musical and art happenings of the town, the hard news that gave the biggest headline.

"EUREKA SPRINGS SLAYER STRIKES AGAIN"

The killer had an official name, as they broke the biggest news story of their lifetime, one that Ryder had yet to learn 'that the notes sent to them did not match those sent to the Star, it was a different killer.' Sitting at a table on the balcony outside of his room at the Crescent Hotel, he tossed the red and white paper down on the table and picked up his phone and dialed it.

"How they did they get this information?" Ryder asked.

"I don't know." Alex's voice replied over the phone. "I am just hearing it myself, reading the report right now." He heard the rustle of a paper and Alex began to read. Heavier strokes on those sent to the Independent compared to those that were sent to the Star. Strokes on those sent to the Independent; a crayon with a blunt point was used, while those sent to the Star were created with a crayon with a recently sharpened point. Heavier stroked indicate female with aggressive behavior or male. While those sent to Star shows type A personality traits Findings: two different people. "

"I don't get it Alex, how come the ones being sent to me, are the same as those that I got in Kansas City, but the notes being sent to the paper are different?"

"Well, you better hold on to yourself." He heard Alex say as he walked down the steps of the balcony as he talked. "I had Bernie do me a favor at the lab; by the way you know that football you used when you made the amazing comeback in the game against Denver, the 24 to nothing game in the fourth quarter…"

"You promised him my football?"

"You said whatever it costed."

"But my football!" Ryder complained, sighed deeply and then said. "What did he say?"

"I had him compare the writing of the notes you are getting to the notes made by Lillian at college. She may have tried to hide it by writing like a child, but he said they are the same person."

"So there is no doubt that Lillian is our murderer."

"You are forgetting the notes being sent to the newspaper, they don't match those that were sent to the Star, and however those sent to you do match those that were sent to the Star."

Ryder reached the ground and gazed out over the woods and at the yellow police tape that was tied across the church property and the bell tower opening. "Could the wrong person really be in jail, Alex?" There was silence from his question. He sat down on one of the cement steps that led down to the church. "We have to find Lillian."

"I am trying." He heard Alex say. "I checked out her last known address, Arch Avenue in Green Forest, but it was just an empty lot. You want me to meet you in Eureka Springs? "

"No, it is Friday, so we are coming back to Cassville, so Yakira can spend the Sabbath with her family. Something about they are going to go see her aunt. So I will meet you there."

"Ricky," he heard Yakira say from behind him and he ended the call. He sat with his hands resting on his knees; he looked back over at his shoulder as she walked over and sat down beside him. "Thom just called, they got the ballistic report back from the revolver found in the Coronet. It is a match, the same one was used to kill them both." He sat, not looking at her as she paused, there was something else she had to tell him. He knew he had to just wait and let her tell him. She raised her head again. "I have been having Jonnie look through the records at the shop; she found an old sale record." She turned and looked at him. "It was sold to Allen Ryder, your grandfather. You know what that means?"

"Yeah,"Ryder said, standing up and dusting the dirt off his pants. "It is time to go see my father."

"When?"

"Tomorrow."

"But that is the Sabbath." Yakira said as she, too, stood up.

He leaned down and kissed her on her the cheek before saying. "I have to do this myself."

Chapter 18

Eureka Springs was quickly becoming like a ghost town, as cars lined up in front of the hotels. Visitors were quickly carrying out their luggage, stuffing it in the trunk, and quickly driving away. The lane coming going out was bumper to bumper, horns honking, drivers screaming for the traffic to move, as a fist fight broke out because of a small t-bone collision in front of the train depot. With the police hunting for a killer, and not responding, the crowd just pushed the wrecked vehicles to the side and the traffic began flowing once again.

The lane coming into town, was nearly empty save the array of TV news vans. All the local stations, ABC, NBC, CBS and the cable outlets FOX, CNN, others from we're trying to find away to fly in only finding that the nearest airport was miles away. The gleam of bright lights from cameras, the over whelming buzz of questions of reporters, the flash of still cameras forever capturing images.

Being back in Cassville was a relief for Ryder. The storm had calmed there were no reporters coming up and asking if he thought the Eureka Springs Slayer was in fact the Kansas City Butcher. The only thing covering him now was the cool shade of a trio of trees outside the county courthouse as he sat on a wooden bench. He sipped from a cup of soda, and snacked on a small bag of chips he had bought from Whitley's Pharmacy, waiting for Alex to arrive. Watching the traffic come to the end of the square and having to decide to turn left or right. Turning left was always the harder choice having to cross both lanes of traffic. He watched as a black Suburban parked on the square in front of a round flower bed. A woman in gray slacks, and matching jacket got out; she checked her appearance, tugging at the collar of her white silk blouse before closing the door and walking down the sidewalk towards the courthouse.

Ryder sat with his eyes fixed on the insurance agency, as the woman turned and walked up to him, and sat down on the bench across from him. He held out the bag of potato chips, offering her some. She reached in, the gold chain bracelet with a green stone, a small cross and a pendant that was engraved 'God gave U 2 Me' dangled from her wrist. A southern breeze drifted over the courtyard; he could smell her perfume. It was delicate like Yakira-honeysuckle, it was more powering, he missed honeysuckle.

"Are you sure you want to do this?" She asked, taking a couple of chips and eating them.

He stood up, finished the chips, wadded up the bag and tossed the bag in the trash can. "What choice do I have?" He asked as he finished the drink and then tossed the cup into the can. "I could wrap up an over forty-year-old murder." He added as he started walking towards his

Charger which was parked parallel to Main Street. She followed beside him.

"It sounds like you want him to be guilty." She said, waiting for him to unlock the passenger side door and hold it open for her. "Do you really want to snap the cuffs on him?" She asked as she seated herself. He shut the door and went over to the driver's side and sat down behind the steering wheel.

"I do what I have to do." He said, twisting the key and bringing the massive engine to life, the scoop sticking out of the hood quivering like a leaf in the wind. Ryder's hands gripped the steering wheel and the shifter as he pulled it down into drive and guided the car out onto the street.

"Are you sure you are going to be all right parked there all day?"

"I told Thom we would be back tonight." She said as they headed back out of town. "Besides, would you ticket a black SUV with government plates?" She offered a small grin as he turned south next to the Ford dealer and head towards the Arkansas state line. It wasn't till then that she spoke again. "You really want to arrest your dad for ..."

"He is not my dad!" He snapped back, interrupting her. He glanced over at her, "He is my father." He looked back down the road, his hands firmly gripped around the steering wheel, the leather covered rim giving him the same comfort as guiding an Italian sports car.

"What is the difference?"

"Any male with a pair can be a father, but it takes a real man to be daddy." There were not many places to past safely on this road, and when Ryder found one he took it the red and gray Dodge quickly passed the slower moving pickup. Ryder asked as he quickly glanced over at Alex. "When you were young and had something planned with your dad, was he there? Did he show up? Or was your mom left comforting you telling you 'that he was just busy that he still loved you.' You ever stand on the stage having to recite something in front of the school, and look out thinking he would be there to give you comfort, and all you find an empty seat." He looked back down the road. "Then one day..." His own words made him grip the steering wheel even tighter. "...you look over and he walks right out of your life, but it doesn't matter he was never there in the first place."

Ryder looked over Alex, he was glad his eyes were shielded by the sunglasses; he didn't want her to see what he was feeling. "You told me you and your dad was close. He was there. You can't know what I feel." He turned and looked back down the road. "A dad cares. A dad loves. A dad sacrifices. A father is name on a birth certificate." Ryder

reached up and pushed adjusted his sunglasses then he became all
business once again. "Besides, this is about murder, not my father."

Not another word was spoken till they reached the Washburn
city limits when Ryder's phone rang and suddenly broke the silence. The
phone was lying on the console next to the shift lever, and it rang again, he
looked down and saw Yakira's photo on the screen.

"Want me to get it?" Alex asked and he nodded. She picked up
the phone and answered it. "Alex here Yakira, we are on our way to Van
Buren." Ryder saw Alex's nose wrinkle up in shock as she gasped out.
"WHAT! Okay I am going to put you on speaker phone. Go ahead."

"Ricky!" Yakira spoke up.

"I am here."

"I figured out the note!"

"What note?"

"The one that was left at the newspaper," He heard her reciting
the note; "'be still, and you will hear the scream of hell's howl. And the
Iron Gate demon will grow still. That shall be time for the kill.' Don't you
get the Iron Demon hell's howl?"

Ryder saw three bright lights heading towards them, they were
part of the Arkansas Missouri freight train on its way to Monett, it blasted
its horn as it approached a crossing. He glanced over at it as it passed by,
three bright red and yellow locomotives leading a multitude of box cars,
grain bins, cargo carts and empty car haulers on their way back to Kansas
City.

"A train," Ryder said turning his attention again to the road.
There was no way Cindy could have had that brochure; it had to be Lillian.
She is going to kill somebody on that train. We have to get on that train. "

"You better hurry," He heard Yakira say. "That train leaves
Springdale at nine o'clock, and it is already eight-thirty." Ryder ended
the call, telling her he would call her later. It was regularly a forty five
minute drive and that was without traffic. His foot pressed down on the
gas pedal and he could feel the horsepower of the 440 Magnum motor
push him back in the seat. Blasting under the overpass at Gateway there
was only more pavement lying out in front of them.

"Got the tapes from Harps in Green Forest, it shows Lillian
getting into a light color Toyota."

"Prius?"

"How did you know?"

"Uncle Tony said he saw a Prius leaving the church just before he got there." Ryder said, his words running out as fast they were moving. His heart pounding so fast it had to be pushing back on the shoulder strap. It was that same feeling that he got in the two minute drill in football. No time for a huddle, shout out the play as he pulled the players to the line, glance down the field to see what was the defensive line up, changing quickly as the play clock ticked down to the last second. "Let me guess: L.P. is missing or…"

"Plates reported stolen; checks back to a red 2002 Ford sedan."

"Time!" Ryder shouted out as he began to back off the accelerator and began to slow as they passed by a brightly colored eatery on Emma Avenue in Springdale.

"Five till the hour." Alex said as Ryder whipped the car into the parking lot, noticing there were five different light colored sedans, but no sign of a Prius. He parked next to a late model light blue sedan with Oklahoma plates. They dashed for the depot, just as the train horn sound four short blasts, indicating it was the last call for coming aboard.

The depot was a mixture of styles with its simple buff colored siding, and white picket fence. It was a throw back to when riding the rails was the way to go; it wasn't about how fast you go there, it was the excitement of getting there. However, with the modern touches of a bright red metal roof, there was no doubt that it was a pair of Alco C-420 diesel locomotives pulling this team of cars and not steam power.

Ryder jerked the door open and quickly scanned for the ticket counter. There was a woman that was an origami figure of skin folds over a skeleton standing behind it. "I need two tickets." He said reaching for his wallet.

"I am not supposed to sell tickets; you needed to make reservations." The ticket lady said as her lips twitched with amusement.

"Tell you what," Ryder said opening his wallet that was full of cash and pulling out a hundred dollar bill and holding it up. 'You sell me those tickets and I will give you a hundred bucks for your trouble."

"You are Rick Ryder!" The woman exclaimed with a resentful gaze that went from his face down to the wallet in his hand. "The one who won the billion dollars in Powerball. ®· You know what I won? Four dollars, four freaking dollars!" She looked at Ryder's wallet, as if she had just crossed the desert, and was now gazing at a glass of clear cool water. "Tell you what." She said with a hungry grin, "give me five hundred and you got the tickets."

"Five hundred!" Ryder snapped back, shocked that she would want this much. Outside the train horn sounded again; it was the last call to board.

"Better hurry, it is getting ready to leave."

"Okay!" Ryder grumpily accepted her blackmail and put down the money for the tickets and the extra five hundred dollars. She handed the tickets to him; he looked at them. "Coach?"

"If you want first class it will be a thousand." She said counting the hundreds as Ryder and Alex dashed for the train.

"Looks like you just made it. " The conductor said. He was a pleasant looking gentleman, just what one would envision a conductor to be. A tad heavy set, pewter like hair partly hidden by a dark colored conductors cap. Of course the large round face with drooping cheeks like an old blood hound, and the bursting mustache that would make any walrus proud.

There were five cars in the entire train; all being pulled by two dull crimson and yellow locomotives, number sixty-four and sixty-eight. The passenger cars on the train were a hodgepodge of styles from wooden cars, to those that had more modern attributes. Theirs was coach # 106 Mountain View, the third car back from the locomotive; it was right out the golden age of railway heaven. The wooden car was long and lean, painted deep green, and the red Arkansas and Missouri Railway logo was painted above the windows.

Inside were small cozy seats on each side, just big enough for two, covered in soft green fabric that seemed to let out a breath of peace as they sat down. The interior was richly appointed in wood. The ceiling was rich and elegant; the side paneling molded and shaped to fit the contoured side above the luggage racks.

The brakes let out a hiss, and Ryder could just envision the days of yesteryear, getting lost in this fancy car on wheels. Where he could imagine himself 'the big cheese, the hard boiled gumshoe hired to stop the torpedo before he could bump off the hoofer with the great gams."

"The what?" Alex asked as the train jerked hard forward and began to pull away from the station, bringing him out of his day dream.

"Nothing." He said letting his eyes roam around the passengers in the car. He was here not to dream but to stop a murder. The car was full with an assortment of people of all ages, but mostly those over retirement age and couples. The train was slow moving at first, the images of faces of those along the street, that would stop and give a wave as the train passed, clear and distinct, but as the people were replaced with trees, there soon became just a passing image on the outside of the window.

"She isn't in this car." Alex said as she twisted around and faced him. "I have checked; it is a church group from the First United Methodist Church from Monett, and the Ozark Mystery Writer's Guild."

"You are kidding, right?" Ryder said with disbelief. "Mystery writers are aboard a train with a murder on board?" It seemed surreal to him, he offered a small laugh.

"I told them we are from a travel magazine and they gladly told me everything." Alex said, her mouth twisting into a teasing smile. "I even got the conductor to allow us to go to the other cars." The train horn sounded just before they went over a crossing. "You think you can take photos with your phone? I told the conductor you were the photographer. Ryder was deep in thought and they both sensed it but it was Alex that continued. "Rick! What is it?"

"Something I saw in her hotel room. A wig and makeup! She could be anybody." Ryder said again, taking a look at the car. He saw the back door of the car open. "There is the conductor."

He approached them waiting for their tickets. They handed them to him, and he tore off a part of it. "So you all are from a travel magazine, which one?"

Ryder really didn't know the name of a travel magazine, but he remembered a magazine that Captain Grosstree always read that might apply. "We are freelance, but hoping to sell it to Train Magazine."

"Good magazine." The conductor replied. "Now that we are up to speed, feel free to move about." Ryder stood up and the conductor warned. "Although, we can quickly change speeds, so be careful." The conductor walked on to the next passenger.

"All right. You go forward and I go back." Ryder said, glancing at Alex. "We keep in touch with texts."

"Remember you're the one taking photos." Alex replied. "So be sure to take them." Ryder pulled out his cell phone and held it up, quickly taking a couple of photos in the car before moving on to the next car back.

It was the "Spirit of Arkansas" a diner-lounge #8322, its dull aluminum outsides held no clue to the brightly colored deep purple and rich wood tone inside. Only a few passengers were here, a young couple from Kentucky on their honeymoon, and two older couples all on the button tufted seats. Ryder took a couple of photos, to promote the facade of being a journalist. Before he moved on to the next car- the Silver Feather.

It began its life as part of the Western Pacific dome coach in 1948 for the famous California Zephyr. Over the years its layout had changed and now there were only tables and chairs in the vestibule portion of the car. In the center were red carpeted stairs that led to an upper dome. Ryder walked up the stairs and he was quickly cloaked in bright sunlight. He glimpsed at the limited number of tables covered with white cloths that seemed to highlight the blue upholstery.

Middle aged males in sports jackets, sunglasses pushed up on top of their heads were talking over a big business deal. To the other side of the car and back one table was a power couple, with enough diamonds on her hand to even outshine the bright sun light that was gleaming through the glass roof. At other tables were two men in polo shirts talking over how to take a stroke off their next golf game. White and green light strained through the glass, casting shadows of tree limbs that shimmered quickly across the floor and to the back of the dome.

There, sitting with her back to the glass wall of the dome, was a woman with long dark hair. She was all alone, and kept her head down; only once did she look up for a few brief seconds, but stared right at Ryder. He didn't know why it was, but he was frozen in his tracks. He wanted to say something, move a little closer to her, but his arms felt as if they were part of the rock ledge they were passing by, and his legs felt trapped in the muck of a bog. He felt the train slowing, but he couldn't stop from staring at her, spellbound by her gaze.

"It's her!" He gasped out under his breath. He quickly brought the phone up and sent a text to Alex. 'Found her. Silver Feather. Dome.' He pressed send and began to take photos, telling everyone they were for the magazine. He started with the power couple and the business men before lifting it back, aiming it at the woman at the back. He clicked the button and suddenly darkness filled the car, they had entered Winslow tunnel.

In the pitch blackness he could hear the train horn blow and someone brush beside him. He smelled the sickeningly sweet smell of flowers. He could feel the brakes kick through each car with a sudden jolt. A flicker of light began to filter through; they were coming out of the tunnel. He tired of adjusting his eyes as the sunlight began to pour back through the glass dome. He was lying on the floor, several people gather around, asking him if he were all right. Alex was running up the stairs, she glanced around the dome and asked.

"Where is she?"

He pulled himself to his feet and looked back at the table; she was gone. He began disrupting the other passengers, lifting up the tablecloths, causing plates to tumble to the floor. "She is not here!" Ryder shouted. He turned to Alex and stood. "She get past you?"

"Not that I know of," Alex said. "There is another car behind us. She could get out that way." The dashed back downstairs and through the car to the exit door into the next car.

The last car in the lineup, the Parlor Car #107 "Explorer, was a dining car. A former star of the Long Island railway company, its brand still appeared in the paper on the ceiling, with red and white panels dominating the interior and small round tables and Pigeon's blood red C-back chairs. Ryder kept his hand clutched on the butt of his pistol under his coat, as he quickly but surely scanned the car. He turned to the conductor behind the wooden counter.

"Did a woman come through here?" Ryder asked, his tone pure cop, making the man quickly answer.

"No sir! But it was dark; she could have passed by then."

159

Ryder motioned quickly with his hand to the back of the train. They pushed past a server and through the door out onto the rear platform; there were three men. "Was there anyone else on this platform?" Again his question demanding a quick reply of...

"No."

Ryder placed his foot down on the step, and hanging on to the rail he leaned down and looked back down the tracks. There were wooden areas on either side, he glanced up the tracks, the wind tussled his hair into a mess. He pulled back. "I don't see how she could have gotten off. She still has to be aboard." He faced Alex.

"You alert the conductor. We will do a sweep search." Ryder nodded as she continued to talk. "I will also contact Van Buren P.D. Get a guard on each exit." She turned to the other men. "You gentlemen need to take your seats right now."

"Who is asking?"

Alex reached into her jacket, pulled out her badge and flipped the ID open. "The United States of America! You have a problem?" They shook their heads and quickly went back inside, Alex following them.

The wind burned at his cheeks, flapping at the tails of his jacket as the shadows of the entwining limbs flashed over him. There is no way she could have jumped, he thought. The train hadn't slowed that much.

He glanced out between the security guard of trees that stood between the track and the houses that were beginning to appear. One, then a few, then an environ of duplexes and triplexes. The enclosure of municipality was quickly closing in once again. The tree guards faded and then Van Buren was coming alive. The scream of police sirens filled the air, as one would die, only to be followed by another and yet another, all stopping in front of the Visitor's Center.

"What is going on?" He heard the conductor say from behind him. He turned and faced him.

"We lied to you." Ryder said his eyes hidden behind sunglasses. "We are not from a magazine. We are investigators. She is an FBI agent; we are hunting for the Eureka Springs Slayer."

160

"Oh my dear God!" He shouted, nearly falling back before Ryder quickly grabbed his arm. "Are you telling me that killer can be aboard the train?"

"Possibly," Ryder said in a calm tone, trying not to frighten the man. "But we need you to remain calm and don't allow anyone off this train. Understand?" He steadily nodded his head and entered the car. Ryder could hear him instructing the passengers to remain seated as they arrived at the station.

The train was slowing as it switched tracks to guide it up to the depot. Ryder again stepped down on the steps and gazed up the tracks. The visitor's center looked as it was an armed bandit; the two large windows looked like eyes gazing out upon a colossal group of police cruisers, their light bars beaming and flashing, causing everyone in town to stop their sightseeing and shopping. The visitors were more interested in the troop of officers that were gathering to meet the train, including one young man in his late teens, with light brown hair that was talking to an officer.

Traffic was stopped on the street closed with an officer sealing off the area with tape and keeping visitors back. He glanced up at the windows on the cars. Faces pressed up against the glass like children watching candy being made, but those were not faces of excitement, but of panic.

Again he felt the jerk and loud pop of the brakes being transferred through the cars as the brakes howled and hissed as if a demon was flying out from the bowels of hell. He glanced up at the train once again. Alex was standing on the bottom step of one of the cars. He nodded to her and she stepped off, and he followed.

Instantly a patrolman approached him, instructing him not to get off the train. "That is one of my associates I told you about." Alex shouted. She turned back to the officers. "I want a patrolman at every door on every car. No one gets off. Understand? NO ONE!"

Ryder walked over to her. He looked back into the crowd that was briskly walking to the other side of the street, but he could no longer see the young teen, and Alex was still giving out instructions. "We will unload them car by car and one by one. We will start with the last car and work our way up. " She turned to a tall muscular man, seeing his rank on his uniform she said. "Lieutenant, get some of your men back down the tracks, look for any signs that she could have jumped off."

A heavy set bald man walked up to them. "I am Chief of Police Cliff Culberson, what is going on here?"

"We have a suspected killer that might be aboard the train." Alex replied as she also watched the officers take their position. But the chief ordered them to stop.

"I need to know a few things before I get my men involved. So why is the FBI. involved?"

"The suspected killer is the Eureka Springs slayer." Alex said before turning to the officers and again ordering them to take their positions next to the doors.

"This isn't Eureka Springs. It is Van Buren. And I am in charge here. Your men will stand down."

Ryder had known and seen Alex handle many different situations, and knew what to watch for when she became angry. She flexed her fingers quickly and then with haste flipped her hair back, making it fall back over her shoulder, as her eyes narrowed and she began to speak. Softly at first, but before finishing yelling her orders, "You know how it works chief- county outranks city, state outranks county and the United States Government outranks all below! Now do exactly what I tell you or—." She opened her jacket and revealed the 9 mm strapped to her side before continuing. "Or I am going to put you down on the ground like a freaking rabid dog! Understand?"

"Yes Sir!" He said, snapping to attention. "Yes ma'am."

"Just yes agent!"

"Yes agent!" He turned and barked an order at his officer. "You men get over there and seal off the cars."

A well dressed woman in a black business suit approached, her hickory- like hair long, but pulled up, styled. One just knew by the way she walked that she was big business, all business. "I am Sheila Longley, Superintendent of Railroad Operations for A&M Railroad. What can we do to help?"

"We want the people to exit one by one. Since Ryder and myself know what she looks like we will position at each end of the car."

"Do you really think that killer is aboard?" Longley said gazing at the train.

"We have every reason to believe so." Ryder said.

The woman turned to the police officer and said. "Then let's get this done. This is not good for A&M. I will contact the conductor." Ryder and Alex placed themselves at the door and one by one the anxious passengers exited the car. Car by car they began to get off, with not a sign of their suspect. When they got to the 'Biloxi Blues', again one by one the passengers got off. At that moment the conductor unexpectedly opened the window and yelled out.

"There is a guy in here. He won't move. I think he might be dead." Ryder and Alex quickly boarded the train. Even through the hustle of activity outside the car, the scream of yet another siren approaching, there was a dreadful dead stillness that seemed overtake the railway car. All the laughter and celebrations were now replaced with sobbing, cries of unbelief, as passengers were being pushed back past the black iron guard rail between the depot and the tracks. Cameras and phones were being held up, documenting everything that was happening, quickly being posted to Facebook, liked and shared over and over again.

Ryder quickly looked over the car and to the still single occupant, a man in his fifties slightly balding and with hints of gray on the sides. Dressed in jeans and a bright yellow t-shirt, he was sitting in a seat in the middle of the car on the right-hand side. He just sat there glassy eyed; staring at a red and white Coke can clutched in his hand. Ryder looked closer. The man's mouth was slightly open with a small stream of blood running down his chin and spoiling his shirt. Ryder placed his hand on the man's wrist, no pulse and limp. Ryder moved his hand up to the man's neck; again no pulse, but still warm to the touch.

"He's dead." Ryder said as he kneeled down on the floor beside the body and began to look around. His eyes were quickly drawn to a piece of paper lying on the floor. It was freezer paper.

"Yep, he is dead all right." Culberson said. "Most likely a heart attack from all the stress you gave him."

"Rick." Alex said with a tone of concern. "Look." She pointed at the seat behind him. Lying there was a dagger with a long thin seven- inch blade, covered with blood. There was something that was bugging Ryder, it wasn't the bone skull head handle, or even the creepy satanic symbol on the blade; it was the why it was lying here. Lillian to him seemed to be a very intelligent woman. Why would she drop the knife? Was she in a hurry?

He looked at the body there was no sign of stiffness, only slight bluing was occurring around the lips. The man hadn't been dead that long. Even the blood that had pooled under him had yet to coagulate. Ryder reached into his jacket and produced the white handkerchief that he always kept, and picked up the knife.

Gripping the knife he brought the blade up and matched it to the tear in seat back. They were not the same size. The one the back of the seat was much bigger. Ryder returned the knife to where he had found it. Using the handkerchief he carefully pushed the body forward the man's jacket was soaked in blood as was the back rest, including a thin smear to his left.

Chapter 19

Van Buren C.I.D. techs arrived and begin sealing the car off and taking photos along with Crawford County Coroner Virginia Jones, who arrived to remove the body. "You are going to find that his heart was pierced." Ryder said sitting in the seat across the aisle a couple of seats up.

"No kidding?' She mocked him looking at him. "I think a blind man could figure that one out. Who the hell are you anyway? What are you doing here this is a crime scene?"

"I am Rick Ryder. I am working with that lady out there. The FBI agent."

"Oh." Her tone suddenly changed it no longer angry. "Well thanks but I knew that."

"Did you know," Ryder said, as he stood up, "that the knife found was not the murder weapon?"

"What! How do you know that?"

"Compare the slashes in the back of the seat and the body to that with the knife. A bigger knife was used." Ryder said as he pointed to the seat. "I would say a Chief's knife."

Virginia looked at the rip in the seat. "Well your killer could have moved the knife."

"Not possible." Ryder said. "That knife is more like a letter opener it is not sharp. If it was pulled it would have ripped not been a smooth cut." Ryder moved closer to the slit on the back of the seat. "No rips. You notice the angle it is wider on this side." Ryder pointed to each side of the slit. "That is your knife."

"How do you know all this?"

"A few years of being with KCPD," Ryder said as he stood back up. "And having a friend who is a Medical Examiner. I also guess you will find out he has some connection to Eureka Springs. "

"Well, that is where is the great detective is wrong." Ryder heard Chief Culberson say as he walked on the train, holding out a wallet in an evidence bag. "His name was Ted Ross from 1120 Pike Road, Trinidad, California."

"Really?" Ryder asked. "What is a person from the west coast doing on a train in the middle of the heartland? Doing one of the things almost all tourists do, I will guarantee you he was staying in Eureka Springs."

"So where do you suggest I check, great detective?"

Ryder thought for a moment before answering. "Try the Crescent Hotel." Ryder looked out the window at the crowd of passengers being separated according to what rail car they had been riding in. Alex was outside questioning those who were on the Biloxi Blues. He turned and headed for the front door of the car.

"Yep, right, so much that you put the wrong person in the prison." Culberson said, just as Ryder started to step off the train. Ryder turned to back to him and said.

"Chief Culberson, why don't you tell your idea to Agent Alexander? I am sure she would love to hear it." Ryder's lips formed a small mocking grin and he stepped down from the car, he knew Alex did not like to be questioned by local flatfoots. He remembered the first time he met her at the K.C.P.D. sitting in a chair swinging that foot back and forth as she watched him approach her, standing and telling him how it was going to be and that she was in charge, and if he felt otherwise there was the door.

The Old Frisco Station with its Victorian style had seen many changes throughout its life. The current one was brick. Its sloping roof lines and large windows that gazed out on to the tracks, had seen many visitors arrive, and the other side had seen those that packed up and left. It was in the early 1960's that the last passengers boarded. It wasn't until later, that the white paint was stripped from the bricks, and their crimson soul appeared once again in the form of a visitor center for the city. Ryder lifted the yellow police tape, and stepped under it. He walked down the brick pathway to a group of people that had been gathered under a canopy on the other end of the visitor's center. It was the passengers of the 'Biloxi Blue'. Alex and two officers were all questioning them.

Excuse me." Ryder heard a timid voice say. He turned and looked down. There was a mousey appearing man standing next to him, wearing large round glasses with heavy lenses that kept making the glasses slide down on his broad nose. He kept pushing his glasses up with his index finger. "Are you one of the policemen that will be asking questions; because I have something to say."

"They will get around to you; you'll just have to wait." Ryder said.

"But sir." The mousey man said as he pulled on Ryder's jacket. "This is about the man on the train, the one that was killed. Everyone is saying he was alone, but—but he wasn't. He was with a strange woman, a—a woman he met at the hotel—the—the Crescent Hotel."

"The Crescent?" Ryder asked, turning and facing him.

"Yes sir. That is where we are staying, him and me and my wife Gertie," he grinned broadly, making his glasses slip, and he pushed them back up on his nose as he continued. "Her real name is Gertrude, but she doesn't like that, so everyone calls her Gertie." Yeah, as if that were any better, Ryder thought. Again the man's glasses slipped and he pushed them back on his nose, and readjusted them. "Anyway, he saw this young beauty at the restaurant. But she was strange."

"How was she strange?"

"She kept asking about marriage." The man replied as he pushed his glasses up on his face.

"She wanted to marry this man?"

"Oh heavens, no!" He laughed sounding as if he had the hiccups. Again his glasses slipped and he pushed them back up on his nose. "She kept talking about a marriage in the hereafter, that if two were joined in death would they remain that way forever. She wanted to know if it wasn't allowed in heaven could it be allowed in hell." He focused his eyes on Ryder's face, looking up at him; the man's eyes looked huge, being magnified through the thick lens. "Then she did something crazy."

"What was that?"

167

"She—well, Ted bought her ticket— he started to get on board, then she went to the bathroom, came out with dark hair, and bought another ticket for the fancy car."

Ryder looked the crowd over. He yelled, "Alex, get over here." Alex walked over. "You have that photo of Lillian? She handed him the photo and Ryder held it in front of the mousy man. "Is this her? Is this the woman he was with?"

The man readjusted his glasses again, moving his head back and forth till the image came into focus. "Yes, that is her but her name wasn't Lillian, it was real fancy sounding uhh…"

"Celeste?" Ryder asked

"Yes, that is it."

"You said she was with him?" Alex asked. "Rick, I checked that car. I remember the man and even this guy, they were sitting across from each other. But I don't remember any woman sitting next to the vic."

"That is because…" the mousy man said, looking at Alex. "…She got up to go to the bathroom, just a little while before you came in asking us questions."

"Rick, I checked the bathroom, there was no one there. How did she get off?"

"I saw her in the Silver Feather; that means she got past us." Ryder said, handing the photo back to Alex. "Did she ever come back?"

"No…well yes, in just a little while she came back and grabbed her bag and went back to the bathroom." The mousey man giggled, sounding as if he was a middle school girl at a slumber party. "I though she must have a weak bladder. My Gertie's sister has that problem; she can't go anywhere."

"Did you see her anymore?"

"No," He said softly. "The only other person I saw was a policeman that came aboard just before we entered the station."

"Before? Are you positive it was before? Before we stopped?"

"Oh yes, most certainly." The mousy man said again, pushing up his glasses on his nose, "She patted Gertie and told her everything was going to be all right."

"She?" Alex asked, " It was a woman?" Alex held up the photo again. "Could it have been her?"

"Yes, maybe, possibly, I just don't remember much."

"What do you mean?" Ryder asked, taking out his notebook form his inside jacket pocket.

"Well, to be truthful sir, I...well just don't even remember pulling into the station. All I remember is this strong flowery smell, and then the next thing I know is we are being asked to get off the car."

Chapter 20

"It is right at the beginning of the next block on the right." The woman at the visitor's center instructed Ryder as she pointed down Main Street. Alex walked up and said.

"Rick, they are going to get the train ready for the return trip in one hour."

"I thought we might stay here." Ryder said as he stood at the edge of the street, the police just now allowing the traffic to start moving again and not being rerouted on Webster Street. "She has to be somewhere in this town."

"You really think we can find her?" Alex asked. "Besides, I have to get back home."

"What is it with you?" Ryder asked, turning and facing her as the locomotive began moving forward on the tracks. The warning bell at the crossing began ringing and the lights flashed as the gate came down, blocking traffic. "When you were doing this in Kansas City you wouldn't stop, we were on her case twenty-fours a day. You act as if you have to be home before dark, what are you the anti-vampire?"

"Not dark, just before sunrise. I promised someone I would be there to watch the sunrise." Alex explained as the locomotive began backing up, switching to another track.

"Do you love them that much?"

"More than I have ever loved anyone else." She said tenderly, with a soft smile, her eyes twinkling as he had never seen them before. She appeared loving, caring, not a hardened Special Agent. "Even more than you." Then the softness faded, the corners of her mouth dropped back down. "Can I have the keys to your car? I will come back and pick you up tomorrow."

"No," Ryder said. "I will go back with you."

"Then how about we go and get something to eat?" Alex said.

Sounds good, but there is something else I have to do." Ryder said as they began walking towards downtown. As soon as they stepped onto Main Street his eyes were drawn to something that rose above all the other buildings. Like a moth drawn to the flame of a blazing campfire, he just kept walking. They would pass by a little sandwich shop, and Alex offered to stop, but he just kept walking, his eyes glued to the witch cap on the building that just kept reaching higher and higher into the clear blue sky with each step he took. Soon the round crown tower made him tilt his head back to see the witches cap and the ornate finial at the top.

"What about this place?" Alex asked, stopping in front of the 'Main Street Ice Cream and Sandwich Shop.'

"Huh?" Ryder answered, clearly not interested in what the choices were; he just kept looking across the street at the old building. "Yeah, this looks fine." He replied as his eyes turned towards the building on the other side of the street. "You go in and get us a table."

"The train is going to leave in less than an hour." Alex explained. "You may not have time to order."

"You know what I like, so go ahead and order for me." Ryder said as he began to walk towards the intersection.

"Are you sure you don't want me to go with you?" She asked grabbing the front door to the shop. He shook his head and said as he crossed the street.

"This is something I have to do by myself."

Ryder was awestruck by the detail this place had. The fish scale shingles design just below the words 'Crawford County Bank', and the horseshoe and bell arches over the windows on the third floor, placed in between the turned columns, that, when he was kid, always made him think of candy canes. It reminded him of standing here with his mother and father, his father telling him how he was going to buy this place someday. The segmented arches and labels around the windows on the second and first floors, slat- like columns that ended in what appeared to be a flower turned around backwards.

Ryder pulled out the slip of paper that had the address written on it, to double check and he grabbed the knob and the door opened with a low groan. It was dark inside, the only light emitting through was that from the windows. Gleaming down on the hardwood floors, the top portion of the windows were stained glass, a rough mixture of red, yellow and green that formed no image. There were several dark colored small round tables with chairs around them. It appeared that at one time this might have been a restaurant. However, the cross on the window made him guess it might have even been some sort of church.

Ryder laughed at the thought that someone like his father could even be in a church without the roof caving in. Seeing a light switch on the wall he flipped it on and revealed the tin plated ceiling. He routed himself around the tables and past the old bank counter that was now being used as a bar, when he heard THUMP from upstairs. He began climbing the grand stair case, runner after runner, each one letting out a muted whine as he climbed to the second floor. When the old bank was being built it was here that the owner and his family lived and now there signs that modern remodeling had been done; a side by side refrigerator, even a microwave on the counter.

Decorated in an inviting appeal of hues in green tones, from the pale tint on the walls, to the medium tones of the trim, to the emerald runner on the hardwood floors of the hall, the bedrooms were a mixture of Victorian style beds, tables, and hot tubs that reeked of modernization. The hall was decorated with a long woven runner and a pair of tables pushed up next to the walls. Ryder had just exited one bedroom when he heard a low groaning moan shattering the stillness around him.

Down the hall a panel door swung into the room. Reaching under his coat, he slipped the Glock from it holster; he drew it up and aimed down its sights, his finger resting alongside the trigger guard. He took a deep breath as a shadowy figure emerged.

A teenage girl appeared in the hall; seeing Ryder she screamed. "Keep your hands where I can see them." Ryder said, the law enforcement training coming out of him. Standing before him was a thirteen-year- old girl, tall; thin as the rails they had just ridden down on, legs and arms longer than other parts of her body, as if she would have trouble just getting accustomed to her body. Her face was pretty. She had long rich sable-like hair that flowed down over her shoulders and coffee colored eyes were frozen in terror; lastly, dimples that appeared as she forced an uncertain smile to her lips as she raised her hands.

It was strange staring down the barrel of the pistol at her, it felt as if it was wrong. He lowered the gun to his side.

"Who are you?" She sobbed; bring a shaking hand to her lightly pursed lips. "What are you doing here?"

"I am investigating a murder." Ryder said. "I am looking for someone."

"A murder," She questioned, tilting her head slightly sideways. "Who— who are looking for?"

"I am looking for…" Ryder quickly stopped speaking as he heard a board a creak from behind him and the cracking click of a revolver's hammer being pulled back. He quickly drew the pistol up, and spinning around pushed his right foot back to place his weight on it. He was staring at a young man at the point where he was breaking from being a kid and becoming a man. He wild bushy sandy hair, with deep blue eyes that were staring down the barrel of a 9 mm Smith and Wesson revolver. Again Ryder's police instincts kicked in. "POLICE! Drop the gun. DROP IT RIGHT NOW!"

Ryder's finger was now over the trigger; he was getting ready to fire. But just as with the girl before, he felt as if there something wrong about this, but the cop instinct in him told him to keep the pistol aimed.

"Rick?" The young man asked with excitement and an innocuous smile that seemed to beam from one side of his face to the other, as he let the revolver slip from his grip and it dropped to the floor with a subdued thump, as it landed on the runner.

"It is you! Isn't it, Rick?" The young man said. Perplexed, Ryder bored his eyes into the young man as he walked towards him. Ryder lowered the pistol to his side as the young man passed by Ryder and over to the young girl. "It is Ricky!" He said again with glee as he placed his arm around the shoulders of the young girl.

"We have heard a lot about you." The young girl said with a grin that again showed her dimples. Ryder's confusion was bristling like a bull thistle to bare feet, as he felt her long arms wrap around him and the warmth of her face against his chest. She looked up at him and flashed her toothy grin as she added. "Know that you are loved."

"Okay," Ryder replied skeptically, as she released him from her embrace and rejoined the young man. "Do I know you?"

"No," the young man said. "But we know you."

Oh gosh, Ryder thought. How do they know me? They probably want money. It seemed that right after he won it, that everyone wanted a hand out. It was then that he decided he would not just give it away, he would invest in people. "If you are looking for money, the answer is no." Ryder said as he tucked the weapon back into the holster on his side.

"I am Jonas, and this Marissa. We are your brother and sister."

"You are—you are—**my what?**" Ryder fumbled for his words as if he were a pimple faced boy at the skating rink, asking the popular girl to skate, only shouting out his last response. "I don't have a brother and sister." Ryder added, perplexed.

"We have the same father, different mothers." Marissa said. Ryder reached up and pulled the sunglasses from his face as he stared at them, oddly enough he saw a resemblance; in Marissa to photos of his grandmother when she was young. Well Jonas and I have the same mother, his father died." Marissa quickly left and disappeared behind the door of a bedroom. She quickly reappeared, holding a framed photograph in her hands. She walked up to him and held the photo out as she asked.

"This is you, isn't it?"

Ryder took the photo. It was of him, his father, and his mother. He was only about seven years old. "I was playing dress up in the attic one day," Marissa said as Ryder continued to stare, remaining immersed in the photo. "I was looking for jewelry to go with my dress and I found this old jewelry box, and that was in there." Ryder looked up at her, his sister.

"Marissa showed me, so I approached the old man." Jonas said as Ryder handed the photo to him. He really isn't my father, but I was only four years old when my dad died. I don't remember him that much." Ryder looked down at the photo and Jonas continued "He wouldn't tell me anything. I kept bugging him every day..." He raised his eyes back to Ryder as he handed the photo back to Marissa. "On Easter morning he told us 'that he had a family before but they all were killed in a car wreck.'"

"Yeah, good old pops." Ryder said with distain. "If the truth doesn't fit, make up a lie."

"Then we saw you on TV; you were talking about the Kansas City Butcher." Marissa said as she clutched the photo to her chest. "That is when we knew he lied. That I had a brother out there; one that was part of me."

"That is when he told us that your mother took you away and he never saw you again, and it was just too painful for him to have the photo of you around." Jonas said as he walked over and picked up the pistol off the floor. "I wouldn't have shot you."

"I know," Ryder said. "Otherwise you would be dead. Everything he told you is a lie. My mother died, and then he married another woman…"

"I know all about it," Marissa said, interrupting him," All about you and Annalisa how she was his daughter and how he divorced your step mother and then married my mom." "I had to do a family tree for history class." Marissa smiled, showing her dimples, making the hardened wall that Ryder had placed up around him for all these years crumble down as it were made of wet paper. "I am so sorry for what he did to you." Again she hugged him.

Ryder was not sure how to respond; he was always the one in control, being it on a gridiron shouting out plays, or in an interrogation room getting that needed confession. Now he stood here struggling to find a word to say. "Uh—are you two hungry?" Ryder managed to say. "If you like we can go to the Ice Cream shop; I have a friend I have to meet."

"Sure." Marissa said. "Just let me leave a note for mom."

There was still a strange feeling inside of Ryder as they walked across the street and towards the Main Street Ice Cream and Sandwich Shop. It felt as if there were a thousand fingers inside of his chest, ticking his breast bone, with another hand squeezing his heart as he pulled the door open and entered.

Walking across the black and white checker board floor, it was stepping back into the 1950's, one could just assume that they could walk down the street and order a brand new Packard from the old ads on the wall. The murder was a thing that was unheard of here, with pictures of Andy Taylor and Barney Fife of the Andy Griffith Show adorning the walls; there was no worrying about calories, as it was here that childhood began again.

Ryder felt as if arms were wrapping around his chest, squeezing the life out of him as Alex looked up from munching on her sandwich and asked the question he wasn't sure he could answer.

"Who are they?"

"This is my..." he paused, because he had never really had to say these words before, "brother and sister."

"You're what?" Alex said choking on the sandwich she was eating, quickly wiping her mouth with a napkin that she grabbed from the red and white Coke napkin holder on the table. Coughing again as she lifted up a glass of pop, she took a drink and returned the gaze to Ryder, to explain further.

"This is my brother Jonas and..." Ryder grinned as he placed his hand on the teen's shoulder as he added. "and my sister Marissa." Alex was still stunned as Ryder seated himself next to Marissa. "Order whatever you would like."

"Usual?" The server asked as she approached the table, speaking to Marissa, and over to Jonas. "What about you?" Jonas nodded and the server continued. "All right then, cheeseburger, light mustard, tomato, lettuce, pickles and onion with a chocolate shake."

"And can we hurry those up." Alex asked. "We need to meet the train."

"Don't worry, you will make it." The waitress said, quickly turning to turn the order in.

"So you are all taking the train too?" Jonas asked. "Me too."

"So, did you meet your father?" Alex asked.

"No, he wasn't there."

"He is in Eureka Springs," Jonas broke into the conversation, "I am going there to meet him, he is supposed to pick me up in Springdale. I will tell him that I saw you."

"No!" Ryder cracked back. "Don't tell him anything about me."

"Wait a minute," Marissa said. "You told me you were there looking for someone? Something about murder, is dad a suspect?"

Ryder could see the uncertainty rising up like a storm cloud over the plains, on her face. He had only met this young lady a few minutes ago, but he felt as if he had known her all his life. As bad as he wanted to make his father pay for the hurt he felt, he couldn't harm her, so he just smiled and reached over to her and said. "I just want to ask him some questions." As he pushed her hair back out of her face he added, "Don't worry."

"I won't." She said with a grin, which once again flashed those dimples that made him feel helpless as a new born foal trying to stand for the first time. The waitress placed their plates down in front of them and left. Marissa lifted the bun off her hamburger and picked up the salt shaker, then began salting her dill pickles. Ryder looked over at her and a small grin appeared.

"Oh, don't mind her." Jonas said as he lifted his bun off and began adding more ketchup on his burger. "She always has been a little strange."

"I only do this because…"

"It makes the pickles taste better." Ryder said with her, before he took the shaker and added salt to his pickles too. "What is strange is …" And again Ryder joined in with her as they said. "Putting ketchup on a hamburger that is for fries." She looked up at him and revealed a small secret smile that could only be between brother and sister.

It was a strange feeling for Ryder; for once in his life he felt connected to this world, not an empty sail searching for a gust of the wind that could guide him. Not to be sitting alone at a TV tray on Thanksgiving eating a TV dinner or to awake on Christmas morning and it was just like any other day. He now had a family.

"So is dad a suspect about the murder on the train?" Jonas asked

"No," Ryder said just as he began to take a bite of his burger. "It is about some kids he knew in high school. How did you know about the murder?"

"I listen a lot to the scanner; know all the codes: one –eighty-seven." Jonas said, before taking a sip of his milk shake. " Homicide."

177

"Yes, but how do you know all that?"

"That is what I want I do. I want to be a cop, just like you."

"That is all he has ever wanted to be." Marissa said after swallowing a bite of her burger. "That was his favorite game to play. He was always arresting me."

Ryder sat listening, trying quickly to finish up the burger and milkshake so they could make the train. It was a little odd feeling that there was someone who wanted to follow in his footsteps, but at the same time Ryder felt a sense of pride as Jonas continued. "So who do you think stabbed the guy on the train?"

Alex said, lifting her cell phone up. "Just got a message, they are starting to board. We have to go!" Ryder paid the bill and left a generous tip as he always did, and they headed outside.

In the distance the blast of the train horn, spread out over the town, warning that boarding was about to begin. "Marissa." A woman's voice shouted out. Ryder turned and saw a woman in her early fifties, plump, friendly and pretty with dark hair in a sensible appearing print dress and white tennis shoes.

"Mom, 'com mere,'" Marissa said, her southern drawl coming out of her. "There is somebody I want you to meet." As the woman approached and smiled, he could see where Marissa got her dimples, along with her dark hair, yet it was shorter and slightly tinted with a hint of gray where it curled around her eyes. She was younger than his father, by more than ten years. "This is our brother, Rick Ryder. This is our mother, Mary."

"It is nice to meet you, Mr. Ryder." Mary said offering her hand daintily to him.

"It is my pleasure to meet you." He said before kissing her hand. "But just call me Rick."

"Ever since these two have learned about you that is all they have been talking about." She placed an arm on her daughter's back and continued. "Especially this one. All I ever hear about is her big brother Ricky. I am making chili for supper; we would love to have you join us...." She looked over at Alex and added, "Both of you."

The train horn sounded again making Alex turn and stared down Main Street at the depot as Ryder and Mary were making small talk. "I can't, but I am staying in Eureka Springs at the Crescent, why don't you all stay there, I will reserve some rooms."

"I have to meet Ryan there in a few days..."

Alex twisted back, clearly upset. "The holidays are coming up. You all can get together then. It is getting ready to leave. I have to get back home! We have to go. Now!"

"How about a photo," Jonas asked, holding up his cell phone with a camera in it. "Get over there Marissa." Ryder got between them and posed for the photo. After goodbyes were said, they raced up the block and to the depot. "Made it just in time again, huh?" The conductor said. "Since we are short one car, it is going to be cramped quarters." Ryder started to explain that it was okay, and get aboard, but before he could move the conductor grabbed him by the arm and pulled him to the side. The conductor lowered his voice so the other passengers and Jonas could not hear. "You think the killer got off, or could she still be aboard?"

"The cops searched the train, didn't they?"

"Yes, but..." He lowered his voice even more till it was barely a whisper, "...they never found her?"

"Don't worry, "Ryder said. "I am sure she is long gone."

The conductor turned back to Jonas and asked in a normal tone "Joining us on the return trip too Jonas?

"Going to go see dad again, with my brother." Jonas said.

"This is him?" The conductors asked looking at Ryder, "The guy that won the big bucks?" Then be our guest, to anything you would like, sir? In fact, we can place you in the Silver Feather; you can have a car all to yourself." He guided them over to the next car. They climbed aboard, and with a jolt the train began its return trip. They sat at one table under the dome portion of the car; Ryder, and Jonas across from Alex.

By the time they reached Frog Bog darkness stretched out like a wing over the train, the howl of the train's horn wailing over the marshland. Alex got up and walked down stairs to the bathroom. Ryder's mind was wandering again as he stared down at the waters that held all

179

kinds of surprises, from fish to frogs and even gators, it was not somewhere he wanted to get stuck.

"You think this could be the Kansas City Butcher?" He heard Jonas ask. Ryder turned his head to him and Jonas continued. "You know, like they are showing on TV? All those dumb people that are protesting, saying you put the wrong person in prison. Makes me so mad!" He said, raising his voice then calming down again. "You got the right person, didn't you?" Jonas reached into his pocket and pulled out a silver coin, and began flipping it over and over his fingers, going from his index finger to his pinkie, and then reversing the direction. "One day I am going to be as good a cop as you are."

"Jonas, I am honored that you want to be like me. But you can't be me; you've got to be who you are." Ryder paused for just a moment, shadows of the night dancing over his face as they passed by a town. "This job isn't like you see on TV, it is not 'shoot outs' every day excitement, there are a lot of times it is nothing. And don't do it to impress someone, especially him."

"You mean the old man?" Jonas answered as the train horn sounded again just before they went over a crossing. Ryder stared out the window at the automobiles, stopped and waiting for the train to cross. He didn't turn back, Ryder just spoke, as he still stared out the window at the ribbons of light of homes as the train passed by. Again he was feeling that emptiness, like a discarded bottle lying along the side of the road.

"What is he like?" Ryder asked.

"What was he like when you knew him?" Jonas answered back as he dropped the coin and it fell onto the table, ringing out like a bell.

"Like someone with a new kitten." Ryder said slowly, turning away from the window as the train cleared the town and vacant countryside once again filled the windows. "When the newness wears off so does the attention."

"And you will do anything to get it back?" Jonas replied softly.

"But there is nothing you can do to get it back." Ryder replied, standing up. "No matter how many touchdowns you make or cases you solve."

"I am going to the bathroom. It is downstairs, right?" Ryder nodded as he saw the lights in the ceiling blink as Alex walked back up the stairs. Jonas had to wait till she passed by before he could go downstairs. She walked over and sat down.

"I was beginning to wonder about you." Ryder said as he sat across from her.

"I thought you two needed some time alone just to talk. After I rushed you off down there."

"Yeah," Ryder said, disenchanted. "This time I thought I was missing out on something, because I didn't have a dad, but if you don't have anything, are you really missing anything?" He relaxed in the seat, draping his arm over the seat back, gazing back out the window at all the landscape that was hidden by the velvet drapes. Only occasionally broken by the blink of lights coming from a farm house along the sides of the track, only to again hide the foes that stalked its prey in the night.

He turned back to her, and noticed the puzzled look on Alex's face, her cell phone clutched in her hand as she draped it out across the table. She didn't say anything at first; her haggard appearance said it all. "What is it?" Ryder asked.

"I just got a call. There has been another murder."

The train horn sound one long blast as Ryder leaned forward and asked "Where?"

"Eureka Springs; the Crescent hotel, they were on the ghost tour. They opened the freezer in the old morgue…" Alex's face became like cinders in a steam boiler. "I don't know how to tell you this." She sighed before adding "It was Dina."

Chapter 21

The shadows of the city of Springdale began falling down through the glass dome, and painting their way across their faces, as the train began to slow and enter the station. "What's wrong?" Jonas asked as he came up the stairs.

"There has been another murder." Ryder said as the train jerked to a stop.

"What! Where?" His reply was of shock.

"Eureka Springs."

"That is impossible! I mean, wasn't our suspect in Van Buren? How could she get up here so fast?" Jonas asked as there was a loud hiss outside as the air brakes released. "It takes over two hours to get there by car."

"I told local authorities we will be there ASAP." Alex said as she stood up.

"I thought you had to get home?" Ryder said still staring out the window, gazing at the sign that read 'Springdale' .

"As long as I am there by sunrise." She replied as Ryder turned his head to face her, she added, "I guess duty comes first. You ready?"

He nodded his head and stood up; following behind Jonas opened the door and jumped out. Ryder and Alex stepped down from the car as they began to make their way back to the Killer Bee in the parking lot. Ryder stopped for just a moment as he stared out across the parking lot a late model Chevrolet bathed in the dim yellow security lights; he saw a face he hadn't seen since he was in high school. Still with a full head of hair, now time had caught up with him and it had become like platinum, with hints of early morning frost at the ends and on his painter brush mustache. Even at fifty feet away Ryder could see the man's features, his come-hither glance in his cold steel eyes, that whimsical smile that lifted only part of his upper lip, creating a trap for women.

"Oh gosh, that is a gorgeous man!" Alex exclaimed as she glanced over, as Jonas began walking towards the Chevy.

"Not if you see what is inside." Ryder grumbled, holding the passenger door of the Dodge open for Alex.

"You mean that is..." Alex said looking back at Ryder and then stole one glance back to his father, who was getting in on the driver's side. She looked back again at Ryder and added. "You look like your father."

"No I don't! "He snapped back, furious that she would even think such a thing. "I look like my mother. Get it!" He said angrily. Alex sat down in the front seat and he slammed the door. Ryder got in the driver's seat. He glanced up into the mirror and saw the Chevy beginning to pull out. Ryder quickly fired the car up and slammed into reverse, and backed out in a hurry. He pushed the gearshift back down into drive and sped quickly towards the exit of the parking lot. As he passed by the side of the Chevy, he floored the car and the tires began to spin, in a smoke filled cloud with a deafening scream. He let up off the gas just a little and the tires caught traction, and the Dodge sped away down the street.

****

Flashing lights were still surrounding the Crescent Hotel when they arrived, and a Eureka Springs officer was swinging a flashing light back and forth in front of the opening to Prospect Avenue, but a quick show of Alex's badge got them inside.

Ryder parked the car behind a city cruiser and they dashed inside. Just heading down stairs to the basement there was a feeling that there was someone walking with them. Restless spirits caught forever, buying into a promise of life, but only receiving death, or could it be Dina's ghost joining all the others already trapped here. Whatever it was, Alex must have felt it too for Ryder felt her fingers gripped around his upper arm, as they navigated down a hallway, past wooden shelves loaded with things, that the mind wondered what did go on down here? The closer they got the creepier it became.

"Thought you didn't believe in spooks?' Ryder asked, slightly turning his head towards her.

"I don't," She replied. "The floor is not that great, and I am wearing high heels."

"Seems pretty smooth to me," Ryder said as his mind recalled the tales of when Baker was running this as a cancer treatment hospital. The bodies of those who eventually died from his 'snake oil treatments, were taken down here and placed in a huge walk in refrigerator, waiting for autopsy. There was a large door partly open, just enough to allow the light from the next room to shine around and under it.

"Oh, just be a gentleman and help a lady."

Ryder pulled the door back. There were several officers in the room roaming about, C.I.D taking photos and collecting evidence. Ryder had been in many morgues with the cold air blowing down his neck, why was it this made him feel that every hair on the back of his neck was standing straight up, and even though there were ceiling vents, he could feel the icy breath of death still all around. Maybe there was something to what Alex said, he reasoned, as he glanced over at the metal table that the bodies were laid upon, a dreary light gleaming down on it.

"You again?" Ryder heard a voice say he turned and saw Detective Ron Shepherd standing there as he scowled at Ryder. "This is really beginning to piss me off! I thought this killer of yours was down south. So how did she get back up here? You want to answer me that?" Ryder did not have an answer to that so he just remained quiet. Shepherd lifted up a bottle of Diet Pepsi, unscrewed the top, took a sip, and then replaced the cap before rubbing the back of his neck with his thumb, before he spoke again. "Well, it is getting more gruesome, this one nearly made me puke." As he spoke he began to lead them across the room.

The tin lined walls had dark stains upon them that looked very much like blood, and the ghostly blue light that was casting from a single drop down light over the examining table was adding to an uncanny feeling that somewhere Frankenstein's monster was going to rise up.

The refrigerator was being blocked by two officers still busy snapping photos. They stopped in front of a smaller room, the walls lined with corrugated tin, with a large wooden door, the green light casting down gave it a supernatural effect. As Detective Shepherd nodded for the officer to stand aside, Ryder saw a true spine-chilling scene.

It was the body of Dina Grosstree resting on the floor, her back up against a blood stained wall. Her body was wrapped in a sheet covering her head on her. Her bare stuck out under the bottom edge of the sheet, revealing her bright pink painted toe nails. Ryder stepped inside the refrigerator. He carefully kneeled down beside her, making sure he was not kneeling in the blood on the left-hand side. He pulled the top of the sheet back and she stared back him, that glassy flat eyed stare he had seen so many times before. On one side of her face, her cheek was battered and bruised, with a small indention that looked like the letter C cut into the flesh of her lower lip, the back of her head her hair caked in partly dried blood.

"Who found her?" Ryder asked sympathetically, not lifting his gaze from her.

"The ghost tour," Detective Shepherd replied. "They came down and the door was closed; the guide opened it and scared the hell out of everyone. At first the guests thought it was a gag, even taking pictures and putting them on Facebook. When they found out it was real, they ran out of here."

"So they come for the ghost but when they find murder they run?" Ryder asked in a sarcastic tone. He carefully lifted the sheet back more, viewing her torso; she was dressed in a pale green evening gown, with spaghetti strip, one that had fallen off of her shoulder. The center of the dress from her breast bone to her pelvis was ripped open, revealing the incision in her abdomen. It was just over eight inches long, jagged, slightly angled. The skin and muscle pulled back hastily, the cut not following the natural line between the abdominal muscles. It was done haphazardly.

There was always something unsettling seeing a face he knew, left him with an icy cold feeling inside, as he tried to choke back any feeling he had. He could feel Alex's hair tickle the side of his face, as she leaned down over behind him.

He could smell her perfume he turned to her and they were nose to nose. "Something look familiar to you?" He asked.

"To familiar," She replied turning away from him. She leaned down and touched the woman's face, right under her eye. Alex lifted her hand and looked at her thumb, it was thick coating of makeup, and suddenly the feel of Alex's hair on him was gone.

"A single stab wound to the back. Looks likes it is the Eureka Slayer." Ryder heard Detective Shepherd say.

"Hotel sheet?" Ryder asked as he stood up.

"Yeah, that is the way we found her, covered up." Detective Shepherd said as he opened up a bottle of Diet pop and took a sip, before replacing the cap. "It is like they wanted to take care of her."

Ryder stepped out of the refrigerator and looked around the room. "Where is Agent Alexander?"

"Your pal the agent went upstairs to question the husband; he is where all the other witnesses are being kept; the Crystal Ballroom."

Ryder walked back up the stairs, and had just entered the first floor when he saw Alex. She was standing there with a far-away look on her face, as if she wanted to be somewhere else. She was talking on her phone.

"I can't make it tonight." She said clearly upset and almost sounding angry. "Yes I know! But I have to work late. I know! Oh course I do." She didn't ever see him, but turned her back to him, pushed her tresses back over her ear and just as if a different person had appeared, a smile broke across her face, and her tone became tender. "Hi baby," Alex said, her smile growing even brighter. "You know how much I love you, don't you?" She paused as she was listening for the reply. "But I have to work late tonight. " Again there was a pause." She lowered her head slightly, along with her voice. "Yes, I have to help someone. But you just go to bed and I promise you I will be right there in the morning and we can watch the sun get out of bed together. All right baby, I love you." She made a kissing sound on the phone and ended the call, turned back around and was face to face with him.

"Uhh—"she hesitated for the words, knowing she had been caught. "Okay, I am living with someone now." She tossed her head firmly, making her hair fall back down over her shoulders as she began to walk down the hall towards the ball room near the front of the hotel, with Ryder following behind her. "I didn't want you to know after, well you know, after our past." She stopped and glanced over her shoulder at him. "Besides, you have Yakira now, and you don't need…"She turned back and continued to walk towards the huge double doors that led into the ballroom. "Why should you care now?"

"How old, Belle?"

Again she stopped; when he called that name it wasn't about business, it was personal. She muffled a phony laugh. "What difference

186

would that make? Maybe I am a gold digger shacking up with some rich old guy, or maybe I am a cougar, and I got me a young stud." She began to reach for the door but Ryder's words made her freeze.

"The child," Ryder asked. "How old is she?" She didn't reply and Ryder continued. "Belle, I know a mother's voice when I hear it."

She slowly let go of the door handle and dropped her head down, as if she couldn't face him and she tenderly replied. "Her name is Ceelia, she is almost three years old, and she is..." He saw the corners of her mouth draw up in a smile again. "...and she is beautiful Ricky, long dark hair, bright blue eyes." She turned back to him, her eyes were misting with tears of pure joy again. She allowed her gaze to drop to the floor. "There is nothing more beautiful than she is."

"Adopted?"

"Huh?" She asked, raising her head.

"She is adopted, right?"

"Yes," Alex replied turning back to the door. "I got her a little while after the K.C. case wrapped up. I just wanted someone in my life after that." Again she tossed her head, and that cold-sober look returned to her face as she added. "We have questions to ask and answers to get."

At first glance, the only way to describe the grand ballroom was one word-grand. With its gleaming hardwood floor, beautiful crystal chandeliers suspended from soaring ceilings, the glimmer of their light twinkling in single crystals, swaying in a gentle breeze that swept across the floor, with not a pillar in sight. It was made for dancing; one could just close their eyes and envision the grand ladies adorned in their sequined and velvet evening gowns, led over the floor by their gentlemen, as the orchestra, led by the grand piano played on. Now all that was left was the piano pushed over to one side. The dancers were now tables and chairs and the only onlookers were the arched shaped transoms above the paned windows that were flanked by crystal sconces mounted on the rich wood walls.

The round tables were dispersed around the ballroom with several Victoriana style chairs around them, white table cloths adorning them like shrouds, waiting for the every Sunday mornings grand breakfast buffet. Death was no stranger to this place; it was the tales of ghosts that fed the appetite, but murder, that was rare. Ryder looked out at a group of fourteen souls gathered around various tables. A veritable multitude of suspects and witnesses, dressed in anything from jeans and well faded t-shirts, to one man dressed in a tie and tails, complete with a top hat, plus Eureka Spring Detectives questioning them.

Sitting at a table by himself was a dark skinned man; it was Ryder's former commander of the Kansas City homicide division, Captain Craig Grosstree. He was dressed in a dark dinner jacket and slacks, the bow tie, hanging loosely around the collar of his white shirt, the top two buttons opened, with a small blood stain appearing just below the lapel of the jacket on his shirt. Ryder walked over to the table. Looking up at Ryder, Grosstree said with anguish "Rick, she is gone."

Grosstree had changed since the last time he had seen him last year. His once dark hair was still showing streaks of silver, as was his bristly mustache, but he was thinner, much thinner. He had lost over 75 pounds so much that his wedding ring and his Black Onyx initial ring twisted around freely on his hand. If he hadn't known that face so well, Ryder might have just passed by him, believing him to just be another witness, instead of the victim's widower. "I heard it could have been the Slayer that got her." He turned his head slightly and saw Alex. "It is god to see you Agent Alexander."

"Has always Captain Grosstree." She said her tone as formal and stiff as a collar ironed with spray starch. "May we sit down?"

"Yes of course." He said.

Ryder sat down at the table, across from him and Alex sat down next to him. It was clear to see that he had been grieving, his eyes puffy, red and swollen. The hotel staff had made coffee and served it. A thin young man approached and Ryder recognized him as one of the bellhops his name was Timmy, he was tall and muscular built, mostly likely an athlete. "Coffee, Ryder?" He asked, remembering that he didn't like to be called Mr. Ryder. "Cream and sugar, right?" He set down a saucer with a cup of tan colored coffee in front of Ryder. "And you ma'am, black." He placed another cup and saucer down in front of Alex. "And you sir, would you like more?" Captain Grosstree shook his head and the young man left.

"I saw her." Grosstree said lifting the half full cup of coffee to his lips with shaking hands and taking a sip. "Damn it Ryder! I thought we had the Butcher" He said.

"We do." Ryder said firmly, clasping his fingers together as he rested his elbows on the table. "She is locked up."

"How can you say that? It is clear that this other woman you have been chasing, she is the killer. She killed my Dina." He turned to Alex who just sit in her chair, turned slightly sideways, her legs crossed staring at him. "What is the damn FBI going to do about this? I demand to know." He turned back to Ryder. "It don't huh? A couple of old Kansas City boys can take care of it right?"

"She didn't kill Dina." Ryder said as he carefully lifted his cup of hot coffee and took a sip before continuing. Ryder again took a sip of coffee and set the cup back down on the saucer. "There was no note."

"What note? Maybe the paper lost it or isn't telling anyone. Come on you have seen these dumb hicks that calling themselves officers, they probably lost it."

Ryder took another sip of coffee before replying. "The ones given to me. Before each murder, before the notes were sent to the newspaper, she sent me a note, address to me. There was no note for this murder."

"So then it was the copy cat." Grosstree said. "Now, I am going to help you and we will find this killer!" He said, raising his voice as he tapped his initial ring face first into the table top. "The department gave me some time off so I will help you find the killer."

"I know about the time off Craig. What happen?"

"Damn it Ryder, it is all these you officers coming in. They don't know what police work is about. Real police work." Again Grosstree slammed his ring down on to the table. "All they care about is sensitivity. Worried that someone's feeling might get hurt. So I told him to 'quit being a little'... well apparently there is no freedom of speech anymore. Young little..." Again he slammed his ring down into the table, leaving a perfect impression in the table top, revealing the prefect letter 'C'.

"You always do that when you get upset. I remember when I was a rookie on the squad and I made a mistake, letting a suspect get the best of me. You chewed me out, banging that ring into your desk."

"I remember that too." Alex said. "When the second murder happened in Kansas City and the FBI was called in. You kept hammering that ring into the desk, telling me that I wasn't needed, that your department and your super detective here…" Alex pointed her thumb at Ryder and continued. …that they could take care of it."

"Agent Alexander, that is before I got to know you and how brilliant an agent you are." Grosstree said.

"Could I see that ring?" She asked as she looked over at Ryder and smiled as she said. "There is a special friend I would like to get one for." He removed the ring and handed it to her.

"Craig, when was the last time you saw Dina alive?" Ryder asked.

"Early this evening, around seven. We were getting ready to go out to dinner at Le Stick Nouveau, you heard of it?" Grosstree said as Alex looked at his ring.

"Good place, good food, perfect for a date night." Ryder replied. "I would recommend it."

"Anyway," Grosstree said as he finished up his coffee. "It was part of this package I won; a second honeymoon and we had to dress in our finest so that the maître d' would know who we are, because there something special that was going to occur. She left the room; she was going to go do something."

"What was she going to do?"

"I don't remember. I was busy getting dressed, trying to tie this blasted bow tie."

"Rick, would you like something like this?" Alex said holding the ring up for him to see and the hard scratches in the onyx.

"You really think that is me?" Ryder asked taking the ring and sniffing it. "I don't like the way this stone smells. I don't want a ring like that."

"If you don't think so, I will let Yakira know so she can look for something else." Alex said and handed Grosstree his ring back, which he slipped onto his finger.

"Now I remember." Captain Grosstree said. "I remember where she said was going. She was going to check about the ghost tour. She thought that might be fun."

"Dressed in an evening gown? She was going on the Ghost tour?"

"Well she was going to go on it and then to dinner."

"But the ghost tour started later that evening your reservations were for seven." Ryder said. He stood up and walked over to the window and looked out into the night. The parking lot was still ablaze with the flashing of emergency lights bouncing off the horrid scene of a body zipped up in a black bag being wheeled out to a nondescript plain white SUV, the traces of blue flashing lights bouncing off his face as he said indifferently. "What happened?"

"What do you mean?" Grosstree said. "I told you, she went to find out when the next ghost tour was going to be."

"That is not what you said. You said she went on the ghost tour."

"I meant she was wondering when she could do that."

"She left the room without her shoes?" Ryder turned back to him and added. "Why would she do that?"

"Why are you asking me this for?"

"Her face had bruises and cuts on it." Ryder spoke as he began to walk back to the table. "It was clear that she was roughed up. That was never a sign in any of the slayings" He walked over to the side of Grosstree and looked down at this man that he considered a friend, a mentor, almost like a father or brother. He didn't want to continue, but he just had to.

"Including a cut on her lip, that looks like the letter 'C' or…" Ryder paused before he added. "One where the letter G that has been damaged and is missing the cross bar." He pointed to the indention in the table. "Just like your ring?" Ryder tone softened asked. "You didn't mean to kill her did you?"

191

""How soon did you know?"

Ryder glanced over at Alex. "Same time she did." He said, and then returned his gaze to Grosstree.

"Thick makeup used to hide bruises," Alex said. "I had seen many times."

"The marks on her face, no sign of a struggle. I knew how Dina was, she would have fought back. But she would have fought back if it was you."

"She had another man."

"What? Who?" Ryder asked as he rested his chin in his hand, his elbow on the table while his index finger slowly stroked the side of his cheek.

"I don't know." Said as he stood and looked across the room at the piano we were going to have a wedding and the reception here, we could have all danced." He turned back and faced Ryder. "You were going to be my best man, Rick." He fought hard to hold the tears back. "Then I found out that this whole freaking trip was paid for by some other guy. We were getting ready to go to the restaurant when someone knocked on the door and he had flowers for her. I demanded to know who was giving her flowers! He told me it the same one that paid for all this. I demanded to know who it was. She stood there and lied, telling me it was because I won it. Then she did tell me she was going to go check when the next ghost tour was. I figured that she was going to go and meet him. So I grabbed her, and yes, I hit her. I saw the blood coming from her mouth. I just wanted to hold her. And tell her I was sorry." Grosstree pulled back the tears with a snuffle, closing his eyes as if it were replaying back over again. "You were right Ryder she fought back, she grabbed some scissors. She had been making this scrap book, there were scissors lying there." Grosstree shook his head and gave a scornful grin. "She came at me with the scissors…" I just pushed her away, and she fell hit her head."

"Why didn't you just report it?" Ryder asked.

"All I could think was who she was going to meet and who it was that paid for all of this? I was so angry; I just had to know who it…"

192

"It was me." Ryder said sternly. "I am the one who paid for all this hoping it might bring you two together." Ryder and Alex both stood up as Alex held out a pair of handcuffs. "You want us to do this, or someone else?"

Grosstree turned and placed his hands behind his back and letting out a shivering sigh as he said. "You." Alex handed Ryder the cuffs and he snapped them down on Grosstree's wrist.

Chapter 22

Ryder didn't say a thing after snapping the cuffs down on his former captain; he just turned and walked out of the ballroom and back into the lobby. Leaning up against one of the wooden pillars, he dropped his gaze down to the floor as the Eureka Springs police led Grosstree out the doors. As the French doors swung closed, Ryder moved towards them and glanced out the emergency light painting across his solemn expression, watching as the man he considered a brother being assisted into the Prisoner Transport Vehicle. Grosstree stood on the back bumper, turned and looked back at the hotel, and gave a slight nod to Ryder. Maybe assuring him that everything is okay. How can it be? Ryder thought as he rested his head on the cool glass, closing his eyes, he could see feel the flash of the P.T.V. then it was gone.

"Need a friend?" He heard Alex say from behind him and he raised his head.

"Want to go somewhere?" He asked, still glaring out the glass of the door.

"Where to?"

"Somewhere? Anywhere, just some place." As he said those words he pushed the door open and stepped outside. He just stood there holding the door open; it was her invitation to join him. She walked out and followed him to the Charger; again he held the door open for her, then got in and began to drive. With no place in mind to go, he was driving, twisting like a serpent searching for prey, then finding it he slammed on the brakes and the Charger slid to a stop. It was just a simple road, off of Highway 62 outside of the city limits. He pulled the Charger up next to the only other vehicle in the parking lot.

In front of them was a group of trees, with a small path that led into the woods. As he stood there holding the door open for Alex, he caught the sight of hope, a warm glow shimmering from the rest of darkness in the woods.

He headed down the path, towards the warm glow. There in front of them was a stunning glass structure- the Thorncrown Chapel. Rising up out of the woods, it towered up with the trees, with a few trees rising above the forty-eight feet, their limbs out-stretched, in the loving touch of a guardian. The warm glow was coming from inside the glass house, beaming through the double door; it appeared as a great jack-olantern, but instead of flowing out fright, it flowed out insight. Ryder felt a smile beginning to come across his face. Suddenly the glow vanished and darkness again surrounded him.

A man was coming out of the glass structure and was locking the door when they quickly approached. "Can we get inside for a moment?" Ryder asked.

"We're closed now." The man said, his attention on making sure the place was locked up. "But if you like you can come back for our Sunday Service at nine."

"How about if I give you a thousand bucks for a half an hour?" Ryder asked, pulling out his wallet. "Or just fifteen minutes?" Ryder pleaded, holding out the cash in his hand. The moonlight was beginning to weave its way through the trees and the man looked at Ryder and the desperation on his face. "Just ten minutes!"

"How about one dollar? For as long as you need it."

"What?" Ryder asked, confused, looking through his wallet; he never carried anything that small anymore. "I don't have a dollar."

"It is on me." Alex said reaching into her pocket and producing a crumpled bill and handing it to the man, who open the doors and once again the light shined out through the glass. She held the door open for them; he looked at Ryder who was walking up the aisle, between the blue cloth-covered pews. "I hope you find what you are searching for. But sometimes the thing we are searching for is inside of us." With that he left and closed the door behind him.

With over 6,000 square feet of glass and 425 windows completely encasing him, there was nowhere to hide here as he climbed up steps that lead to the altar stage. Alex stood there in between two pews, watching him. The moon hid like a blessed bride behind a veil of high flowing cirrus clouds, suspending its light for a moment. As Ryder kneeled down at the back of the structure in front of a cross in the glass, he could feel the coldness of the stone floor soaking through the thin fabric of his slacks. It was so still and peaceful, as if he were in the very mind of God. He didn't know what to say, what to pray. All he wanted was an answer.

"Why am I so weak?" He asked softly.

"What do you mean weak?" Alex asked, still standing, her fingers gripping around the backs of the pews. "You are the strongest person I know."

"If I am..." Ryder paused, staring out through the glass at the tree trunks that were wrapped by the light that was coming from the cross shaped lamps on the side pillars between the windows. He glanced back over his shoulder at her. "... How could I let a friend down?"

"How did you let him down?" she asked, climbing the steps to the stage. "You did what was right? That is what makes you strong." He felt her place her hand on his shoulder. "You remember we were talking about fathers, well it was my mother that didn't believe in me." She lifted her hand and walked over and looked out through the spotless glass. "I told her what I wanted to do-joining the FBI, she called me silly, saying what I needed was to get married and give her grandchildren, because my sister sure wasn't going to do it. It was only my dad that believed in me." She turned back and faced him, still kneeling on the floor as she added bluntly "'Anyone can stand where everyone else does, but only the strong stand where only they stand alone.' That is what he told me the day I became an agent, two days before he passed away. "She walked back to him and added. "I try to live by that, but you excel at it."

"I just want answers." Ryder said softly, closing his eyes, wanting to see a light that could only be seen when the eyes were closed. What he got was darkness. He heard Alex's footsteps as she crossed the stage, followed by the complaint of the bench legs as she sat down at the piano. Three notes rang out that were so familiar to him, three notes that any classic rock fan would know. It was the opening of 'Carry on My Wayward Son' by Kansas. She began to sing the words. He could see the light flowing through his eyelids as the bride of the sky removed her veil as the moon came out from behind the clouds and shined down through the glass opening at the peak of the roof, and down on him and on Alex at the piano, playing and singing. He stood up as she continued to play and sing, she had a remarked god voice. Ryder walked over to her. She stopped as she looked over at him and he asked with great curiosity.

"Why did you pick that?"

"I don't know, I just sat down and that is what came. Why?"

"That is my answer. I just-I just carry on." Ryder stepped down from the stage and stood in the aisle. "You know this isn't the end of these murders?" He said as he lifted his head up to the cross beams that supported the walls and the roof, the light shining through the diamond shaped openings. "The press is going to go crazy on this. Saying he was the killer all along."

"Unless this is what Lillian wanted all along, to get her mother released? She said peacefully as she walked up behind him. "You remember what we did the night we caught Celeste and she confessed?"

"I can't! I am — you – I am with Yakira."

"Not that." She said with a small smile. "When we watched the sun rise up over Blue Springs Lake, let's do that."

"But you promised your little girl that you would be there for her to watch the sunrise together." Ryder said. "You shouldn't break a promise to a child."

"Well, she is going to have to learn that is not the way the world works. You get your feelings hurt and promises are broken." Her smile widened as she added "Besides, you need a friend more."

At one time the White River flowed freely through Arkansas and Missouri, its source in the Boston Mountains of northwest Arkansas, in the Ozark–St. Francis National Forest southeast of Fayetteville. The river flowed northwards, looping through southwest Missouri, through Branson, Missouri, before diving back down into Arkansas and emptying into the mighty river itself,-the Mississippi. It's cold waters offered some of the best trout fishing that could be had. However, nearly every time there was a heavy rain, flooding would occur, farms would be washed away. To control the flooding, dams were put into place holding the water back, creating large lakes like Table Rock, Taneycomo, and Bull Shoals, and Arkansas' Beaver Lake.

Farms, bridges, even small towns were flooded over and the lake's water spread out. As the waters of the lakes called out, the people heard, and they came, bulldozing the acres of woods to build their cookie cutter homes so that they could live next to the water's edge. It was getting harder and harder to find a spot where there were no homes, but Ryder knew of one place. It was down a narrow country road, to the east side was Beaver Lake, and to the west was a row of homes. There was no country or farm land; there was just the reach of the city. However there was still room to build at the end of the street. It was wide open, flat and not a tree or a high power line in sight.   It was the perfect place to just sit on the hood of the Charger as the sun rise up over Beaver Quad.

"I don't get it." Alex said, looking into one of the sacks that they had picked up from Mc Donald's before they got there; 12 biscuits and sausage, 2 Cinnamon Melts, 2 Fruit 'N Yogurt Parfaits, 2 Chicken and Biscuits, 2 orders of hotcakes and 5 coffees and two cartons of milk. "Why all the food?"

"You never know when you might have company." Ryder said with a grin, just as the rays of the morning sun began to rise up over the distant hill on the other side of the lake.

"Like who?" She said just when the chop-chop sound of an approaching helicopter could be heard; she looked up. It was just a small red dot on the horizon at first skipping across the sky, but it turned and began an approach towards them. As it got bigger the sound became a loud roar. Soon the image of the Robison R44 copter filled the sky, the rumble of the engine rattling glass. Ryder was sure it was awakening the home owners, but he didn't care. The ruby red helicopter squatted down, the rotor blast flatting out the grass in the bare lot.   Alex, who was sitting next to him on the hood of the car, looked at him strangely.

"You never know who may drop in!" Ryder said, raising his voice to be heard over the roar of the rotor. Soon the motor became still and the rotor began to wind down as Alex, who was holding a cup of coffee looked back at the helicopter as one of the doors popped open, and out stepped a woman, Alex's sister, cradled in her arms was a small girl with long dark hair.

Alex turned and looked at Ryder, who smiled and said. "You never break a promise to a child," He paused as Alex set her coffee down on the hood of the car, then added. "Ever."

"Mommy!" The little girl yelled wiggling to get down. Alex dashed towards them. The little girl was wearing a bright blue princess dress with puffed sleeves and a flowing hem line that just twisted with each running step she took towards her mother.   Alex scooped her daughter up in her arms. Lifting her up she spun her around, drawing her closer to her in an embrace, the sheer cape the girl had tied around her neck billowing out behind her.   Out of the copter climbed the pilot and Yakira, as Alex walked back towards the car still carrying Ceelia, the little girl's arms wrapped tightly around her mother's neck.

"Thank you." Alex mouthed out the words; Ryder lifted his cup of coffee in a salute. "Ceelia," Alex said, shifting the girl's weight to her hip. "This is your…" She paused before continuing. "This is our good friend Rick Ryder." Alex brushed her daughter's hair out of the little girl's face. She looked at Ryder still sitting on the hood of the car as she added in a hopeful tone. "You can call him Uncle Rick, if you want." Ryder like that idea, just yesterday he had got up an only child, today he had a brother, sister and now a little niece. His smile told Alex it was okay. He watched as the little girl smiled, flashing her little dimples, her eyes like precious sapphires that just jolted through him, as she began to enlighten Ryder on her adventure.

"Uncle Ricky," Ceelia said with glee that could only come from a child whose imagination was yet untainted by the muck of the world. She held her arms out like a bird as she said. "I flew! High up in the air. I flew over the lake." Ryder tilted his head slightly as he looked at the little girl as she continued to tell of her adventure aboard the helicopter. "I am just like a Super hero!"

"But you are dressed like a princess." Ryder said slightly tugging at the lace collar of her dress.

"I can be both."

"Yes you can, Ceelia. You can be anything you want." Ryder said. Out of the corner of his eye he could see the dazzling glow of red and yellow beginning to fill the sky. "But I want you to do something for me. Right now I want you and your mother to turn around and look out over the lake."

"The sun is getting up Mommy! He is getting out of bed."

Ryder turned and looked at Yakira as she sat down on the hood of the car beside him. He lifted the side of her face and gave her a kiss on the neck. "Now the sun can rise, you're here." He said tenderly, letting her hair fall back down on her shoulders, her bangs in a slight curl resting over her eyebrows. The sun rose up over the hill, the edge of the brilliant orange light gleaming through the trees, before it became a dancing glimmer up on the rippling water of the lake, and long shadows behind them. Another day had begun.

After breakfast it was time to leave again. Ceelia hugged her mother and said. "You have to go help people again, Mommy?" Ceelia said.

"Yes I do." Alex replied, then her daughter gave her a kiss and then ran over to Ryder, grabbing the edge of his jacket, she pulled on it. She tilted her head back and looked up at him and asked, just pure of heart. "Would you like a hug, Uncle Ricky?"

The little girl embraced him. "All the money I have couldn't buy anything better than that." Her hand slipped down his side and touched the butt of his pistol and she glared down at his side and asked in an innocent tone.

"Do you help people too, like Mommy?"

Yeah, I do." He said.

"Then you need a kiss too." Ceelia said before kissing him on the cheek. Confused, Ryder drew back and asked.

"What was that for?"

"In case you don't come back." She said warmly, turning and dashing toward Yakira standing next to the helicopter. Ryder stood numbed by the little girl's words, tears moistened his eyes as he took his thumb and rubbed along his cheek where she had kissed him, and he looked at his thumb. Then back over at the bright red metal bird. Ceelia had to give Yakira a hug before the pilot lifted the little girl into the rear seat.

Feeling Alex walking up next to him, Ryder spoke, but still keeping his eyes on the helicopter as Yakira dashed away from it as the rotor began to spin.

"That is some kid you got there." Ryder turned to her. "Don't ever forget that."

"I won't." Alex replied as Yakira walked up and the roar of the chopper filled the countryside, the wind whipped the leaves about, making the grass surrender face down as the helicopter quickly rose into the air and flew away, becoming a small red dot that disappeared over the horizon.

"So where do we go now?" Yakira asked as the three of them began to walk back towards the car.

"Back to the Springs," Ryder said, slipping his sunglasses over his eyes.

Chapter 23

A wave to the Round House, a tip of the hat to the dining rail cars-waiting patiently for later in the day when they would greet diners who had to choose between prime rib, chicken or gourmet trout- by the 'rainbow houses' and sign after sign that invited the weary to their "house" to rest. Once again they were in the town of the ghost.

Ever since the first murder the town had been holding its breath, waiting for the next murder. With the arrest of Captain Grosstree the city had exhaled, thinking the killer had been caught. The mayor was quick in reacting; holding a news conference in front of the courthouse, telling everyone to come back; that the city was safe once again.

Ryder shook his head in disbelief as he pulled the Charger into an all day parking lot under the guard of a flowering Dogwood tree. He paid the fee, and they began 'walking a beat' towards the heart of the city. Into the Grand Central Hotel, to the shops in Great Basin Bath House, where they showed a pair of women Lillian's photo, but they hadn't seen anything. It was at this point they split up, Ryder and Yakira heading up the metal steps to the balcony and across the bridge to Spring Street, while Alex continued on down Main Street.

Ryder looked across the street at the stone wall and the building marked with the words 'Park Place', before looking up the street, his eyes gazing at the largest building on the street- The Basin Park Hotel. He motioned with his hand that they should continue up the street.

A large blockade was across the street with a sign 'Street closed to traffic' tacked to it. Yellow police tape surrounded a large hole in the street. The hole nearly swallowed the entire width of the street. The hole was ten feet deep and attached to a tunnel that ran along the sidewalk. Curiosity was driving Ryder to take a closer look, but the sweet aroma that was drifting from the store was enticing him more.

Entering the store that specialized in making candy was a sensory fantasy. The aromas of homemade chocolate and fresh coffee were just overwhelming and required a cup of coffee and a sample of walnut fudge.

"What is with the hole in the street?" Ryder asked, chewing on the fudge, savoring the rich sweetness.

"I didn't know we could have earthquakes here, I moved from California to get away from them." The woman behind the counter said, as she wrapped pieces of candy and was placing them in a box. "I never heard of the Kimberly Fault before." She explained about the fault line that ran along the top edge of Arkansas and to the New Madrid fault, which was responsible for the largest earthquake in the continental United States, and also for creating the Kimberly Lake for which it was named. Ryder always had to shake his head and offer an unseen laugh for those coming from California to escape earthquakes, he lifted the cup of coffee to his lips to hide the grin, but her next words intrigued him, he also didn't know about the underground.

"Underground?" Ryder asked gazing out between the letters on the front store window at the hole in the street.

"According to the locals, Spring Street use to be a lot lower in the early days of the town," the woman behind the counter stopped wrapping up candy and moved closer to him, leaning over the counter. "In fact, this is originally the second floor."

"What?"

"The basement was originally the first floor; when they built the street up the second floor became the first floor. It is like that with most buildings on this street, and Main Street."

"That is interesting." Ryder said as he reached into the inside pocket of his jacket and produced the photo of Lillian. "Have you seen this woman?" Ryder asked, holding up the photo. She shook her head and Ryder replaced the photo, then he and Yakira walked out of the shop.

He didn't know what it was, but there was something that was drawing his attention to the Basin Park Hotel across the street. He even stopped and stared at the arch shaped entryway, before returning his attention to the shops that lined along the street. At this point the street quickly divided, one way still Spring Street, the other one Central Street. They continued down the right hand-side of Center Street. Again, showing the photo and asking.

"Have you seen this woman?" Every answer was the same, just a simple shake of the head. They crossed the street and began entering the shops on the other side. Again the answers were just a plain "no" or a shake of the head, till they came to a shop that touched both Center and Spring Street, its red awnings quickly drawing the eye of a woman shopper who quickly cut in front of them and went inside.

Ryder was instantly hit with an aroma that smelled like the loveliest basket of fresh laundry coming in from being hung on an old-fashioned clothesline, like the ones that used to be in most backyards. A grandstand of hand stitched quilts, hung as if they were grand works of art, created in patches of brown, blue, rust, black, pumpkin, olive green or dark red with simple geometric patterns. It was the first time entering a shop that Ryder removed his sunglasses.

A middle aged woman with salt and pepper hair that was in a bun on top of her head approached them. "What can I do for you?" She asked, the corners of her lips slightly drawing up. Ryder had made copies of the photograph, a 5x7 size that made it easier to carry around. He held it up for her as he asked.

"Have you seen this woman?"

"Yes." She replied, which left Ryder thunderstruck, he had been in shop after shop and had almost started to give his standard reply of 'thank you' and leaving. He couldn't make his mouth ask his follow up question. Lucky for him, Yakira could.

"Where did you see her?"

"Across the street, in the hotel," She said. "I saw her there this morning when we opened up."

"Was she alone?" Ryder finally managed to ask.

"No, she was with some man." The clerk looked at Ryder and added. "He kind of looked like you." Ryder pulled out his wallet and pulled out a pack of photographs that were tucked into the pocket behind his driver's license. "Is she in trouble? Did she do something?" Ryder looked up from his wallet, wondering why she was asking this. He knew from basic training he could tell her the truth, it could scare her and if a witness is frightened, they would likely try to remain quiet. He had to apply the old stand answer.

"No, we just need to ask her a few questions. About something she had seen." Ryder sorted through the old discolored photographs, some even in black and white, till he came to the bottom photo. Ryder held it up. It was a man and a small boy. It was of him and his father; he knew it was a stretch. Maybe it was the fates of the muses of law enforcement, or

204

an angel from heaven itself, but something or someone was telling him to ask this question. "Is this the man?"

The clerk looked long and hard at the worn photograph; even the upper corner was missing. "He may look a little different now, but is this him?" Ryder added, hoping it would help her remember.

"Well..." The clerk drew out before saying. "Yes, that is him. Is this about the murders? I heard from my friend Jessie that the FBI was asking questions about it, but they caught that killer..." She paused for a moment before adding anxiously, "...didn't they?" Ryder's refusal to answer just made her more uneasy. "It wasn't him, was it? I knew it! The killer is still around. Oh my God, it is her! She is the killer!"

"Ma'am," Ryder said, placing his hands on her shoulder and leaning down. He offered a warm friendly grin; he placed one of his hands on her cheek. "Don't be frightened..." He placed his other hand on her other cheek. "You are a very observant person; you just keep your wits about you, and you will be okay." Ryder reached into his jacket pocket and pulled out a business card with his phone number on it, and handed it to her as he said. "Now if you see her again, I want you to give me a call."

Ryder slipped the photo back into his wallet and stepped outside of the shop, up the steps that led to Spring Street. He gazed up at the eight-story stone monster that stood before him. With the bright face of the sun shining on the entrance of the hotel, Ryder's eyes slipped from floor to floor, then onto the Balcony Restaurant on the second floor and to a face that he didn't want to remember- Ryan Ryder-his father- sitting at a table near the rail. Ryder drew in his breath as he felt their eyes meet. He handed an extra photo of Lillian to Yakira and said. "Why don't you hit the rest of the shops? I am going in here."

Yakira took the photo and looked up at the man at the table. "Are you sure you don't want me to go with you?" She asked.

"No," Ryder said with a shake of his head as he stepped into the street. "This is something I have to do myself." Ryder walked across the street and pushed the door to the hotel open.

He was engulfed by a huge lobby that gave him that feeling he should have tied up his horse to a hitching post outside. The colors were subdued, nothing flashy here, just deep wood tones of the support pillars and trim doing the talking to any guest who entered, and the deep color of the hexagon tile floor, made it was clear this was a design from years ago. A fireplace to his left showed signs of many cold winters, the soot staining its rocky face. Ryder's eyes drew up to the sign on the wall that read "Balcony Restaurant 2nd floor.' He climbed the stairs and entered the restaurant, and the hostess wanted to seat him, but he told her.

"I am meeting someone." His low tone was full of angst as he pushed the sunglasses up on his nose and proceeded over to the table where his father sat. The tables were oblong, with a faded red marble pattern. Ryan was sitting with his back to the door, gazing out over the Basin Park below. He looked up from his glass of Bud Lite®.

"Well, look at what the cat drug in." The man said his voice low and deep. He grinned in almost a snarl. "Sit down, son. I will buy you a beer."

Ryder pulled out one of the metal backed chairs and sat down across from the man. "I don't drink beer." Ryder replied as he leaned back in the chair.

"Oh yes," The man replied as he lifted his glass of beer. "You never like the bitter taste." He took a sip and set it back down on the table and asked, "Then how about a root beer? That is a boy's drink."

"Is that what a father buys his son," Ryder cocked his head slightly sideways as he asked, "after being gone all these years?"

"Well, how about a steak? His father asked again, raising his glass of beer to his lips. "Or would you prefer a Hummus Platter? Being the big man of the city after winning all that money."

"I am not here to eat, Mr. Ryder."

"Then what are you here for, boy?"

"I am here to ask you questions."

The man laughed, deep and hollow. "Son, I heard you are not a cop anymore." Ryan started to lift the glass again as he added, "Heard you quit, because you couldn't take it. Always knew you weren't. " Ryder grabbed his arm and pulled the glass down.

"Now, you can answer my questions here, or I can get Judge Weber to issue a warrant and have Carroll County pick you up. Then, I

206

will come and get you and take you back to Barry County. Ryder took the glass and dumped it on the weathered floor and turned the glass upside down on the table as he added. "That is if you make it there, old man."

Ryan rubbed his fingers over his mustache and day old growth of whiskers on his chin as he stared at his son. "What are the questions about?"

"Murder."

"Oh yes! Jonas told me that you were investigating those that happened here. What does this have to do with me? He told me you were looking for a woman. Do I look like a woman to you?" The man raised his hand to get the server's attention to order another beer. As the server approached Ryder turned and scowled at the woman as he said.

"We will order later." Making her turn and walk away. Ryder pulled a photo from his inside breast pocket and laid it down on the table in front of his father. "Why were you seen with this woman?"

"I don't know her." Ryan said as he dropped his gaze down to the photo. "I wasn't with her."

"Don't lie to me! I have a witness that says you were with her."

"Then your damn witness is lying! I was not with her."

"Same old crap you spew all the time. Just like you told me you were not with Maureen?"

Ryan again rubbed his hand over his face. "Son, I am not lying!" He picked up the photo and noticed how beautiful she was. He rubbed his hand over his whiskers and grinned sinfully as he added. "Damn! Though she is a beauty."

"And mom wasn't?" Ryder bristled.

"Your mother was a great woman; it's just that she was sick and she couldn't...well, a man has needs." He laid the photo down on the table and with his fingers pushed it back across to Ryder as he said, "I don't know who this woman is."

Ryder picked the picture up off the table and placed it back in his pocket. "Okay, let's go on to the next murder."

"Another one? How many of them you got, son?"

Ryder didn't answer his question, instead he calmly said "Roaring River. March the first."

"You are talking about Greg Anderson and Karen. You found them, didn't you?" Ryan's voice lowered, almost showing sorrow as he rubbed his hand over his chin again. "When I heard about that blasted eggplant…" He rolled his eyes, up his steely blue stare looking at his son and said, "I need a beer, son."

Ryder held up his hand and ordered a specialty beer; the server came over and set it down in front of Ryan, with a glass of water for Ryder. Ryan picked up the Pilsner Glass and took a sip of the rich dark ale before he spoke again. "You found the car?"

"You are the one that buried it?"

"Yes, but I didn't kill them." He leaned back in the chair, and looked out across the town and at the street below as he held the glass in his hand. "That night after I saw what he did to Karen, I wanted to kill him."

"What did he do?" Ryder asked as he pulled out a notebook and began writing in it.

"He beat her up. Real bad Rick, Real bad. Karen didn't deserve that. She was the most beautiful girl in school. Real jerk of a guy."

"Yeah you would know."

"I never once, ever hit a woman. I never hit your mother."

"No you just leave them." Ryder grumbled.

"You want to hear about them or not?"

"Go on." Ryder said only briefly looking up from his notebook.

"It was because she was getting tired of him messing with young girls and making her go along with it." Ryan took a large swig of the beer, downing nearly a quarter of it.

"Like Monica?"

"Yeah, that whole scene with her father really upset her." He downed another big swallow of the beer, it was now more than half gone, and Ryder ordered him another beer. "That is when I asked her." The server set the second beer down on the table and moved away. Ryan quickly finished the first beer and started on the second dark ale.

"To marry you?" Ryder asked as he reached into his jacket pocket and pulled out the ring wrapped up in a piece of cloth. He laid it down on the table in front of his father and unwrapped it and said, 'and you gave her great-grandma's ring. And she said yes at the campfire."

"Yeah, but first she had to talk to Greg and tell him it was over." Ryan turned back to face his son. He took a drink from the second beer, and continued. "She was gone for about an hour, and then she came back. He had messed her up; her mouth was swollen and bleeding. Greg had found some young blonde girl and raped her, made her hold her down. She told me 'that we would never be able to be together as long as he was alive.'"

"So you agreed to help her kill him?"

"I chickened out. I told her I had a gun in my car, it was under the front seat on the passenger's side. I went to talk to your mother, but before I got down to the old lodge, I heard a bang from the woods, it sounded like a gunshot. I went looking for Karen. That is when I found them, him lying on the ground next to a large rock near the Pibern Trail, the gun still in her hand." Ryan quickly took a large drink. "She said we could be together, if I helped her get rid of the body. That is when I remembered the large hole that was dug for the cattle that had been killed. We were going to get rid of him and then we were going to leave town. If we buried him and his car and the gun, everyone would just think he left town because Karen broke his heart."

"If Karen was still alive, what happened to her?" Ryder asked as Ryan began to take another drink of his beer. Ryder placed his hand over the top of it and forced it back to the table. It was clear that he wanted him to continue.

"We placed his body in the trunk. And she sat down in the passenger's seat, when she remembered we had left his letterman jacket back there and it had blood on it. I went back to get it when I heard another gunshot. I ran back and Karen was dead, and I saw your mother running away. So I buried them both."

Ryan lifted his glass of beer to his mouth and paused for just a moment before he carefully took a drink. "I have kept that secret all my life; I never even told your mother what I saw. That was why I married her. It kept us all from going to jail. As the legend grew, I just went along with it."

"Mom didn't kill anyone. She walked up on it after it happened. Where was the gun at when you went back to get the jacket?"

"It was lying in the trunk with his body."

"And where was it when you came back?"

"Floorboard of the backseat." As Ryan spoke Ryder closed his notebook and placed it and the pen back in his jacket pocket. He picked up the ring and stuffed it into the side pocket of the jacket and stood up. "Any more questions for me, son?"

"Only one," Ryder said as he readjusted the sunglasses on his face. "You loved mom enough to marry her so you wouldn't have to testify; why didn't you love me enough to stick around? What did I do to make you leave?" Ryder asked as he reached up and pulled his sunglasses off. "I tried to be the best son I could be. Winning all the awards in sports, I even ran for a touchdown myself." Ryder paused and curled his lips into a sneer as he slipped the glasses back over his eyes.

"You remember the tornado that hit the farm when I was seven years old, and how I felt your strong arms around me while we were in the cellar, trees crashing down and the old barn caved in? I was so scared, because it was so dark and you told me everything was going to be okay?"

"No, I don't remember that."

"That is because it never happened. Mom left you to take care of me while she went to Cassville to get groceries and you left me all by myself while you went to the bar. That was the story you made up to tell to mom. Instead the truth was that I went to cellar by myself, but I didn't bring a flashlight, it was so frightening down there, hearing the rain drip on the floor, feeling the cold water on my bare feet and wondering if the old maple tree was going to fall and crush me in the cellar. Then after the storm you came home and yelled at me, and warned me that I better not tell mom the truth. I never told her, not even when she was dying. Every since that day I wondered what did I do? What did I do to make you make you leave? What did mom do to make you not want her?"

Ryder shook his head and stared down from the balcony at Yakira, waiting for him at the Basin Park. Though he felt nothing but bitterness now, seeing her made him want to smile. "I could never do that to someone I loved. Uncle Tony thinks I should forgive you." Ryder turned back to his father, she small smile he had was gone. "But he is wrong! There is no damn way I am going to forgive. When I needed you the most you weren't there." With that he turned and walked away only to hear his father's voice.

"Come back when you are not such a little bitch."

Ryder felt tightness in his chest and sickness in the pit of his stomach, as if he had been gut punched. He stood outside of the hotel and gazed out across the across the street as the fluffy clouds soared above, the minutes just before occupying his mind like an unwanted squatter. He turned to his right and walked under the same balcony, where just a minute ago he had said the words he had wanted to say for years, yet he didn't feel any better.

He crossed over to Basin Park. A cement island of sanctuary in the city of forgotten time, it was where it all began. The very heart, nay, the very soul of the town, it was the spring waters that were bubbling up here, causing the Native Americans and soon others to claim the healing resources. Today with the serene setting of fountains, trees, and dark green benches, it served as a resting area for worn out shoppers. Ryder scanned over the park, she had been sitting by the statue of the 'doughboy' that was erected in WWI to honor those who served from this area, but now she was gone.

"Ricky!" He heard his name shouted and looked up at the band shell, and saw her wave. He went up the steps to the top of the stone wall at the back, maneuvering around the neatly trimmed evergreen bushes and up the steps to the stage.

"What are you doing up here?"

"I wanted to perform, thought I might sing a song." She said with a small smile that barely moved her lips.

211

"I have heard you sing." Ryder mocked. "This town has suffered through murder; don't you think it has suffered enough?" He stifled a giggle. Unaffected, she just shook her head, throwing her hair back and began bouncing around the stage, acting as if she were playing lead guitar as she began to belt out at the top of her lungs:

"Give me, give me, give me your love. Your Love!" With those words she screamed even louder as she dropped to her knees, leaning way back, acting as if she was finishing playing the guitar, the five other people that were sitting on a bench in the park clapped. Yakira stood and took a bow. She looked up at Ryder.

"Is there any way to shut you up?" He asked as he wrapped his arms around her waist and pulled her close; she pushed up on her tip-toes and wrapped her arms around his neck as she said softly.

"Only one way, Sweetie."

He lowered his face to hers and had just begun kissing her when suddenly a voice rang out. "Rick! Yakira!" It was Alex; she was standing in the park next to the fountain. She was looking up at them and yelling so she could be heard. "I found her. I found Lillian!"

Chapter 24

Ryder and Yakira quickly descended the steps to the retaining wall, and Ryder leaped down to the ground of the park. He then helped Yakira down and raced for Alex. The leap had flared up the pain in his damaged knee as he moaned slightly, grabbing at it. "You okay? Alex asked.

"Yeah," He said, moaning again as he straightened his athletic frame. "Never mind about me, where is she?"

"I didn't actually find her." Alex confessed. "What I found is someone who said they saw her going into a shop here."

"With some guy, right?" Ryder quipped back. "Been there and done that. It didn't turn out. "

"No, this happened moments ago. She went into a jewelry store, just up the street. They told me she works there part -time." They began the ascent up the street along the sidewalk, passing by the shops, all up hill. The street took a hard jog to the left and they still continued following it, till they came to a jewelry store.

A quaint little shop that sat at the beginning of a two-story brick building, dwarfed by tall buildings around it. It seemed almost out of place, yet at the time its size made it seem quaint and inviting. Ryder opened the door and held it for the ladies.

Ryder remembered his mother's tales of what heaven was going to be like. Streets of gold, and emeralds, rubies, and sapphires lying as if they were glass-like streams. With the glimmer of precious stones twinkling like multiple colored Christmas lights, in a dazzling blend of yellow, green, reds and blues, it was the closest thing to heaven on earth. Drawn like moths to a flame, both women were drawn to the one color, which had no color, the one of pure light- the diamond. Yakira stood there, her palms resting on the glass on the top of a case as she stared into the cosmic ray of brilliance, with the hungry look on her face like that of a famished soul gaping through the glass at an all you can eat endless buffet, starving to death before they could make up their mind. Alex, too, seemed to be put under the spell of the glimmering stones. Ryder didn't understand; all he saw were price tags.

Ryder removed his sunglasses and saw the two women behind the glass counter. One was tall and thin, one more heavy-set, Betty, with dark hair and Madison, with blonde hair. Betty approached, asked if she could help him.

Instinct kicked in as he looked down at her hand; there were only two rings on her finger. A simple wedding set, with a single third carat princess cut diamond, and on her pinky, a simple silver band. He glanced over at Madison's hand. There were so many rings he almost couldn't count them. At least one on every finger, except her thumb, each one a work of art itself. On her left hand was not a diamond engagement ring, but a large crystal blue sapphire, with small, yet almost perfect diamonds, creating a halo around the main stone.. He quickly gazed at the rings in the case and then at the one on the blonde's hand. Just as any master's brush strokes can be detected; so can a jeweler's work. This quickly told him either this was the jewelers wife, or his daughter. Depending on the age of the jeweler, Ryder's eyes quickly looked over the walls, searching for a photo, a family photo. Finding it, he turned to the blonde woman and asked.

"Where is your dad?" By asking the question that way, he sounded more like a local and not just some tourist, which might help with the next question he was going to ask. "Need to ask him a few things."

"He went for a late lunch." Madison said. "But maybe I can help you?"

"We are looking for Lillian." Ryder said, holding out the photo. The woman looked at the photo, as did the other woman. Ryder watched as the eyebrows of the dark haired woman lifted up, meaning she knew who this was.

"I can't discuss our customers." The blonde woman said.

"But isn't she an employee here?" Ryder said as he reached into his jacket pocket and pulled out the photo, and showed her. "This is her."

"That is Celeste!" Betty spoke up, but then seeing her bosses' frown stepped back.

"She was just in here, she walked in and quit, didn't even give me a warning. Now I have to work her shift." Madison said. "She took her check and said something about she was going to meet someone at Basin Park."

"Could I get her address?"

"I cannot give that out." Madison looked at him and then at Alex before she said. "I know who you two are, and unless you have a warrant, you are not getting that. Now if there isn't anything else? If you do not wish to buy anything, would you please leave the store?"

Ryder huddled with Yakira and Alex around him and whispered "You two go back down to the hotel, there is something I need to get here." They turned and walked out and Ryder turned back to the counter.

He reached into his jacket and pulled out the ring that was wrapped up, he unwrapped it. "Can I get this cleaned up and resized?" Madison looked at the ring and said "smaller or larger?"

"Smaller."

"We can do that, take a couple of days." Madison placed the ring back down on the counter and ordered. "Betty, write him up a ticket." Then she turned and walked into the office at the back of the store. Ryder grinned broadly at the dark-haired woman and said as warmly as he could.

"Maybe you can show me something else?" Ryder knew there were two ways to get information out of someone. You can intimidate them and scare it out of them, or charm them. "I think that the ladies in my life would like to have some jewelry. Maybe some pendants or earrings." He pulled out his wallet as he looked down into the case at the shining jewels. He looked up at Betty and his next words made her have to place her hands on the glass case to keep from falling on the floor. "And let's forget anything less than five hundred dollars, that is just so pretentious."

The woman began showing item after item after item, as he selected a dazzling collection of emeralds, rubies, sapphires, and of course diamonds. "And what about that?" Ryder asked, pointing to a small crown decorated with gleaming stones.

"The tiara, sir?" Betty asked reaching into the case and picking it up and handing it to him, "It is just for display; it is just CZ's."

"Doesn't matter, a princess isn't a princess without one. Toss it in." When it was all totaled up Betty's hand trembled, and she took a deep breath and said

"That will be fifty two thousand three hundred dollars and fifty two cents."

"Can I get all that gifted wrapped?" Ryder asked, "Except for the tiara. I want to place that on the princess myself." After a short time she returned with the packages all wrapped up and placed them in a bag. She handed him the bag to him and said.

"I hope your little girl likes the crown."

"Oh. she is not that little." Ryder said as he leaned over the counter and placed the jeweled crown on Betty's head. "Every woman should be a princess." He said with a pleasant smile and leaned down and gave her a kiss on the cheek. He watched her face flush with pink and she placed her hand up to her cheek where he had kissed her. Betty looked over at the office to make sure that Madison was not watching and whispered.

"The lady you are looking for. She lives at the end Peacock Road. It is just outside of town on highway 62. You can't miss it. It is an old spooky house."

Chapter 25

After leaving the jewelry store Ryder got a text that seemed to make him smile. Even when Alex told him she was going to try and do this all legal, by going to the Carroll County judge and get a warrant to search the old house. Ryder gave her keys to the Killer Bee and told her to meet them at the Mud Café.

Compared to the other shops along Main Street this café could easily be overlooked, there were flashing lights, declaring it to be open. If you looked in through the window you didn't see bustling tables, instead it was a staircase that led down under the street.

It was a true trip back in time, back to when the streets were dirt and spring water ran under them and the streets turned to mud; that was the time when this was street level. Pulling the door open at the bottom of the stairs, the bustle of the traffic above is gone as the door closes. Open timber beams on the ceilings and limestone walls covered with paintings from local artists. It was usually the century oak bar with beveled mirrors that drew one's eye, but it was a painting that was drawing Ryder's attention.

It was the 'Garden of Eden' large, taking up nearly the entire wall. Ryder stood there thunderstruck; gaping at the nude blonde woman-Eve-that was kneeling at the edge of the stream with a leopard beside her and a peacock sprouting its tail flume behind her. Yakira cried out his name but he just stood there, bewitched by the beauty of this woman.

"It's her," He said quietly as he reached out and touched the woman's face.

"Sweetie," Yakira said. He didn't answer; he just stood there, mesmerized by the woman's face in the painting. Even when the hostess tried to show them to a seat he just stood there. "Rick, Ricky! RYDER! Yakira said, nearly shouting, finally breaking his attention away from the painting.

"Where would you like?" The hostess asked.

"Anywhere, just away from that!" Yakira said, pointing to the work of art.

"Has to be big enough for six," Ryder said as the hostess showed them to a large oval shaped table. "I have more guests coming." Ryder held the chair out for Yakira and she sat down. He sat down in the chair next to her, at the head of the table, placing the bag he was holding by his feet. "We will wait to order when they get here." He looked out at the young woman, her long crimson-like hair piled up on top of her head. "But bring us a couple of your coffees."

"What kind?"

"Your house special, and we will need cream and sugar with it."

"So, who are we meeting?" Yakira asked.

"My brother and sister," Ryder replied.

"Your what?" Yakira replied, stunned. "You have a brother and sister?"

"Well, half of a sister and half of a brother. It seems when the old man left he had another family. I invited them to come and stay at Crescent." The waitress set the mugs of coffee down in front of them, along with cream and sugar.

"And your father," Yakira asked tenderly as she mixed cream and sugar into her coffee. "Is he invited too?"

"I guess," Ryder replied, his tone still showing his distaste for the man as she poured cream into his coffee, followed by sugar. "I t doesn't mean I have to accept him." "My little brother and sister," Ryder said, laying down the spoon and raised the white mug to his lips. "I have a family." He added just before taking a sip of the dark roast blend. He swallowed the slightly acid tasting fluid, the taste lingering on his tongue.

Yakira raised the mug to her lips and took a careful sip of the hot coffee. "Why are you seeing her all the time?" Yakira took another sip of coffee and then said "Lillian. It was her you saw in the painting, wasn't it?" He gazed across the room to the wall where the painting was. "Why does she have this hold on you?" Her words just fell away as he sat staring at the painting. "Rick! He turned to her. "What is it with her? What does she have on you?"

"I don't know." He replied, taking another sip of the coffee. "I see her in everything." "I..."He paused, looking over his shoulder, scouting out the women that were in the café. He turned back. "I feel her

218

now; as if she is somewhere just watching me. I can't sleep without dreaming of her. I can't get her out of my head."

"I don't like it! Do you love her?" She asked. He looked at right at her and didn't answer. "Do you love her!" She repeated her question; this time as more of a demand.

"No, I have no feelings for her. She is a murder suspect, that is all." He said, raising the mug back to his lips. "That is all she is, that is all she will ever be," his words sounding as if he didn't believe his own statement. He looked up. Entering the café were Jonas, Marissa, and their mother, Mary. Ryder waved for them to join them, as they approached Ryder stood up and held the chairs out for the ladies.

"I don't get it?" Jonas said, "Why do you do that? I mean, women are just..."

"Princesses," Ryder said as he reseated himself at the head of the table, his step brother and step mother, Mary, to his left and Yakira and his sister to his right. "And every one of them needs to be treated as such."

"I don't know," Jonas said as he reached into his pocket and pulled out a Kennedy half-dollar coin and began flipping it over his fingers. "A good looking girl at school, okay, but your sister and your mother; that sounds sort of weird."

"All ladies!" Ryder said, grabbing the young man's hand, causing the coin to fall to the table with a resounding ring.

"Even those who murder?" Jonas asked as he picked up his coin, and started flipping it over his fingers again. "The woman you are looking for, should she be treated like a princess?"

"Kiddo, don't get into things you know nothing about." Ryder said with a slight snarl, lowering his voice, making it harsh and coarse. "Would you treat the devil as God?"

"Of course not!"

"Why not?" Ryder asked, lifting his mug and resting his arms on the table as he gazed over at the young man. "You can ask him for things just as you do God, and he will give them to you."

"For a price," Jonas replied as he let the coin slide down between his fingers into his palm, and clutched it tightly as he added, "My soul."

"The devil doesn't deserve it, because he doesn't give respect. Same for a killer, they don't deserve respect." The expression changed on Ryder's face as he leaned over and picked up the bag and placed it on the table. "I got gifts for everyone."

"Yeah, presents." He heard Marissa say and watched her put her cell phone on the table. She smiled, showing those dimples. "Me first?"

"Yeah, okay," Ryder said, opening it up and looking down into the bag, pulling out a small package wrapped in light blue paper and a darker blue ribbon. She opened the velvet box and saw a round brilliant cut blue sapphire pendant necklace, the central stone surrounded by tiny clear blue topaz stones, as if the sky were surrounding a dark blue thundercloud. Seeing it, she quickly reached over and grabbed him around the neck.

Ryder reached back into the bag and pulled out a pink wrapped present and handed it to Yakira. "I saw you looking at these." She opened the present; it was the emerald earrings that she had been looking at in the store. The earrings were fashioned from white gold, set with teardrop shaped deep green emeralds in the center and surrounded with alternating marquise shaped diamonds and emeralds. She gasped at their beauty, they were stunning! She took them out of the box and immediately slipped them onto her ears, carefully placing the backs on them. She got up and hugged him and gave him a kiss before returning and sitting down in her seat. Ryder reached back into the bag and pulled out another small package wrapped in blue foil and white ribbon; he handed it to Mary. "Didn't know what your favorite stone was, so I got something I thought would match those green eyes of yours. She unwrapped the package and held up an irradiated diamond pendant set in 14K white gold, as Ryder explained," the radiation sometimes turns normal colored diamonds to green".

The waitress returned and everyone ordered cheese burgers and iced tea. "Sweet with…" Ryder began, and his sister joined in as they finished together. "With a half twist of lemon." Sweet tea for Yakira, and unsweet for Mary and Jonas. Ryder's phone dinged and he picked it up. It was a text from Alex that read:

'On my way. Need to talk about tonight. Order for me.'

"And for the other guest, she will have the chicken club; go very light on the mustard with chips and a diet coke to drink."

Ryder turned to his brother and said. "Don't think I had forgotten you, brother, what I have for you isn't in this bag. I talked to the dean at MSSU; you are ready to attend class this fall. All four years have been paid."

"I don't know what to say." Jonas said, hunting for the right words to say. "I have been—I mean have—I didn't know where I was going to get the money."

"He even tried to get me to sell the bank building to a developer so he could have the money. I just couldn't do it; it has always been my dream to turn that place into a nice B and B, I think it will make great location right downtown. It could be a whole family thing."

The waitress came by and refilled his cup and Yakira's, and poured coffee for the others. Mary continued, "Your father even thought you might like to join us." She looked over at Yakira and added, "You also."

"I don't get it. He wants me there?" Ryder asked as he started to lift his mug again, but quickly set it back down. "I just saw him today, why didn't he ask me then?"

"He is a proud man, Rick. He is ashamed of what he did. He couldn't bear to tell you that. He never forgot about you. When you played with the Chiefs we would go every Sunday to Neosho to visit my sister so we could see the game and he could cheer you on."

"I don't..." Ryder's words were cut short as he saw Alex walk in. Ryder could see the exasperation on her face, teeth clenched down, her eyes narrowed slightly, even the wiggle of her finger motioning him over was quick and furious. He stood, excusing himself and walked over to her. Before she even spoke he knew what it was that was upsetting her.

"That stupid nitwit judge," She said, trying to control her volume so no one else could hear. "He wouldn't give me a search warrant. Saying we didn't have enough proof that she was the killer. Maybe if she murdered someone in front of him, then he could see. You know what this means we have to do?" Alex reached into her jacket pocket and pulled out a packet of M&M's and poured a variety of colors into her hand and popped them into her mouth."

"Ten O'clock tonight?" Ryder asked. She nodded her head, popping more M&M's into her mouth.

Chapter 26

Ryder stood at the top of the steps at the back of the Crescent Hotel once again, gazing down at the yellow police tape ruffling in the breeze that was sweeping across the yard, and the leaves on the trees that were exposing their underbelly. It was a true sign that rain was on its way, as was the flash of lightning filling the sky. He waited but no rumble of thunder came.

"What is the meaning of this Mister Ryder?" He heard the mayor complain as he walked up behind him.

"I told you, don't call me that." Ryder warned. He continued to watch as the lightning flashed in the sky and could be seen through the opening of the bell tower.

"What is the meaning of this?" The Mayor demanded, holding up a photo of Lillian that had been left at a store downtown. "You are asking people about this woman. The killer has been caught. Don't be scaring everyone with your fantasies. You ruin my daughter's wedding; I will make sure you are arrested."

Ryder slowly turned to him. Ryder was dressed all in black, black jeans and black button down shirt. He looked at the mayor, the wind flapping the tails of the mayor's navy blue windbreaker.

"With all due respect, take that and shove it under your equator. The murder here in the hotel was not the Eureka Slayer." Ryder looked down at the photo in the mayor's hand. "That is your Slayer."

"This gorgeous woman?" the mayor questioned, holding up the photo. He looked again at the picture. "Are you telling me this beauty is behind the murders? You really expect me to believe that!" The mayor crushed it in his hands and let it fall to the ground. "I am warning you and your two girlfriends. Stop this or I am making a call to the governor." It was at this moment that Alex and Yakira, also dressed in black walked up. The mayor turned to Alex and warned her. "Then he is going to call the A.G."

"There are going to be more murders, mayor." Alex said as lightning flashed, now filling the entire sky.

A low rumble of thunder was heard in the distance as the mayor spoke again. "I am warning you; I want this to stop. The laws of this town

223

must be obeyed. And I am the law!" The mayor turned and began to walk away. Ryder leaned down and picked up the crumpled up photo, he stared at the mayor walking back towards his car.

"All laws, mayor?" Ryder said coldly at him as another rumble of thunder could be heard. The mayor stopped walking and turned back to Ryder. Ryder held up the wadded up picture. "What about littering? You lie to this people, Jesus won't be the only one crucified in this town." The mayor let out a huff, got into his car and drove away.

Rubbing Yakira's leg was a fluffy gray cat. She reached down to pet him and he rolled over on his back, tucking his front paws in, looking up at her and meowing, trying to get her attention before rolling back up right, allowing her to pet him.

"Did you get your family checked in?" Alex asked as she checked the 9mm that was strapped to her waist.

"Everyone has a room of their own." Ryder said as they began to walk down the steps toward the street below. He reached into his pants pocket, pulled out a key, and handed it to Alex, "Including one for you and Celia and your sister Natasha." He mispronounced the child's name and Alex corrected him.

"It is Ceelia with two e's, just like the sea holds passion, she holds my passion."

Ryder stopped at the bottom of the steps as another flash of lighting streaked across the sky, as if it were neon sign flashing its warning that the storm was coming. "That is beautiful. I think that is the first time I have ever heard you say something like that." He held the door of the 'Killer Bee' open and flipped the seat back up so Alex could get into the back seat.

"What can I say, Rick? Seeing that face every morning changes everything else in the world." She placed one foot on the floorboard in the car and started to tuck her head under the roof when she pulled her foot back out and looked at him and said sincerely. "Promise me if anything happens to me, you will make sure she is taken care of. That she has not everything that she wants, but everything she needs."

"Nothing is going to happen to you. I promise you that. You will see the next sunrise together."

224

"Promise me that you will be the one that takes care of her." She stressed her plea as a streak of lightning filled the sky.

"I promise, Belle." He said, calling by the shortening of her first name. She smiled, knowing when he called her this he meant what he was saying. She got into the backseat, Yakira slid into the passenger's seat. He shut the door and got in the driver's seat and they drove away.

Just outside of town; it was the third cross roads and to the right. It was a narrow strip of pavement; at first there was the trickle of household lights beaming, then there was darkness, there were no more houses down this road. The sign that read 'Dead End' didn't help anyone's nerves. He felt Yakira's hand reach over and grip his leg, and in the back seat the rustle of a bag of M&M's was being torn open, he heard them pour into Alex's hand, and heard the crunch of the candy in her mouth.

"Anyone want some? They are with peanuts." She said, holding the package in between the seats and filling each of their hands from the large yellow bag. "Tried to find the mint but couldn't find any."

There was nothing but darkness to the sides and behind them. In front lit only by the warm yellow glow of headlights and occasionally interrupted by a bolt of lightning streaking across the sky was a small road. The further he drove the narrower the road became, till nothing but trees filled the windshield. The road had come to an end. Ryder braked the car to a stop; just to the left was a small road, which was more of a path that led off between the trees. Ryder held his hand back over the seat.

"Hit me !" He said as she poured some more candies in his hand and then Yakira's. Ryder left off the brake and guided the car down the hill, tall grass swatted at the sides of the car and then they went back up the hill, the headlights caught sight of something- an old house.

In the lightning flash he could see it, a huge three story Queen Anne Victorian style, with turrets at each end, a wraparound porch and a balcony above. Thunder rumbled like a stampede of a hundred rushing bulls across the sky. Ryder stood outside of the car holding the door open; staring out across the weed infested yard, the weather worn wooden gate swung effortlessly back and forth in the breeze, slapping at the leaning fence post. Lightning streaked across the sky again.

"Why is it always storming when we do things like this?" Alex asked as she crawled out of the back seat. "I could be home reading a bedtime story." Again thunder rumbled as she added. "Instead, I am living a nightmare." She reached into her pocket and popped a couple of pieces of candy in her mouth.

A single drop of rain fell from the sky, landing on the windshield, streaking down in a long tear trail, quickly followed by another drop, and another. "We better get inside before it hits." Yakira said, shutting the passenger door. He just stood staring up at the windows in the forward tower. He thought he saw a face, looking down at them, soulful eyes begging him to come to her.

"Ricky!" Yakira screamed and he turned to her with a look, wondering what she wanted. "We need to get inside." The rain was getting heavier. He nodded and said.

"Get the flashlights out of the trunk." He reached in, took the keys, and unlocked the trunk. He handed a Maglite ® to Alex and another to Yakira and then took the last one for himself. He could hear the rush of sheets of rain coming. He slammed the lid down and they ran for the house, making it under the roof of the front porch just as it began to pour. The wind was whipping the rain, driving it sideways.

Ryder griped the knob and twisted it and the door swung inward. He shined the beam of the flashlight through the foyer, the old gray paisley print wallpaper partly peeling down from the wall. Above them were twelve-foot high ceilings with a seven branch crystal chandelier swinging from a chain. Over to the side was a semi-circular grand staircase, with hand-turned newel posts, with a lion's head carved out of the wood and placed on the end cap of the handrail.

As he swung the light back around the beam caught the mirror on the wall and reflected the light back on them, before finding the sitting room over to the left. Lighting flashed again, casting the shadow of a square grand piano across the hardwood floor, its legs like that of a stalking beast creeping towards them. Thunder rumbled and rain drops were so large they sounded like hail hitting the roof.

"You two search down here," Ryder said, shining his light into the darkened room and then up the stairs. "I will search up stairs."

"Do you think it's wise to split up?" Alex asked, shining her light around the sitting room. "It is against standard procedure. I think we should stay together."

226

Lightning cracked outside and thunder rattled the glass in the windows. "We don't have time." Ryder said. "Alex, you take that side." He pointed to his left. "Yakira, you take the other."

With each step Ryder took, the treads let out a squeak or a moan. He reached the second floor just as lighting flash painting ghostly images of the curtains on the floor. He went to the bedrooms, they were well decorated with old Victorian style beds and dressers, but there was nothing unusual there, and the dust and the lint on the covers showed that no one was staying there. He walked to the end of the hall, where another set of stairs led up into the tower. As he stepped on the first stair, that cop instinct hit him like a cold slap in the face. He reached under his jacket and slipped the pistol free from its holster and continued to climb the stairs.

The streaks of lightning were creating frightful shadows, shadows that only belonged in a horrendous tale, or a late night fright movie, of twisted legs like of a giant spider, lurking, waiting in its web across the windows. Another flash and it was shadows of a lab, of glass beakers and flasks blubbing their wickedness over a Bunsen burners. Ryder gripped the flashlight with his left-hand and rested the butt of his gun in his right hand as he entered the room at the top of the tower.

It was a large octagon-shaped room with six windows on the front side; something was growing over them. It wasn't a spider, it was-a plant-a flower. Twisting and tightening on the sides of the wall, with funnel shaped flowers that were pink, yellow and white. Lighting flashed again, casting the shadows of glassware on the other side of the room. He shined the light over to a large work bench. There were several pieces of red construction paper and a brand new black crayon; it was lying in front of a large amount of glassware. Ryder had seen this stuff before in the crime lab at KC, and in professional meth labs, but this was no meth lab. There were glass beakers full of the trumpet shaped flowers; next to them were flowers in flasks soaking in some sort of liquid solution and bubbling under a flame, the liquid running through a tube to a distiller that was creating a bright red liquid that was dripping into another smaller glass flask. There were three bottles next to it, one he quickly recognized as a bottle of Vodka, it was grocery store special, the type that was only drank by 'town drunk', he wouldn't use it to cook it with, but it would make a good infusing agent. The other two bottles were smaller, white plastic. He picked one up; it was half full of a powder that was colorless. On the label it read 'C17H21NO4' and beneath the compound was the words 'Devil's Breath.'

227

"What in the world?" He questioned softly to himself. Suddenly smelling the rich aroma of flowers; he had smelled them before-at the hotel- he realized what it meant but it was too late.

Suddenly the smell became overpowering. He felt weak and he let the flashlight and gun slip from his hands. It was as if he was out of his body looking down on himself, spread across the floor. Now it was as if he was back in his body, but he could control it. He saw a shadowy image across the room. A woman was there, dressed in a long dark cloak, her face partly hidden by the hood. As she took a step closer to him and the lightning flashing through the window he could see gripped in her hand was a long thin bladed dagger. The lightning flash again and he saw her face-it was Lillian.

He wanted to shout out for help, he could her hear her voice but her lips did not move, she said for him not to move or say a word. "You seek the trumpet of death, do you not?" Her words were soft and seemed to spin around him, echoing off the walls. She reached up and lowered the hood, revealing her beauty as she stood over him.

"My beloved," She said, kneeling down beside him. She was holding a pink trumpet shaped flower in her hand. Her golden hair fell down on his face as she straddled him and lightly traced the flower over his lips. "This is the trumpet of death. It can kill. It's very scent and soul belongs to the night, just as my scent makes your very soul belong to me." She leaned closer to him, he could smell her perfume. It was so intoxicating he was charmed like a cobra and her voice was the flute. "I am in everything you see, everything you touch, everything you feel." She lowered her lips to his ear and whispered, "The time grows near, when our love shall bond forever." She kissed him fully on the mouth, her lips tasting like tart cherries, her eyes glowing as if they were hot embers of passionate blue light. She placed something in the top outside breast pocket of his jacket. She stood up, replaced the hood over her head and said. "Forever, my darling is forever." With that she raised her hands and fire consumed her.

Ryder was awakened by a loud crack; the glass in the window had shattered from the heat. Flames were consuming the flowers and the wall, nipping and devouring the wood like a hungry beast, feasting on a fresh kill. He coughed and gasped for air. The smoke was stinging his eyes, so that he could barely see.

228

"Ricky!" He heard Yakira call out, followed by Alex.

"Are you up there?"

He pushed himself up to his hands and knees and crawled towards the sound of the voices. He crawled partially down the tower stairs until he could make out the beam of two flashlights in front of him. He coughed again and reached for his weapon, but the flames blocked it.

"Yakira! Alex!" They came running towards him, the beams of their flashlights hitting him square in the face. He began to slip down the stairs head first. They quickly grabbed his hands, helped him to his feet, and down the rest of the tower stairs.

The smoke was beginning to fill the second floor hall; he couldn't really make out any faces, just voices. It was Alex.

"This place is going up like a freaking Roman Candle! We've got to get the hell out of here!"

He nodded, waving his hand for them to continue on down the hall and head for the stairs. "It was her!" Ryder said, trying to see through the smoke. "It was Lillian! She was telling me..."

"Never mind!" Alex shouted as they reached the top of the staircase. "You can tell us when we get out of here." From up above there was a low groaning sound, and suddenly the wall gave way, collapsing on the stairs in front of them, the timbers burning, blocking their path.

"How are we going to get out of here?" He heard Yakira's voice from the other side of him, feeling both of the women's grip tighten, squeezing his upper arms.

"The back stairs," Ryder said as he gestured to continue on down the hall.

"I didn't see any back stairs!" Alex said as he placed his arms around their waists, their arms around his. They had to hold on to each other; they could not get separated. They bent over as low as they could, trying to get below the thick dark black smoke that was making them all cough as they gasped for air. As Ryder saw the lighting streak across the sky through the window, he thought about jumping out, but they were still two stories high, and the landing below was a sloping hill with rocks.

229

Jumping was out of the question. He let go of Alex just long enough to feel the door; it was cool. He opened the door and they walked in.

It was the maid's room, complete with an old antique bed, which Yakira quickly took the cover off and placed it at the bottom of the door that led out into the hall. "There are no stairs in here." Alex said jerking open a door. "Just a bathroom and closets."

"Only one closet!" Ryder said, jerking open another door and revealing a flight of steep stairs that led down to a closed door that was locked with a pad lock. "Give me your gun!" He shouted, holding his hand out to Alex. She handed him her 9mm. He aimed the gun at the door.

"You can't shoot a lock off." She said," that only works in the movies".

"I'm not!" Ryder said. "I am going to weaken the wood. He fired off the rounds, placing bullet hole after bullet hole around the bracket holding the lock. The gun empty, he handed the weapon back to Alex and turned to Yakira. "Please tell me you have your Bulldog with you?" Yakira reached down and pulled the revolver from her boot and handed it to him. He cocked the hammer back. "Only six shots, but a 357 magnum; it should do it." He fired again into the door, splinters of wood were sent flying. The powerful blast inside the small stair way was nearly deafening,. He handed the empty gun back to her. He banged his shoulder into the door, but it wouldn't give.

"Okay, all three of us." Ryder said, but the step was not wide enough for three of them, he stepped up one step and allowed Yakira and Alex to stand on the first step. "On three! One...two...three." All three banged against the door, it gave a little. "Again!" Ryder shouted, he again counted off and this time the door opened. Ryder became over balanced and they all fell to the kitchen floor. The back door was also padlocked, and to make matters worse, it opened inward towards the kitchen. There was no way to get out the door.

"Get back!' he warned. Ryder grabbed a chair and tossed it through a window over the sink. "Okay, Yakira." He said, grabbing her and picking her up, there was a large rumble that shook the entire house. The ceiling in the dining room, just outside of the kitchen had fallen, crushing the antique Queen Anne style table.

Yakira climbed up in the sink and out the window, just as there was a moan and groan from the ceiling above and a flaming rafter fell. Ryder could feel the heat of the flames on his face, he felt like he was raisin in the making. Again he could hear the moaning of the ceiling above them. If they didn't get out of here quick he wasn't going to make it to be a raisin, he was going to be wine, crushed under the weight of the entire second floor.

"Now you, Belle!" Ryder shouted as he used his cupped hands, just as more flaming ceiling tiles began to fall to the floor she too climbed out the window. Smoke was beginning to fill up the kitchen. Again he could hear the moaning of the ceiling.

Come on Ricky, get out of there!" Yakira screamed. Ryder climbed up onto the counter and went head first out the window. Rolling to his feet, he, Yakira, and Alex dashed away, leaping off the porch. There was a loud crash, and hot embers flew out of the window. The rest of the ceiling had caved in.

The rain poured down on them as they as they sat in the wet grass watching as the walls of the house fell inward and the roof tumbled as the flames leaped higher into the air, even outshining the flashes of lightning above it.

"You guys all right?" He heard a voice ask; it was Jonas.

"What are you doing here?" Ryder asked.

"I was doing my own investigation. I found out that Lillian was staying here. When I got here I saw her running away, and the place was on fire." Jonas' face was covered in soot running down the side of his face like cheap mascara at a wedding, in the rain. "I saw your car. I was trying to get in." In the distance there was the wailing of a fire truck approaching. "I called the fire department."

"She is going to kill again." Ryder said as he watched the rest of the roof cave in, then he added, "Then she is going to kill me."

Chapter 27

The rain continued to pour from the sky, as Ryder stood on the upper step, looking out the door that led out onto the balcony of his hotel room. He watched a single drop of rain as it streaked down the pane of glass, hitting the wood and finding itself pulled in two different paths.

He was in the largest suite that the Crescent had to offer- The Governor's Suite; two bedrooms with king size beds, a sitting room, and a full bath with a Jacuzzi. The sound of the water in the bathroom stopped.

The sitting area of the suite had eight sides. The distinctive trait of the room was that a doorway led to each of the two bedrooms, the bathroom, or the wet bar in the entrance hall. The furniture was Queen Anne style, the color complementing the pink floral pattern of the wallpaper, and the mint green wood work. There was a large oval shaped coffee table, with a white robe lying on it.

Ryder turned and stepped down onto the floor and looked at himself in the mirror over the fireplace. His hair was mussed, lying flat against his scalp; black soot was on the side of his cheek and he reeked of smoke.

"Next!" He heard Alex say as she exited the bath, wrapped in a large white fluffy towel, with a small towel clutched in her hands drying her mop like stringy hair. Yakira exited one of the bedrooms dressed in a white robe that nearly dragged the floor as she walked, she headed for the bathroom.

"I won't be long." Yakira said, closing the door behind her; once again the sound of running water was heard.

Ryder could see Alex's reflection in the mirror as she walked over to the couch, leaving behind wet footprints on the low pile green carpet. She sat down on the sofa, crossing her long slender legs, her bare foot moving back and forth as she continued to dry her hair with the towel. Lightning flashed in the window behind her and it took a few seconds, but thunder's echo replied. She pushed her hair back down over her bare shoulders.

"So what really happened in there?" She asked, laying the towel down beside her on the seat of the couch and leaning back. Keeping his back to her, he answered.

"What do you mean? I told you all that happened in there. That she appeared and set the place on fire. That was all there was to it." He reached up and pulled out what Lillian had placed in his pocket- a folded piece of red construction paper. It was heavily damaged by water spots, making it hard to read. He held the paper in his hand as he watched Alex's reflection in the mirror.

"She gave you a note, didn't she?" Alex stood up and walked towards him. He didn't reply as she held out her hand and he handed it to her. He watched as she unfolded it and saw the words written in black crayon, words that he had already read more than once. She read out loud

'Now the dream is almost over'

'The visions that lay upon the clover'

'The light guides my path that I shall take.'

Under the feet of the sun the next shall lie.

For it is Sara's step is the five that you make,

That will allow her to die.

"You have any clue what this means?" Alex said, handing the note back to him.

"Not a one. How about you?" He asked, laying the note on top of the mantle.

"Maybe Sara's step is a place around here?" Alex said, standing beside him, as she stared into the mirror too. "But what do I know?" She turned around and leaned back against the cold white marble. "You didn't answer my question." She said, looking up at him. "She put you under that spell again didn't she?"

"What do you mean?"

"Come on Ricky, Yakira told me about the painting. I saw how you stared up at the window. Are you in love with this woman?"

"Are you effing crazy? I don't want her; it is just..." He heard the water in the bathroom stop as he stepped away from the fireplace. There was a small flash of lightning now, just barely seen in the distance. It was that flower that she called ...." Ryder struggled to remember as he removed his rain soaked jacket. "You ever hear of something called 'Devil's Breath?' "

"Devil's Breath!" Alex exclaimed as she quickly turned around.

"Yeah, that is what the bottle had written on it." Ryder said picking up a black trash bag on the floor that they had been placing their clothes in. "Have you heard of it? " He said, removing the empty holster, and beginning to unbutton his shirt.

"It is called the zombie drug."

"What?" Ryder asked, puzzled by this name, as he unbuttoned the sleeves of his shirt and then removed it, tossing it in the bag. He stood there with his muscular chest bare, still showing its quarterback form, and waiting for her response. She turned her back to him and walked over to the large window that was in between the couch and a rose colored settee; she pulled back the sheers and looked out into the night, before she continued. "Didn't you read her thesis? That's what it was all about. She developed a formula by blending angel trumpet flowers and Scopolamine; she developed the biggest mind alerting drug there is. The real reason she left school was not what the professor told us. She was she thrown out after she tested it on staff and students." She started to look back at him, but she could see in the dark reflection of the glass that he was continuing to disrobe; her own body blocked his image, so she continued to stare out the window as she continued to speak. "She had the girls coming to class naked, the sports team throwing games, professors giving out A's to everyone."

Ryder laughed at these things as he stuffed his clothes into the trash bag, and slipped on a robe, tying it in place. Then her next words wiped the smile from his face. "She also controlled class elections, getting every student to vote for the least popular person on campus. And the big one- she almost got another student to stab her best friend, it was only because she stopped it before it happened." She stopped talking and quickly turned around. "Rick!" She gasped. "If she got you under the influence of this stuff there is nothing you can do to stop her; you can't refuse her. If she asked you to kill me or Yakira you can't refuse her."

"That is crazy, I wouldn't do that. No one can control me."

She walked over to him, reached down, and took a hold of his hand. "I have seen just Scopolamine at work in New Orleans. It was given to a banker and he robbed his own bank and didn't remember it. This stuff is a hundred times more powerful. It is as if she is in control of your soul." His face went blank. "What is it?" She asked.

"She did say something- 'like as my scent makes your very soul belong to me.' Could she be wearing it?"

"There was a part in her paper that said she was creating an antidote to it. It could be she is using that or that she has developed immunity to it." She brought his hands up to her lips and kissed them softly. "That is a blessing, and a prayer." She headed for the front door.

"What was the prayer for?" He asked, just as the bathroom door opened and Yakira emerged.

"That you don't trust this woman." She said as she held the door open. "And that her spell on you will leave you." Alex stepped out into the hall and closed the door behind her. Ryder walked over and locked the door.

"What was that about?" Yakira asked, drying her hair with a towel, the robe tied around her.

"Nothing," Ryder said. "Just Alex being herself, don't worry about things."

"So we are going to be here by ourselves?"

"Till Double T arrives here with our clothes. I had him stop by your house and pick up clothes." Ryder said, giving her a kiss. He walked towards the bathroom door and grabbed the knob.

"I heard you talking." He stopped as she spoke, wondering just what she did hear, as she walked toward the fireplace. "Lillian. That is what this all about? Leading you on, so that she can kill you."

"Possibly," Ryder answered, just as unassumingly. "I have put a lot of murderers away, and some of their families have placed a..."

"A Blood Curse upon you." Yakira said, turning back to face him.

"It is just a silly fairy tale, Yakira."

"Just like the spell she has on you." She hesitated; her voice beginning to reel with anger. "I don't like her hold on you. The way you looked at that painting, she's..." Again she paused. "Can I ask you a question?"

"Always." Ryder replied.

"Do you find me attractive?" She asked moving closer to him and looking up at him.

What kind of dumb question is that? You are beautiful." Ryder said, releasing the door knob and placed his hands on her shoulders.

"Then why haven't you made a move on me?"

"Is that what you want? I thought you wanted to wait until your wedding night?" He said tenderly as he let his hand slide up to the sides of her face, her damp tresses resting over the back of his fingers.

"I don't, maybe." She said as she pulled away from him and turned around and faces the mirror above the fireplace before she continued. "This is all new to me. But you did have other girls didn't you, lots of girls?"

"But you are not those girls." He said walking up behind her, and again placing his hands down on her thin framed shoulders. He could see her face in the mirror, crumpled with sorrow. He wished he could say he could have waited for love, but it was all part of the football star package. "You are more than that."

"You didn't love them, even Alex?" Her words brought memories back that he didn't want to remember.

"She is a friend." He tried to explain.

Yakira turned around and faced him. "I am not talking about now, I am talking about then. Did you love her?"

"I don't know. As friend..."

"What about Lillian?" She asked as she walked over to the window and pulled the heavy drapes back and gazed out the window, the storm was now nothing more than a distant flash of lighting barely visible over the distant hills. "Do you love her?"

"Are you crazy," he barked back. "She is a lunatic!"

Yakira dropped the drape and looked back at him as she asked. "Then why do you call her name in your sleep. I have heard you." The tears puddle in her eyes as she turned once again away from him and walked over to the fireplace.

"It is not because I want to." He said compassionately. "It is that every time I close my eyes, she is there. It has to be the perfume she is..."

"You know what is like to grow up and not be the beautiful one in your family." Yakira said interrupting him. "To be called cute, but not the beauty your sister is?" Her words made Ryder look at her. She paused for just a moment, before she looked at herself in the mirror above the fireplace. "As beautiful as Annalisa was, she would an ugly duckling compare to this woman. How can I compete with that?" She placed her hand to her face. "Maybe if I get my nose done."

Ryder walked over to her and placed his hands yet once again on her shoulders, carefully brushing her long hair back over her shoulders. She turned and faced him "Don't you dare," he said his hands cupping the sides of her face. He drew his face down closer to hers, and looked into her eyes as he added softly. "This is the face of beauty I see; you don't change a work of art." He gently kissed her lips and added. "You are a masterpiece." She smiled and he released her face. He turned and walked back toward the bathroom.

It felt good to take a nice warm bath, to just lay back and relax, to get rid of the smell of the soot. However, that sickeningly sweet smell of the flowers, no matter how hard he scrubbed and scrubbed, he just couldn't get it out of his senses. And when he closed his eyes she was there. He let the water out of the tub and was wrapping himself in the robe when he heard voices outside. Many voices, they must be back with the clothes.

He opened the door. Marissa, Jonas, and Mary were standing there along with Double T, who had returned with four suitcases, including pajamas. Yakira was still in her robe. She was holding the red construction paper note, pacing dramatically back and forth. Mary had gone to the wet bar and fixed a drink, Scotch on the rocks. She brought it to Yakira, who took the glass.

"Ricky, is this the note she gave you?"

"Yeah, but I have not been able to make heads or tails out of it." Ryder said, concerned that the glass in Yakira's hand was shaking as she lifted it up and took a sip. He had never seen her drink hard liquor before.

"I know who she is going to try and kill next." Yakira's words hit him like a 300 pound linebacker sacking him to the ground; he had to steady himself as he sat down on the edge of the coffee table.

"WHAT!" Ryder snarled back. "How could you know that?"

"Every note she has left has been to lure you in." She stressed her words. "You took her mother away from her. Now she is going to…" She paused as the hotel room door opened and in walked Alex, who was now dressed in a robe. She looked at Yakira.

"Somebody give me a five dollar bill." Yakira said. Alex handed her the bill she was holding in her hand. "You know too, don't you?" Yakira asked and Alex nodded.

"Well, will somebody let me in on this?" Ryder was getting upset.

Yakira held up the bill as she explained, "You can make money, the man of the five is Lincoln, his sister was Sarah. Don't you get it?" Yakira glanced over at Marissa, sitting on the couch, and then she looked back at Ryder, who face was as pale as his robe. "She is going to try and kill Marissa."

Chapter 28

Three hours had passed when Ryder opened one of the bedroom doors, and the light from the sitting room filtered in and fell upon Marissa's face, asleep in the king-size bed. He stood there for a moment, watching her face scrunch up, complaining of the intrusion of the light, finally turning over on her side. Ryder quietly closed the door. He opened the other bedroom door and saw Yakira curled up on her side in the other bed; he carefully closed that door also. He turned to Alex who was sitting on the couch now dressed in light blue PJ's.

"It is two in the morning Ryder; you need to get some sleep." She said as she sipped on a cup of herbal tea, hoping it would help her sleep.

"I can't," Ryder said, now dressed in checkered sleep pants and a light blue t-shirt. He yawned and rubbed the back of his tired sore neck. "We know Lillian can get in here. You told me you found lock picks in the house. That is how she has been getting into the rooms."

"I know you are trying to protect your little sister but you are not going to do her any good if you are not alert. You should be in there—." Alex pointed the bedroom where Yakira was asleep. "—cuddled up to next to her, living life."

"Work has to come first." Ryder said as he walked over to the mirror above the fireplace. He looked tired, even to himself. His eyes were heavy and blood shot, dark bags underneath them. She finished her tea and set the cup and saucer down on the coffee table. She stood up and walked over behind him, he could see her reflection standing behind him in the mirror.

"That was what I used to believe till they placed that little girl in my arms. The world changed then, Ricky." She placed her hand on his back. "You have a whole world here yourself." He turned and walked away from her, going over to the wet bar and dropping ice in a glass, but changing his mind, he set the glass down. He walked over to the window and pulled back the heavy drapes, looking out over the warm light that was reflecting in the fog that had gathered over the town.

"You remember how you told me that after that storm you were not afraid of anything?" Alex said as she walked over behind him again; he could see her reflection in the glass. "That is not true is it, you are afraid of one thing…" He dropped the drape down and turned around to confront her. "You are afraid of caring." Ryder walked around her and sat down on the couch.

Alex walked over and stood in front of him. "She is your sister."

"What is that suppose to mean?' He asked looking up at her

"Stop treating her like she is a witness. It is okay to get emotionally involved. It is okay to tell her you love her." Alex said a small grin beginning to show.

"We go to zone defense. There are only two ways in to this place. The front door or the window. I will stay out there and you are in the bedroom with her."

"There you go again, all business." Alex said. "When are you going to let someone in?"

Ryder dropped his gaze to the floor, not wanting to look at her as he said. "How did you change Alex?"

"Looking into that little face, how can I not?" Alex said as she sat down on the coffee table in front of him. "The world may still suck but somehow when I see her reach out her arms for me, it seems all right, and it is a reason to get in the morning."

"You don't have to say something for someone to know it. He said as slowly raised his head till they were face to face.

"True but, sometimes that is all someone wants to hear. But it a lover, a sister or a..." She placed her hand on top of his as she said. "A friend." She let go of his hand and stood up, and heading for the bedroom where Marissa was asleep.

"What do you about the ones that let you down?"He asked making her turned back to him. "Those that leave you, or those that disappoint you because they are not who you though they were?"

"There is something that Uncle Tony told me that I try to remember. 'If you never swallow heartbreak, you cannot ever taste the sweetness of love.' "

"She will be here before sunrise." Ryder said. "Your little girl, I got her on a chopper, she will see the sunrise with you."

"You are wonder man." Alex said. "I love you."

"Belle," He said softly calling a short version of her first name. "I— I—I ..." he just couldn't get the words out.

She smiled brightly, showing her teeth, she said. "I know," she said softly, before she disappeared behind the bedroom door.

There were a blanket and pillow lying on the settee, and he picked them up and placed the pillow at one end of the sofa, laid down and covered up with the blanket. It wasn't long till he was asleep.

'Tap. Tap.' Ryder was awakened by a light rapping on the door, it was barely a knock, and the morning dawn was just beginning to break, just before the sun rose. Ryder rose up, remaining still and gazing out into the darkness. He began to reach for his side arm, but remembered he had dropped it on the floor at the old house, it had burned up. He heard the door unlock, and the door moaned as it opened and the light from the hall leaked in, he could see a shadowy image on the entry hall wall. Ryder quickly rose to his feet. His mind flashed back to basic training, hand to-hand. He quickly moved over to the side of the wall where the opening to the sitting area was, he could hear the footsteps on the thin carpet. He drew his hands back ready to attack. The shadow was in the door way.

He moved quickly and fast, not even thinking of what to do. He attacked from behind. Quickly grabbing an arm, twisting it around, and bending back against the elbow, before twisting it around behind his back and with Ryder's other arm he placed it around the neck and with his weight forced the figure to the floor. There was a cry of pain. And suddenly the room filled with light, as Alex darted out of the bedroom with her gun drawn.

"Son, you wanta' get off me." Ryder heard a muffled voice say from underneath him. "You are about to break my neck." It was his father. Ryder released his grip and stood up. He held out his hand and helped his father to his feet. Marissa stood in the doorway to her bedroom, her hair mussed, and standing up on one side.

"How did you get in here?" Ryder asked as Alex lowered the gun to her side and Ryder walked over to the couch and sat down. "And what are you doing here?"

Ryan held up a key. "I gave him my key." Yakira said as the noise had caused her to awaken, and she was standing in the doorway of the bedroom. "The storms grounded the chopper so I called your father and had him go get Ceelia."

"Mommy," Ceelia's small voice broke the silence as she twisted her head around from behind her Aunt's legs and looked over at her mother. Alex handed Ryder her weapon and kneeled down on one knee.

"Come here, baby!" The little girl raced to her and Alex wrapped her arms around her, holding her close. Then releasing her from the embrace and placing her hands on her shoulders, she looked at her daughter and in a soft kind tone she told her. "I don't want you to ever be afraid of guns, or any of this stuff you see." Alex looked up at Ryder. "Uncle Ricky was trying to protect his little sister."

Ceelia pulled back from her mother's embrace, turned her head, and looked up at Ryder. Reaching out she took a hold of his hand, allowing her small fingers to twist around two of his fingers as she said. "Can we see the sun get out of his bed?" He nodded and led her over to the balcony door. He opened it and helped her up the steps, and then down on the metal rail balcony, he lifted her up in his arms so that she could watch as the sun rose up over the hillside, spanning out across the tree line, beaming behind the towering Christ of the Ozarks.

"Look Mommy!" Ceelia said, as she gaped at the sunrise, the bright orange sky now filled with bright pure sun light. "Jesus is shining!"

"Could you get some agents to watch her?" Ryder asked, motioning with his head back towards the room. "Can you get them to watch Marissa?"

"Uh—hh..." She drew out, almost hesitating to answer. She took Ceelia and led her back into the room and over to her aunt, and asked her to watch her as she stepped back out on the balcony and shut the door. "That is what I wanted to tell you." Again she hesitated, placing her hands on the balcony rail, wrapping her fingers around tighter and finally getting the courage to say it. "I have been let go from the agency."

"What! How, why?" Ryder's tone was coarse and harsh as he demanded answers, then when he realized it was because of him, his tone suddenly softened as he placed his hand on her shoulder and added. "This case, you are not supposed to be working on it, are you?" She shook her head. "Why? Why did you do it?"

"You are my friend. You needed help." She rose up and turned to him. "It was what I had to do. They put me on a desk; it was what I thought I wanted. But when I saw that note was from her, I..."

"You knew she was after me all along?"

"Yes." Alex said as she walked over to the other side of the balcony and crossed her arms in front of her. "I don't know what I am going to do. Maybe I've got enough money saved for a couple of ..."

Ryder placed his hands on her shoulders and turned her around. Do not worry about money."

"No!" She said firmly. "I don't want you giving me money. I told you that right after you won it, and wanted to give me a million. We will get by."

"I am talking about you coming and working with me."

"Doing what?"

"What you are good at, being an investigator." He smiled slightly as he added. "I can promise you great benefits." Ryder replied as he turned, hearing the door open, and saw Yakira standing there, with Marissa behind her.

"Like what?" Alex said.

"Never a dull day. Fee health care, education provided for your child, including college. Plus, a boss that—would be very happy to have you here."

"Well now, I would be a fool to turn that down, wouldn't I?"

He placed his arm around Alex and turned to Yakira and said. "Alex is officially one of us now."

"That is good, Ricky." Yakira said rather somberly. Noticing the tone, he lifted his arm up off Alex and asked.

"What is it?"

"Detective Shepherd called this morning; the newspaper got another note."

> You try to protect the one you love
> As you look down upon me from above
> I will soon see your tears fall
> Then it will happen again-
> For I will strike when she is having a ball-
> So say the slayer of sin-

Chapter 29

Ryder had sent Jonas down stairs for breakfast for everyone for he could no longer trust room service. There was a loud rap on the front door. Thinking it might be him, Yakira opened it, and in walked the mayor shouting as he marched past Yakira

"What is the meaning of this Mr. Ryder?" Ryder looked up from a cell phone where he was reading a copy of the note the Detective Shepherd sent him. Ryder didn't say a word he just dropped his eyes back down to the screen. "I thought we had this Slayer crap all wrapped up. What the hell is this Sin Slayer?"

Ryder slowly lifted his eyes up from the phone and stared at the man. "I told you before the Eureka Slayer is a different person."

"Again with this gorgeous blonde? I am not buying that." He stormed on into the room and looked at everyone that was there, and then back over to Ryder. "Where is your uncle? The so called priest! If you ask me, this Sin Slayer that would be right up his alley. Why was it that he found the body of that woman? And he knew the other woman, he was seen with her. You ask me, he could have done this."

"Are you accusing my uncle of murder?" Ryder said as he handed the cell phone back to his sister. Ryder slowly walked over to the mayor. "You pompous blow hard."

"Makes more sense, than a beautiful blonde."

Maybe it is you mayor?"

"Are you accusing of murder?" The mayor's word was hard hitting trying to make himself sound more important than he was. "What motive would I have?"

"Maybe because the number one trending on the web for the last three days has been Eureka Springs, it has been the talk of all the cable shows, even the Tonight Show is making jokes about."

"But it is bad news."

"Ever hear there is no such thing as bad publicity?"

"I talked to Chad at the desk downstairs…" As Ryder spoke he could hear the front door open again and looked over and saw Detective Shepherd walk in. Ryder returned his stare at the mayor and continued. "He tells me the hotel is full, everyone is coming for this gala this weekend.

It seems that the thought of a beautiful killer is just helping you get more visitors."

"That is insane!"

"Prove it! Cancel the Grand Gala Street Ball."

"That is what I am going to tell you mayor," Detective Shepherd said. "It is pretty clear she is going to strike at the ball, we can't risk this."

"I am not cancelling it!" The mayor snapped back. "This is the biggest thing we have ever had going in Eureka Springs. Even the Travel Channel is going to be here filming it. I will not have it cancelled. He turned to face Ryder. "And you Mr. Ryder I don't care about all your money." The mayor said pointing his finger at him. He turned to Detective Shepherd. "I want him, and all these people arrested."

"What for?"

"Interfering with a murder investigation."

"With an investigation that you gave him permission to investigate," Detective Shepherd said as he walked over next Ryder.

"That is when she was with the FBI, she isn't any longer with them."

And how would you know that? Alex asked, disgruntled, "I couldn't figure out how they knew." She looked at Mayor. "I should have known."

"I want you out of here right now." Ryder said pointing towards the door. "You got thirty seconds."

"What if I don't leave?"

"Then you leave by the window."

"You heard him!" The Mayor shouted turning to Detective Shepherd. "He threatened me! ARREST HIM!"

Detective Shepherd ran his hand over his chin before saying. "With all due respect Mr. Mayor, Get the hell out of here!"

"I have your badge Shepherd!" The mayor warned as the he walked out of the rom.

"So why are you doing this? You could get fired." Ryder asked.

"Because I can't shave in the dark. If I don't try to stop this, knowing it is going happen how can I face myself? You are not going to get the Gala cancelled. So how are we going to protect everybody?"

"We don't. I know who she is coming after; it is Marissa. She won't be going?"

"What!" He heard Marissa gasp as she walked out of her bedroom. "You can't do that! That ain't fair. I have my costume ready and everything. I am going to dance with Zack; he asked me, it is my first real dance. You can't do that!"

"Who is Zack?" Ryder asked with a tone that was more big brother and not a detective, but quickly changed back. "Doesn't matter, you are not going!"

"You are not my father!"

"You're damn right I am not. And I am telling you that if I have to, I will tie you down to something. You are not going to that dance."

"That is not fair!" Marissa shouted, stomping her foot on the floor as Yakira walked up next to her. She turned to Yakira with a pleading look on her face. "You too? Daddy!" She yelled, walking over to him. He stood in front of the fireplace with a low ball glass in his hand.

"Please!" She begged her father, pressing her hands together and making her eyes as big and sad as she could, pushing out a pouting lip.
Well, I don't see no harm in letting her..."

Mary, her mother quickly broke in. "Rick is right. You are not going to the dance. There will always be more dances. But here is only one of you."

"I hate you!" Marissa shouted at her mother, then turned back to Ryder and added, "I hate all of you!" She stomped into her bedroom and slammed the door behind her. Everyone else was quiet, wondering what to say next after that display. Alex stood looking at Yakira, watching her walk and move, noticing her face and how young she appeared.

"We have a problem then." Alex said.

"What is it?"

"Lillian is going to be watching. If she doesn't see Merissa leave, she is going to come in here, or more likely she will attack someone else at the gala,. I don't care how well we have it guarded, there is no way we can watch everyone there."

"So what do you have in mind?" Ryder asked.

"We use bait to draw her out."

"No!" Ryder said forcefully. "No one is using my little sister as bait."

"We don't have to," Alex said, again looking over to Yakira. "With the right hair do, and a mask..."

"No!" Ryder shouted again. "We are not putting Yakira in there."

"She looks young enough to be a teenager. If she is armed, she can take care of herself. "

"No," Ryder stated as he placed his arm around Yakira and pulled her close.

"Come on Rick, they are the same height, about the same built, if we just lighten her hair."

"No!"

"But we know she is going to be at the gala, we could be there. We lure her in..."

"NO, I said. We will catch her some other way."

"If we don't do this, you told me she was brewing up a large amount of that toxin; she could release it on to the crowd." There was another loud rap on the door, Yakira went to open the door, but she returned holding a box. She handed it to Ryder and he lifted the lid, what he saw made the color in his face drain away. He reached in and picked up what was inside, a Glock pistol. He examined it carefully, turning and twisting it around. One of the hand grips was slightly melted and the other on the very end had the letters R.R. carved at the end of the grip.

"It is mine," He said softly. Then he looked over at Yakira and Alex. "It is my service weapon!"

"But you dropped that in the house."

"Yeah, only one person could have gotten it out of that house!" Outside in the hall there was a loud crash and Ryder dashed to the door. He jerked the door open and gazed down the hall where Jonas stood, at his feet was a tray, and shards of broken coffee cups and saucers, spilled coffee spoiling the carpet. He was pointing down the hall.

"It was her!" He shouted. "It was Lillian! She was standing outside the door; she ran for the stairs!

Ryder quickly turned back to Alex. "Take the elevator! Head her off." He turned to Shepherd and Yakira and said," Stay here in case she comes back, and get somebody on the balcony." Ryder then turned and ran down the hall, his service weapon clutched in his hand. He pulled the stair door open and listened carefully for footsteps, he could hear them going down stairs. He quickly followed, running down the stairs. Landing on the bottom floor, he held the Glock out in front of him, spanning it across the lobby.

He heard the elevator doors open and Alex stepped out, her weapon already gripped in her hands. "See her?" She asked. Ryder shook his head and then looked around, slowly making his way along the wall, as Alex went the other way. They went deep into the lobby toward the front desk. Seeing Timmy behind the counter Ryder asked.

"Did you see anyone pass by here?"

No," he said, shaking his head. "I haven't seen anyone in the last thirty minutes." Ryder saw Alex out of the corner of his eye. He turned to her, she shook her head.

"If she was here," Alex said, lowering her pistol to her side. "She is gone now. She must have another way in."

"Maybe she found the tunnel." Timmy said.

"What tunnel?" Ryder asked as he lowered the pistol to his side.

"You know about the tunnels under the town." Ryder nodded as Timmy spoke, "Well, there are tales that there is also a tunnel that goes to this hotel."

"Where is it?"

"No one knows, no one has ever found it. I think it is just a legend."

"Ricky," Ryder heard Yakira say as she walked up behind him, she was holding something in her hand. "There was something else in the box." She held up a note. She handed it to him and he read it.

I know where she is.

You cannot hide her.

The game must be played

She is next move.

Then it will be you.

Chapter 30

That last note changed the way Ryder looked at the whole thing. It was clear to him that Marissa was to be the next victim, and Lillian knew where she was; still the hotel was the best place she could be. Ryder called up favors, importing help with Father Anthony and Double T outside in the hall and Brian on the balcony, and himself, Yakira and Alex in the room, Lillian would have to run a gauntlet to get to her.

This was all much to the displeasure of Marissa, who was feeling like she was a prisoner facing her own execution, in embarrassment and humiliation of having to tell her friends that she couldn't go to the gala, but she couldn't even do that, as Ryder wanted no communication, and no visitors. The hotel staff was not even to enter. The maid would leave the towels and sheets outside the door and they would make the beds themselves. Someone would go and get the food; no one would bring anything in, unless Ryder or Alex cleared it.

Marissa was confined to her bedroom, the sitting area or the bathroom, she was not to go near windows or open up the drapes. To get into the hotel room required a special knock; three at the top of the door and then two lighter knocks on the lower portion of the door. Marissa could have anything she wanted to eat, get anything her heart desired; Ryder would buy it and have it brought to her, but she was not happy. Ryder heard about it through slammed doors in the night as yet another day passed.

Once again the morning sun rose, its light beaming across the town. Just as in the days before, Ceelia, in her mother's arms watched. "The sun is getting out of his bed, Uncle Ricky." The little girl said as the sun beamed behind the statue of the Christ of the Ozarks. Knowing she may not be able to explain, he turned to Alex. Who smiled, and placed one hand up to her ears revealing dangling ruby and diamond ear rings.

"I never got to thank you for the ear rings, and the lovely pendant you got for Ceelia, I think we will wait till she is a little older before I give it to her." Alex said. "

"Rick there is a package here for you." He heard Yakira say as she stepped out onto the balcony.

"I have been expecting that." Ryder said walking over to her and taking the bag. He looked into the bag as Yakira retuned and went back into the room. Ryder reached into the paper bag and pulled out a gleaming tiara. "Every princess needs a crown." He said placing it on the little girls head. Alex gazed at the gleaming jewels on the silver crown. "Don't worry," he said. "They are not real, and it adjusts, so she will always have it. The little girl quickly reached up and felt the crown on her head as she said.

"I real mommy, I princess."

"Yes you are." Alex said "You want to thank Uncle Ricky?"

"Thank you Uncle Ricky!" Ceelia said wrapping her arms around his neck and hugging him as tightly as she could and kissing him on the cheek she added with a bright smile. "Love you."

"Love you too little girl." He heard him say something he thought he could never say.

"She gets to you don't she?" Alex asked, as Ceelia once again wrapped her arms around her mother as Ryder reached into the bag once again and pulled out a small black velvet box. "Is that for who I think it is for?"

"Well I decided to take your advice and let those walls down a little." Ryder said as he turned and headed back towards the doors that lead into the room from the balcony. Before stepping inside he took one last look across the landscape at the sun glimmering behind the leaves, and creating a golden glow around the statue of the Christ of the Ozarks.

Ryder stepped down into the room. He saw his father over next to the wet bar pouring gin over ice in a glass. "Father," Ryder said formally as he walked up to the man, more than a day's growth of beard showed on his face. He turned and looked at Ryder and rubbed his hand over his chin. "A new day has begun."

"So it has, son." The man said raising the glass to his lips and walking by Ryder.

"It has for us, too."

"What does that mean?" His voice was coarse, rough, and much deeper than Ryder's; he sat down on the couch and gazed up at his son standing before him.

"It means…" Ryder hesitated for a small moment; these words were hard for him to say, and they were coming up out of his mouth as a vile tasting bitterness, which over the years had fermented into unresolved hatred. "…I am forgiving you."

"Am I asking you for it?" The man said, raising his heavy dark colored eye brows up to him.

"No, I am giving it to you."

"That sounds like the garbage that Tony says." His father said as he stood taking his glass in his hand and refilling it at the wet bar. "I really don't go for that mumbo jumbo stuff you hear on Sunday morning. That where you got it from?"

"No," Ryder said, looking over to the window and watching as Alex helped Ceelia down the steps, "Someone much wiser." He turned back to his father and added. "I have to forgive you. So I can do something more important."

"Yeah, what's that?" The man said, taking a sip of the oily bitter tasting drink.

"To forgive myself," Ryder said as he watched the man walk back to the couch.

"That is the dumbest damn thing I ever heard son, a man doesn't forgive himself." He took a swig of the gin, the ice clinking on the side of the glass.

Ryder looked over at Yakira kneeling by the window, crawling and acting if she were a monster going to get Ceelia, the little girl screamed as she giggled and ran. Behind her and through the glass he watched as the breeze drifted through the trees as if it were tickling at the leaves. "He does if he wants to be his own man." Ryder turned back to his father. "All my life I thought it was something that I did. Something I could have been better at. Something that I did wrong, and that was the reason you left. It was you. All you! It is just the way you are." His father looked up at him, the glass clutched in his hand as Ryder continued. "I was so afraid I was going to be like you. I am not you, I am me, and I will never be you."

The man looked up at him and swigged down the rest of the drink before he asked sarcastically. "You done? Have any more to say?"

"Not to you." Ryder said as he walked over to the window, reaching down he took a hold of Yakira's hand. "Come with me." He looked over at Alex and added. "Can you hold it down?" She nodded and he led Yakira to the front door. "There is something I need to tell you." He grabbed the door and opened it. He nodded at Uncle Tony at one end of the hall and at Brian on the other end. Then he led her into the elevator and the doors closed.

"What did you want to tell me?" She asked.

"Not here." He said, watching the elevator count down to the ground floor. The doors opened, and still holding on to her hand he led her through the lobby and out the French doors. They went down the long steps that led to the parking lot then to the street below. They went across the street to the St. Elizabeth church and into the bell tower, which was no longer sealed with police tape.

"This is the place," He said, turning her around to face him, "Before the very eyes of God himself." He took a step down, and kneeled down on both knees, so that she was looking down at him. "This is where you belong and that is where I want you to remain. So I am never looking down on you, so that I am always looking up to you."

She was confused; she didn't know what to say, but he held his hand up for her to be still as he took a hold of her hands, brought them up together and kissed them.

"I love you, Yakira." He said looking up at her, with the sun shining behind her she looked like a true angel. "I know I haven't told you that much. I guess I never really told too many people that. But I do love you." He reached into the pocket of his jacket and pulled out the small box and opened it up, revealing the tear drop shaped diamond ring that was his great grandmothers. It gleamed brightly now, the shaft polished brightly; the stones cleaned and polished. Seeing the ring she began to tear up as he spoke.

"My tears are your tears. I don't cry. You don't cry...." He took the ring out of the case and held it out as she held out her hand and he slipped it on her finger as he said, "But now that we have found each other, we weep no longer." Yakira trembled with delight as he asked the question she had been waiting to hear since she was eight years old. "Marry me?"

"OHHH, YES!" She squealed, her words echoing out over the yard and the hills, racing back up to the hotel. "Yes, YES, YES!" He rose up from his knees and she grabbed him, wrapping her arms around his neck as he lifted her up off the floor. His lips took a hold of hers as they shared a passion-filled kiss, her feet dangling loosely. "I love you." She said as he placed her back down on the floor and she looked up at him.

253

Her tone turned somber. "You can't do this anymore, Ricky."

"What?"

"Trying to catch Lillian, she is going to kill you. You-you…" She lowered her gaze, placing the top of her head in his chest. "You can't leave me. We have to leave; get out of here."

"That isn't going to do any good." Ryder said, lifting her head up and making her look at him. "It doesn't matter where we go; she is going to come after me. The best thing we can do is draw her out."

"Then in that case," she said, turning and not wanting to look at him when she said this; she paused and took a deep breath. The wind whipping across them, blowing strands of hair into her face. She pushed her hair back out of her face as she spoke carefully. "I know how we can draw the shiska out, if you will go for it." He turned to her as she added. "Give her what she wants."

Chapter 31

As he and Yakira climbed the steps hand in hand, up the hill back to the hotel, Ryder didn't have much to say. His mind kept going to the possibilities of how he could stop Lillian; he knew from other profiles that if the plan was set, she was going to do whatever it took to get to Marissa, then come after him.

"It is the only way, Ricky." Yakira said as they reached the top of the steps. He wanted to continue walking but she stopped and pulled back on his hand, making him turn to her. "I am trained; I know how to use a gun. You are going to be there; Alex will be there."

"No," he said without a hint of emotion, and pulled on her hand to make her follow him back to the hotel, through the lobby and into the elevator. As the door closed and they began their ascent, she pleaded her case again.

"If I am wearing a mask she wouldn't know I am not Marissa. We could grab her." The elevator doors opened, and he led her down the hall; they stood in front of the door. He gave the secret knock.

"Who is it?" He heard a soft voice say from behind the door, he quickly recognized that it was Mary.

"It is little Red Riding hood, were you expecting the big bad wolf?" He joked and heard the door being unlocked and it opened. He and Yakira had just walked in when Mary looked right at Yakira and then over at Ryder. She grinned, throwing her arms around him in an embrace.

"Congratulations!" She released him and then hugged Yakira as she asked. "When is the wedding?" Ryder's puzzled look quickly darted over to Yakira and then to Alex, she was the only one who know what he was going to do.

"You told her?"

"I didn't say a thing." Alex pleaded

"I could see it on this face." Mary said placing her arm around Yakira's shoulders and patting her face with her other hand. "You can always see it in a woman's face." Mary lifted Yakira's hand up and examined the ring.

"Ryan, come and meet your new daughter-in-law."

"What?" He offered his tipsy reply.

"A wedding!" Ryder heard Marissa squeal with delight from the far bedroom as she came running into the sitting area, tagging along with her was Ceelia. "Who is getting married?" Standing behind her was Ryder's father, another glass of liquor in his hand.

"I must thank God for being such a lucky woman." Mary said, looking at Ryder and saying. "I got a son and now a new daughter."

"So going to take the plunge, big brother?" Marissa said, walking up to him and punching him in the arm, before she grabbed and hugged him around the chest.

"I want you to be one of my bride's maids." Yakira said, facing Marissa.

"Really?" Marissa's face drew with glee. "Oh that would be awesome!"

Turning to Alex, Yakira asked. "And you my maid-of honor?"

"Me?" Alex asked stunned. "Why would you—I mean..." She paused and Ceelia ran up to her. She picked her child up, the little girl wrapping her arms around her mother's neck as Alex added. "I am touched; I don't know what to say."

"Well, how about yes?" Yakira grinned.

"Okay, yes."

"Can I be in the wedding too, aunt Kahari? Ceelia said, reaching out her hand, trying her best to pronounce her name.

"Of course you can! You can be our flower girl."

"Gonna have ourselves a wedding. I guess that is a reason to celebrate." Ryan said as he walked back over to the wet bar, pulled out a bottle of whiskey and began pouring a drink. "What does everybody else want?"

"Ryan, it is not even ten o'clock yet." Mary said as she walked over to him and placed her hand on his, trying to stop him from pouring the drink.

"Gosh Dammit woman, my son is going to get married. I have a damn right to celebrate." He said as he pushed her hand back before taking the bottle and the glass with him and head for the couch. He placed the bottle on the coffee table and plopped down on the sofa. He raised his glass to Ryder. "With all your blasted money it ought to be one hell of a blow out." Then he took a large swig of the drink. It grew still till Mary's question broke the silence.

"So who is going to be your best man, Rick?" Mary asked.

Ryder walked over in front of his father, and his father looked up at him, with his eyes blood shot and blinking stupidly as Ryder asked. "Dad…" Ryder took a breath, causing the man to begin a grin, even to set his glass down beside the bottle on the table.

"Yeah, son?" He asked, righting himself to his feet.

"Where is Jonas? I have something to ask him."

"Oh, him!" Ryan said, dejected, as he flopped back down on the couch, picked up his glass, and took another drink. "He left!"

"Where did he go?"

"Don't know. Don't care, not my flesh and blood." He raised his glass and took a drink. Once they get certain age my job is done, makes 'em tough." He took another drink, swallowing down the golden liquid and rolled his eyes up to Ryder. "Made you tough didn't it?" He let his head turn and look at Marissa and added. "What I have with you about a couple more years? You are sixteen right?" He struggled with his words trying to get them out. Ryder saw the disappointment in his sister's face as she spoke.

"I am only thirteen, daddy."

"Oh great got another five freakin' years." He muttered as once again he raised his glass and took a large drink. "You ae a smart one may—I—I can let you go even quicker. I'll get rid of you all."

Ryder wanted badly to just throw his father out of this room, and get of him, but he kept his mouth shut and instead, just let his finger twist in between Yakira's as she walked over next to him.

"I hate to be the doomsayer here." Alex said as she leaned down and placed her child back down on the floor, allowing her sister to take her and leave the room before she continued. "There is no way we can have a wedding if Lillian is still around."

"I could draw here out." Marissa said.

"No!" Ryder snapped back.

"You asked me! Now I want a wedding and there is no way I am going to let her stop it!" Yakira said, as she walked over to the side of

Marissa, and Ryder noticed they were the same height, same built. Yakira turned to Marissa and asked "What costume were you going to wear?"

"An ice princess."

"Does it have a mask?" Yakira asked.

"Only over my eyes."

"See, it won't work." Ryder said. "We will find her some other way."

"I can get a bigger mask." Yakira said, "I can cut my hair, get it lightened. It is the only way."

"We will be right there, Ryder." Alex said. "Yakira can handle herself; she is a better shot then either of us."

"I can do it, Sweetie."

"All right!" Ryder reluctantly agreed. He placed his hands on her shoulders and looked into Yakira's eyes as he said. "I don't like this. But I don't see any other way to draw her out." He let his fingers slide up her neck to the side of her face, pushing her hair up, letting it curl around his thumbs. "After we catch her I am going to take you to anywhere you want to go for your birthday."

"You remembered?"

"Of course."

"Anywhere? Anything?"

"Sure."

"Can we get married? You said anything."

"Okay." Ryder said tenderly.

"Nah," Yakira said with a grin that beamed from one side of her face to the other. "That way you would only have to buy one present; I think I will pick another date." He stood there for a moment just staring at her, maybe he was mesmerized by how beautiful she was in his eyes, and then again maybe it was because he didn't want to let her go. He slowly lowered his lips to hers and kissed. He stood watching as she and Mary walked out of the room closing the door behind them.

Within a few minutes he heard a knock on the door. "Who is it?" Ryder said, loud enough to be heard. Alex drew her gun up from the holster on her hip.

"It is Timmy from the desk. I have a note for you."

Alex took a position next to the wall as Ryder unlocked the door. Ryder saw Timmy standing in the hallway. He handed Ryder a sealed up envelope with his name printed on it.

"Who left this?"

"Don't know." Timmy said. I went to the bathroom, I came back and there were two notes on the counter; one for you and one for your brother, I gave it to him and he ran out screaming that he was going to get the witch." Ryder tore the envelope open. It was a photo of Lillian climbing down into the hole on Spring Street. He handed it to Alex who lowered her gun.

"In these tunnels, is there any place that someone could be hiding?" Ryder asked.

"Yes, there are old store fronts down there."

Ryder turned back to Alex and said. "Go get changed, we are going underground."

Into the hole

Ryder had seen it when he had first come to town, baring its naked soul to the heavens. The hole was still wide open, like a sore cavity in the tooth of the city's smile; it was just begging to be filled. Parked next to the Basin Park was a large dump truck, its bed loaded with white gravel, behind it was a bright yellow front loader. Ryder had changed clothes into something suitable for what they were going to undertake. Jeans, t-shirt and wind breaker that covered the Glock tucked into the holster on his side, and boots. Ryder approached the hole, a black canvas back pack draped across his shoulder. Alex stood next to the hole; she too was dressed for the trip underground.

"Got brand new batteries," She said, handing him one of the head mounted flashlights, placing the other one on her head. "They are extra-long life."

"I got supplies." He said sitting the backpack down and slipping on the headlamp. "Chips, protein bars, a couple of bottles of Gatorade, and..." He unzipped the bag, reached inside, and pulled out a bag of M&M's. He looked up at her and handed her the sea foam green bag. "Dark chocolate Mint, your favorite?"

"You remember?." She said offering a small smile, as she brushed her hair back over her ear.

"I am a detective. I know things."

In the hole there was a ladder leaned up against the side of the opening. They crawled down the ladder and into the hole; to the side was the beginning of a tunnel. He flipped on his headlamp, as it began to cut through the darkness there was nothing grand or elegant about the facade of the tunnel. Most of the store fronts were sealed off by stone walls that continued around, above, and to the other side, creating more of a storm drain like effect, complete with rain water a couple of inches deep on the floor. Even through his leather boots Ryder could feel the cold water soaking in on his toes. As he pushed back the cobwebs and continued forward, sloshing in the water, up ahead he could hear water running. Not a gushing geyser, instead just a trickle, but then a drip, drip, as water ran down the sides to the stone walls of the tunnel and collected in a pool, the light spilling from the purple crystals overhead on the sidewalk, creating a radiating hue of Amethyst that gave the tunnel a little less of a cave like feeling, easing Ryder's fears that it was all going to come crashing down on him.

They continued on down the tunnel, the light of the opening becoming smaller and smaller with each step they took. Again they stopped under one of the crystals in the sidewalk above. Ryder set the backpack down on the floor of the tunnel and opened the bag. He pulled out a bottle of Gatorade, opened it and took a drink before handing it to Alex; she took a drink and handed it back to him.

"Do you think there is anything down here?" He asked, taking another drink.

"I don't know; all we can do is try." She said, trying to look further up the tunnel.

"It is possible she could hide in one of those…" He had just replaced the lid on the bottle, when he suddenly stopped speaking then turned his head and gazed back down the tunnel, the way they had just come. "You hear that?" He asked in a whisper. She listened carefully and replied in a normal tone.

"It is a bell."

It is not a bell, it is a beeping. It's a truck backing up!" Ryder's tone changed to panic and he dropped the bottle as he shouted "It's the dump trunk! They are going to fill the hole!" They both took off running back down the tunnel as hard as they could, their feet plowing into water, soaking the legs of their pants. The daylight from the hole was growing brighter the closer they got. Ryder could hear the deadfall sound of gravel scraping across the metal bed and falling into the hole, at first just a dribble, like a shovelful of dirt upon a grave.

"STOP! We are down here!" Ryder yelled out. He could hear the dump truck bed being raised more and the gravel poured in furiously, the grave was sealed. They were buried alive.

Chapter 32

Ryder coughed and gasped for air as the dust filled the tunnel, and darkness once again reigned. "Oh dear Lord! No, STOP! " Alex cried out with force, before her voice softened with a tone of hopelessness. "Ricky, we are buried down here." He turned back to her as the dust began to settle once again on the floor of the tunnel. He could see the beam from her headlamp gleaming in the water on the floor. "I am never going to see my little girl again."

He had to admit it; his heart was heavy in his chest and worry was running through his own mind. He had to keep his senses about him, and he had to keep Alex from losing hers; they both had to keep thinking straight. He coughed again and reached down and took and a hold of her shoulders, and made her stand up.

"Belle," He said tenderly as she looked at him. "I need you to remain strong." She nodded her head. "Ceelia needs her mother." Again she nodded her head. "Now we are going to get out of here." He placed his hands on her cheeks and he lowered his face to hers and added. "I promise you."

Suddenly there was a rumble from above and the dust again began tumbling down on top of them. He used his body as a shield, wrapping his arms around her and holding her close as she yelled out.

"Stop it, Stop it! You are burying us alive!"

He heard the rumble of the back hoe and the deathly scrape of the bucket across the pavement as it smoothed out the gravel, thus sealing them in a tomb, the beep, beep sound as it backed up becoming like the sound of Gabriel's trumpet. Again the vile sound of the bucket being scraped across the pavement made a chill run through him as he shuddered. He hoped that with her own shaking in his arms, she couldn't feel his fright. As the back hoe backed up to take another run, he released her from his embrace and grabbed her hand, leading her deeper into the tunnel, back to the purple hue of the crystal in the sidewalk. He bent down and picked up the bottle of Gatorade. He wiped the dust from it as he seated himself on a rock; he opened the bottle and took a sip before handing it to her. He bent down and picked up the bag and pulled out the goodies, opening up the chips.

As she took a drink from the bottle she looked over at him with amazement showing on her face. "Are you crazy?" She gasped out as she lowered the bottle from her lips. "This is going to be our grave and you are going to have a picnic?" He handed her the bag of chips after taking a handful. She looked up as the sound of the bucket being slammed down on the gravel rang through the tunnel.

"We are going to get out of here, but we can't get dehydrated or get weak." He said again, pushing the bag at her, "Eat!" She took the bag and sat down on the rock beside him,

Again the sound of the backhoe bucket banging on the gravel rang through the tunnel. They lowered their heads and Ryder shielded the food as dust fell down once again. There was another beeping sound, and the muffled sound of pouring on the street, it was pavement being placed over the gravel. If the gravel was the sealing of their grave, the pavement was the headstone. She placed her head on his shoulder. The sound above them grated as the crew gathered the equipment up and then it grew still.

"I always pictured us dying together in a shootout." She said before lifting her head and looking at him, offering a petite smile. "Taking down a big terrorist group, saving America from another 911, we would be held as heroes. Our families would tell tales of how proud they were of us. Little kids would hear about us in history class. We would be somebody." She leaned her head back down on his shoulder as she added, crestfallen. "Never thought we just wait to die." He stood up, making her lift her head. He walked back towards the pile of gravel. "Well, if we are going to die down here there is something I need to tell you." She said, her words penetrating the darkness and echoing off the stone walls as he stood in front of the gravel, gazing out over it and looking up at the top.

"The tunnel also went this way."

"Yes, but it is sealed over, there is only a small opening. We can't get through that." Alex said as she stood up and walked back to him. "I was going to tell you a secret. "

"You can tell me when we get out of here!" He said as he began climbing the pile of gravel towards the top of the tunnel. He began using his hands; he began digging like a dog, scooping the gravel out between his legs. "Are you going to help or not?" He asked, glancing over his shoulder. She climbed up the gravel pile next to him and began digging. Soon there was a small hole. "Ladies first." He said with a wave of his hand.

"No, no! A gentleman should lead the way."

"Beauty before age." Ryder said.

"That's age before beauty, but how about this- there is no blasted way I am going first."

"And here I though you believed in equal rights." Ryder laughed as he laid down on his belly on the gravel, sticking his head into the hole; he slid down, his feet quickly disappearing.

"Rick." Alex called. "You see anything?" He didn't answer her. "Rick!" She placed her head in the hole when suddenly Ryder grabbed her by the shoulders and pulled her in. She let out a squeal and she landed face down in a puddle of muddy water. She got up and wiped the mud from her face.

"We are in luck." He said helping her to her feet. He too was covered in the mud. "It looks like the earthquake may have opened into another tunnel." It was clear that at one time the tunnels were not connected or that they suffered damage, as the stones were piled in the new tunnel. To the right was nothing but darkness, cobwebs so thick it just gave him a nervous feeling. Straight ahead was another opening, nothing more than just a crack in the ground.

Above Ryder could hear the stop and go traffic at the intersection of Main and Spring streets. With each passing of the vehicles above, the dirt and rock would fall down. The crevasse was just wide enough to make it through if one was to crawl through one at a time on their bellies, falling down hands first into the other tunnel, rolling onto their feet. As with the tunnel before, this one also had amethyst crystals on the sidewalk, allowing light to enter. They had walked only a short way when they saw a door that had originally been on the first floor. It was open.

It opened into a brick corridor that led to a set of rickety stairs and to another door. Ryder turned to Alex; covered in mud she looked like a creature from the underworld. He laughed. "You smell like rotten eggs."

"Don't laugh buddy, you're no rose yourself." She said as he reached down and grabbed the door knob but it was locked. He smashed into the door and it barely moved. Again he drew back to slam the door again. He quickly stopped as the door began to open. There standing in front of them was a tall pimply face young man with wide eyes. His eyes rolled back in his head and he hit the floor like a bag of wet cement. Ryder and Alex quickly walked over to him. The name tag on his uniform read 'Neil.'

He awoke looking up at them, his eyes blinked," Ghosts!" He shouted as he jumped up and backed into a storage rack, knocking it over. The metal rack landed with a loud clang on the cement floor, spilling the cleaning towels that were stacked up on the shelves.

"We are not freaking ghosts." Ryder said, trying to calm him down. "We got trapped in the tunnels."

"Oh." He seemed relieved. "The tunnels, my grandfather told me tall tales of those, and how he was looking for the one that went up to the hotel."

"The Crescent?" Ryder questioned.

"Yep, that would be the one." The young man picked up a couple of towels and handed them each one, so that they could wipe their faces.

"Did he ever find it?"

"I don't know," the young man said. "Pappy told me that the tale was that young girls were run up to the Crescent from the church for the big shots to play around with. They used a tunnel so no one would see them."

"How old were these girls?" Alex asked as she wiped away the stinking sulfur caked mud from her face.

"Anywhere from twelve to fourteen," Neil replied.

"That is sick!"

"They ran them up from the church, you are sure?"

"That is what Pappy said."

******

It seemed strange to be walking through the bell tower of St. Elizabeth's, going down the steps, along the sidewalks and past the stations of Christ. All the while his head twisted back and forth and Alex, walking beside him said, "What are we looking for?" She asked, as she too began searching.

"Any sign of something being moved." Ryder said as they walked towards the church. "If she is getting into the hotel that way there has to be a sign, dirt moved or something…" His voice trailed off as he noticed that she was no longer to the side of him, he turned and saw her kneeling. "What are you doing?"

"Giving thanks," She said, standing up. "That we got out of that tunnel."

"Can I help you?" He heard Father George say from behind him, thinking they were a homeless couple by the way they looked, with their clothes torn and dirty. "If you would like a hot meal, shower, get you some clean clothes." Ryder turned and saw him standing there in work clothes, carrying a large bucket of soapy water in one hand and a large brush in the other.

"What I want is answers, Father George."

"Ryder?" He questioned, looking intensively at him, staring through the layers of stinking mud. He gazed over at her and said. "Alex, what happened to you?"

"The killer is using a tunnel to get into the hotel." Ryder said.

"And you think it is here?" Father George said passing by them and walking back toward the marble figures along the sidewalk. He stopped in front of the one where the murder had occurred and set the bucket down. "Believe me, there is no tunnel from here to the hotel." He stooped down and plunged the brush into the soapy bucket. Scooping up a lot of suds and water, he began to scrub the blood off the figurine. "Believe me, if there was a tunnel I would have found it."

"But what about the tales that young girls were run up from the church to the hotel back when the big wigs were here?" Ryder asked.

"That proves it!" Father George said as he stopped washing and stood up. "Back in that day, there wasn't even a church here."

"I don't get it. If there was no church here, how could the tale even be told?"

George let the brush fall down into the bucket of soapy water and it splashed on the ground. "It might be where the church used to be. I have heard tales that there was a tunnel in the old school."

"What old school?"

"It is now known as the Mount Victoria Bed and Breakfast."

Chapter 33

As Ryder guided the Killer Bee up the narrow strip of pavement known as German Alley, two things were racing through his mind. One, he hoped he didn't meet any traffic here as the street looked more like a long driveway and was barely wide enough for one car, let alone two. The other was the more impressive point, how did they get into the place, and try to find the entrance of a tunnel that may or may not be there. As they crossed over the main artery of town, suddenly the street name changed to Howell. He glanced over at Alex, her long hair plastered straight to her head, mud streaking the sides of her face. There was no way they could just walk in.

They needed a diversion. It may have seemed an odd thing to pray for, but his Uncle-Father Anthony-always told him he could pray for anything, and that is what he did. Now Uncle Tony always said there are no coincidences in this world; all the sudden happenings are part of God's plan, while Captain Grosstree would have told him it was police thinking. Be it God or just training, something was telling him to turn right.

French Street was another steep narrow twisting tale of pavement that was the story of this town. Even though the sign warned 'Do Not Enter', Ryder turned left and maneuvered up the narrowest strip of pavement he had been on so far, it even warned 'steep and narrow locals only'. Twisting like a viper coiling, ready to strike, it twisted first one way then the other till suddenly that street vanished, replaced by another street. This one was not as challenging as before, still not that wide, but straight, allowing Ryder to see cars parked along both sides of the road. He grinned and looked up and whispered. "Thanks."

"What?" Alex said as Ryder pulled the bright colored Dodge over behind a light gray BMW sedan. He glared out up the street at the guests filling the yard.

"It is a wedding." Ryder said, glancing over at her again. "That is our diversion. Every eye will be on the bride. Including the guests, and the owners, we just walk in." Ryder said as he opened the car door, and Alex followed him, both creeping up the side of the street, staying low behind the row of cars on the street. He looked up at a sign that read "No parking this side.' That made it even better; this pure disregard of the law told him it had to be some big shot in the town or state's wedding. Which meant lots of big important guests, meaning without a doubt the owners of the cars, and all the guests staying at the inn were going to be watching this event.

Ryder looked up over the hood of a stretch black limo and gazed over the round tables with their black table cloths. "What are you doing here?" He heard a deep firm voice say. He looked up over his shoulder and saw a large man with dark skin dressed in a chauffeur uniform.

"I will give you a hundred bucks to look the other way." Ryder said loud enough that the man could hear, but not enough that it interrupted the wedding.

"If you're here to interrupt the Mayor's daughter's wedding, I will give you a hundred bucks. She is a true 100% first-class witch." The man said, standing beside the car and surveying the crowd.

"Or something that rhymes with witch?" Ryder asked as he saw the man grin sideways reaching up and pulling down on his hat as he spoke.

"For sure, one hundred percent prime class Grade A number one!" The breeze changed direction. "Phew!" The man said, his face crinkling up, trying to wave the smell away from his nose. He looked down and saw them still wearing the headlamps. Have you two been in the crap mine? Smells like you hit the mother lode."

"It is a long story." Ryder said scrunching down behind the limo. But we need to get in there," Ryder said pointing to the inn. The chauffeur grinned unmercifully as the wedding march began to be heard and the bride made her way up the aisle between the chairs, her multi thousand dollar gown with ten foot train covered with satin rose petals rustling up the aisle.

"I will help you for a price."

"How much?"

"Your jacket."

"This thing wasn't even fifty bucks when it was new."

The chauffeur grinned again. "Yeah, but it smells like crap, don't it?" He reached over and opened the rear door of the limo. "Just shove it under the seat in there somewhere; they won't be able to find it." Ryder removed his jacket and wadded it up and shoved it under the rear facing back seat. The chauffeur closed the door. "You are in luck; they are going to pray now. When I drop my head you get moving." He dropped his gaze. Ryder and Alex raced for the open front door.

They quickly made their way past the lobby; it was strange and seemed almost uncanny, the place being empty. It was as if you were a space explorer, on another planet wondering what you might find on the next turn.

"So where would an opening to a tunnel be?" Alex asked as she crept through the house.

"Haven't you watched enough Scooby Doo cartoons?" He moved over to the fireplace and pressed on the stones.

"Enough not to believe everything I see." Alex said. "Maybe we should find the library and pull out a book."

"Do I detect sarcasm, dear?" Ryder said, showing as much scorn as he was asking for. Suddenly he stopped walking. He could hear voices, muffled by the walls, but they were in the next room that sounded like the kitchen.

They entered another room. He quickly looked the room over and out the window behind the couch. Not watching where he was going, he bumped into the low coffee table, causing a large book to tumble off onto the floor, alerting someone in the next room. There was only one place to hide- the closet. They hurried across the room and into the small closet.

He closed the door behind them, but left it open just a crack, so he could peer between the door and the frame at what was going on. At the same time Alex lightly tapped her foot on the hardwood floor.

"Will you stop that?" Ryder whispered, glancing back at her, and then quickly back to between the door and frame, as he saw a man enter. He was heavy set with dark hair and a goatee; he was wearing a light gray chief's jacket, buttoned up, except for the top two buttons.

"Ryder." She said very softly.

He motioned for her to be quiet, as he watched the man walk over to the table and pick up the book that Ryder had knocked off the table. The man glanced around the room, as if he were looking for something out of place.

"It is hollow under here." Alex murmured as she got down on her knees and pressed on the floor, trying to get it to open, then she began pressing on the sides of the wall, trying to find a trigger that would open it up. "This is the opening." She whispered again. "I just know it."

"What?" Ryder asked looking down at her still on the floor.

"The tunnel is under here."

Ryder looked out between the crack between the door and the frame again. He watched as the man saw the door of the closet open; he was walking towards them. Ryder pulled back and leaned back against the wall, as Alex stood up, her eyes still searching the wall paper pattern. Suddenly her eyes opened wide as they gaped at a symbol just to the side of him-a crescent moon. It was just part of the pattern of wallpaper; she quickly brought her fingers up and pressed in on it.

Ryder heard a muffled click under his feet and the boards in the floor popped up, he moved his foot back closer to the wall and reaching down, lifted up a trap door. Alex quickly flipped on her headlamp, and descended the rickety ladder that was propped against the wall. Ryder followed after her; it was nothing more than a handmade ladder, covered with cobwebs and a thick layer of dust on the sides. The closet door was opening. Ryder quickly reached up and closed the trap door. It was the tunnel- they had found it.

Chapter 34

At the bottom of the stairs, he reached up and turned on his headlamp. The beam cut through the darkness, as he twisted his head around, the light panned over the stone lined walls and ceiling. It was filled with cobwebs, except for right in the middle. He looked back at the ladder. Cobwebs lay broken to the sides, waving freely in a breeze that was coming in around the gap of the trap door.

"Ghost again?" He heard a muffled female's voice say from above, at the same time, someone stomped on the floor above.

"I know you think I am crazy, but people go in here, and never come out." The man's muffled reply could be heard saying. Ryder tapped Alex on the shoulder and motioned that they should continue on down the tunnel. Darkness closed in behind them.

The break in the cobwebs told him that someone had been through here before they were. Ryder lowered his head to shine his headlamp on the floor in front of him. There in the dust on the floor size seven footprints led him deeper into the tunnel.

The tunnel was over a block long; it was long and straight, even though he couldn't see it, he knew that they were heading for the Crescent Hotel. Suddenly the tunnel widened into a small room that was ten-foot-square, when suddenly the floor became stone embedded in the dirt.

The room was like the tunnel, the walls and the ceiling were made of hand cut stones, except for one small opening where a ladder rose up and disappeared into the darkness. "Ryder!" He heard Alex say, startled. "Look at this!"

Ryder turned and let the beam of the headlamp shine across the room. There were four wooden chairs around a large wooden table. Alex was staring down at the table. "Ryder, get over here!"

He walked over and looked at the table. It was covered with pictures of him. Some at the hotel, others around town, with Yakira, with Alex, while he was sleeping, while he was changing, getting on the train, going into the Crawford County Bank. Alex picked one up showing Ryder and her on the balcony with Ceelia clutched in her arms." She turned to him and said with a tone of worry.

"She has been watching us." Alex laid the photo down. Ryder picked up another. It was of him in the Mud Café sitting at the table with Yakira and his family, there was another photo of him when he proposed to Yakira standing in the bell tower. There were other photos taped to the sides of the wall, of Ryder with Annie Peters, a red mark across her face, Captain Grosstree and Dina, red marks across their faces.

"Ryder." Alex said, concerned as she picked up a photo in an old silver frame, which was sitting in between a pair of pewter candleholders with trumpet shaped flower handles holding three blood red candles. She handed him the photo- it was one of Marissa and her mother with Ryder standing beside them- it had been taken just outside the Ice Cream Shop in Van Buren. Ryder set the photo back down, moving his hand over the candle that was in front of the photo he could feel the warmth lingering. He pressed down on the top of the candle, the wax stuck to his finger. It was only a short time ago that these candles had been burning.

"She is going after Marissa!" He waved towards the ladder and added. "Ladies first."

"Not when it is like this, a gentleman leads the way into danger."

"You know, for a hard core FBI agent, you are a wimp." Ryder said as he started to climb up.

"Former F.B.I. I work for you now. And the boss always leads."

"Who says?"

"Union rules." She smiled as she began to follow him; he climbed higher and higher in the darkness. She started singing "look for the union label…." He stopped climbing and looked down at her, and wrinkled his brows at her. "There you go, the man keeping the working woman down." She joked as he began to climb again.

He looked up. They were under the staircase. He couldn't go any higher. Over to the side of the tunnel was a large oak framed door with a handle. He could hear voices outside, talking about the ghost that roamed the halls. He grabbed the handle and lifted up the bar. There was a loud click and a moan as the panel under the staircase opened. Ryder peered out at three frightened people, including Timmy, who just stood frozen there with a pair of bags in his hands. The other two were newlyweds, a young bride who leaped into her groom's arms as Ryder crawled out, and Alex followed.

Still covered in mud and reeking of sulfur, Ryder placed his arm around Alex and with a mocking devilish grin he said in a deep voice: "Greetings, from the underworld. The tomb just couldn't hold us." Timmy fell back, sliding down the side of the wall. Ryder looked over at the couple and smiled as he added. "Boo," which resulted in screams that ripped through the hotel, after all the excitement died down Ryder and Alex went back upstairs and he knocked on the door, using the secret knock.

"What happened to you?" Mary asked as she opened the door.

"We fell in a mud puddle." Ryder said as he entered the room.

Mary looked at him from head to toe. Before she replied, "Looks and smell like." She quickly placed her hand over her nose.

"Yeah, I know." Ryder grumbled as he looked around the room, noticing the door to the bedroom was opened the bed was messed up and he could see Marissa wasn't in there. He turned to Mary and asked. "Where is Marissa?"

"She is sunning herself out on the balcony."

"She's what!" Ryder shouted as he marched towards the door that out on the balcony. It has a quarter of the way open, and he pushed it open and saw that she had taken a blanket off the bed and placed it on the balcony and was lying on it. She was dressed in a two piece green and white stripe bikini, lying on her stomach, her head twisted to the side. Ryder quickly reached down and grabbed her by the arm.

"What are doing out here!" He demanded as he pulled her up to her bare feet, clutched in her hands was her cell phone.

"I was just getting some sun, I am wearing sunscreen."

"I told you, you were not to leave the room!"

"I am on the balcony." She said trying to smile and show those dimples.

"Get back in there!" He said pulling her back towards the door.

"Why are you being so mean?" Marissa complained as she stood with one foot on the balcony and the other on the step in the room.

"You stink."

"I know," Ryder said. "That is what all sisters think."

"No," She said screwing her face up and holding her nose. "I am saying you reek!" She looked back at him as he forced her inside and he climbed through the door. Shutting it behind them and pulling the drape closed.

"I have to go to that dance! He is going to be there. This is my first dance." She pleaded with him, when he heard her cell phone ding, a message was coming in. She lifted it up and looked at it. "He says he is looking forward to dancing with me. Please I have to go?" He didn't say anything. She turned and stormed into the bedroom slamming the door behind her. She flopped down on the bed in a huff, and Ryder barged in.

"Don't you know how to knock?" Marissa asked folding her arms in front of her. She rose up and faced him. "Get out of my room!" He didn't move, so she started to walk around him, but he grabbed her arm and tossed her down on the bed.

"Don't you get it?" He raised his voice, leaning right down in her face. "She wants to kill you! This is not some freaking video game we are playing, you get killed you can reset and play it again. Death is forever!"

"I know that!" She huffed again.

"You know nothing about death," Ryder said. He looked over his shoulder at Mary and Alex staring into the bedroom. He looked back at his sister. She didn't answer, she just sit there pouting her still folded across her chest, as tears began to puddle in her eyes, and run down her cheeks. His tone softened. "Marissa, I just found you. I don't want to lose you." Ryder walked over in front of her and placed his soiled hands on the sides of her face, squeezing her cheeks; she looked up at him. He smiled at her, and took his thumbs and wiped the tears from her eyes and placed them up to his eyes and spoke in a low whisper.

"Your tears are my tears. You don't cry. I don't cry." He moved till he was nose to nose with her. "But if we weep...we weep together." He released her and she looked at Ryan who had entered the room he was holding a new bottle of whiskey in his hand, he was standing outside the bedroom door. Ryder stood up.

"You think that makes it all better?" Her tone was sweeter than Saccharine laced with honey, but her words bitter. "Please! If you really loved me, you would let me go." She looked at her father, hoping he would intervene. He didn't say a thing. He just turned and walked back to the wet bar. He turned back to her.

"And you are not to use this anymore either." He said reaching down and grabbing her phone.

"I hate you." Marissa huffed as she pointed at the door. "Get out of my room!" Ryder walked out the door and she flung herself on the bed face down, sobbing as Ryder shut the door.

Ryder looked around. Only Ryan and Mary were in the room. "Where is everybody?"

"Ceelia and Natasha went to Alex's room to rest. Yakira hasn't come back from the salon, and Jonas; I haven't seen him all day." Mary said as Ryder stood there watching his father walk back over to the sofa after pouring another drink. "Do you really think this woman is going to try and murder our little girl?"

"Only if she gets through us," Alex said as she walked towards the entry hall. "I am going to go get cleaned up, if you need me…"

"Yeah okay," Ryder said allowing his eyes to roll over to her as she walked out of the room before he looked back at his father. Alex walked out and shut the door. Ryder walked over to his father and grabbed the glass out of his father's hand. "And no more of this," Ryder dumped it down the sink. "I need you sober. And more importantly…" Ryder grabbed his father by the shoulder and pointed at the bedroom door, "She needs you!"

"Son, you stink!"

"Yeah," Ryder said, releasing his grip on his father. "Mine washes off, how about yours?"

Ryder turned and walked into the bathroom, and filled the tub with water and soap, creating a bubble bath that he could sit and soak in, as he scrubbed away the grime and smell, it took a long soak and having to let water out and put more hot water back in when it got cold. He had just finished the second filling of hot water when there was a knock on the door.

"Can I show you what I look in my costume?" The voice was low and soft.

"Marissa you are not going."

"Please, I just want to show you."

"Can't this wait till?"

"Please!"

"Okay," Ryder said making sure the bubbles covered him. The bathroom door open, a young woman lady walked in wearing a bright blue ice princess costume; it was long and flowing, covering her feet, with an icy silver band around her waist, and a sheer cape with snowflakes and white fur trim. Covering her face was a blue, glitter mask.

"Marissa, you look beautiful, but are not going to the gala. Now get out!"

"Don't plotz, sweetie!"

"Yakira?"

"So you think I will fool the shikse?" She asked, removing the mask from her face.

"As long as you don't speak," Ryder said hinting at her thick Jewish, yet part hillbilly accent.

"How about if I do this…" Yakira lowered her voice, sounding hoarse. "I tell everyone I have a sore throat." He raised his eyebrows meaning that was not going to do it. "Or I could just nod a lot."

"Make it softer. Like you before." He said. Yakira lowered her voice to almost a whisper. "That can work, but don't talk too much." Ryder continued scrubbing the mud that was caked on his arm and asked, "You do have protection with you, don't you?"

"Sweetie, just what did you have in mind?" Yakira laughed.

"This is no joke, honey. Do you have your gun with you?"

"Yes." She said, lifting the hem of her dress up to reveal a small pistol that was tucked in a holster, strapped to her lower leg. "We have handled these kinds of situations before, why are you so worried?" She asked pulling the hem of her dress down.

"No, we haven't. This lady is off the rails she is..."

"Meshuggeneh?"

"More than just crazy, she has lost touch with reality, and you are pretending to be the person that she plans on killing next. You have to be on guard tomorrow night. Anyone and everyone that approaches you...Wait a minute. Tonight is the Sabbath, shouldn't you be..."

"What can't I miss once?" She replied interrupting him.

Ryder wrung the washcloth out as he spoke. "Maybe if we do this right, we can end this tomorrow night. If we don't, then..." His tone was so grave that he frightened himself with what would happen if they failed, so he quickly changed the subject. "Have you had supper yet?" She shook her head. "How about you order us up something and we have a nice meal together."

"To celebrate," she said, holding up her hand and showing the ring.

"Okay." He said. "But go down and get it. We can't trust anyone here." She closed the door and he finished his bath, dressed in sleep pants and a robe he walked out. The lights of the sitting room had been lowered, only the brass stand lamp on its lowest setting was lit, and in front of him was a rolling table. He could see Yakira standing beside it, lighting two tall white taper candles. There were two chairs pulled up to the table. He looked around the room.

"I sent Ryan and Mary to their room, and gave Marissa a burger she is still in her room." Her eyes sparkled in the candlelight as she smiled at him. He walked over and pulled the chair out for her and she sat down. He seated himself across from her. On the tray was a pair of plates, each covered with a silver dome lid, to keep the food warm. In the center of the tray was a bottle of red wine, which had been opened, allowing it to breath, and two glasses, along with crystal glasses of water.

He poured the wine into the glasses and then lifted the covers off the plates, revealing the meal; a ten-ounce Beef Tenderloin grilled to perfection, red and warm in the center, allowing the juices to flow when he cut into it that mixed with the Chive Garlic Butter that melted on top of the steak. On the sides were Smoked Gouda Mashed Potatoes and steamed asparagus with Hollandaise sauce spooned over it.

"To a long and happy life..." She said, raising her glass as a toast.

"Oh, yes." He said, lifting his glass. "To us, may we have a long and wonderful life together that is full of love and..."

"And mystery." She said with a quirky smile as they clink their glasses together.

"Of course," Ryder said. "What is life without mystery?" He watched her cut into her steak, and the red juices ran out. He drew back in puzzlement. He knew that under Jewish law the eating of blood was forbidden. She looked up at him as she took a bite. "Isn't that a big no-no?"

"I told you Sweetie, I fall of the kosher wagon every now and then."

She cut into the thick piece of steak again and the warm red juices flowed out into the potatoes. "That is more like leaping off head first." He said as she savored the bite, the juices running down her chin. He took his napkin and began to wipe it away, but found a better way. Placing his lips on her chin he sucked the juices away. He drew back and looked into her eyes as he placed his fingers under her chin, guiding her face around.

"We could always start with dessert." She said with a low sultry voice, turning her head slightly and parting her lips; he moved forward, their lips almost touching, when there was loud banging on the door.

"Rick. Ryder. Somebody. I found her!" It was Jonas.

"I have to go let him in." Ryder said softly, leaning back into his chair.

"I know." She said as she stood muttering, cursing in Hebrew meaning, "I hate this job."

"Come on, somebody let me in!"

"Just a second, Jonas," Ryder said, walking towards the entry way and turning on the ceiling lights and opening the door. "Jonas walked in.

"I have been searching everywhere for her." He said, passing under the ceiling light, revealing that his clothes were filthy with dirt. Yakira rolled her eyes up and blew the candles out as he walked into the sitting room. He flopped down in her chair and took her glass of water. He swigged it, looking down at the meal and then how they were dressed and he asked.

"Am I interrupting something?"

"No," Yakira mockingly replied. "Nothing ever happens here." She reached over him and grabbed her glass of wine and she patted Jonas on the back, getting some dirt on her fingers. She brought it up to her nose and sniffed, and then sniffed it again and shrugged her shoulders before sitting down on the couch and taking a sip of her wine. Letting out a sigh of frustration she crossed her legs and leaned back.

"Like I was telling you, I have been looking for her all day. Even in the underground of the town. I couldn't find her..." He looked down at the remaining piece of Yakira's steak. He turned to her. "You mind if I have a bite? I haven't had anything to eat all day.'

"Ma ratsa" She said.

"Huh?"

"Whatever floats your boat, buddy!" Yakira said, standing up and walking in the bedroom across the hall as Jonas began cutting up and devouring the steak. He began explaining that he went through the Main street tunnels but hadn't found her. Yakira returned with blankets and a pillow.

"You can sleep out here." She told Ryder. "I am heading to bed."

"Wait, Yakira!" Jonas said, reaching into the pocket of his jeans. "I finally saw her down town. She was near the Basin Hotel. I lost her again, but she dropped this." He handed Ryder a folded up piece of paper; it was from a costume rental shop here in town. I talked to the guy there, he remembers her, particularly her eyes, he told me she rented this costume and she told him this is what she was going to the gala as tomorrow. Ryder looked at it.

280

A&J Costume Rental

1-Female Id 235-Marie Antoinette

Chapter 35

" You are cordially invited this Saturday to the Eureka Springs Masquerade Street Gala. A city wide costume party, of merriment, and dancing, … let your ambitions go, be not who you are, but be who you want to be."

Celebrations were nothing new to the city, the town flourished with celebrations of one kind or the other every week end, but this party was" the party"; part Halloween and part Mardi Gras, complete with a parade on Main Street and that night the prima-donna of the event, the grand gala costume ball. Every face was covered with a mask, it was a mystery that bubbled up, like the springs that once drew in souls in an effort to cure the ills of the human body; only this time it was the sweet sounds of the Arkansas Symphony Orchestra that cured the ills of the human spirit.

The Orchestra was arranged in the Basin Park, dressed in their finest, even their faces were covered with black or silver masks. The grand conductor standing up on the stage, directing the great highs and lows of the harmony. Spring Street was blocked off from the bridge to the Basin Hotel. Now it was a grand outdoor ballroom, with twinkling clear lights strung across the street and the park.

Ryder stood on the sidewalk at the edge of the crowd, dressed as a French Highwayman, complete with a full length dark button up coat, which worked wonders in hiding the Glock that was strapped to his side. His head covered with a tricorn hat, and a black mask covered his face from his forehead to his mouth. It almost seemed ironic that he was dressed as a robber and acting as a detective, but in a way maybe he was robbing Lillian's last kill from her, something that he was determined to do.

The sounds of "Concert #5 in D Major" rang through his ears as he watched the couples twirl themselves about in pretense of dance, some wondering who the other person was that was hiding under the mask. Others knowing exactly who it was, but pretending, just for tonight, that they were strangers meeting for the first time. Others were just wrapped too tightly in their own lives to just let go and dream.

He watched as Yakira, as Marissa, danced with a young lad. Ryder made a quiet wish that he could be out there with her. As the dance ended, Yakira offered a curtsy as her partner bowed. Ryder walked over to her and held out his hand and said.

"Dear sister, would you please do me the honor of allowing me to have the next dance." He saw her smile, and again pulling at her dress she dipped down, bowing her head, and not saying a word, she offered her hand as the Slavonic Dance No. 10 for orchestra in E Minor B. began. He took her and glided over the pavement. Looking up at him, he could see her eyes beaming with life. He wanted so desperately just to grasp her in his arms and hold her close, so close that they could feel each other's heartbeat. However, for all purposes she wasn't to be Yakira, she was to be his sister. So instead, distance remained between them as he effortlessly spun her around, displaying her, as dancing should be, like a fine work of art.

"Have you seen anything?" She asked softly, matching his steps, again twirling around.

"Nothing," he said as he looked briefly over her head at the crowd that had gathered around them, watching them as they danced. Just at the right moment with the beat of the music, he spun her around again, gazing over the crowd. "But I feel her, she is here, watching."

Ryder spun her yet again, not for just the beat of the music but also to check out the crowd. It was an array of everything from Court Jesters dancing with warrior princesses, to Caped Heroes dancing with Fair Maidens. Watching the spectacle was an assemblage of knights, executioners holding their axes of death, wizards, and witches, princesses looking for their prince, a fair haired woman dressed as a Can-Can dancer kicking up her heels, even a Lady Pirate.

As the conductor instructed the ensemble to bring the music to a halt, Ryder whispered in her ear. "Be careful, I love you." He stepped back, placing one foot in front of the other he offered a deep bow as he said out loud for all to hear. "Thank you Mademoiselle, for the dance," She bowed her head, again not saying a word. "Now I will return you to your prince." Ryder added as she held her hand out to the young teen that was standing next to him. Yakira rose and looked at the young teen. Still pretending to be Marissa, Ryder looked at the young man and said. "Top that if you can, kid." Ryder grinned as he added a warning, "But remember, big brother here will be watching."

"You are the one that was the cop?" The teen asked nervously.

"Yeah, and I still have my gun."

Ryder stepped back as another song began playing, he couldn't help but grin even more as the teen, with shaking hands, took hold of Yakira's hands and tried to guide her, but failed miserably. He spun her around so fast it nearly knocked the hat from the top of her head. She had to let go of his hand quickly to catch the steeple-cone style hat before it fell to the ground, after repositioning it and the light blue scarf with its snowflake shape pattern, she turned to Ryder and even though most of her face was hidden, he could see the amusement as she offered a small shake of her head.

Ryder backed out of the crowd and slipped his hand into his pocket of the Highway's coat. He pulled out a small walkie-talkie and raised it to his lips.

"Alex, you spotted anything?"

"Negative." The lady dressed in the red and black pirate outfit over next to the park said. "I have seen everything from Adam and Eve, to a couple dressed as a Zebra, but no Marie Antoinette. Has anyone approached our subject, except you?"

"Two young boys," "Ryder said into the gadget, looking around making sure no one was watching him. "They seem to be taking turns asking her to dance. One is dressed like a caveman, at nine o'clock; the other is dancing with her right now and is dressed like Prince Charming. You heard anything?"

"Only a gaggle of teen girls, if I have to hear 'OMG he is so cute' one more time....can I please shoot them?"

"Only if they shoot first," Ryder said, quickly and then releasing the key waiting for her reply, almost knowing what it was going to be before she said.

"Oh! you are no fun!"

Ryder turned and looked across the crowd up toward the Basin Hotel at Jonas dressed as a vampire. "Jonas, how about your end?"

"Nothing Rick." He said into the walkie-talkie before turning around and trying to stare down the blocked off Center Street, at a crowd of guests not in costumes that had gathered along the sidewalks there. "It is mostly older people that don't want to get dressed up." He turned back to the crowd of dancers; haven't seen a sign of her."

"Double T," Ryder spoke again into the device. Not getting a response he repeated. "Double T! Where are you?"

"I am on Main Street! I think I see her," came his breathless reply. "I will try to catch up with her."

"You need assistance?" Ryder asked, waiting for a short time before speaking again. "Thom. DOUBLE T!"

"Forget it. It wasn't her. It was a Ghost lady."

"You sure?"

"How many Mexican girls you know with blonde hair and blue eyes? She had dark hair, dark eyes. I will keep looking. Her name was Selene."

Ryder replaced the device in his pocket when the woman dressed as a Can-Can dancer walked towards him, her face mostly covered with a bright red glittery mask with black outlines that encircled her baby blue eyes. Her hair was pulled back and tied with a large black and red bow. "Dear Sir, I would like to ask for this dance." She said, her voice soft and almost angelic sounding she pulled her skirt back, revealing long luscious creamy white legs in black fishnet stockings. Ryder didn't want to dance but as it was announced, it was ladies choice. Besides, it would give him a different view of those there and he could keep a better eye on Yakira, who had to choose between her two suitors.

Ryder took the lady's hand and led her out onto the street. The orchestra began to play a slow waltz; he took her into his arms, she tilted her head slightly back and looked up at him. "You are a wonderful dancer, sir." The young lady said, but Ryder didn't look down at her, he just looked over her head at the crowd, twirling her around so that he could see Yakira dancing with the boy dressed as Prince Charming again.

"They say a good dancer makes a great lover." The Can-Can dancer continued to speak. "I saw you dancing with the young lady. But she is so young. You need a real woman." He spun her around again at the edge of the crowd; He saw a fluff of towering white hair at the far edge of the park coming down the side wall in front of the band stand, still the young lady continued to speak.

"I bet you are a great lover. Maybe you could come up to my hotel room after the dance?" Her question made him look down, her pouting lips parted as she smiled, making her blue eyes glow even brighter.

"What did you say?"

"I am staying at the Crescent, here is my room key." She said, almost purring as she rubbed her face up against his chest, and dropped a key chain into the pocket of his coat. She then leaned up and kissed him on the lips. Ryder's eyes blinked as she released him and said. "See you soon." He stood watching her walk away.

"Ryder!" Alex's voice suddenly broke through. "She is heading right towards Yakira!" Alex's words snapped him back, and he again began searching the crowd, but it closed in around Yakira. He twisted his head back and forth, but dancing with the other woman had allowed him to lose track of her. He couldn't help but feel the tension inside of him growing. He didn't want her to do this in the first place, that was all that was running through his mind, as he pushed through the crowd and out into the sea of dancers. Again his head twisted back and forth as the music played. He raised the radio to his mouth and spoke frantically.

"Alex, where is she?"

"I lost her! I can't find Lillian either! EVERYONE MOVE IN!" He heard Alex shout over the airwaves. Ryder carefully unbuttoned his coat and slipped the Glock from the holster holding it closely to his side. He gazed across the crowd, searching for either Yakira or Lillian dressed as the French queen; all he saw was the crowd and Alex moving in on the other side, her weapon drawn, clutched in her grip by her side. She looked right at him.

Ryder and Alex had worked together so much they had developed their signals. So when she made a cutting motion with her finger across her lips, he knew that meant to go to radio silence. He reached into his pocket and switched off the radio. Ryder pointed at her, then at his eyes, before he took his index finger and scratched the mask on his forehead. She nodded it meant have you seen the suspect.

She raised her hand with her fingers spread out; she bent her ring finger and crossed her thumb over it, indicating 'seven', seven o'clock from her position. He twisted his head slightly to the right. He saw the woman dressed in a ghostly white costume, her face completely covered, a large white powdered wig covering her head. She had her hands down to her sides.

He looked back at Alex; she made a motion with her fist as if she was stabbing, Ryder nodded, knowing she meant that Lillian was holding a knife. She glanced the other way and then held up her thumb and two fingers. 'Three', three o'clock! Yakira and the boy were dancing right in front of the killer.

Ryder looked at the far side of the crowd; he could see Double T, he hoped he had remembered all the signals that they had used when playing war when they were kids. Ryder held up his hand and waved it back and forth. He felt relieved when he flashed Ryder the okay sign, and started moving in. Alex watched him and together they matched their steps, moving toward the woman.

The music was swirling around reaching the finale, the crescendo growing. The young man twirled Yakira around with her back to the woman; she raised the knife in her hand. Ryder pushed a couple dancing out of the way; he drew the Glock up and clutched it in both hands, and using his best police voice yelled out:

"Don't move!" He aimed down the sites of the weapon, pointing right at the center of the woman's chest. Suddenly Alex moved, drawing her weapon and screaming.

"You as so much as twitch I will put you in the ground!"

With that Yakira twisted her dancing partner around and shoved backwards to the pavement, and he took her down with him. Yakira landed on her back, but quickly pulled the Bulldog revolver from the holster on her leg and aimed it at Marie Antoinette.

"Drop it, Queenie!" She shouted. The crowd screamed and yelled as they ran for cover in the park, causing the orchestra to stop playing. Some stumbled over their own feet, falling to the street, as others trampled over them.

The woman dropped the knife and landed with a dull thud on the pavement. "Kick the knife away towards me." Ryder yelled, still keeping the weapon aimed right at the woman's chest. She kicked the knife towards Ryder.

"Down on the ground!" Alex shouted at the woman, making sure the little white dot on the sights was aiming deal-square at the woman's back. Her finger slipped from the side of the trigger guard and over the trigger when the woman did not respond. "I will not tell you again! Down on your knees!"

The woman complied and it was then that she spoke. "Please!" She begged. "It was just a joke. The knife is not even real."

"What?" Ryder questioned, quickly picking up the knife, he jabbed the blade into his thigh, the rubber blade bending. "It's plastic!" He said curtly as he walked up to the woman kneeling in the street and jerked the wig from her head, allowing long dark locks to fall down on her shoulders. Even more upset now, he ripped the mask from her face revealing that she was a teenage girl.

"It was a joke! We were just playing a joke," the young girl begged, looking up at Yakira, and pleading. "Please Marissa, tell them who I am. I just didn't want you dancing with Zack all night." The girl watched as Yakira removed the mask, revealing who she was. "You are not Marissa! I could have had him all this time!"

Ryder jerked the mask from his face and slung it to the street, kicking at as he cursed "Oh for the love of Mary!! This is all about some teenage pimple faced twit?" Ryder kicked at the mask again, sending it sailing across the street. Alex lowered her weapon, reached up, and removed her mask.

"This had to scare her off," Alex said. "She could be anywhere by now."

"Or anybody..." His words trailed off as he began to once again search the crowd over with his eyes.

"What is it?" Alex asked, following his gaze.

"The can-can girl, the one that danced with me," He said, pulling the Walkie-talkie back out and turning it on. Alex, watching, did the same with her radio. "She set us up Alex, she knew all along it was Yakira. "

"She was the can-can dancer, she gave her...." Ryder remembered the key she placed in his pocket; he reached in and pulled it out, the words written on it made a cold shiver go down his back bone. It read, Governor's Suite.

Chapter 36

The masks were removed, the faces revealed, the music grew still, and the sound of sirens filled the hollows. The lights grew dim, replaced with those flashing against the walls of the Crescent once again. Ryder didn't even wait till the cruiser came to a stop before he leaped out and was running up the front steps. He had pushed opened the French doors and was half-way up the stairs, before Yakira and Alex even entered the hotel. Alex shouted to him as they entered the elevator, but he just kept running. Detective Shepherd and a uniformed officer followed behind him. He ran down the hall, and stood in front of the door. He had just gripped the knob when the elevator door opened. Click!

The door opened. This was against his orders; he wanted it locked at all times. He pushed the door open. It was dark. Ryder reached down and slipped the Glock from his holster. Sliding along the wall, he flipped the light switch on and the darkness was shattered. He glanced around the edge of the doorway into the sitting area. Ryan, his father, was draped over the couch, a glass in his hand. He quickly went to Marissa's bedroom and opened the door; he turned on the light. Her bed was rumbled, the sheets and the blankets tossed in a heap on the floor, as if there was a struggle. Marissa was not there. He entered and noticed something dark red and sticky on the floor.

He checked the other bedroom; it was empty. He twisted the door knob of the bathroom, but it was locked. Inside he could hear the running of water, he knocked on the door and called out her name, but nothing was returned. From behind him Detective Shepherd entered the hotel room. Ryder drew his foot back and with a couple of hard kicks the door opened. He saw Marissa stretched out in the bathtub, her head lying back on the rim, covered mostly in soapy water, except for one leg that stuck out of the tub, resting on the edge, exposed clear up to her thigh, which was still under the sudsy water. Her eyes were closed and she was not moving at all. Her clothes were lying in a heap, stained with the same dark red substance he had found in the bedroom. He yelled her again, but she did not move.

He felt a sinking feeling in his chest, as he walked up to the tub and kneeled down. He reached over the tub and placed his fingers on her neck, which was quickly followed by a scream as Yakira stormed into the room. Marissa's eyes quickly opened and she looked up. Seeing all these people in the bathroom, she quickly pulled her leg back into the tub and sunk deeper down under the suds in the bathtub, leaving only her head exposed, and pulling the headphones off.

"What are you doing in here?" She asked her brother, crossing her arms over her chest.

"I thought something had happened to you! I saw the red stain." He said, picking up her blouse and holding it up for her to see.

"It is cherries."

"What?"

"You wouldn't let me go to the party, I felt bad so I had mom get a cherry cheese short-cake." It is like strawberry short-cake with a layer sweetened pie crust and whipped cream but used cherries instead of strawberries and a layer of cheese cake in between the shortcake. "But I spilled it on me before I even got to eat it. So I thought I would take a bath and go to bed."

"Why didn't you answer me?"

"I was listening to music; I must have fallen asleep."

"Rick! What the hell happened?" He heard a nervous Brian ask as he turned around and saw him standing in the sitting area.

"Where were you?"

"I had to go to the bathroom. She was in the bathtub, so I went downstairs to get a bite to eat; besides her dad is with her." Ryder stormed past Brian and into the sitting room, where Yakira was trying to get Ryan to wake up.

"Damn you!" Ryder said grabbing the man by the collar and slamming him back against the wall. He reeked of booze, his eyelids heavy, his eyes blood-shot, and his cheeks rosy.

"Hey, son…" He spoke and his words were slurred and drawn out, a partial grin breaking across his face as he placed his hand on Ryder's shoulder. "You know how proud of I you was when you won the national championship?" He spoke, his words out of order.

291

"Get me that bucket of ice." Ryder said, turning to Yakira as Alex entered the door after checking on her child and sister.

"Everyone is fine." She said, her words trailing off at the end as she watched Yakira take the ice bucket from the wet bar and hand it to Ryder. "How is Marissa?" She asked just as the teen walked out of the bedroom.

"She is okay." Ryder said through gritted teeth. "No thanks to this moron!" He pulled Ryan's collar back and poured some of the ice down his shirt, then the rest right over the man's head.

"What the hell, son!" He grumbled, and Ryder slapped him hard.

"You almost got Marissa killed!" He looked over at the empty bottle on the table. He grabbed it and shoved in his father's face. "Because of this! THIS!" Ryder flung the bottle across the room and it shattered.

Marissa had stepped of the bath tub and was wrapped up in a robe. His father was having trouble trying to keep awake. Ryder pushed his hand under the man's chin, pushing his head back onto the wall as said. "Wake up!" He shouted again, his fingers curling around the man's collar. He pulled him across the floor into the bathroom. Grabbing his father's hair on the back of his head, he plunged the man's head below the water in the tub. Ryan struggled and bubbles came up as he lifted him up. "You awake now?" Ryder yelled at him as water ran down the man's face and onto his pants as Ryder pulled his father back to his feet.

"What's the big deal, son? Mary is here."

"Where? Where is she?"

"Rick, mom went down to the lobby." Marissa said as she walked up behind Ryder. He turned and looked over his shoulder at her. "She was hoping she could get something to eat."

"When did she leave?"

"About thirty minutes ago."

Ryder turned to Alex. "Stay with her!" Alex nodded, and he turned to Yakira and added. "Come on; let's see if we can find her." In the lobby they looked all over, asking the staff if they had seen her, they hadn't. Suddenly a radio call from an officer standing next to the door made Ryder stop and listen to the dispatcher.

"City 112." Detective Shepherd callout. "See the woman at 935 Passion Play Road possible 10-100." 'Ten-one hundred. That code rang through Ryder mind, like a coal train through Kansas it was going full speed ahead and nothing was going to stop it. It was a code that he had heard so many times- DEAD BODY.

Without saying a word Ryder grabbed Yakira's hand and they raced out the front doors, down the steps and across the parking lot to the Killer Bee, it hadn't made sense to drive downtown, so they just had taken the trolley; the car was still here. He had already sped away by the time Detective Shepherd had made it back to his car.

Spending the last two weeks here, he had gotten pretty good at finding places, including short cuts. He pushed down hard on the brake pedal and cocked the steering wheel hard over and the Charger slid sideways. He straightened the wheel and slammed down hard on the gas and rocketed up Magnetic Drive. The headlights were sucking down on the yellow line in the road, like a babe upon his mother's breast. Both windows were down and the night air whipped through the interior, making Yakira's long locks swat her face with the fury of a jungle cat with its prey. The road narrowed, and in the distance he could hear the approach of sirens. He had to get there first; he just hoped that the modern suspension could make the car stick to the road.

They topped the hill; again he braked and turned hard to the left, the Charger's tail end swung out with tires screaming and howling, almost clipping a mailbox, he corrected, turning into the skid, and the car straightened and sped forward. The road split; one to the left and one to the right, even though it was narrower, he took the one on the left.

It was here that the Passion Play was enacted; there were thousands who came every year to watch the greatest gift of love ever given played out. In a flash they passed by East Jerusalem, the white domed Memorial Chapel, and the gift shop; this was the address. However, it was the note Lillian had left behind that made Ryder drive on. The words, "at the feet of the sun." It was typical, using the wrong word to appear more childlike. It wasn't the sun of the sky, it was the Son of God, and it was at the Christ of the Ozarks. He slid to a stop just outside of the gates. The sound of sirens was quickly approaching.

Ryder hopped over the gate and ran towards the towering giant bathed in lights almost seven stories high, he couldn't help himself, he looked up in the sky at the huge face looking down on him, the arms outstretched, even though the cross wasn't there, he could see it in his mind. He stood at the foot, and dropped his head down partly in thanks, and another in relief, there was no body at the feet. He lifted his head slowly, as he thought about the ten-one hundred call.

"She is over here." He heard a female voice say, clearly showing signs of distress. Standing next to a row of evergreen bushes in front of the statue was a woman, middle aged, slightly overweight with dark colored hair, wearing a flowery print sun dress. She dabbed her eyes with a rolled up tissue as she motioned with her hand. "She is around at the back."

The sound of sirens grew louder and louder, piercing through the night and rolling over the hills and into the valleys below. Ryder rounded the corner, just as the sirens, like a katydid's- song dies down; so did the siren. He stood there seeing the profile at first; he felt a hand grab his, it was Yakira. He moved closer.

Stretched across the stand the held the plaque with the information about the artist was a woman. She was sitting on the ground, her hands bound to the cable that surrounded the statue with white twine, which was stained with her blood. Ryder kneeled down in front of her. There was a large pool of blood on her left side that had stained her dress.

"Ricky," Yakira said softly as another siren grew still. In the distance another siren broke the silence. He looked up at her. "I am sorry you lost a mother again." He felt her hand rest on his shoulder. "I guessed wrong, I really thought—I really thought it was going to be Marissa." Ryder didn't say a word; he just carefully lifted up Mary's hand and examined it, "No defensive wounds," He said standing up, noticing that there were several coins under her, coins that had been tossed at the statue of Christ, just as the guard had told him.. He turned and looked down, and saw large silver with blood on it he heard the police approaching. He searched for a cloth, but being still dressed in the horseman costume, he didn't have one. Instead he grabbed the pocket of the jacket and ripped it free. He carefully lifted the coin by the edges. His fingers wrapped around it just as Detective Shepherd approached.

"You know the Vic?" Shepherd asked as a uniformed officer also arrived.

"Yes," Ryder said humbly. "Mary Ellen Ryder."

"Ryder? Any kin?"

"She was my step mother." He said as he placed his arm around Yakira's shoulder and turned to her.

"The Slayer?"

"Yeah, and I am next." Ryder said as he carefully slipped the cloth with the coin into one of his pockets. "That is what this is all about, getting to me, because I put her mother in jail."

"So we will put a full time guard on you."

"No you won't!" Ryder said forcefully as he turned and faced him then he turned back to Yakira and continued. "You didn't guess wrong honey. We just made it where she couldn't get her target and she selected someone else." Ryder paused as another officer appeared. "You do that; she will just kill someone else." He turned and with his arm still wrapped around Yakira he started to walk away.

"You keep playing with her, there is only one way this is going to end." Detective Shepherd said making Ryder stop walking.

"I know," Ryder said. "One of us is going to die."

Chapter 37

It is death's unclaimed conclusion. If someone is loved, someone will weep, each single tear but a memory, falling as droplets of rain into a valley that suddenly becomes a rushing river, filling the heart with either despair or hope.

Funerals were always a mixed breed of emotions for Ryder, it was so permanent. Visions of the sight of the mourners all dressed in their best, gathering around a casket. The sounds of hymns being played, softly in the background, the wafting smell of fresh cut flowers, just barely making their presence known, tickling the sensitive nose and the heaviness of a heart, as the minster speaks the last words. The mourners become like ants following in line to a peaceful setting just outside of town, nestled on the grassy meadow, with trees around the edges, their shades offering a little comfort, maybe even an embrace of a departed loved one.

Yet as he looked skyward in to the crystal blue ocean of air he felt as if life were just a moment, and death a tick of a second hand that barely moved; that new life awaited somewhere. He stood all dressed in black, in the cemetery several feet away from the services, under the shade of a pine tree. He was close enough so that he could hear the services, but far enough that he felt he didn't belong. "Thought I would find you here," Father Anthony said as he walked up to him. "You belong with your family."

"You are my family." Ryder said, turning and facing him, his eyes hidden behind the sunglasses, then turning back and gazing out towards the grave.

"So are they. An adorable sister and loving brother and…"

"Wonderful father?" Ryder questioned, not even believing his own pun as he turned to him, lifting a mocking eyebrow. "Sounds just like a TV show family. Maybe we should get a reality program."

"You sound angry. Are you angry with God?"

"No," Ryder said. "Disillusioned maybe, but I left anger a long time ago." He turned away from his uncle and watched as his sister carefully took a tissue and wiped the tears from her eyes. "It just seems that everywhere I turn all I see is death."

"And you are telling me this?" His uncle asked, unbelieving that his nephew could be this dense. "When they call you it is over, when they call for me it is just another beginning." Ryder turned back to his uncle and saw the emotion on his face, of giving those dying last rites. "I give the dying comfort; you give those left behind answers."

"Don't you ever get tired of the question you can't answer. 'Why?' Why does God allow these things to happen?"

"It is not God that caused this. There are always two paths that can be taken. You have to choose." Ryder reached up and pulled the glasses from his face as he looked at his uncle and said.

"Are you telling me, that she is there because she chose to know me?"

"You, God, even Mary herself is not to blame for this. The only one that is to blame is the one who murdered her." As the father spoke, Ryder placed his sunglasses back on his face and stared down at the ground. "I know you see mystery in everything, but there is no great mystery to life, it is just life. We live and we die. It isn't what we do in life; it is what we do with our life that matters." He paused making Ryder turn and look over at him, he saw him grin as he turned back and saw two women about the same size, approaching him. It was Yakira and Marissa; they walked up to him and Marissa held her hand out and said.

"I need my big brother."

"You've got one in Jonas."

She flashed that grin, making her dimples appear. "I want you."

"Because of me your mother was murdered."

"No it was because I wanted something, she went to get it for me..."

"It is not your fault! It is Lillian's she is the one that murdered her." Ryder said interrupting her.

"Then how can it be your fault?" She looked up at him smiling flashing those dimples and he reached down and took a hold of her hand.

"So you forgive me?"

"You mean all that I hate you stuff," Marissa said. "You don't forgive family; you just learn to love them a little bit more. My mom told me that."

Yakira and Marissa led him across the cemetery, where the services were starting. He was seated on the front row next to Marissa, who never let go of his hand. As the survivor's names were read he was shocked when they read his as a step-son; he felt Marissa's hand grip his tighter, telling him that it was her doing.

The final words were a prayer by the minister. The visitors all passed by, offering a hug or a shake of the hand. Ryder hung his head, not looking at those that went by; only occasionally would he glance over towards Marissa, and Jonas who was sitting next to her, who was sitting next to Ryan. He would look over and see Yakira sitting next to him.

"Darling, do not worry," He heard an angelic like voice say, as he saw a hand reach down on his. Perfect skin and porcelain like, with blood red ruby painted finger nails. It made him look up. Her face was covered with a dark veil, but through he could see her eyes of blue flame, and hints of golden locks. "Death is but only a breath away, weep no more. You will soon see them again." Before she left she dropped a flower down onto his lap, a single white Angel Trumpet.

He was startled at first, not even being able to shout out what he wanted to say, he just sat there watching her walk away from him. Finally he stood up and shouted out. "It is her!" He pushed through the line. "It is Lillian!" He stood and gazed out at the crowd of mourners that were walking back to their cars. His head was twisting back and forth, searching for the woman in black, but everyone was in black. There was a woman with her back to him, getting in a light-colored sedan. He ran up and grabbed her by the shoulder, spinning her around.

"What is the meaning of this?" The woman asked.

"Who are you?" Ryder demanded releasing her trying to look into her car, cupping his hands over his eyes and looking through the tinted windows of the Mercedes. He turned back to the woman and again demanded "Answer me!"

"I am Beverley Weaver, from Weaver and Young Realty; I was just here to offer my condolences." Ryder felt like he was losing his mind, he knew what he saw, but she couldn't have just disappeared. He gazed down at the woman's hands; they were covered with Victoriana style lace gloves.

"Did you say something to me a while ago in the line?"

"I told you I am sorry for your loss."

"You didn't say anything about death being just a breath away. Or call me darling?"

"I don't think so." Beverley said as she patted him on the arm. "I mean you are a gorgeous man, but just not my type, a little high strung. Besides, what would I tell my husband?" She turned and smiled as the rest of the family walked up. She pulled out one of her cards and handed it to Jonas and said. "When you are up to it give me a call, but know the buyer isn't going to wait long."

"Didn't you see her?" Ryder asked Marissa and then Yakira, they both shook their heads no. "But I swear it was her! "

"You see what kind of crap you cause, son." He heard his father say. Ryder turned to him. "You just couldn't leave it alone. You had to come back. Because of you, I lost the woman I loved."

"I am sorry Dad I thought she was Marissa. I don't know it was...please forgive me."

"Forgive you?" The man grumbled, his eyes staring into Ryder. "Well it ain't ever going to happen. I want you out of our lives. I don't want your damn money. I don't want your help, I don't want you." He turned and looked at Yakira and continued. "All I want is for you and your little girlfriend to get the hell out of town and leave me and my family alone." He rubbed his hand over his chin, turned and walked away.

Ryder stood there feeling just as alone in the world as he had before. "He doesn't mean what he is saying." Marissa said, her voice almost cracking. "You are my brother. I don't blame you." Ryder bit down, clenching his teeth and watching as this man walked out of his life just as he did before. "Ricky! " Marissa called out to him and he turned back to her. "You are my big brother. I need you." She grabbed him in an embrace. He lifted a shaky hand up to her, wanting so much to embrace her back, but if he did it would have just caused the hurt to be even more. So instead he just gave a quick pat on the back of the head. "I love you."

299

"Yeah, I uh..." He couldn't utter the word out.

"Marissa!" Ryan yelled. "Get over here right now!"

"I got your number, we will talk." She sobbed as she released him from the embrace and he could see the tears in her eyes even as she forced that smile, showing those dimples again.

"You know I..."

"I know..." She said with another flash of those dimples. "We will talk. "All he could do was nod as she added. "I promise," before she ran to meet her father.

"Well, I am nineteen now, he doesn't tell me who I can or cannot see. When I make it big, nothing is going to stop me. I will throw him out." Jonas said. "Besides, I am heading for college next fall."

"Jonas! Get over here! I am leaving with or without you." Ryan shouted.

"I guess I better go." Jonas said. "You know, for Marissa's sake."

"Yeah, for her sake." Ryder managed to get out.

"Oh! By the way, you dropped this when you got up." He said handing Ryder a piece of paper and then he left. It was a piece of folded up red construction paper. He unfolded it and read it.

> THiS deATH HAS ONLY MAde iT STRONgeR
>
> YOUR HEART, YOUR BODY, YOU BeLONg TO Me
>
> MeeT Me ACROSS FROM WHeRe SECONdS TiCK AWAY,
>
> TOMORROW TONighT MY dARLiNg YOU WAiT NO LONgeR
>
> ONe KiSS, TWO KiSS, ANd THe THiRd KiSS We CReATe FOReVeR.

Chapter 38

"I don't like it! And I don't want it!" Yakira fumed as she stood in front of the fireplace in the Governors Suite of the Crescent Hotel. Her fingers gripped tightly around the edge of the mantle. She turned her head slightly to the side, her long locks still looking like Marissa's falling in front of her chest. She narrowed her gaze at Ryder. "I am putting my foot down on this!" Her tone softened as she turned back and laid her head down on the mantle. "I can't lose you."

Ryder was sitting at a fold away table in one of the wood armed chairs around it. The table was covered with photos, files and papers; Lillian's college records, her medical records, photos of the victims, autopsy reports, blood analyses, crime scene reports. Across the table was Alex who was studying the medical report from the college. Looking out the window was Jonas.

Suddenly the door of the bedroom opened making Jonas quickly turn around. Thom emerged holding a blood type test paper. "Well," Ryder asked.

"You were right about the blood on the coin," Thom said handing the coin back to Ryder, who pulled out his wallet and stuffed the coin inside. "It was not Mary's her blood type was A- the one on the coin was O positive."

"Lillian's is O positive." Alex said as she looked at a medical report.

"Yes, but so is a few other billion in the world. It is the most common type."

"My father was O positive," Jonas asked sitting down in the other chair at the table. "Can you get a DNA match?"

"Possibly," Thom said as he walked over to the wet bar. "But it will take a while for the results to come in, but you will also have to have a sample from her ideally it being blood."

"Did you get the other test results I asked for?" Ryder asked watching Thom as he filled his glass up with ice and then dark colored pop.

"Yes, and guess what your blood contains heavy concentrations of Brugmansia, just like every victim of the slayer, the only one that didn't have it was Mary. And she was the only one that fought back. Also you were right about the train; the man also had heavy doses of Brugmansia."

"And the others?" Ryder asked.

"It took some doing," Alex said. "By the way you owe Bernie another football. "But the toxicant was found in both Anne and Cindy."

"And Mary?" Ryder asked.

"Don't know yet." Thom said. "I am having it rushed through hoping to get a call soon." He paused for just a brief period. "Rick it is also in your blood. But there seems to be acting like a drug on you just at the point that..."

"Stop it! Ricky I don't want you to do this." Yakira said cutting him short as she walked over behind him. "She is a crazy dumb woman."

"She may be crazy, but in no way is she dumb." Thom said as walked over to the couch and sat down. "What she is doing with Angel Trumpet," he took a sip and set the glass down on the coffee table, standing up he retrieved a paper from a soft leather briefcase, and tossed the paper down on the table in front of Ryder. "Matter of fact, I would say she is smarter than anyone else in this room, in this hotel, even the state, maybe the whole United States." Thom said as Ryder picked up the report.

"Why do you say that?" Jonas asked as he flipped the coin over his fingers. "She is crazy, right? I mean that is why you...why we all think she is the killer, right?" He slipped the coin in between his fingers, palming the coin; he laid it down on the table.

"That is what the professor told us." Yakira said as she wrapped her arms lovingly around Ryder's neck and pulled him back to her chest. "Is she really that smart?"

"I can't wrap my head around this." Thom said as he picked up his glass and walked back over to the wet bar to fill the glass with soda again. He took a sip and turned to them. "I even contacted a friend at the Mayo Clinic, they couldn't figure it out. The way she has fused the compounds of the flower and scopolamine, she has made it a hundred times stronger, yet made it where it can kill, or mind control." Thom picked up the glass and took a sip before continuing. "That is the big thing, the person being affected would not know if it is real or not."

"Like Ricky?" Yakira asked.

"What you have told me about the dreams definitely." Thom said as he set the glass down on the coffee table in front of him. "According to her reports it works like hypnosis, it could be a trigger word, a smell…"

"Perfume?" Ryder asked.

"Possibly."

"So how do I fight back against it, resist her?"

"You can't." This stuff could be the greatest gift or the biggest weapon of mass destruction there is. "Whatever she wants you to do you are going to do. You can't refuse her."

"So she could make him kill someone? Even someone he loves, like Yakira or Marissa. I mean, she wanted Marissa dead. Could she do that?" Jonas asked as he picked up the coin off the table and once again began to flip it over his fingers.

"Without a doubt," as Thom said that the coin fell from Jonas' hand and landed on the table with a dull clang. He quickly picked up the coin and shot back.

"WHAT? I could be the only surviving member of family!"

"The thing that bothered me about the stabbings is a stabbing is a horrific murder. It is usually very violent. It is very hard to get a single stab wound that kills, unless you have been trained like a Navy SEAL or you are drugged."

"What about Mary?'

"Say way single stab wound to the back. No sign of a struggle." Thom raised his glass of soda to Ryder and added. "There are three reasons to murder. Money, revenge or passion."

"She wants revenge, for me putting her mother in jail.." Ryder said as he reached back and placed his hand on Yakira's that wrapped around him.

"Alex did too why has she not gone after her?" Thom asked before taking another sip of soda. " I read these notes you take out all the freaky stuff, I would say they are love notes."

Yakira suddenly released Ryder and stood up as she forcefully asked. "Are you telling me there she is in love with him?"

"Well…" Thom paused. Ryder glanced over at him, studying his actions, having known him since the beginning of school and being friends since then he could read through him like a wet paper towel. He didn't say anything; he just waited for him to say it. "It might possibility be about her mother, but why go through all this? She had you in the hotel room she could have killed you easily. She would have had her revenge."

"What if we run away?" Yakira said as she released walked over in front of Thom. "Would he be safe?"

"Possibly," Thom replied before taking another drink of the dark colored liquid. "But eventually she is going to find him again."

"Then we run away again!"

"I don't run from things." Ryder replied.

"Well, can't we just set her up and when she comes near Rick we just take her out?" Jonas asked, picking up his coin up off the table again.

"Little brother, we just don't kill people no matter how bad they are. We follow the law."

"Thom," Yakira asked. "She has been doping him with this stuff, right? If we get away from her how long will it take before it is out of his system, and no jokes, please?"

"There are no jokes here." Thom said as he down the rest of his soda and placed the empty glass on the coffee table again. "The pharmacological half-life is about nine hours, but dose after dose will build up in his system; it could be ten days or even more." Thom stood up and walked over to Ryder, placed his hand on his buddy's shoulder and sympathetically stated. "It is going to be tough. Like drug withdrawal, you are going to be sick to your stomach, throwing up, paresthesias of the hands and feet, dysphoria, and hypotension. It could be that you can't do it by yourself."

Yakira walked back over behind Ryder and grabbed him around the neck again, she lowered her head next to his, placing them cheek to cheek. He reached up and his fingers entwined with hers. "You just asked me to marry you. Ricky, let's just leave. Let's get out of Eureka Springs. We could get out of Missouri. "As she spoke he felt her grip tightening around his neck, he moved his grip from her fingers to her wrist. "Please, we have enough money; we could just leave the country. Take me to Paris. I have always wanted to go there."

"What we do when we she finds us?"

"Then we pick up and we go somewhere else. Please, Ricky!"

"That will mean saying goodbye to everything and everyone we know."

"I don't care." He heard her sob and felt her long locks tickle the back of his neck as he stared down at the toxic report. "As long as I have you, that is all that matters. "

"Rick, I am not one that usually tells you to run away from something..." Thom said, as Ryder looked up to him and said.

"But?" Ryder looked over at Alex sitting across the table from him; she sat sideways in the chair with her legs crossed, in front of her. On the table was a glass of diet pop, she slowly twisted it in her fingers, as she gradually lifted her gaze to meet his eyes and said.

"You got to do, what you got to do, my friend." Just as slowly she lowered her gaze back to the glass she was twirling.

"All right," Ryder grudgingly agreed to Yakira's request. "But we are going to need some more clothes. " He turned to Thom and asked. "Double T, can you take her back to the house and get some more clothes?"

"Sure."

"Jonas, I want to say goodbye to Marissa. Can you find some way to get her here, without your dad knowing it?" Ryder asked as he stood up and gazed at himself in the mirror over the fireplace.

"I think so."

"Go do it!"

"Are you going to be okay?" Yakira asked as she, Thom and Jonas headed for the entry way.

"I am in good hands. I have a former FBI lady looking out after me." Alex didn't speak; she gazed up at them while she twisted the glass in her fingers. "Besides, it will give us time to say goodbye to each other."

They left and Ryder walked over to the wet bar and poured himself a glass of pop then returned to the table and sat back down. "So what do you think?" He asked before taking a drink of the ice cold liquid.

"I told you," Alex said, lifting her glass and taking a sip. "You got to do what you got to do."

"In your opinion, if I do run and I don't face her, what is she going to do?"

"It is hard to say." Alex said again, twirling the glass in her fingers. "She may just give up and disappear. Some killers are like that."

He watched as she twirled the glass around and around in one direction, then the other. "I am not asking my friend Belle, I am asking former agent Isabelle Alexander. What profile does she fit?"

"She is psychotic, she hates you and at the same time, she is madly in love with you. That is why she refers to you as hers. But that is what is bugging me. If this was all done to get your attention, so that it can lead up to what she wants... " Alex uncrossed her legs and turned and faced him, leaning over the table. "Why pick Mary?"

"She wanted Marissa...."

"Exactly!" Alex said with enthusiasm as she started searching through the pile of papers, and picking up the note that had been left. She held it up. "Every other note was vague; it never told who was to be killed, why suddenly make it about who it was?" She picked up another note as she continued. "And why be so specific to say, 'I know where she is?' It doesn't make sense, Rick."

"She couldn't get to Marissa so she chose another target." Ryder said as he leaned back in his chair cupping the glass in both hands. He brought it up to his lips and took a drink before asking. "Doesn't that make sense?"

"No, just the opposite," Alex said, again leaning forward, "If I was madly in love with you, would I not take out those that stand in my way? You did not know who she was at the dance. She could have easily come up and killed Yakira, we couldn't have stopped her. Why is it that she has never gone after Yakira or..."

"You?" Ryder asked with a tone mixed with compassion and curiosity as he sit staring at her his finger supporting his chin as his elbow rested on the arm of the chair.

"Okay, it would make sense for me, we have a past; we have a connection. Mary as the victim doesn't fit it. There is more to this Ricky, I know there is. I just can't put my finger on it."

Ryder finished his drink and stood up, picking up her glass also, he walked back to the wet bar to refill the glasses. He walked back and set her glass down in front of her, and again sat down as he asked. "What was it you were going to tell me, something I needed to know?"

"What?' She asked, picking up her glass and taking a drink.

"Down in the tunnel when you thought we weren't going to get out."

"Oh that," She said, taking another sip before she continued. "I was just going to thank you for being my friend, I don't have too many real friends; in fact, I guess you and Yakira are it."

"You are not friends with anyone at the agency?"

"We talk about work, suspects, but just to go out and have a drink, or eat dinner, even tell a joke to, no." She said softly, she looked down at the glass and twirled it in her fingertips. "Even when I had Ceelia, I never got a party, no one even said congratulations." She stopped twirling the glass and looked up at him. "I guess it's because I always stayed by myself, always thinking about the case I was working on, I always figured you and I had that in common." Again she glimpse down at the glass in her hands. "But I see you have lots of friends."

"Alex," Ryder said affectionately leaning up and placing his hand on hers he continued "Belle, you will always have a place in my life. There are not too many friends that would give up their job." He lifted his hand off of hers and leaned back in the chair once again before adding. "I want you to watch over Yakira."

"You are going after her aren't you?" Alex asked. "You know where she is going to be." He didn't answer her, but just like he could read her thoughts, he knew she could read his. Suddenly placing her hands on the table, Alex stood up and said. "She isn't going to kill you right away; she wants something from you. I could put a tracer on you. When she grabs you I can follow to wherever she takes you and grab her then."

"You got one?"

"Back in my room," Alex said before leaving quickly returned holding a small bright yellow cube, along with a small pen knife. Using the knife, she cut a small hole in the lining of his jacket, turned on the device, and the lights blinked, indicating that it was linking to the home base that she pulled out of her other jacket pocket. The home base beeped wildly. She dropped the small tracking device down into the hole on his jacket.

"You know she is going to be watching?" Ryder said as Alex double checked the tracer was working.

"This has a five-mile range." Alex said. "I should be able to stay out of sight, and be able to trace you." Ryder pulled the Glock from the holster and double checked that it was loaded and ready to go.

"If she grabs me and I don't..." He stopped speaking as he shoved the pistol back into the holster on his side; he stared at Alex, not able to say the same words just hoping she understood.

"She tries I will stop her." Alex said placing her hand on his shoulder. "I promise you that." Ryder gave her one last nod and started to walk out the door. Holding it open he stepped back into the room. He leaned down and kissed Alex on the cheek. "So you know you are my best friend and I love you." He turned and walked out of the room.

****

It is alive during the day, the city bustling with shoppers going from shop to shop, visitors finding the perfect gift for Uncle Frank, but after the sun goes down comes a new life, those going out for dinner, or to hoist back a few at the local tavern, hearing a big tale of woe or just a chance to forget for a moment, and pretend to be something they are not. However, at the witching hour, the city sleeps. The sounds of nothing is all that can be heard, or if one held their breath and listened with all their heart they might hear the faint sound of a coyote's howl, as the bright light of the full moon gleamed on Ryder as he stood on Main Street in front of a clock shop; catty-corner across the street was the Eureka Springs courthouse.

The courthouse that stood proudly was one of the stars of the town, constructed of hand cut native limestone it rose up three stories. In the center was a tower, four stories high with double windows on three sides, each side appearing as eyes, with a red dome roof as its hat, it was a centurion guard over the town.

Ryder walked across the street, glaring up at the tower, noticing the dim glow of a single candle burning in one of the windows, at the top of the tower, which faced the street. He walked up the steps, it should have been locked, but the door opened and he stepped inside. He had heard no ghost tales about this place, but hearing his footsteps echoing off the hard floor and walls, gave him the creeps more than anywhere else he had visited. It was dark and he slowly made his way down the hall. It was also alerting her he was coming so he bent down and removed his shoes; the hard floor was cool on his feet. He remembered the small pen light on his key chain. The bright blue beam gave him just enough light to guide his way. Every door was closed and locked; he wondered where she was hiding. He shined the beam around and saw something lying on the bottom step of the stairs. He bent down and picked it up; it was a flower- A white Angel Trumpet. He gazed up the stairs and began climbing. At each flight there was another flower. He kept climbing till he reached the top.

It was the crowning arena of the court house, looking as if it were a bell tower missing its bell. High above him on all four sides were arched windows; the moonlight gleaming through and casting on the floor, drawing him closer to the double windows on one side, noticing the glass in one of the windows was broken out, and folded up lying on the window sill was something white. He moved over to examine it more carefully when from behind he heard a soft voice say-

"Forever begins tonight." He turned around. Lillian stood there holding a pistol on him. She stood on the step next to the top. She had followed him up the stairs. He glanced down at her bare feet, peering out

from under the white gown she wore.   Made of white lace, it was part
wedding dress, part night gown.

"Now sweet darling, I want you to reach in with your left hand
and remove that nasty pistol."   He did as he was told, holding on to the
butt of it with only two fingers.   "Now toss it out the window."   He
reached out the broken window and let the gun fall, hearing it crash on the
cement below.

"Okay Lillian," Ryder said as he moved towards her, but she
made him stop, pushing the gun towards him. "I am yours. What do you
want?"

"It is our wedding day, my darling."   She spoke effortlessly as
she moved across the floor keeping the gun aimed at him, her index finger
clutched over the trigger. He couldn't make a move towards her; one
squeeze and he would get hit squarely in the chest, and be killed. Now
with a family and Yakira agreeing to be his wife, he had a reason to live.

"So that is your wedding dress?" His question seemed to amuse
her at first, almost making her laugh before her lips became a perishing
grin, her bright blue eyes burrowing into him, as she moved to where the
moonlight shone behind her. The lace revealed the ravishing curves of her
body and the fact that she was nude underneath. Ryder drew in a
quivering breath as he realized what this gown was- a death shroud.

"Today forever begins." She said, as the moonlight flowed over
her and the candle twinkled; he noticed what a great beauty she was. The
soft curves of her cheek and angular chin, golden hair, parted in the middle
that flowed down over her shoulders. However, it was those bright eyes
that were frightening and at the same time hypnotic, almost willing him to
walk over to her, to hold her, to do what to her whatever she asked. "Now
you must be dressed. Take off all your clothes, throw them out the
window, and put on what is behind you."

"But, this a thousand dollar Armani jacket," Ryder pleaded, "It is
perfect for a wedding." He knew once the jacket was gone, so was his
hope that Alex would find him. He removed the jacket and begged once.
"It is perfect for a wedding."

"Where we are going gold lines the streets and jewels fill the
streams." She said in a tone of glee as she motioned with the gun for him
to toss the jacket out the window, and he did so, feeling his hope sink just

as much as the jacket that glided down, landing on the parking lot below. There was no way to trace him now.

"To enter the city of light we must leave this world just as we came into it, with nothing, wearing nothing." Again she moved the gun, encouraging him to remove the rest of his clothes. He removed the holster and tossed it out the window and began unbuttoning his shirt. He thought it was time to get answers.

"Why me," Ryder asked. "I am the one that put your mother in jail. Don't you just want to kill me?"

"This isn't about my mother," Lillian replied. "Oh silly darling, is that what you think? That this has been about her? This is about you and me, and the promise made to me."

"And what would that be?" Ryder asked, slipping off his shirt, exposing his bare muscular hairy chest. Which she seemed to enjoy, as she lifted her eyebrows and let her eyes roam over his bulging biceps, wide shoulders and down to his taut stomach. He held the shirt out the window and flapped it like a flag, hoping Alex would see it, or maybe a local officer.

"Oh, don't think that Eureka's finest will help you." She said as Ryder let the shirt fall. "They are all taking a long well deserved nap."

"You killed them?" Ryder asked.

"I killed no one. They are just sleeping, like the others; if they die it is their fate." She said as.

"Just like the others, the ones that you stabbed, they are just sleeping?" Ryder asked as he unbuttoned his pants, and let them fall to the floor.

"I hurt no one, I am not my mother!" She said, sounding almost bashful as she watched him slide his pants down to the floor. She dropped her gaze, offering a modest smile, before she quickly let her steel like eyes roam up from his feet, calves, up his hips. "I just want her to keep the promise that she made to me." Ryder tossed the pants out the window.

"And that is?" Ryder said as he slipped out of his underwear.

She grinned like a blushing bride, a virgin on her wedding night, not sure as what to do or say, or how to act before saying "She said 'That I could have you.' "

Me?" Ryder said, tossing his underpants out the window.

"It has always been you," Lillian said, but paused. "Now the socks." He pulled them off and tossed them out the window. He stood dressed as a new born babe before her; she let her eyes caress his body, every muscle from his head to his feet, then slowly back up to his face. She moved closer to him.

"All of this is because of you." As she spoke he picked up the white garment; he realized it too was a death shroud. As he pulled it down over his head she was standing directly in front of him. She reached behind him and let the gun she was holding slip from her grip. He could have easily overpowered her, but there were questions that were nagging at him.

"What do you mean, all because of me?"

"My mother promised you to me. I saw you in Union Station; I had just turned of age. You were so handsome, dressed in a tuxedo, you took my breath away. She moved even closer to him, he could smell the sweet aromas of flowers on her. She placed her hand behind his head, and drew his mouth closer to hers. "I even dedicated the song to you because the lyrics say what I couldn't." She let her hand slide down his head to his back, and pulled him closer. "I came to see you, and tried to tell you how much I love you, but you did not hear."

"They didn't understand, all I wanted was love." She stepped back from him and he saw rage building in her. "All they wanted was death and destruction." She shouted out.

"And you gave it to them." Ryder asked.

"I told you, I hurt no one!"

"But your mother, she did?"

"You were promised to me." She took another step away from him before she continued. "Every town let her down, even your wonderful hometown, she came to Roaring River just to have fun, and some jerk hurt her, because all men hurt her. But she showed him one bullet and he shut

312

his mouth forever. And the one that held her down, she thought she could get away. She didn't even see it coming. After that she said it became easy for her and no one was going to hurt her again."

Ryder's mind was reeling. Never did he think the murder at Roaring River, over forty years ago, would be connected to these today. That it was Celeste that shot the two teens. "She couldn't understand." Lillian continued. "I told her you were different, that you would not hurt me. But you wouldn't notice me. Then mom said 'you were a homicide cop; there was only one way to make you notice. But one murder would not be enough.' "

"Oh dear lord," Ryder could barely let the words fall from his mouth, realizing that all the murders that she did Kansas City, were because of him, they couldn't place a motive on Celeste. All she would do was keep saying 'you know why'. Now he knew why and he felt heaviness on his chest, pure guilt. "She murdered those people just to get my attention?"

"How else was she supposed to do it?" She said softly walking back over to him, placing her head on his chest. "I wanted you. I was the flower, you were the water, I needed to grow. Like a flower without water I would wither and die in the heat of the sun's passion." He could feel her warm breath on the side of his neck; just before he felt her lips softly kiss him, before feeling her teeth sinking gently into his flesh. He winced in the pain, before she moved her head around to his Adam 's Apple, which she kissed before looking back up at him.

"And those in Eureka Springs, did they hurt her too?" She took a step back away from him, drawing her eyebrows down, clearly upset as she shouted at him.

"Enough of this!" She let eyes drift up to the ceiling and spoke. "Did you not hear? The Queen of Heaven has spoken. You now take me as your wife." She lowered her head and looked right at him. "And now I take you as my husband." She grinned broadly, her eyes beaming with life. "Our child shall be a beauty, she will have golden hair and blue eyes, her name shall be 'Forever'." She quickly brought up a bottle and the sickening smell of flowers filled his senses.

Chapter 39

Now what happened was just a blur in Ryder's mind; of rings being exchanged, of him and her arm in arm, grinning just as any other newlywed couple marching out of the courthouse and down the middle of Main Street, to a light-colored sedan, him face down in the back seat driving. Of course a toast of champagne, and what all couples dreamed of the wedding night, filled with passion that filled every sense, every fiber of his being, before everything went black.

He awoke to find himself in a place he had never been before. The room was small, barely wide enough for a small cot that was placed across the far end. The walls were once white, but were now peeling and cracked, a single incandescent bulb hung from the ceiling, housed in a faded white metal shade. There were no windows at all, and only a solid metal door at the front with small wire encased glass window in the door, cracked.

He was sitting on the floor. He tried to stand, but it was difficult, he was restrained his arms in front of him, he was in a straight-jacket. He was still dressed in the death shroud, he pushed his back up against the wall and using his bare feet against the floor pushed himself to his feet and walked over to the door and peered out the window.

Twisting his head slightly, he could see a long hall, again once painted white, the paint peeling and tagged with graffiti, overhead fluorescent bulbs were either burned out or buzzing loudly and flashing like warning lights. He realized where he was. An abandoned mental hospital, from the furnishings that he could see it appeared it hadn't been used in years.

He cried out for help placing his head up next to the window on the door, he saw a shadow approaching. When Lillian appeared, he just lowered his head resting it against the glass.

"What is the meaning of this?" He yelled lifting his head up again. "What am I doing in here? I thought we were celebrating our wedding night. " She turned her head towards him; pure hatred flowed from every pore on her face. Her breath was coming in short spurts as she marched over to the door.

"It is not so fun being in here, is it?" She asked, looking intensively through the window at him. "Tied up and you can't move, soaked in your own filth." Her voice became shaky and her eyes filled with tears as she continued. "Wondering what they are going to do to you next? Someone looking at you like you're dessert on an all you can eat buffet." She turned her back to the door and she began to cry, sliding down the door. "And it was your entire fault!"

"How is it my fault?" Ryder struggled against the straps on the jacket, trying to break free.

"Because I met you," She replied tenderly, even though he couldn't see it he could see her smile just by her tone, but with her next words it would fade away. "I thought it would be magical, that you would sweep me up in your arms and we would live happily ever after. But you didn't want anything to do with me. You hurt me, just like mother said you would."

"When was that?" He asked as he saw her stand up and faced him through the glass as she explained.

"Just before the last murder, I was a witness. You bought me coffee and a doughnut and put your jacket around me." As she spoke she placed her hand on her cheek, and again a small smile appeared. "I thought you loved me." As she spoke Ryder began to remember the beautiful girl that claimed she had found the body. She was crying and shivering, he was just trying to comfort her so he could get her statement, he was doing whatever it took to get her to calm down; he even… "You gave me a kiss."

"It was on the cheek."

"It was a KISS!" She shouted out. "You loved me. I told everyone that. I told them ALL THAT!" She walked over to the other side of the wall and leaned back on the wall and stared at him through the window. "Every time I told them you loved me, they would do things to me!" She sobbed out.

"What kind of things?"

"Bad things! They hurt me. And the doctor gave me shots. Telling me over and over again that you didn't love me that you never loved me…" She ran back up to the door and tilted her head down, and placed her left hand up on the glass. She was wearing a wedding ring.

"I am sorry Lillian that they hurt you. I would never want to hurt you." He could see this woman was not stable he had to just humor her; it was his only hope to get free or wait long enough for Alex to find him.

"Because you love me?" She said softly bringing her hand up and wiping away the tears from her eyes. "Say IT!" She shouted

"Yes Lillian, I love you." He replied "Is that why you murdered them, to prove your love to me?"

"I told you!" She snapped back viciously. "I didn't kill anybody. I am not my mother. I gave you the notes and then prayed that it would happen, but…" She turned around, resting the back of her head on the door, swinging back and forth as she grinned and looked up at the ceiling tiles that were barely holding into place as she said blissfully. "I guess the faiths of heaven were smiling down on me because they died." She turned back around and faced him again. "It allowed me to watch you, to be with you, even if you didn't know it. I was sorry when Mary got killed. I didn't want that. I didn't pray for that." She brought her hands up to her face and they shook, she appeared frightened, and her tone changed to show it too. "That is when the darkness came! I saw it! I saw her die! I saw the shadows take her."

Like a bathroom light being switched on in the middle of the night, her mood again changed as she stepped back in the middle of the hall, she held her hand over her tummy and began dancing about as if it were in praise. "But our daughter will change that. Forever, will be forever, can you feel it?" She asked with excitement as she ran back to the door and looked at him. "Her spirit is here, she has been born."

"Lillian," Ryder said warmly, again resting his head against the door. "Why don't you let me out of this room and this jacket; we can make love again."

"NO!" She snarled back. "It can't be! Only Forever's spirit can change the world. She will bring love to the loveless, hope to the hopeless. It cannot be any other." He saw her walk away; he twisted his head, trying to see where she went. She went to a room across the hall and opened the door. Inside the room was a ring of white candles. Lillian knelt

316

down in the middle; she picked up a knife that was lying on the floor. Holding the large knife in her hands, she spoke gibberish before she held it up above her head, then she bowed down placing the knife in front of her. She stood up and picked up the knife and walked to another room and she opened the door. Inside it was like a bedroom, with a luscious soft bed, and here too a circle of candles were burning around the bed that was also covered with red roses, their stems tied into loops. She had taken the pillows and placed them on top of each other in the center. The bright white silk sheets were pulled back and folded, the pillowcases had wide draped ruffles, and it looked like the insides of a casket. Ryder swallowed hard as he leaned his head against the door, as he grasped that was exactly what it was- a death bed. It was to be a murder- suicide that way they would be joined in death.

"Come on Lillian, you don't want to do this!" Ryder pleaded his voice begin to crack from the stress. "Let me out of here, we can go somewhere and we will live together and watch our little girl grow up, and give us grand kids and die together of old age. Lillian!" He screamed out as he watched her use the knife to slice her hand open, as the blood gushed out she carefully wiped a spinning circle in the center of pillow. She laid the blood stained knife down on the bed and spoke.

"The curse that was laid upon us will now be released as love marries death." She walked back up to the door and continued. "Those in the coats want to keep us apart, it is death, and it is the only thing that can seal our love so it can never be broken."

Ryder didn't know what to say or how to respond to her. He just soaked in the silence that emitted between them until she broke it as she spoke softly. "I am ready." She kissed her bloody fingers and brought them to the glass as she added. "And you, Rick Ryder, are you ready to die with me?"

"No!" He cried out struggled against the straps in the jacket as hard as he could. Suddenly a thick mist appeared in the padded room, emitting from vents in the ceiling, it was thick as fog and he could feel it collecting like water on his hair. He tried not to breathe, but he couldn't hold his breath and he sucked in the poison.

He felt as if he was floating out of his body, falling to the floor like a leaf tumbling slowly the ground. As before it was as if were dream, of

317

her and him gliding across to the hall over to the bed. He was free, he could move his arms, but he couldn't do anything as she laid him back on the bed, his head resting on the blood stained pillows. Gripping the knife in both hands she straddled him across his waist, raising it above his chest. She looked down upon him and spoke, her words echoing in Ryder's mind.

"Love can only be, if forever is you and me." She began to plunge the knife into him when suddenly a bright light appeared, flooding the entire room. She turned, holding the knife with one hand she faced a shadowy figure. "No, this is not right! She demanded. "You promised me if I helped you I could have him. You promised me!" The sound of a gunshot rang out. Lillian's body jerked straight up as blood began to stain the front of her gown; she looked at Ryder and moaned out one word. "Forever!" Before falling face down on top of him. Her arms spread over him, her head over his shoulder, and her face next to his.

There were voices echoing, he couldn't understand any of it. Shadowy, blurry images were moving about, then Alex looking down over him as she said, "It is going to be okay, a chopper is on the way." He struggled, reaching and grabbing for her arm and pulling himself up, trying to open his mouth, wanting to tell her what he had found out. That Lillian claimed she wasn't the slayer. He couldn't speak; it felt as if a hand were squeezing around his neck. The poison was taking effect; he couldn't breathe, he tried to gasp or scream he couldn't make a sound. He fell back on the bed.

Chapter 40

The glimmer of a new day was rising as those all over Springfield, Missouri were awakening. As they sipped a cup of coffee, the mug came down quickly as they gazed on the headline in the News leader; "Eureka Slayer Shot Dead."

Those caught in the throat of the beast of traffic-known as the James River Freeway, were not in that much of a hurry to get to work. Instead, they were tuned to 104.1 KSGF as the host of the morning show, and forgoing the usual politics, answering calls from listeners as they were shocked by the "Beautiful, but deadly killer."

Televisions were flipping off the umpteenth showing of the Andy Griffith Show, leaving the fantasy of Mayberry behind for the harshness of reality as they tuned into the local news stations. Soon, like seed thrown out for hungry birds in the winter, it became the lead news feed on all the internet sites, and cable news outlets picked it up, and the nighttime talking heads promised to get to the bottom of: 'how can the beautiful kill?"

Children stood in line, waiting for the yellow beast to come and gobble them up, while in their mind they were counting the days that were left until that last bell rang, but eventually the talked grew into tales, as teenage boys, bragged 'they would do her, and teen girls stated "She ain't that pretty."

Meanwhile, there were those professionals, so wrapped up in their own little world, who only had time to quickly grab a toaster pastry, were shocked by the congregation of media outside the Mercy Hospital, and no idea of the patient that was being attended.

The red, blue and white Eurocopter, once a buzz of life, now was sitting silently, perched in the middle of the cross on the roof of Mercy Emergency Room. Down below, just as still, sitting in the waiting room was Yakira. She just sat there, holding her own hand, staring down at the pink diamond in her ring.

"Two sugars and cream, right? " She heard Alex say, she looked up and saw her holding two cups of coffees, and handed one of the foam cups out towards her. Alex sighed slightly as she added, "Just like he likes it." Yakira took the cup, but didn't say a word, not even a thank you. She took a sip of it, and Alex sat down beside her.

"I fell for it didn't I..." Yakira asked, starting to take another sip of her sweet coffee, but stopped and set it back down, closing her eyes in agony as she said. "What happened, Alex? I... he and I— well, I thought we were going to leave, get married and..."

"Live happily ever after?" Alex said with scorn carefully taking a sip of her coffee. "You didn't fall for that lie, did you? That only happens in the movies. This is real life..." Alex took another sip of coffee before she added. "Sometime the story ends with the words 'Life sucks '." She held the coffee cup in both her hands in her lap as she leaned back and closed her eyes, tired from the long night before.

"Haven't you ever wanted the fairy tale?"

"You mean, I would have a wonderful prince that comes in and rescues me, and live in a big castle with no worries? Maybe once, then I woke up." Alex said before taking another sip of the coffee.

"I mean, when you have the worst day of your life that there is someone there to give you a hug, let you know it is going to be okay." Yakira said as she stood up.

"You mean like today?" Alex said, looking straight out across the waiting room, instead of at her.

"I don't get it. Why did he go to her?"

"Yakira," Alex said, turning to her. "You really didn't think he was just going to run away, did you? You've known him longer than I have, did you ever see him back away from a fight if he believes it was right? Did you think he would change, even for you?"

Yakira walked over to the large glass windows, and peered out, watching the sun reflect off of the windshield of a car in the parking lot. She remembered her grandmother telling her that was the smile of God. Alex followed Yakira and stood behind her. "This is the first sunrise I have seen without my little girl."

"Did you think of her when you saw it?" Yakira asked, resting her head against the pane, feeling its coolness on her forehead.

"Yes, there isn't a moment that goes by that I don't."

She turned back to face Alex, and said. "Then she was there, wasn't she?"

"I am sorry for the way it went down Yakira, if I could have…"

"What happened?"

"We can't do it in here. Let's go outside." Alex led the way out through the sliding glass doors, past the awning with its red letters that spelled out EMERGENCY, across the driveway, past a security cruiser, and seated herself on a rock under the tree, the shadow of the hospital looming over them. Yakira seated herself next to Alex.

"I put a tracer in his jacket; I didn't know that she would make him get rid of it. I guess Thom was right; she was smarter than any of us. She had him strip down to nothing that way she could see if he was wired. Then she placed his clothes in a car that was leaving, it was halfway to Rogers before I got it stopped. Luckily I got her Psychologist to finally open up her files and I saw her plan, about putting him in the old psych ward. That was where she was going to kill him. I…"

"Eight years old."

"What?"

"That was the first time I fell in love with him. He was eighteen-years, old the quarterback of the Wildcats. Each year of my life I waited and waited until that time span didn't matter." She turned and faced Alex. "Now that it is forty and thirty-one, it doesn't seem that far apart."

"Thirty-one?"

"Today, is my birthday. Some birthday present, huh?"

"I would wish you a happy birthday but…"

"I just wish I had a birthday cake so I could make a wish."

"Yakira! Alex!" Double T yelled, standing under the awning of the emergency entrance. Yakira felt her heart sink into her stomach. She hurried across the parking lot with a mixture of emotions, praying it was good news, but wondering what she would do if it was bad news. Seeing his bleak expression made her heart pound hard in her chest, pushing up against the pink blouse she was wearing.

321

"They are moving him up to ICU." Double T said, there was a little relief and she tried to show it with a small smile. "That doesn't mean he is out of the woods just yet." She waited for Thom to make a joke, if he just joked about it, then she would know it would be okay. "They just don't know what to do; CDC has not a clue. Poison control told them to treat it as chemical pneumonia. A Pulmonologist from Barnes in St. Louis is flying in."

"Can I see him?" Yakira whispered.

"Yes, but they said only for a short time. He is on the fourth floor."

She ran across the drive and took the north elevator, as it zoomed straight up she steadied herself gripping the bar, within a matter of seconds the doors opened onto the fourth floor. She quickly stepped up to the desk. "I want to see Richard Ryder." She said using his real first name.

A tall thin nurse with long yellow hair and a serious over bite approached her, looking her over before asking. "Are you a family member?"

"I am his fiancée. " She replied, holding her ringed hand out for the nurse to see.

"Mmmm huh?" The ICU nurse replied. "I am not sure that will be good enough."

"Please! I am all he has."

"I wouldn't be so sure of that." The nurse said, her gaze drifting over to the waiting room. There seated together were Marissa and Jonas. "Now, like I have told them. Go over there and wait."

"No more waiting! Do you know who he is?"

"I know exactly who he is, and who you are Miss Rosen. Everyone in this hospital has heard what happened. I want to assure you that Mr. Ryder is under acute care right now, and also has a Critical care team with him. Still, you have to wait with the others." Yakira walked over and sat down across from Jonas.

"He is going to be all right, Yakira." Marissa said, flashing those dimples of hers.

"How do you know?"

"I just know so."

"Sure of it?"

"Positive!" Marissa said getting up and sitting in the chair next to Yakira. "I can feel it!" She grinned brightly, making Yakira truly want to believe her. "I can feel him in here." She pointed to her chest," I always have. Even when I didn't know anything about him, I knew there was someone else out there. It is a brother and sister thing! You've just got to believe it, Yakira." Marissa wrapped her arms around Yakira, and she hugged her back.

"It is the truth, Yakira." Jonas said, "When she would get mad at me, she would storm off, saying she was going to find her other brother. I thought she was crazy, and should be put in a..." He paused, catching what he was about to say, and his tone softened as he added. "I didn't like seeing him there, locked away in that cell. But now that she is gone, I guess everything is...well, I guess we don't need to talk about it."

Marissa looked at the ring on Yakira's finger, and grinned again, saying. 'Let's talk about something better. That you're going to be our sister; I never had a sister before. So when is the wedding going to be? Summer is coming up, June is the time for weddings, but I think that is so passé, everybody wants to get married then, you don't want that. But it could be outside! That would be so cool, don't you think. Oh-oh—how about in the winter, in the snow, we could clear out paths that you could walk down. The icicles, hanging on the brushes and in the trees, we could hang colored lights and they would reflect in the ice. I have always wanted a wedding in the winter; I just think it would be so cool. When it snowed I would pretend like I was a princess and getting married, I would wear a blue veil because I was..."

Yakira hadn't known this young girl very long, and the time she had known her, she never had much to say, now suddenly she was hearing every thought that was coming out from her mind and right out of her mouth, if there was speed limit in thought, she was breaking it. However, Yakira was listening, it dawned on her why Marissa picked the costume she did for the Street Gala.

"An Ice Princes," Yakira said, interrupting Marissa.

"Yeah," she replied with that smile that flashed her dimples; she had charm, much the same way that Ryder had, she had always assumed it had come from his mother because of the way his father was, but she had it too. She glanced over at Jonas; however, he didn't seem to have the gift, and maybe that was what it was: a gift. "So what are your colors going to be?"

"I don't know. I guess pink, I like pink." Yakira said which sets Marissa off on a two minute speech of how good pink looked on her before she asked. "How about pink and ice blue? That would look good, don't you think?" Yakira was deep in thought as she stood up and walked around the waiting room, every once in awhile looking over at the door that led into the ICU ward. She would go back to the nurse's desk and ask, "Is there any word?" then back to her chair.

"Don't you think those would be good colors?" Marissa asked again; all the while not stopping talking.

"What?"

"The colors for your wedding?"

"Oh yes," She replied without any feeling. "Where is your dad? I thought he would be here."

"We asked, but…well, he still blames him for what happened to mom, even though it wasn't his fault. But it doesn't matter, we are here." Marissa said, the grin leaving her face only for a short time before it returned. "So where are you going to register? At Macy's, J.C. Penney's? Dillard's? We will have to go to the mall and get you set up."

"I would like to get you both something special for your wedding." Jonas said "Maybe a silver tea service set."

"Those are very expensive, Jonas. You don't have to get us anything." Yakira said.

"I want to. He is my brother. Besides, Marissa and I are going to inherit the Crawford County Bank building and there is a guy that is offering us big bucks for it."

"I don't want to sell it, Jonas." Marissa said. "I want to start a B and B, like mom wanted to do. We could get Ricky and Yakira to join us and it can be a family thing. So tell that guy no, okay?"

"All right sis. I will tell him."

"You can go in and see him now." The nurse said. "But only two of you."

"Go on," Jonas said. "You two go in I'll—I'll call this guy and tell him no."

Yakira and Marissa entered the ICU and walked over to Ryder's cubical. The steady beep of the Cardiac monitors was the first thing Yakira noticed, followed by the ensuing hiss of the ventilator. She followed the soft white endotracheal tubes from the machine by the bed over to where he lay, the cup placed firmly over his nose and mouth. She watched his chest expand as the machine forced rich oxygen into his lungs. His eyes were closed and his skin was pale, his hands were lying out on top of the blanket, his fingers had a bluish cast, attached to his finger was a pulse oximeter, a white clothespin like item that monitored saturation of oxygen in the blood. On his other arm a needle was inserted and a small drip flowed from a large IV bag, followed by another line that dripped from a bag of blood.

His blood pressure was low, 65 over 45, as was body temp 94.1, pulse 50. She reached down and took a hold of his hand. It felt so cold, it felt like death; she pulled her hand back. She couldn't help it; the tears began to fall down her cheeks.

"Tell him you are here." Marissa said as she took a hold of his hand, the coldness not seeming to bother her. "He can hear you. I know it" She said softly before she turned to Ryder, and flashed those dimples. "You are getting out of here, big brother. When you do, I am going to make you a special cake just for you. What do you like? Butter yellow with Chocolate Buttercream frosting?

"He likes carrot cake with walnuts, black walnuts." Yakira spoke up, wiping the tears from her eyes. "Bubbie makes it for him."

"I love carrot cake too." Marissa smiled again as she knelt down beside the bed, cupping his hand in both of hers. "Especially with strawberry cream cheese frosting." She looked up at Yakira for only a moment before her gaze returned to her brother as she continued. "Yakira is here and she loves you, and so do I...." she looked up at Yakira and her bright eyes glistened with tears as she added softly "tell him." She looked back down at her brother and said, letting go of his hand. "Okay big brother, now you just get better and I will make you that cake." She leaned over and kissed him on the forehead. "Now I will be back. But Yakira's here. You take care."

"I don't know?" Yakira asked. "How do you know he is going to be okay?"

"God took my mother, he won't take my brother. He wouldn't do that. Just believe now and go to him. You are the best medicine he can have." Marissa walked away. Yakira approached the bed again, the beeping filling her ears. She gripped his hand in hers, it was so cold, but she didn't let go.

"Sweetie, if you think you are going to get out of marrying me by dying on me, you are sadly mistaken. When a Jewish girl says yes, she means yes. Besides, Bubbie will come in and beat your tukhus." She leaned over closer to him and whispered, "I have been planning this since I was ten years old, so you had better get ready to be become a groom." She leaned back, cupping his hand in both of hers. She brought his hand up to her face and caressed her cheek as she spoke. "Sweetie, I don't know where you are now, but Marissa says you can hear me. Then come back to me."

"Miss," The nurse said in almost a whisper. "It is time to leave now." Yakira kissed his hand and laid it down on the bed. "Dr. Rogers would like to speak to you and the family in the consultation room."

The nurse led her into a small room with a long table and several chairs around it, sitting there were Marissa, Alex and Jonas. Yakira seated herself at the table. The door opened and in walked a stocky built man dressed in surgical blues, a stethoscope draped around his neck. He was middle aged, with dark hair. He held out his hand. "I am doctor Erin Rogers; they brought me in from Barnes-Jewish in St. Louis. I would like to tell you that everything will be fine. But…"

"You don't know what you are doing? You are just a nebbish." Yakira spoke up.

"I do feel insignificant and worthless."

"You understand me?"

"I work at a Jewish Hospital; I have heard the word before." He paused to go back to the discussion. "It isn't that we don't know, it's that there has never been a case like this before anywhere. Snake bite we give anti-venom, cyanide there would be steps that we could take. However, there is no name for this poison, if we had the person that made it, possibly they could tell us how to counteract it."

"That isn't going to happen." Alex said, "She is dead." Alex looked over at Marissa and then to Yakira as she said uncomfortably, "I shot her. Ironic, isn't it, I shoot her to keep her from killing him, yet in doing so I may have done just that." Alex let out a heavy sigh as she pushed the chair back and said. "I am sorry—I—have to get out of here." She walked out, closing the door behind her.

"I didn't mean to upset her." Dr. Rogers said, crossing his legs. "Is she close to him?"

"Yes." Yakira replied. "Very close. That is his best friend."

"A woman?' the doctor questioned.

"Yes, she loves him, we all do." Yakira said as she heard the door click as it opened, turned and saw Father Anthony creeping in and walking over the empty chair next to her and sit down. He was dressed in clerical collar.

"Father it is good to see." The doctor said. "Did someone call I don't know if you are needed here."

"That is my nephew, I am going to be here." The father reached over and took a hold of Yakira's hand. "How are you doing my child?" She tried to smile. "You don't worry about a thing. My boy is tough fighter, and he isn't going to leave you."

"I am glad you have that much faith in me father." The doctor said.

"Not in you doc, in someone higher up," The father cupped his hands around Yakira's and added. "What can we do to help?"

"I would say what you are already doing." The doctor uncrossed his legs and leaned forward and continued his tone showing the seriousness of it. "I don't want to give you any false hopes. We are flying blind here. There is no known treatment for this. We are just going to have to guess, and I am warning you that treatments may end killing him. Right now we are treating it like Organophosphate poisoning."

Yakira looked at him, puzzled, and drew one eyebrow down. "Doc, all I did was graduate Cassville high school. What are you saying?"

"It could be reacting like a kind of nerve gas, but not a violent reaction, but also as the Scopolamine."

"So what are you going to do for him?" Father Anthony said.

"When he arrived he could barely take a breath, they administered 0.5 cc 1:1,000 concentration of Epinephrine. I feel this is good choice and I am continuing 1 mg of the same concentration of epinephrine to 250 ml of dextrose 5% in water through an IV. We will be continuing the oxygen therapy, with almost pure oxygen, hopeful that will push it right out of his system. We are monitoring his blood gases. We are trying to get his BP back up, along with medication for any seizures that he may have".

"Doc, you are scaring me to death, but okay, I am going to ask." Yakira said. "What happens if these levels don't increase to normal?"

Doctor Rogers took an inward sigh, one that is taught to every doctor, to not show emotion, to remain disconnected; he turned a page in the file as he spoke. "He won't be able to breathe on his own; he will either have to remain on the ventilator or..." He paused and looked down at the paper before him before he continued. "...you will have to make the decision regarding life support..." He looked over at Yakira and said. "I see by his 'Quality of Life' statement you are the one listed that will make that decision."

Chapter 41

Yakira found herself wandering the halls, lost in a maze of halls that suddenly came to an end, with no way out, except to turn around, return, search for another turn that led to an elevator that only returned her to the place she had begun this journey, with no way out- more wandering long halls, which suddenly turned and all the while the words of the doctor, 'that she would have to make the decision'. This was a part of love that she didn't want, somehow she found herself in front of another elevator, and she wondered- can this one take me out of here? She stepped inside and pressed the button marked for the first floor; again in what seemed like only a couple of seconds, she was back on the main floor.

She found herself facing the hospital cafeteria, a warm aroma drifting over towards her. Considering it was almost noon, and she had skipped supper and breakfast, she was getting hungry. The smell of roast beef was drawing her in. She almost stepped inside until she caught sight of a woman in the alcove. Her face buried in her hands, her long mane dropping down hiding her fingers, it was Alex. She walked up to her and gently placed her hand on Alex's shoulder.

"Alex," Yakira said, and Alex lifted her head up, turned and looked over her shoulder at her.

"If I could have gotten there sooner," Alex said through her clinched teeth, angry at herself. "I could have stopped her. It wouldn't have had to end that way. If I could have been able to talk to her, if…"

"Alex, it isn't your fault. You had to do what you had to do. Of all people you should know that…"

"I missed the sunrise." Alex said, interrupting her. Alex stood up and Yakira could see that her eyes were red and swollen. "Have you seen more sunrises or sunsets?"

"I guess sunsets; I am not an early riser."

"I have seen more sunrises. I remember my dad getting me out of bed on an early Christmas morning, there was a fresh snow on the ground, and the sun was just coming up, and the sky was so clear, the orange glow painted over the snow, the sun making icicles gleam like jewels. The morning of his funeral was the most beautiful sunrise I had ever seen." Alex took the waded up tissue in her hand and dabbed the tears from her eyes and she grinned, just enough to make her lips curl up. "If I see the sunrise I know everything is going to be okay because Dad is watching."

"That is why you do it; it reminds you of your dad."

"You love him, don't you?" Yakira asked "Ricky, you love him?"

"Not the way you do?" Alex said tenderly. "I know we may have not always got along, but I consider you friend."

"You are my friend Alex."

"I never had that many friends, even in school I was a loner. I didn't even go to my prom. I was kind of a nerd."

"I don't understand Alex you are very attractive."

"Rick sort of helped me find myself. Encourage me to become who I could be. Even before he was rich he was helping people. And because of me, he may now die."

"No he isn't, Alex. Marissa has been trying to make me see it; we have to believe that he will make it." Yakira grabbed Alex's arm and added. "Come on, let me buy you something in the cafeteria."

"I've got a better idea." Alex said, placing her arm around Yakira's neck. "How about we take a taxi over to my house; I will make some breakfast for us. You will also have a place you can get some sleep."

The taxi's ride was almost like being in her mother's arms, rocking her softly to sleep; in fact, she had drifted off. Only to be awoken by Alex's gentle shake to tell her they were there. It was a typical middle-class suburban neighborhood, with cookie cutter homes in a development right at the end of a cul-de-sac street. The yard was shaded within pin oaks, and fresh cut green grass, inside it was the same middle class styling, with a small living room being the dominating room that first greets you as you enter the front door that graduates into the dining room. The front room had blue wing chairs and a large ottoman in the center, in front of the window was a red sofa with comfortable looking pillows decorating the ends of it. In the dining room was an old-fashioned pull down chandelier from the 1960s, this illuminated the round table with four ladder-backed chairs around it. In the corner of the room was a small China cabinet with Pink Depression glass dishes arranged in it.

"Just make yourself at home." Alex said as she walked back into the bedroom to change her clothes. "I have some of that beef bacon that Rick gave me, would you like that?" She heard Alex's voice from the bedroom.

"That would be great!" Yakira said as she walked over to the bookcase that lined the far wall of the living room that contained the TV. Yakira began to look at the photos that were displayed in frames on the shelves. One of her and Ryder having a picnic next on the bank of the river, other photos were of her in her hospital bed holding the newborn Ceelia, and many other photos: of the little girl at her first birthday, Ceelia trying to make a cake for her mother, with most of the frosting on her face. On the bottom shelf was a six inch tall white porcelain bell; on top of the handle was a pair of Cherubim. Yakira picked up the photo that contained Ryder. Alex entered the room.

She was now dressed in light gray sweats, her hair pulled back in a ponytail , thick brown plastic framed glasses over eyes. "This is the real me? What do you think?"

"You look like a mom."

"Thanks," Alex said with a grin. "That is what I enjoy being the most." She looked at the photo in Yakira's hands."That was taken the week after we arrested Celeste." Alex said, and Yakira turned to face her. "Right after that, he quit the force. I didn't see him again until…"

"You investigated Annalisa's murder?"

"Yes, I mean I would see pictures of him in the paper with all the big shots of K.C. but he never said a thing to me." She paused. "If he dies because of what I did…"

"Stop it!" Yakira said, placing the photo back on the shelf as she walked over to her grabbed her by the arms. "We can't think this way! Marissa says 'We have to have good thoughts.' I think she is right. Now I don't want any more of this feeling it is your fault."

"I haven't got to see him." Alex said.

"I will make sure you do." Yakira said offering a small grin. "Now where is that little girl of yours?"

"Natasha takes her to pre-school, it is part of the Rick Ryder education program..." Yakira saw Alex choke back the tears and she spoke up.

"He is going to be all right. Uncle Tony tells me that. Marissa tells me that. I just don't believe God would take him from us." Alex went into the kitchen and made breakfast. Beef bacon and scrambled eggs topped with salsa. After breakfast Yakira was really growing tired. She started to get and go lay down when Alex said

"Hold on, I've got one more thing for you." Alex came in, holding a single cupcake on a saucer with a small lit candle stuffed into the top of it. "Happy Birthday, Yakira." She said, sitting it down in front of her. "Make a wish and blow out the candle." Yakira leaned over and blew the flame out, a whorl of smoke drifted across the table. "Hope you get your wish." Alex said, removing the candle and laying it on the saucer beside the cupcake.

"I will." Yakira smiled as she looked over at her. Then, she took a knife and sliced the cake in two, exposing the creamy center. She picked up one half. "Want to share with me?" She asked. And Alex took the other piece. After their cake, Alex showed her back to the guest room. Yakira didn't even bother to crawl under the sheets; she just removed her shoes and curled up on the bed using the quilted comforter for her blanket.

Yakira's eyes blinked open to see a bright shining face staring at her, her little chin resting on the mattress, her dark hair parted in the middle. As she saw Yakira's eyes open the little girl grinned and spoke the way only a three year could.. "Hi there aunt Yahhie" Ceelia said, trying her best to say Yakira's name. "Mommy said 'we could have icy cream when you woke up. You woked?"

"Yes," Yakira said as she brushed the child's hair back over her ears. "I am awake." Ceelia quickly grabbed Yakira's hand and pulled on it, trying to get her to get up. Still holding on to her hand she led her out into the living room. The little girl proudly announced as they entered. "She is up, Mommy! Can we have icy cream now?"

"Supper is almost ready, Ceelia; you can have some if you eat a good supper." Alex said as they walked out from the kitchen dressed in red sweatpants and a long sleeved shirt, the sleeves pushed past her elbows, a flowery print apron tied around her. It was strange to see Alex that way, the only way Yakira ever thought of her was in business attire and a semi-automatic strapped to her side. Alex's sister was sitting on the sofa watching TV; it was KYTV, the local news headline was about the killing of the Eureka Slayer, the reporter was in the town interviewing the locals on how they felt now that the threat is gone, the mayor proclaiming that Eureka Springs is once again safe, and that he thanked Rick Ryder for this and wished him a speedy recovery and prayers for him and his family.

"Antie Yahhie," Ceelia said, pulling on Yakira's dress. "Is Uncle Ricky sick?" The child's question brought silence to the room as Alex's sister muted the TV; Yakira stooped down, and picked the child up in her arms.

"Yes Ceelia, he is very sick," Yakira said holding the child close to her. "He is in the hospital that was why your mother couldn't be with you to watch the sunrise." The child turned to her mother and said.

"That okay Mommy, I saw and thinked you, so you were there." She turned back to Yakira. "Then we pray for him?"

"Yes, we should." Yakira said. "You want to do it?" Ceelia nodded before bowing her head and said:

"God, Ricky sick. He need to be better. Jesus say so. Amen." Ceelia lifted her head and looked at Yakira. "Was that a good prayer, Yahhie?"

"That was the best prayer I have ever heard." Yakira said giving the girl a kiss before setting her down on the floor and she ran over to her toys near the fireplace on the floor. Dumping her shoebox of crayons out, she spread out in the floor on her stomach, feet in the air, as she began to color on a piece of paper.

"Supper will be ready in a few minutes." Alex said.

"I—I am not that hungry. " Yakira sputtered out. "I was thinking about going back over to the hospital. I will call a cab."

"You don't need to do that." Alex said, walking back into the kitchen and returning with a set of keys. "You can take my car."

"I thought the department took it back."

"They did, this is my personal car." Alex said, handing her the keys. "It isn't much to look at, but it does run well. You are free to use it."

Yakira held the keys in her hand. "I wish you would stay and eat with us. I would like to have a friend here too."

"Okay," Yakira said with a nod.

"I am not sure what you can have, is steak smothered in golden mushroom soup okay?"

"It would be fine," Yakira said. "Can I help?"

Alex laughed. "Ricky told me about your cooking skills, Can you make the tea?"

"That I can do," Yakira stood in the kitchen at the counter that separated the dining area and the kitchen. She was dipping the tea bags in the hot water, while she watched as Ceelia lay on the floor on her tummy, her bare feet sticking up, bouncing back and forth with the rhythm of a song she was singing, words that only she could understand. In front of her a piece of paper, which she was intensively drawing and coloring in. Suddenly the little girl sneezed. She wiped her nose and mouth with the back of her hand as she looked up and said.

"Mommy, I got bless you on it." She stood up and ran over to her mother who was standing at the counter over an electric skillet, checking to see if the meat was done. "I got bless you on it." She held the paper up for her to see.

"It is okay, honey." Alex said as she squatted down and looked at the picture. "That is beautiful, what is it?"

"A get you well. It is for Ricky." As the little girl spoke Yakira stood and watched her, she could see herself there, well maybe not in the kitchen, but she could see herself as a mother. She had never felt that way in her life; to her kids were something for someone else to have. "You write it?"

"Why don't you have Yakira help you?" Alex said, pointing to her. Soon there was the patter of bare feet racing over the tile floor and Ceelia holding up the drawing.

"You write, Yakiree?" Yakira picked her up and placed her up on a stool, and sat down on the next one beside her. She laid the drawing out on the counter. She handed her the crayon she had been holding and said "You write, Yakiree."

"Okay," Yakira said, taking the crayon. "How about we write, 'Ricky get well soon. Love, Ceelia." To the child it was a masterpiece, to Yakira it was just circles and scribbles of color.

"You give Uncle Ricky?" Ceelia said, holding up the paper. Yakira took the paper and looked at it. It just looked like blue and red scribbles.

"What is this?"

"Bells! They make angels come." Ceelia said as she slid down off the stool, and as before, she ran across the floor, as fast as her little bare feet could take her to the white porcelain bell and took it from the shelf and the bell rang out. "This make angels come. " She turned to her mother and said "Right, Mommy?"

Again tears began to puddle in Alex's eyes as she brought her hand up over her mouth and gasped. "My dad gave that to me, it was a bell for his Belle. He was getting real sick. He told me when he was gone if we wanted to see him to ring the ring the bell."

"Ricky. Need bells. He need angel." The child raced back to the bar, and jumped up grabbing the paper in her hand, and raced back to Yakira and handed it to her saying. "You give Ricky."

Alex was right, her car, a Chevrolet Laguna Type S-3 was nothing to look at. Dull white paint, peeling red tape stripes along the sides and deep red bucket seats that required a couple of pillows, one under her and one behind her back, to allow Yakira to drive it, as Alex said it ran well, having no trouble at all making it back to the hospital. There was only one way to the ICU on the fourth floor and that was through the Emergency Room and the north elevator.

Yakira approached his bed and heard muffled voices and she stopped. She noticed that Marissa was standing beside his bed again, holding his hand and talking to him, outside the cubical stood Ryder's father, staring at his son in the bed. "You must talk to him." She heard Marissa say.

"I don't have anything to say to him. It isn't my fault that he is here." Ryan's coarse voice carried throughout the ICU unit. "What should I have to say to him? Because of him, someone…"

"Why? Because mom is gone," Marissa said, letting go of Ryder's hand and walking out of the cubical, "It wasn't his fault, it was that screwball woman that killed her, and if mom was here she would smack you upside the head and tell you to get in there."

"And do what? Forgive? Why should I do that when I've done nothing to be forgiven for? "

"Because, it just might help him get better!" Marissa said raising her voice, making the nurse look. She lowered her voice. "Because that is what a real father does, his children come first, over his own needs, own wants, own desires, but you have never been a good father. How many times I wanted to see you out there when I was in the school play. I had the part of Emily Webb in 'Our Town.' In my big graveyard scene I look out and what do I see? An empty chair because you are outside guzzling down a bottle of Jim Beam. You were never there. You were never there for him, Jonas or me." Marissa said pointing to herself. "You were never there for anyone, except yourself. For god sakes Dad, he could die, are telling me that you could live with yourself with that, that you could go to his grave and…" She stopped speaking and looking at her father with sorrowful eyes. "What the hell am I saying, you would never see him again, and if it was me in this bed it wouldn't be any different, would it?"

"You done bitching at me now?" Ryan snapped back at her again, making the nurses look. "Let's go! It is either you go with me or you stay here."

"You are asking me to choose between my father and my brother." She said, her tone rising and clearly showing shock that he could ask this as the nurse approached. "What kind of father are you?"

"Choose! If you choose him, then he will have to take care of you because I am through with you." Yakira approached silently behind him and he turned to her and said. "You probably think I am an Asshole too." Yakira didn't respond, she just stood staring at him. "I bet you all think I am. Well guess what- I don't care. I am a good man!"

"Sir, you need to leave." One of the nurses said. "Right now! And please don't come back."

"No worry on that!" It was at that moment a woman that was younger than Ryder appeared; she stunk of cheap perfume, with a dress that fit tighter than skin. She looked over at Ryan and shouted.

"Can we go to Hot Springs now?"

He looked back at his daughter. "You comin'?"

"She is staying." Yakira said, placing her arm around her. "We will take care of her."

With that he walked out the door. "Honey," the nurse said to Marissa. "You are better off without a father like that."

Yakira hugged Marissa. "Are you okay?" then she looked over the girl's shoulder at Ryder, his hand was twitching and moving, his finger's grabbing into the sheet. "Nurse! Nurse!" Yakira yelled and they came running to his bed. Ryder was struggling to sit up. Struggling to speak.

"Who, who?" The oxygen mask that was still over his face and the tube down his throat made it all come out jumbled. He reached up and pulled the mask from his face and the tube from his throat. He gasped for air; as the nurses tried to reattach them, he pushed them away. Trying to get out his words, he reached for Yakira, grabbing her arm and pulling him to her. "Who?" His voice was low and gravely, as he still struggled for air. "Did her, Lillian, who shot her?"

"Alex did."

Chapter 42

The next day Ryder was transferred to a regular room on the same floor, where he continued to receive oxygen treatments, and was under observation as he started the raging symptoms from the withdrawal from Scopolamine and Angel Trumpet. Violent vomiting, sweating, his hands feeling as if they were on fire, and a thousand needles were giving him their sting, nausea to the point that he couldn't eat.

"All right doc, when am I going to get out of here? I have things to do." Ryder complained as he laid back in the bed, his hands tucked under his head. "I am going crazy in this place. How much longer?"

"Likely it is going to be another three weeks before…"

"Three weeks!" Ryder shouted back.

"Hi, Rick." A twenty something nursing student appeared in the room, grinning and holding a stack of magazines. "I was wondering if you would like a magazine to read, hold. Or to hold anything?" Even with his tummy feeling as if it were on the high seas, you knew she was referring to herself.

Dr. Rogers said in a whisper so she couldn't hear. "They are going to be catatonic when you leave." Then Dr. Rogers raised his voice so she could hear. "No Ms. Mannington, we don't need anything." The young nursing student quickly left. He turned back to him. "You do realize the girls hold drawings on who gives you a sponge bath."

"Ricky !" Another young twenty something nurse appeared. "Is there anything you want special for lunch? I will gladly go anywhere or do anything you want me to."

"No Renee,' I am fine, I have someone bringing me something."

"Would you like a back rub?"

"No, I am fine. I will see you later, okay?"

"I think we should hose them down with ice water, don't they know you are married?"

"Uh?" Ryder used the controls to raise the bed up. "I am engaged, but I am not married."

"I just assumed." The doctor said, as he opened up a drawer in the night stand next to the bed and pulling out a small plastic bag. He shut the door. "You came in here with not much on, the only personal effect you had was this." He opened the bag and dumped out contents into Ryder's hand. It was a gold wedding band, from his nightmares.

"It was real." Ryder said, turning the ring in his fingers.

"That's not..."

"It is from Lillian, the woman that tried to kill me. I remember some strange things, things that she did, things that she said." Ryder said, stopping on that word before he continued. "Doc, is there anyone out there waiting to see me?'

"Three women, one young, one tall and one..."

"The one I need to see, send her in."

Yakira stepped in and walked up to his bed. "Hey Sweetie," she said, wrapping her arms around him, and he returned the embrace before releasing her as she said. "You want me to get you something to eat, or a milkshake?"

His tummy rolled like the wildest roller coaster ride. "Let's forget that for a while." He said, taking hold of her hands. He guided her to sit on the side of the bed, her right hand resting on his thigh. He watched as she gazed down at the ring on her hand.

"Mom is going nuts over this. Calling and emailing everybody she knows, it is the number one thing trending on her Facebook page, people that she doesn't even know are giving her likes. Marissa and I were thinking we could have the wedding this summer, maybe outdoors? Maybe next month? "He took a hold of both of her hands, he gazed at her seriously.

What is it?" She asked worriedly. "You still want to get married don't you?"

"You just need to know that—what happened between me and Lillian, I..."

"I don't need to know!" She said, steadfast, as she stood and walked away from the bed and over to the window, pulled the drapes back

339

and said more calmly. "And more importantly, I don't want to know!"
She dropped the drape down and turned back to him, crossing her arms in
front of her turning her back to him. "That is all in the past." We need to
forget all of it!"

"I don't know if I can." Ryder said, looking at the ring. "She
married me, it may be legal, Yakira."

"No!" She snapped back as she tromped back to his bedside, "I
don't want to hear about that!" She placed her fingers on the sides of her
head and messaged her temples, as she calmed down and spoke. "It
doesn't matter what you did with her, I told you that was over, it is in the
past. I don't want to hear it anymore." Again she walked away from the
bed to the middle of the room.

"It was all because of me," He said faintly as she turned and
looked at him over her shoulder, and then turned around to him. "All the
murders, those that Celeste did, and those in Eureka Springs, all because
she wanted me." She swallowed hard and gazed down at the ring on her
hand.

"Are you saying—," Again she swallowed hard, getting up the
nerve to ask the question. "That you don't want to marry me?"

"I am not saying that." He said as he reached out for her as she
walked over and took his hands. Once again he motioned her to sit down
on the bed. "It is just in that short time I was with her I got to know her.
When she was a suspect, I hated her, when I knew it was me she was after I
was afraid of her…"

"And now?"

"I feel sorry for her. All she wanted was to be loved. But she was
afraid it would go away, she was a lot like me." He cupped his hands over
her face. "I am afraid you will go away."

"I am not going anywhere, but she was a killer!" Yakira said.
Ryder lowered his hands and his face told the whole story which prompted
her. "Wasn't she? She was the Slayer wasn't she?"

"I don't think so." Ryder drew out.

"Who else can it be?"

"What kind of gun was she shot with?"

"Nine millimeter." She said quickly, "Alex shot her."

"Ballistic match?"

"Alex admitted it, so they didn't even check, what you are thinking?"

"Lillian was not afraid of whoever shot her. It was her partner, the one that shot her," Ryder said as he pushed himself in the bed.

"But that was...!"

"Yeah, send her in."

Yakira left and Alex appeared in the door. "Did you want to see me?" Ryder waved her over to the bed and moved his legs over so she could sit down on the bed, which she did. She handed him a folded up piece of paper and he looked at the scribbles of crayon. "Ceelia wanted to send you some more bells, so that the angels would come." He grinned, folded in quarters and laid it on the nightstand.

"There is something I need to know."

"So what do you want to know about?"

"That missing night? And all the lies being told."

"What do you mean?" Alex said clearly flustered as she stood up, helping herself to a drink of water from the pitcher by his bed. "I don't know any lies."

"Who shot her, Alex?"

"I did."

"So you went, from nearly being in Rogers then found me in the insane asylum in Nevada and got there just before she killed me."

"I got it out of her doctor..."

"I talked to the doctor; there was nothing in her report about her wanting to lock me up. He was shocked by the fact that she would want to do that to me. How did you know?"

341

"It was a lucky guess." She said downing the water and walking over to the windows and pulling the drapes back. "I can see my car from here; I've really got to get a new one."

"Belle, we don't lie to each other. Why are you doing it now? "He said making her turn back and face him. "I know you. Shooting her when she wasn't a threat is something you wouldn't have done. You would want her alive so that she could have given you the antidote to the poison, so who was it?"

"I don't know. And that is the truth!" She walked back over to his beside. "When I was in Rogers I got a strange call, it was from some man. He told me that she wasn't the killer, and where she was holding you." She sat down on the bed beside him. "I called in a favor with Robert at the department, he got me a chopper. When I got there she was already dead, lying on top of you, and you were barely alive. I kept giving you mouth to mouth just to keep your lungs going till we got to the hospital."

"So why did you take the blame for it?"

"I thought it would be best. For you and Yakira. If you thought I killed her and she was dead, there wouldn't be any case left to investigate. If you knew that someone had called me and had killed her, you would have to find out who murdered her."

Ryder swung his legs over the edge of the bed, placed his hands on the bed and slid onto the floor, his bare feet on the cold vinyl. He tried to stand. "She was not the Eureka Slayer, in fact, she killed no one."

"She could have been lying. That is what murderers do."

"No," Ryder said, placing his weight on his wobbly legs as he tried to take a few steps towards the window, he placed his hand on his stomach as he felt so sick. "This was about killing me, and then killing herself. It was not about anything else." He placed his hands down on the bed rail, to steady himself. He looked over at Alex, "Get me something to wear. We have to go see a real estate agent."

Chapter 43

Yakira and Alex returned with clothes, underwear, socks, charcoal colored slacks and a jacket, and a light blue shirt, along with loafers. Ryder was still weak, but he got dressed and put the ring and the paper that Ceelia had colored for him in his jacket pocket.

"When he saw the nurses were not watching, he walked out with Yakira and Alex on each side of him. They had just made it outside, when he saw Jonas and Marissa walking up.

"They let you go?" She asked as Alex went for the car.

"I let myself go." Ryder said, moaning from stomach pain, sweat running down from his brow.

"You need to get back in there in the hospital," Marissa said, trying to take his arm; he quickly pulled away from her and moaned out.

"I need to stop the next murder."

"She is dead—I mean—she was the slayer, right?" Jonas asked.

"No," Ryder said as he waited for Alex to arrive with the car. "The killer is still out there." He looked over at his sister. "Alex was right. There was no reason for your mother to be the victim, unless she was the intended victim all along. Everything else was for a cover up." Ryder again nearly bent over as the pain ripped through his insides; he rubbed at his hands wishing the tingling feeling would stop.

Alex drove the car up. She got out and opened the door and twisted the passenger seat around. Ryder braced himself on the roof of the car, his finger digging into the vinyl top as he looked back at Marissa and then at Jonas. He reached over and grabbed his sister's hand as pain again wracked through him. He looked at Jonas and said. "I want you two to go back to the hotel. I still have a room there. I will call Double T and Brian to look after you." His face wrinkled up as he felt as if he was going puke, but he took in a deep breath and then added. "You don't leave that hotel for any reason."

He fell onto the back seat face down, as Yakira got into the passenger seat and Alex into the driver's seat and drove away. "Where to?" She asked.

"The airport, we are taking a chopper."

It is funny how some will say no they will not do that, for it is against the law, it is against morals, but everyone has a price, and for the chopper pilot it was a hundred times his going rate, or ten grand. For that amount allowed him to put the chopper down right in a parking lot next to Weaver and Young Realty in Van Buren.

Ryder didn't wait hardly for the blades to stop spinning, as he slid out the chopper, ducking his head and making his way toward the front door, with Alex and Yakira following him. He pushed the glass door open.

"I was getting ready to close." Beverly said, and then seeing who it was, said "Oh. It is you; what do you want?"

"Name!"

"What name?"

"The person that wants to buy the Crawford County Bank?"

"I can't give…"

"You are going to give it to me if I have to beat out of you." Ryder groaned and held his stomach. "They could be a murderer."

"I assure you, he is not a murderer Mr. Ryder, he just upped his offer to a million and a half. And Jonas agreed."

"He can't do that…" Ryder felt even sicker than before. He reached into his jacket for a handkerchief ,but instead pulled out the drawing that Ceelia drew for him. "Bells, "he said softly. "It didn't ring." She twisted around and faced Yakira. "You got my wallet?" She nodded and handed it to him. He opened it and pulled out the coin that had the blood on it, it was a fifty cent piece. He flipped it in the air and it landed on the hard floor, landing with a dull clang. "It didn't ring!" He said, again clutching the paper tightly into his hand. " We have to get back to Eureka Springs right away. Before there is another murder."

Chapter 44

Ryder's question was answered and he didn't care for the answer, and if he didn't make it back to Eureka Springs in just a matter of minutes there was going to be another murder. There was a flutter in the sky, buzzing, then the guests at the hotel heard the flutter and gazing up at the sky, the flutter became a full roar as the chopper settled to the pavement in between two police cars that were creating a landing zone. As soon as the chopper was down Ryder opened the door and leaped out, tucked his head down, the rotor flipping his jacket like cheap colored flags at a used car lot.

"Is this what you wanted?" Shepherd said, placing something in Ryder's hand, Ryder nodded and raced up the street and to the hotel. He raced up the stairs and pushed open the doors. "Chad! " Ryder yelled out as Yakira and Alex ran into the hotel behind him, followed by Detective Shepherd. "Where is my family? Where is my sister!"

"She is in the Crystal Dining Room, having dinner with Jonas." Timmy said as Ryder raced for the restaurant, pushing past the host and waiter and nearly knocking over a tray that he was carrying. He saw Jonas raising a glass to his sister, wanting her to make a toast.

"Don't drink that!" Ryder yelled, placing his hand over the glass and forcing it back to the table. His hair was now plastered with sweat.

"Ricky, you need to get back to the hospital right now!" Marissa said

"If you drank any of that," Ryder belched, tasting the sickness in his mouth. "We both may be going there."

"I hope you don't mind, I just had them charge it to your room." Jonas said.

"Here, let me pay for it." Ryder said as he flipped the coin in his hand. It landed on the table and bounced to the floor, where it rang out like a bell.

"The coin didn't ring."

"What does that mean?" Jonas asked, wiping his mouth with cloth napkin.

"Ever since I met you, when you get a little nervous you start playing with that half-dollar piece of yours. But you're not really that good at it and you drop it and it would ring out like a bell. I found a silver coin near your mother's body. What is your blood type?"

"What? Why are asking that?" Jonas said watching as Yakira walked up behind Ryder.

"It is O positive just like mine." Marissa said as she stood up for the table. "Why are you asking this Ricky?"

"Your brother here was going to murder you."

"What! I don't believe it. Why? What reason would he have?"

"A million reasons, with you out of the way. He could sell the old bank." Ryder said as his stomach twisted in knots, bending him over.

"This is crazy Rick!" Jonas said, "I would never hurt Marissa."

"Drink it!" Ryder moaned out as he pushed Marissa's drink over to him. "Prove to me you didn't lace that with the rest of Lillian's poison."

"I don't have to prove anything to you!" Jonas said pushing the glass over and spilling on the table.

"The coin didn't ring."

"What the hell does that mean?"

"After your mother was killed, you dropped the coin again and it didn't ring, for it was not silver."

Alex walked in and said. "It was just like you though it was. They found it in a down stairs closet."

"An Arkansas State trooper uniform, just like the one they saw on the train." Also, when we first met you pulled a 9mm pistol on me, the same type that was used to kill Lillian. Want to bet they match?"

"I had to do that Rick she was going to kill you."

"So you were the one she was working with?"

"No!"

"I was just following after her. When she was trying to kill you I called Alex."

"One way to prove it," Ryder said. "When Double T handed me the coin back I put it in my wallet. Do you still have your coin?"

"Yes, I do. " He said reaching into his pocket and pulling out a half dollar. "See, I still have my coin." He flipped the coin and it landed on the floor, ringing out like a bell. "See, it is silver."

"For someone who wants to be a cop, "Ryder said, walking over and picking up the coin. "You really blew it. The coin I used was one that I got from Detective Shepherd. The man had entered the room and Ryder flipped the coin at him. "Thanks." Then he turned back to Jonas, and said. "If you truly knew police work and how evidence is gathered you would know that an officer carves their initials into them. If you look carefully on the coin just above the eagle's wing you will find two letters 'RR' inscribed into the coin. Since Lillian made me throw this out the window, the only way the coin could have gotten switched was that you had to be helping her, and you switched it."

"You know what it is like having him for a father. Hearing all the time how you were a great guy or Marissa was the great daughter but I am… I was a nothing. I wanted out. I wanted to be somebody. Have money, but mom was happy just the way she was, she wouldn't listen. I figured I could be like you. Rich and powerful, I see how all these idiots would snap to attention around you. They would go downtown and get something for you. And Lillian, she was the most beautiful woman I had ever seen in my life. I took her to Little Rock, every guy there wanted to be me. She let me touch her once, just once because she wanted you. I told her if she helped me make everyone think there was a serial killer loose, I would arrange it to where she could have you. I also figured that if mom was just one of the victims, the cops wouldn't even look at me. They would blame Lillian and if she was dead…"

"You were going to kill me?" Marissa asked interrupting him

"You, were just like mom, you wouldn't sell. You thought more of him as your brother than me. You were going to have it all. I got nothing. What else was I to do?" Jonas said as he looked up at Ryder. We are not blood so you wouldn't you have given it to me?"

"Blood doesn't make family. You were my brother, all you had to do was ask." Ryder said, as he turned to Detective Shepherd and said "Get him out of here!" The detective handcuffed him and led him away. Marissa held her head down; Ryder leaned down and grabbed her hand, letting his fingers grip around hers as he looked down at her. He moaned out and then collapsed in the floor.

Epilog

Ryder spent the next 21 days in the hospital recovering from the effects of Lillian's Devil Brew', the first week was the concoction itself. He lost twenty pounds, and some muscle tone, but the next week was able to slowly start building back with therapy and modern exercise. Now he stood in the purple end zone of the Robert W. Plaster Stadium of the Missouri State University campus, and looked down field of the Astroturf. Clutched in his hands was a football, as his fingers gripped around the laces; he stared up into the empty stands.

"I figure if you can do this," He heard doctor Rogers say, who was standing beside him in the end zone. "Then you can go home." He glanced over, and standing on the side of the field was Yakira, Alex, Marissa, and Thom. Ryder looked at him.

"I need the best center the state of Missouri ever had," Ryder said as he tossed the ball sideways to Thom, who caught it and stepped out on to the field. He walked up to Ryder and Ryder said. "Seems like old times, huh Double T?" Referring to him by his nickname.

"Yeah," Thom grinned, as he looked up into the stadium seats then back to Ryder. "Wildcats are down by six on the three yard line, we need the Pale Ryder." Thom twisted the football in his hands and stepped out in the end zone and on the three yard line and bent over.

Ryder looked over to his other side, there stood a young man, wide receiver for the Bears, barely six foot tall, but was lean and trim. "You want to go for a couple of warm ups? You haven't done this for a while, and I am heading for the pros this year."

Ryder laughed and said, "Son, it is like sex. You never forget your first time, and it just gets better from then on out. We are going for it all." Ryder lined up behind Double T and placed his hands under his behind. He looked back at the receiver who was in hunched position. "You fast?"

"Fast enough."

"I will give you the count of five, and you had better be past the Bear's eyes." Ryder said as he looked down field at the center logo at the fifty yard line. "All right Teeny Tiny; let's show this kid some Wildcat pride." Ryder then yelled out his commands. "Twenty-one red twenty-one red Camaro, Hike!" Ryder slapped his foot down and Thom hiked the ball, and the running back took off running. Ryder ran back and to the side as he counted "One, two, three, four, five." With that he leaned back and the ball left his fingers with a tight spiral, perfectly spinning over the field, past the mid-field and right into the player's hand, who just couldn't help but run all the way to the end-zone and spike the ball.

"Well this may be the strangest place I've ever done this." Dr. Rogers said as he walked over and picked up a clipboard, and signed a paper on it. He removed the paper and handed it to Ryder. "You are free to leave the hospital."

"Good because there are a few things I have got to do." Ryder said as he walked across the field to the track and up to Marissa. "So what are you going to do now, sister?"

"I don't know," she replied uncertainly. "I don't know where I am going to go. Dad doesn't want me. My Aunt Vera will take me, but— I guess—" She dropped her gaze down to the track and continued, "Because I guess nobody else wants me." She carefully rolled her eyes up, but not moving her head hoping he was watching.

"How about a brother," Ryder said, waiting for her response, and seeing it as she lifted her head up, smiled showing those dimples and said.

"Really?"

"Ryder there is only two bedrooms at the lake; will we have enough room?" Yakira asked.

"I bought the old Warner Ranch; it seems he owed back taxes, fifteen hundred acres and lots room big enough to start a family."

"You mean?" Yakira said with a tone of joy of that built up into a scream of delight as he said.

"You better get busy planning that wedding." He looked over at Alex and said. "You know, there are two houses on the ranch, and there is an old shed that could make a nice castle for a certain princess."

"You want me to move in there?" Alex asked sounding confused.

"Why not? Let just say it is part of the package for working with me." Ryder grinned brightly as he added. "Say a dollar a day for rent?"

"Mr. Ryder." He heard a voice say from a distance, and he turned to him. He was tall and thin, dressed in a dove gray suit. "Richard Thomas Allen Ryder?"

"Yeah."

""I am from the law firm of Taylor, Newman and House. Our client instructed us to give this to you." The man said handing Ryder a manila envelope. Ryder opened the envelope and inside was a folded up piece of red construction paper. May be it was the stillness running through those standing there, or just looking down at the piece of paper, but Ryder felt a coldness running through him. He unfolded it.

"What is it?" Alex asked.

He couldn't answer her, instead he just handed her the paper and Alex read it out loud. "'Hickory Dickory Dock,, the time has run out on the clock. What is but one flower, when it I that has the power. Hickory Dickory Dock." Alex paused and looked up as she said. "Signed Mademoiselle Celeste."

"Who gave this to you?" Ryder demanded of the man.

"I can't tell you our client's name, all I can tell you it was a man."

"We have to get to the prison." Ryder said.

"There are thunderstorms between here and there, you will never get a chopper. " Alex said. "Besides we can't get in till tomorrow.

"We will take the Killer Bee."

Early the next morning they arrived, it strange the line of people carrying signs marching across the street and the media that were lined up like covered wagons, raging their own war against death were all gone. All was left were the signs as isf they were suddenly dropped and those marching gave up.

Ryder parked the Charger in the parking lot and he, Alex and Yakira walked inside and was met with a guard. "I thought you might be showing up." The guard said calmly, Ryder didn't seem to hear the guard and marched right up to the counter.

351

"I want to see Velour! Right now! " Ryder demanded slamming his hand down on the counter. "You know who I am. If I have to I will call the governor and…"

"You are too late." The guard replied.

"What do you mean?"

"Ms. Velour passed away."

"When? How? Ryder replied shocked.

"Around midnight in her cell we found her unresponsive. No pulse, not breathing, she was even turning blue. She was rushed to the hospital, they pronounced her dead. Doctor said it was heart attack." The guard said leaning back on the front counter.

"Where is the body?" Ryder demanded

"It was already claimed."

"Who?"

"Her brother claimed it. It was sent to Fenton's Funeral Home here in town."

It was strange to drive up the business and see lights on, the sun was just beginning break over the horizon. As Ryder held the car door open for Yakira and Alex in the back seat. Yakira stopped and sniffed the air and asked.

"Do you smell smoke?"

Ryder turned and looked at the Alex as she stepped out of the car. They both raced for the door the funeral home, it was open and they dashed inside with Yakira right behind them. There were only a few lights on in the outer room the long hallway was dark, and they continued down the hall running on to a man.

"We are not really open, you need to …"

"Velour, Celeste Velour! Where is her body?"

"I am going to call the cops if you crazy people don't get out of her." The man said. "She is dead now. You can't save her." Ryder grabbed him by the collar of his shirt and slammed him against the wall of the hall.

"Where is her body?"" Ryder said yelling his warning.

"She is back there." The man said pointing to the door at the end of the hall. The sign on the door read 'Crematory'. Ryder pushed the door open; the large room was dominated by a large furnace. He could see through the glass doors the casket was fully engulfed by bright orange flames

"You are too late. You idiots can't save her." Ryder heard the man say. He turned back to him.

"Who declared her dead?" Ryder asked.

"Doctor Hunter."

"Doctor Ron L. Hunter?" Alex asked, "Ryder, Ron Hunter? He is the doctor that…he is Lillian father."

"Did you see the body?"

"Of course."

"You saw her in the casket before you put her in the crematory."

"Yes she was in there!" The man said. "The family had their goodbyes, they closed the lid and I sent her into the finance."

"Come on Rick," Alex said pulling on his arm. "It is over. Let's get out here. Let's go have breakfast."

They flowed the hallway back outside and Ryder stood next to the Killer Bee and unlocked the doors, watched as the sun rose higher making shadows grow long. He held the door open so Alex and Yakira could get inside the car. He walked around the car and sit down in the driver's seat.

"Where do you want to eat at?" He asked, but they didn't answer there were fixed on the rearview mirror. He glanced up and there he saw it tied in a loop around the mirror was a single red rose.

THE END

Mr. Mulvaugh spent most of his childhood growing up on a dairy farm a few miles north of Cassville, MO. When the chores were done and playtime came, because his siblings were much older than himself, he found that his imagination was his greatest ally, allowing him to create cities and characters in his mind. He always makes up stories. At the age of eleven years- old his sister gave him a typewriter for Christmas, more stories followed. That was just beginning a lifelong career as a writer.

Today Mr. Mulvaugh lives in Monett, MO with his wife and three cats. He is the author of the author of the 'Blood Series' featuring detective Rick Ryder. Mr Mulvaugh likes to blend fiction tales and places with real places.

The first book in the 'Blood Series' Blood Necklace.

Former homicide detective Rick Ryder has just won the largest Powerball® jackpot of all time one-billion dollars , he is the toast of the town. However, when his high school sweetheart Annalisa comes to ask for help he is too busy to help. When she is found murdered in his sports car in Roaring River State Park he returns to his hometown to solve the murder. What he finds is a twisting tale of murders and secrets that will keep you guessing till the very end.

www.ingramcontent.com/pod-product-compliance
Lightning Source LLC
Chambersburg PA
CBHW061314170626
46817CB00001B/175